Praise for MICHAEL CORDY's previous novel
THE MIRACLE STRAIN

"Fascinating . . . a highly suspenseful thriller."
San Francisco Examiner

"Michael Cordy spins a swell yarn . . . a sharp, science-based thriller that should get Michael Crichton's competitive juices flowing."
Detroit News

"A potent cocktail of high-tech science and apocalypse . . . clever twists, plenty of action, and a whizbang climax . . . [Cordy] keeps pages turning until the last revelation."
Publishers Weekly

"An inventive genetic thriller."
Chicago Tribune

"An engrossing and intelligent work that reads like a cross between Michael Crichton and Umberto Eco."
San Francisco Chronicle

"A taut, gripping tale."
The Times (London)

Also by Michael Cordy

THE MIRACLE STRAIN: A GENETIC THRILLER

CRIME ZERO

A NOVEL

MICHAEL CORDY

HarperTorch
An Imprint of HarperCollins*Publishers*

This is a work of fiction. Names, characters, places, and incidents are products of the author's imagination or are used fictitiously and are not to be construed as real. Any resemblance to actual events, locales, organizations, or persons, living or dead, is entirely coincidental.

HARPERTORCH
An Imprint of HarperCollins *Publishers*
10 East 53rd Street
New York, New York 10022-5299

Copyright © 1999 by Michael Cordy
ISBN: 0-380-73043-X

First HarperTorch paperback printing: May 2001
First William Morrow hardcover printing: July 1999

HarperCollins®, HarperTorch™, and ◆ are trademarks of HarperCollins Publishers Inc.

Printed in the United States of America

Visit HarperTorch on the World Wide Web at
www.harpercollins.com

10 9 8 7 6 5 4 3 2 1

For my mother and father,
Betty and John Cordy

Acknowledgments

My greatest debt is to my wife, Jenny, who has always been my true partner in crime. From the start she helped research the plot and characters, developing the good ideas and editing out the bad. Even at the end, when disaster struck and I thought I had lost the entire completed typescript, she alone kept calm and recovered the computer file.

The other major thank you is to my editor at Transworld, Bill Scott-Kerr, who invested an unusual amount of time, effort, and patience to vastly improve the story.

To research *Crime Zero* the following sources were invaluable: *A Mind to Crime* by Anne Moir and David Jessel, *On Aggression* by Konrad Lorenz, *Virus X* by Dr. Frank Ryan, and *In the Blood* by Steve Jones. For providing first hand scientific advice I am grateful to Susan Robinson and Sejal Patel, both of whom used their respective Ph.D.s to weed out and modify my more fanciful inventions. I thank Betty Cordy for reading numerous versions of the manuscript and providing me with consistent feedback and encouragement. I also thank Bill Reinka, Simon Hoggart, and Richard Cordy for their contributions.

Last, but certainly not least, I thank my excellent agent, Patrick Walsh.

Certainly there is one gene which is shared by most criminals—and its complete DNA sequence is known. It is the single small gene, carried on the Y chromosome, which makes its carriers male. Most criminals are men: the criminality gene has been found! Needless to say, no one suggests that geneticists should do anything about it.
> —STEVE JONES, professor of genetics, University College London

Prologue

It wasn't his pain that denied him sleep. It wasn't his fear that filmed his skin in clammy sweat and made him rise from drenched sheets to piss for the tenth time that night. And it wasn't his suffering that urged him to take his own life after seven years on death row.

It was *their* pain that made him do these things, their fear, their suffering.

Something had changed deep within him. He didn't know what it was or why it had happened, only that it was somehow fundamental, irrevocable.

Karl Axelman had taken many lives in his fifty-six years but had never once considered taking his own. He had always been untroubled by his past, savoring his conquests, using his photographic memory to summon up some exquisite detail of the girls he had raped, tortured, and murdered for his pleasure. But now their faces came unbidden, tormenting him day and night. For the first time in his life he could hear their pain, smell their fear, and understand their suffering.

After returning to the bed in his five-foot-by-ten-foot cell in San Quentin's East Block, he stared up through the bars at the faulty lamp in the corridor outside. But he found no comfort in the light. The beacon only exacerbated his distress, intensifying the gloom that surrounded him.

1

Sitting up, he looked around the cell that was his universe: the stainless steel basin and toilet in the corner; the shelf above the sheet metal bed stacked high with neatly ordered newspapers. He turned to check his pillow again. Strands of silver flecked the yellowed linen. His thick hair, although silvered with age, had always symbolized his strength. But now it fell in clumps from his scalp. His handsome face, once bait for his prey, was pitted with weeping acne more acute than any teenager's. Yet as he clasped his clammy palms together and his pounding heart drowned out the sounds of despair from the neighboring cells, he ignored these physical indignities.

He was aware only of dry-mouthed, heart-palpitating anxiety, an emotion he had never experienced before. Unwanted images of vulnerable flesh intruded on his mind, arousing the familiar desire to control and humiliate. Yet even as his erection hardened, his whole body crawled with revulsion. And the bile of acid guilt rose in his throat.

Reaching up to the narrow shelf above his bed, Axelman's hands shook as he selected a copy of the *San Francisco Examiner*. Except for a shoebox at one end, the shelf was bowed beneath the weight of crisply folded newspapers. Knowing what was happening in the outside world had always given Axelman a sense of control, allowing him to imagine he was influencing events. But no more.

Carefully unfolding the paper, he ignored the warmongering headlines about Iraq and the latest polls on the first ever female presidential candidate running for office in a week's time. These issues no longer concerned him. He would be gone by then. There was only one issue to resolve.

He turned to page three of the paper and studied the flash photograph of a man carrying a naked girl wrapped in his jacket out of a cemetery late at night. The headline said: FBI MIND HUNTER SAVES VICTIM NUMBER FOUR. Axelman stared at the man. Then he reached for the shoebox containing all the personal belongings he was allowed to keep with him. The old faded color photograph was on the top of the letters and other paraphernalia. Squinting in the flickering light, he compared the faded photograph with the newspaper picture, as he had done countless times before. Finally he reread the text in the article, noting once again the age and the sur-name.

Axelman sighed. He was sure he was right. But even if he was wrong, he would still confess all the details to this FBI agent for the first time. He had once savored frustrating the police and prolonging the mourning and pain of the relatives by keeping the location of the bodies to himself. But now their pain was his pain, and he could no longer keep the information secret. This man could do something with the knowledge.

Listening for the footsteps of approaching guards, Axelman carefully replaced the photo and newspaper. He then knelt on the floor and lifted one corner of the bed. After slipping two long fingers into the hollow base of the tubular leg, he extracted a steel belt buckle from the chewing gum wedging it in place. The pin had been removed from the large biker's buckle, leaving a squared-off figure of eight about two inches wide and three inches long.

The buckle had cost six packs of cigarettes eighteen months ago, and the con who had sold it to him had smiled while pocketing the Marlboros. With no pin the buckle was useless and harmless. But over time he had chamfered one beveled outer edge against the concrete floor, the iron bed, and even the bars of his cell, filing the end into a crude but keen blade. At first, sharpening the steel buckle was something to do, a small act of rebellion, but now it had taken on a new significance.

Sitting on the bed, he passed his thumb over the nicked edge of the blade and drew blood. His atrophied testicles involuntarily retreated into his body, and for a moment Axelman wished he could wait for the executioner. Release would be so much easier if administered by a different hand. But this wasn't just about release; it was about punishment. He himself must remove the source of the dark urges.

Rocking back and forth on the edge of the bed, Axelman didn't bother to lie down. Sleep wouldn't come, and if it did, he would gain no sanctuary there. He touched the buckle blade again, strangely reassured by its presence. Soon it would be dawn, and later he would unburden his soul to the FBI agent. He could do no more to find peace. After that he would play out the final act. And then, redemption or no redemption, at least the torture would end.

Part 1

Project Conscience

1

His head aches, and he wants to go home, but he still waits in the cemetery under cover of the short fir tree. The damp bark smells as strong as any perfume. It is 1:57 A.M. The two San Francisco Police Department officers left an hour ago. After three days of staking out the area, they and their replacements have been recalled to follow up other leads. The police say they will return in the morning, but he knows they have lost the faith. Fourteen-year-old Tammy Lewis is missing, and they are concerned she will end up like the other three. Special Agent Luke Decker should leave too; he has only adviser status here, and other cases are piling up on his desk at Quantico.

But Decker can't go yet. He knows deep in his gut that the killer will return here at night and bring the girl with him—perhaps even alive.

The night air is cool on his face, and above him through the branches of the fir a crescent moon gazes down. Seventeen miles from San Francisco and nine miles from Oakland, the Gates of Heaven Catholic Cemetery is still. Nothing moves, and even nearby Interstate 80 is silent.

He retrieves a pair of night vision glasses from his coat and rereads the inscription on the headstone twenty yards away:

Sally Anne Jennings
Taken August 3, 2008
Aged 15 years
You were taken from us too soon.
But we shall meet again in a better place.

Decker grinds his jaw, remembering the crime scene photos of Sally Anne's violated body. The killer's most recent victim must also be his last.

Car tires on gravel break the silence. He turns to his right and sees a Domino's pizza van pull into the cemetery's deserted parking lot. Sweat breaks out on his forehead. Decker knows the psychological profile of the killer because he wrote it. And the pizza van fits. His heart is beating fast now, but he feels no triumph about being right again, no excitement of the chase, just weary sorrow and a vague disquiet that he should know the mind of a killer so well.

A sudden scream from the van rips through the night. It is short and quickly muffled, but Decker crumples inside, feeling her pain and terror himself. He reaches for his cell phone and calls the incident number.

He whispers urgently that the suspect is here. He needs backup.

A sleepy detective snaps awake. "Two squad cars will be there in ten minutes—max," he promises.

The van's rear doors open, and a muscular young man with red hair and a black T-shirt drags something white out of the back and drops it on the gravel. Decker realizes then that ten minutes will not be soon enough. The silent white bundle is moving, and even before he puts the night vision glasses to his eyes, Decker knows it's a naked girl. Tammy Lewis is gagged and bound, her eyes round with terror. The young man is strong because he easily lifts her over his shoulder and carries her toward the cemetery.

Decker reaches for his gun and releases the safety. He has won the FBI shooting competition at Quantico with the SIG semiautomatic every year for the last five years. But he dislikes using the gun for real. It means he's failed. But he has no choice now. If he does nothing, the man will carry Tammy Lewis to Sally Anne's grave, where he will lay her down, torture, and rape her. Then, when he is satisfied, he will kill her and defile her body. Decker knows this with a gut-wrenching certainty as absolutely as if he'd already witnessed the crime.

He waits for the man to lay Tammy down on the grave and

*start to untie her ankles before coming up behind him.
Decker is ten feet away when he sees a knife flash in the
man's hand.*

*"FBI," he shouts. His voice sounds alien in the stillness
of the night. "Drop the knife, put your hands up, and back
away from her."*

*Crouching over his victim, the red-haired man looks over
his shoulder, his long face surprised and uncertain. He hes-
itates.*

*"Now," orders Decker. But the man doesn't drop the knife.
He turns and raises it high into the air. The curved blade
mirrors the white sickle of the moon as a bellow of rage cuts
through the darkness. Then in one furious movement he
brings it scything down toward the girl with the force of a
guillotine. . . .*

"The defense calls Dr. Kathryn Kerr."

It was her name that jolted Luke Decker from the events
in the graveyard nine weeks ago and back to the warm,
stuffy chamber of the San Francisco Court of Appeals.
Above the judge's bench the clock showed 10:07 A.M., and
the calendar below it the date: Wednesday, October 29,
2008. The hushed oak-paneled courtroom carried every
sound, but when the woman's name was called, Decker
couldn't believe he'd heard it right.

What the hell was Kathy Kerr doing here?

Reorienting himself, Decker blinked his green eyes and
ran a hand through his cropped blond hair. Shifting in his
chair, he looked around the paneled court. The judge, a bald
man with a permanent pained frown, sat at the front of the
chamber with both the prosecution and defense teams
arranged facing him on either side. Decker sat with the prosecution behind the district attorney. This wasn't a full trial,
and there were few people in the public gallery behind him,
except some junior press. No relatives of the dead girls had
come, but Decker gained some satisfaction from noting that
Tammy Lewis's family wouldn't have been among them. At
least she had been saved.

Turning to his right, the first person he noticed was

Wayne Tice, sitting beside his defense attorney. The red-haired killer's right arm was still in a sling from where Decker had shot him in the shoulder. Tice caught his eye and flashed his crooked teeth in a cold, unrepentant smile. Decker ignored him. The man had been found guilty and condemned to death almost a month ago. This hearing was just an attempt by his defense team to gain Tice leniency and a chance for rehabilitation. As the FBI forensic psychologist responsible for catching Tice, Special Agent Decker had been asked by the DA to comment on his psychological state and ensure the man wasn't allowed back on the streets.

Now it appeared that Kathy Kerr, the woman he hadn't seen for almost ten years, was here to help Tice.

He watched her take her seat and be sworn in. Decker couldn't help staring at her, although she seemed oblivious of his presence. She was slimmer, and her glasses were gone, no doubt replaced by contacts, and her navy suit was smarter than the jeans and T-shirt she'd favored in their Harvard days.

"Please state your name, occupation, and qualifications please," requested Tice's attorney, Ricardo Latona.

The witness unconsciously raised a hand and attempted to run it through her dark, glossy hair before remembering it was tied back into a French braid. A flash of memory intruded on Decker's thoughts. No doubt she had tried to restrain the long cascade of unruly curls in order to look more authoritative. Decker guessed that many people still underestimated the formidable intellect behind the packaging of open smile and Celtic coloring of fair skin, freckles, and pale blue eyes.

"My name is Dr. Kathryn Kerr, and I am a research fellow in behavioral genetics at Stanford University. I have a degree in microbiology from Cambridge University in England and a Ph.D. in behavioral genetics from Harvard."

Her voice had lost none of its soft Edinburgh burr. In many ways Kathy Kerr had hardly changed, and Decker wondered whether she would think his appearance had altered so little. The woman he had known all those years ago still seemed vulnerable and wild at the same time, both of which were only half true. He couldn't help wondering whether she used her maiden name professionally or was she still unmarried.

"Could you briefly outline the nature of your work?" requested the attorney.

"I specialize in the genetic science of criminal and antisocial behavior. Apart from teaching, most of my research work at Stanford is funded by the biotech company ViroVector Solutions and the Federal Bureau of Investigation."

Decker raised an eyebrow. He didn't know she'd returned from England, let alone that she was working with his people at the bureau. He wondered how long she'd been at Stanford.

"I realize that many aspects of your work with the FBI will be confidential," said Latona. "But isn't it true that one aspect of your research involves identifying the genetic risk factors for criminal behavior?"

"Yes."

Her blue eyes met Luke's for the first time. He tried to read her gaze, but for once his famed powers of perception failed him. Although he had had no idea she was part of the bureau project to explore the genetic roots of crime, he had heard of it; everyone had. After all, nature, not nurture, was now the new religion at the FBI. Criminals were born, not made, so the senior hierarchy believed, particularly Madeline Naylor, the first female director in the bureau's long and illustrious history.

Decker had always disagreed with this philosophy. In his experience criminals, and their victims, were shaped by their backgrounds. At thirty-five Decker was one of the youngest ever heads of the behavioral sciences division at the FBI's training academy in Quantico, Virginia.

His unit had once been the glamour division of the bureau; Hollywood films had been based on its exploits. It specialized in helping police forces target suspects for serial killings, bombings, or other apparently motiveless crimes by developing psychological profiles of possible offenders based on the methodology of the crime.

But under the new regime the behavioral sciences division had become ghettoized. Physiology, not psychology, was where all the money went now. The criminal brain was far more interesting than the criminal mind. PET brain scans, adrenaline levels, skin conductivity, theta activity, and serotonin neurotransmitters were seen as the future of crime control, crowned, of course, by the promises of genetic science.

The new ideology had prompted Decker to tender his resignation last month and accept the offer of a professorship at Berkeley to teach criminal psychology. He had done his time on the front line and could achieve more now by training and inspiring a new generation of mind hunters. Plus ten years in the minds of the sickest killers had taken its toll. His mother's sudden death eighteen months ago had also made him realize that he hadn't seen enough of her or his grandfather in the last ten years. He had been living out of a tiny apartment in Washington, D.C., traveling the country, and putting no roots down. It was time for him to settle back here on the West Coast, where his grandfather still lived, and sort out his life, rather than try to save everybody else's.

McCloud, the deputy director of the FBI, had refused his resignation, asking him to reconsider. But with every day that Decker stayed, the more he knew he had to go. He had already picked his successor. So after finishing off this case and interviewing Karl Axelman in San Quentin this afternoon, he would return to Quantico and tell McCloud his decision was final.

"Thank you for agreeing to come here today, Dr. Kerr," said the defense lawyer with a smile. Ricardo Latona was a squat man with thinning dark hair. He turned to the judge. "The reason we requested this hearing and asked Dr. Kerr to give evidence today is that we believe a new approach to crime is long overdue.

"It is now apparent from all the research that biology is a central factor in crime, interacting with social, cultural, and economic influences. This knowledge raises key questions. If someone is biologically predisposed to crime, should he be punished or helped? If he is sick, do we *dare* treat him? Or do we feel that treatment somehow excuses 'criminality' and robs us of the need to punish? Is society civilized enough to equate justice with merciful treatment of a disease, or must it always be linked to punishment?"

Decker watched Latona pause and turn to Tice, a man who had abducted and murdered three girls and would have murdered a fourth if Decker hadn't prevented him. "Wayne Tice has done wrong," said Latona in his soothing, reasonable voice. "No one denies that, and he has been convicted of terrible crimes. But we intend to show that they were the result of genetically inherited biochemical factors beyond his control, for which a just, humane society would seek medical treatment, not the death penalty."

Decker groaned. He was no advocate of the death penalty, so long as dangerous people were kept off the street. But the idea that genes determined violent behavior was abhorrent to him and to his work over the past fifteen years. Criminals already had enough excuses to avoid taking responsibility for their actions, without blaming their choice of parents too.

"Dr. Kerr, could you please outline the key scientific evidence that demonstrates that biology is a central factor in violent behavior and crime?"

Kathy Kerr cleared her throat and paused for a moment. "Let me start with a few facts. Firstly, biology is only *one* of several interrelated factors, including cultural, social, and economic influences, which lie at the root of violent crime. But the more we have learned over recent years, the more important we now understand it to be. Secondly, the biggest biological factor is gender. The world over, it is *men* who commit over ninety percent of all violent crimes."

Decker remembered back to their Harvard days nine years ago. His criminal psychology Ph.D. on using patterns of behavior to diagnose an offender's state of mind and determine his likelihood to offend again, rather than rely solely on the patient's own opinion, had been much praised. But Kathy Kerr's Ph.D. paper on behavioral genetics entitled "Why Men Commit 90 Percent of All Violent Crimes" had been so groundbreaking it had been published in *Nature,* one of the world's two most prestigious science journals. He hadn't agreed with it, but he'd had to concede it was brilliant.

Kathy continued, warming to her subject. "The male brain is different from the female brain, and understanding these differences is pivotal to understanding the small subset of criminally violent males. A chemical mixture of neurotransmitters and hormones drives the brain. Let me deal with neurotransmitters first. They are the chemical messengers controlling the flow of electrical messages in the network of nerve cells that allow the complex neural networks of the brain to communicate with one another. They influence and facilitate the thoughts of our mind and the actions of our bodies.

"There are four key neurotransmitters. Three of them—dopamine, adrenaline, and epinephrene—are very similar. They fuel the brain, stimulating many of our emotional and physical impulses, such as the fight or flight reflex. The fourth is serotonin; this is the vital brake that inhibits and modifies our waking behavior. Its specific function is to link the impulsive limbic part of the brain with the more civilized cortex. Put simply, without serotonin we would have no conscience or inhibitions.

"While neurotransmitters are responsible for the instigation of specific actions, hormones influence the broad pattern of behavior, although the interaction between them is complex. Again put simply, the higher the level of androgens, particularly testosterone, the higher a man's aggression and the lower his empathy with the pain or feelings of others."

Nodding, Latona stepped in. "So overall the male brain is more specifically wired and fueled for aggression, impulsiveness, and crime than is the female brain. But this doesn't mean that all men are violent criminals."

"Of course not," said Kathy with a wry smile. "Violent criminals are the small minority of men well outside the norm, for whom these natural differences have become amplified, exaggerated. There exists a range of physiological tests on which they can be reliably assessed versus the norm. For example, we can measure in the blood levels of MAO, an enzyme that acts as a marker for the neurotransmitter serotonin. And we can monitor levels of brain activity with PET scans and electroencephalograms—"

"OK," interrupted Latona. "So violent criminals are physiologically different. But how exactly does genetics fit into this picture?"

"The recent invention of the Genescope has enabled scientists to read an organism's entire sequence of genetic instructions. By conducting aggression studies on primates, my team and I have identified seventeen key genes that code for the production of critical hormones and neurotransmitters in male primates, including humans.

"These interdependent genes effectively determine man's aggressive behavior. And depending on how each gene's promoter, or volume control, is set, we can tell how loudly that gene will express its instructions. For example, we can predict dangerously low levels of serotonin or high levels of testosterone by studying the calibration of these genes. What we have discovered is that although everyone's gene settings change in reaction to particular stimuli, almost every individual has different base settings. If you see these seventeen key genes as cards, then every man is dealt a slightly different hand."

"Is it true that although this work was done originally on apes, it is now relevant to humans?" Latona asked.

"Yes, much of my recent work confirms these findings in men."

"So a man's genes determine if he is going to become a criminal or not?"

"To an extent. But I stress what I said earlier. Environmental, social, and cultural factors also have an influence. However, the crucial point is that humans are different from animals because they possess consciousness. This means that they are aware of the consequences of their actions. So regardless of any genetic predisposition, free will still plays a significant part in the choices humans make. But certainly some men, regardless of other influences, will find it more difficult than others to behave as society expects them to. The genes they inherited from their parents give them little choice."

Decker smiled. She sounded convincing. But then she had always been a good teacher with a flair for simplifying the most complex problem. As far as she was concerned, the world was one big puzzle that, if she thought about it hard enough and long enough, could be broken down into its component parts to find the one overarching rule that explained everything. To her the whole was never greater than the sum of its parts. That had been their problem. To him the whole was everything. He could never understand how humanity could be reduced to a line of programming. In the short time Kathy Kerr and Decker had been lovers during that last summer at Harvard they had spent most of their time in heated argument. The only area where they hadn't been incompatible was in bed. He thought of the five or six half-serious relationships he'd had in the last nine years and quickly realized that despite or perhaps because of the friction, none shone as vividly in his memory as those few summer months with her.

"You're aware of Wayne Tice's family history, aren't you, Dr. Kerr?" asked the lawyer, pulling out a large board and placing it on an easel by the judge. The network of names and lines on the board formed a simple family tree.

"Yes. That's why I agreed to be involved in this case."

As the lawyer turned to the chart, Luke knew what was coming. He too had studied Tice's family, and he shook his head as Latona explained that the spidery lines leading to boldly typed names revealed how four generations of Tice men had, with two individual exceptions, been drawn to crime. All were famed for their tempers and aggressive drives. "Think twice before you marry a Tice" was a watchword in their hometown.

The chart infuriated Decker. What did Tice have to complain about? He still had both parents, and he had a brother. Apart from his domineering mother and his successful brother making him feel inadequate, Tice had had it better than most. Decker would have given anything to have a whole family and to have known his father.

Fluent in Russian, Captain Richard Decker had been an interrogator with the U.S. Navy at the height of the Cold

War. As a child Decker often fantasized about his father's using his psychological skills to prize a piece of information vital to the safety of the free world from some recalcitrant Red admiral. Decker's mother used to reassure him that his own uncanny and unsettling ability to see into the minds of others must have been inherited from his brilliant father. But of course the Russians hadn't killed Captain Richard Decker; some street punk in San Francisco had. That was one of the reasons Decker had joined the bureau: to fight the war on the streets.

Turning back to Kathy, the lawyer asked, "Dr. Kerr, you have applied your battery of tests to my client and his immediate living family?"

"That's correct. I conducted a gene scan on Wayne Tice and a series of ancillary tests, checking serotonin, testosterone, and adrenaline levels. I also gave him a PET scan to probe brain activity on his frontal lobe. Tice's readings put him in the top five percent, in terms of propensity to violence. His male relations also have dangerous readings, although not nearly as high."

"So would it be fair to say that he and most of the menfolk in his family, through no fault of their own, carry a gene calibration that makes them predisposed to aggressive behavior and crime?"

"Yes, but—"

"But broadly speaking," interrupted the lawyer, eager not to let nuances of interpretation cloud his crucial point, "isn't it the case that Wayne Tice dances to the beat of a more violent drum?"

"Yes," said Kathy cautiously.

Latona smiled and turned to the judge. "So, Your Honor, Wayne Tice was born with a particular set of genes, calibrated in such a way that he had to commit murder."

"That's not what I said," protested Kathy. "I am talking about predisposition. No more. No less. Ultimately a person decides—"

"Excuse me, Your Honor." The lawyer deftly corrected himself before the frowning judge could intervene. "He was *predisposed* to commit violent crime. But the point is, How can Wayne Tice be punished for his actions? He should be counseled, not executed. He was doing only what he was born to do."

Latona paused and turned back to Kathy Kerr.

"How can we put a young man to death for simply doing what came naturally?"

2

After giving evidence to Latona and then the district attorney, Kathy Kerr retook her seat. Glad her session was over, she began to relax. Unless she was teaching, she always felt uncomfortable speaking in public, especially in court, where any words could be twisted to suit a purpose. After Latona had finished with her, the DA had given her a tough time, but she had expected that. Latona angered her, though, trying to use her evidence to shift all responsibility for the horrific murders from Tice. She had agreed to testify only because Tice was a classic case and would make an excellent research subject, if ViroVector received the expected FDA approval to begin the Project Conscience Phase 2 efficacy trials. Kathy didn't support the notion that Tice's genes allowed him to shirk all responsibility for his actions.

There was one other reason she had felt uncomfortable giving her testimony. She had known that Luke Decker was going to be here.

Watching the tall FBI agent take her place on the witness stand, she was surprised how much he'd changed. His appearance was similar, the lean physique a little broader perhaps, the blond hair shorter, and the face more defined, but those penetrating green eyes had lost none of their sensitive intelligence. It was his bearing that was different. He had more presence somehow; his gait was more confident, as if the hunted younger man she had once known had now become the hunter.

Like most of America, she'd seen the press coverage of Decker carrying Tammy Lewis from the graveyard near Oakland, his face a mask of rage. She'd recognized that look from years ago, when his night terrors used to wake her at three in the morning.

Back then they had been lovers. She'd known Luke Decker was different from that first time she'd walked into him in the Harvard library, knocking his pile of books all over the floor. Each book had been about the darker side of humanity, from biographies of Jeffrey Dahmer and Ted Bundy to textbooks on the criminal mind. But as she'd apologized, he'd just laughed and piled his books up under his chin, making a joke about how heavy a bit of nighttime reading could be.

Even then she had discouraged men's advances, refusing to be distracted from her work, but she could still taste the disappointment when those soft green eyes had examined her, smiled again, and then moved on. Decker had made no attempt to exploit the occasion, so she'd had to stammer something about helping him carry his books, the least she could do after knocking them over.

"If you like." He'd shrugged with a casualness that had both frustrated and delighted her.

They couldn't agree on anything they discussed, but within two weeks they made love, and for those precious, magical moments they were in total accord. After that they had become inseparable, but he always seemed to retain some small part of himself. Kathy felt she caught a true glimpse of his soul only during those terrifying nights when he would sit bolt upright in bed, drenched in sweat, his eyes wide open. He would start speaking to some invisible presence directly in front of him, his voice angry: "You wanted control, didn't you? That was why you did it. You didn't actually want them dead. You only wanted slaves who would do whatever you wanted without ruining the fantasy. That's right," he'd conclude, having solved some puzzle troubling his subconscious. Then he would lie down again. At first she'd tried to soothe him, until she realized that he'd remained asleep throughout. In the mornings he would remember nothing, except resolving something that had been worrying him. It took her weeks to realize that he had an ability to understand man's baser desires that went beyond normal experience. And that this ability haunted him.

His mother told him his intuition came from his father, but Kathy knew Decker felt it was more than just intuition. He was scared that somehow he was tainted.

While still at Harvard, he would follow national cases and write in advice to the relevant police authorities or even the FBI. She always felt he was driven by some inner force, always trying to exorcise something deep within himself, something she could do nothing to reach, let alone soothe.

She could handle the arguments and the fact that they couldn't agree on anything, especially their views on the roots of crime. It was his reserve she found the hardest to take. He could never relax and just be. He always seemed to be on the defensive, always on guard against himself. As independent as she was, she needed at least one thing from their relationship: to be needed.

But now, as Luke answered the district attorney's questions, she found herself asking what might have been if the timing had been different.

When she returned to the States from Cambridge, she often heard of him through her dealings with the FBI. But on the few occasions she made halfhearted attempts to contact him he had been unavailable. In fact he seemed to be forever in transit around the country, helping solve crimes or teaching local police forces profiling techniques. Despite the new regime's reliance on hard science and biology, time and time again Special Agent Luke Decker had proved himself indispensable in solving the more intractable cases. She'd heard that his colleagues, no mean mind hunters themselves, called him Luke the Spook, a tribute to his ability. She only hoped that by hunting down the demons in others, Luke had found some respite from those warring inside himself.

"I don't know whether Tice should be executed or not," she suddenly heard Decker say. His voice wasn't raised, but from his tone she could tell he was angry. "That isn't my province. My only concern is that he isn't allowed out on the streets again—ever." For all his faults and distrust of the genetic revolution, Decker had one quality that she admired above all others: an almost naive integrity.

But when Latona took his turn to question him, the defense lawyer soon realized that Decker was no patsy. "Surely after hearing Dr. Kerr's evidence, you must concede that Tice needs help? That he's genetically programmed to do what he did?"

Decker smiled, a wide, disarming smile that seemed to say, "Surely you don't expect any reasonable human being to believe that." Then he turned toward her. "Dr. Kerr and I disagree on the relative importance of genetic predetermination. Genes may well be a factor, but they are only that, one in a series of factors. And they certainly aren't an excuse. Yes, I believe your client does need help, but I'm also convinced he will always remain dangerous whatever treatment he may or may not receive. Let me tell you something about how he came to be the way he is." At that moment Decker turned toward Tice. Decker was still smiling, and his smile was genuinely compassionate. For the first time in the glare of the court's attention Tice looked self-conscious, his cocky, defiant grin frozen on his face.

"Wayne Tice is now twenty-one and until his arrest lived at home with his parents. His elder brother, Jerry, is a successful manager for a major insurance company. Jerry attended UCLA and had a string of girlfriends. He has recently married and has a beautiful wife. Both parents doted on Jerry, whereas they told Wayne not to expect too much from life. His mother continually reminded him that he wasn't as smart or good-looking as his brother."

Still looking at Tice, Decker began to address him directly, sounding as if he were Tice's best friend and confidant. There was no judgment or censure in his voice. "Your first overtures with girls weren't happy, were they, Wayne? They couldn't look beyond your crooked teeth, freckles, and red hair, could they—"

Latona interrupted, his voice betraying a sudden slip in his slick composure. "Excuse me, Special Agent Decker, but

I don't believe that manipulative questioning of the defendant—"

Decker's eyes remained locked with Tice's, oblivious of Latona, of everything except his connection with the killer. He continued to talk. "And you felt shy. You wanted them to like you, but they were unkind. They laughed at you, didn't they?"

Tice looked uncertain now.

"Your Honor, this line of leading interrogations is outrageous," said Latona.

The judge looked from Tice to Decker as he considered. "This isn't a trial, Counsel. This is a hearing, and I want to hear where this goes."

Decker continued. "So every day you went to the gym to get stronger and stronger. How much can you press now? One-fifty, one-sixty?"

"Two hundred," said Tice without thinking.

Decker raised an eyebrow in surprise. "That's more than me, and I'm about three inches taller than you. That's pretty impressive."

Tice smiled.

"You do martial arts too, don't you, Wayne? Karate, isn't it?"

"Yeah."

"What belt?"

"Black."

Again Decker looked impressed, and this time he smiled the smile of a proud elder brother. "Only ever got to brown myself."

Kathy saw Latona start to object, but the judge waved him down, watching the exchange. "Must have really made you mad to have achieved all that and still be regarded as a loser by your mother," said Decker. "I would have been pissed."

Tice said nothing, just stared at Decker, as if he were the first guy in the whole goddamn world to understand his shitty life.

"But you loved your mother and couldn't hit out at her. So you thought you'd teach one of the girls a lesson, one of the pretty girls who'd laughed at you. One day a young girl about the same age as the ones who used to dis you at high school came into the pizza parlor, and although she was real nice, you knew she was mocking you. She didn't even realize that you'd grown up, that you'd improved. You could now press two hundred and had a black belt at karate. But she was still giving you the brushoff like you were some geek at school."

Tice looked white, his eyes wide.

"Am I right?"

Tice didn't actually nod, but Kathy could tell he wanted to.

"Killing her and the second girl felt good, didn't it? You got what you wanted: the control. You taught them that you weren't some loser. You taught them respect, and then you killed them. But the third girl was different, Wayne; you covered her head when you killed her. You felt bad about Sally Anne Jennings, didn't you? She liked you. Came to visit you at the pizza parlor and talked to you—*really* talked to you, like you were a regular guy. Am I right?"

Kathy saw Tice's Adam's apple bob in his throat; then he gave a definite nod.

"But you killed her anyway. Mistaking her kindness for something else, you made a pass at her, and when she got scared, you killed her. You felt bad about it, so you covered her face, tried to depersonalize her. But you still felt bad about it afterward, couldn't get her out of your head. You thought she was judging you. So when the next girl came along, Tammy Lewis, you decided to take her to Sally Anne's grave. You wanted to show Sally Anne that she didn't have any hold over you." Decker shook his head then. It was a gesture of sadness. "But I was waiting for you. If it's any consolation, Wayne, it wouldn't have worked. You still would have felt bad about killing Sally Anne, however many girls you raped and killed on her gravestone. In fact it would have got worse."

Tice sat slumped in his chair, shaking his head. He looked as stunned as the rest of the silent courtroom.

Then Decker turned quickly to the judge and gestured at the chart of Tice's family tree. "This isn't about genetics. In fact, Tice's own brother is in many ways a model citizen. This is about a man whose programming came from the screwed-up signals of sex, violence, inadequacy, and love he received from his family and his peer group. Tice, like all of us, is a creation of his past. But ultimately he *chose* to do what he did, and the responsibility rests with him. Tice is a very dangerous man. He has acquired a taste for controlling women he can't win through normal mating rituals. And the risk is very high that he will revert to this behavior in the future. It's not in his genes; it's there in his head."

Kathy could tell from the look on the judge's face that any chance of Tice's original sentence's being changed had gone. Not long after Decker retook his seat, the judge's stern voice confirmed her fear, announcing that Tice's appeal was denied and he was to return to death row pending execution. Kathy shook her head. She didn't agree with the death penalty any more than any other kind of killing. All her adult life had been focused on one aim: developing a way to modify the genes that coded for senseless violence, making it a thing of the past, an eradicated plague like smallpox. Tice would have been a good subject for her trials if the Food and Drug Administration approval came through on Project Conscience as expected. Dr. Alice Prince, her sponsor at ViroVector, was confident of getting that approval.

She watched Luke rise, shake hands with the DA, and then walk toward her. She stood, uncertain what to do. Suddenly nervous, she remembered how they had last parted, he seeing her off at Logan Airport, both of them making vague promises to stay in touch, both recognizing the end. A kiss good-bye and then not a word exchanged between them for nine years.

"Kathy, what a surprise. And I do mean surprise." There was a fleeting pause before he extended his hand in greeting.

"I know," she said with a smile as she took his hand in hers. Up close he looked tired. "I guess I had a small advantage. I knew you'd be here. Although a courtroom's not exactly the place I thought we'd meet again," she said. "Certainly not on opposing sides in a murder case."

Decker smiled. "I thought we were always on opposing sides."

"Perhaps," she said, feeling the old abrasive itch return. "Anyway, you won today. Another villain safely tucked away on death row."

Decker's eyes flashed for a second as if he were about to meet her challenge. Then he shrugged in that deceptively casual way of his. "You're looking good, Kathy. What are you doing in the States? I thought you were in England."

"I was for almost a year, but then I got a grant from ViroVector to come to Stanford University and continue my work."

"So you've been back in the States eight years?" He frowned.

"I've tried to contact you a few times," she said quickly. "But you were never around when I called, and well, it didn't seem right just to leave a message somehow. . . ." She trailed off.

"Yes, I've been busy, far too busy. So what brought you back? What about that brilliant offer from Cambridge University? The one that made you go back to the U.K. in the first place."

"Excellent academically, but this was better for practical reasons. You know? All the normal stuff, unlimited funds, access to the resources of a leading biotech company, learning from the great Alice Prince. Plus of course the cooperation of your crowd, the FBI. I've been working directly with Director Naylor, and access to the FBI DNA database alone was enough to convince me." She felt as if she were showing off. But she couldn't help it. "Perhaps we could go for a drink or something?" she said, not knowing what else to say. "We could catch up."

"I'd like that," Decker said, checking his watch. "Damn it. But not now. I've got to interview a killer on death row in less than an hour."

Kathy smiled. "I haven't heard that excuse before."

Decker grinned, and in an instant his face changed, and he was the younger man she had known at Harvard. "I'm sorry that didn't come out right. Believe me, I'd much rather have a drink with you. But I can't. I can't do it tonight either, I'm afraid; I'm seeing my grandfather. And I'm due back to Washington tomorrow." He reached into his jacket pocket and pulled out a card and scribbled something on the back. "Look, I'll be around San Francisco more often in the future. This is my grandfather's address; it's the old family house in the Marina. Give me a call, and we'll catch up when I'm next here. For all I know, you're married with kids by now."

Kathy paused to look into his eyes, but they were giving nothing away. "I've been far too busy to get married, Luke," she said simply. In fact she'd had only three relationships worth talking about in the intervening years, all of which had been at best forgettable. She wasn't short of offers, just offers from people she liked. And apart from the occasional dinner date, usually with men who turned out to have less charm than the contents of a petri dish, she had been single and celibate for the last thirteen months and three weeks, not that she was counting. She reached into her jacket and handed Decker her card. "Anyway, here's where you can contact me when you're next here."

"Thanks," he said. But as soon as they both pocketed each other's cards, she knew they probably wouldn't meet again for at least another nine years. There was simply no reason to. It surprised her how sad this made her feel.

She shook his hand. "Good-bye, Luke. I hope your killer on death row tells you what you want to know."

3

Baghdad, Iraq.
Wednesday, October 29, 5:13 P.M.

Salah Khatib could barely see for the sweat pouring off his brow. But his condition had little to do with the heat of the windowless chamber beneath the barracks of Baghdad's Al Taji Camp.

"What are you waiting for? Shoot them!" hissed the captain, his face inches from Private Khatib's ear, his breath hot on his cheek.

Khatib locked his elbow and aimed the heavy pistol at the nearest of the four men kneeling on the floor in front of him, but still he couldn't prevent his hand from shaking.

The four men in uniforms like his own had been caught trying to desert two nights ago. The rumors of the advance south to retake the province of Kuwait had excited most of his fellow soldiers. After all, they were the Northern Corps Armored Division of the elite Republican Guard; it would be their invincible tanks that led the assault. But these four cowards had chosen to desert, not from some conscripted troop but from the well-fed, well-trained Tenth Brigade. These dogs deserved to die. Bullets were a kindness to their shame.

He even knew two of the men and hated them. They had made his life hell when he first joined. But now, given the opportunity to kill them, he couldn't pull the trigger.

28

And he couldn't understand why.

Khatib loved the army, wanted nothing more than to obey its orders. He had joined two years ago and had never been more content. A twenty-one-year-old mechanic from the back streets of Tikrit, he had been caught in a failed gang robbery, but because of his gift with machines, he had been given a choice of jail or the army. The armored division had given him a sense of direction and belonging he had never felt before. Only a week ago he had received the full batch of vaccinations for going to war. He was destined to be a hero. So why couldn't he obey his captain's order?

Two of the men were looking up at him now, as if aware that something was wrong.

"Shoot them!" The captain seethed, his lips almost touching Khatib's ear.

"Sir, *we* can shoot them," whispered Ali Keram, one of the five other soldiers standing at the back of the chamber.

"No," said the captain, his face red with rage. He pulled a revolver from his holster and pushed it into Khatib's temple. "I gave an order to Private Khatib, and he will obey it. If you don't follow my orders, I will shoot *you* dead. Now do your duty."

Using the sleeve of his tunic, Khatib rubbed the sweat from his face, the rough fabric scratching the pustules and acne that had broken out on his cheeks. Black flecks stuck to his sleeve. His hair had started falling out four days ago. He tried to clear his mind, but it was impossible. Last night he saw hallucinations of people he and his old gang had robbed in the past. They'd come to him in his bunk back at the barracks, taunting him, admonishing him for his petty sins. Now he felt so torn and confused he didn't know what was happening to him. Over the past few days he had been beset, on the one hand, by surges of raging aggression and, on the other, by sloughs of guilt-ridden depression. He had tried to disguise his mood swings, but now he didn't even want to go to war. He could even understand why these dogs had deserted.

Standing there in the gloomy underground chamber staring at the soiled walls, leveling his pistol at the men, he was unable to pull the trigger. As the snout of the captain's revolver ground into Khatib's temple, he felt such mental torment that he found himself closing his eyes and pushing his head against the officer's revolver, willing him to fire. He was terrified of dying, but at that moment it seemed like an escape.

Slumping his shoulders, Salah Khatib dropped his gun onto the stone floor.

He didn't hear the captain's order to the other soldiers or see them step forward, heard only their shots reverberate deafeningly around the confined space. Opening his eyes, he saw the deserters jerk to the ground, a pool of red spreading from their bodies, adding to the marks that already soiled the stone floor.

It was with a sense of relieved detachment that Khatib heard the shot fired from the captain's pistol before the bullet plowed into his brain.

San Quentin Penitentiary, The Same Day, 3:19 P.M.

Driving over the Golden Gate Bridge from the courthouse, Luke Decker turned off the car radio. He was sick of hearing about the Iraq crisis and next week's presidential election. Pamela Weiss already had his vote; a woman couldn't make more of a mess of things than her male predecessors. He adjusted his Ray-Bans and glanced out across the bay. The sky was a clear pale blue, and the darker sea below was bejeweled with reflections from the afternoon sun and the small armada of yachts and boats. The scene reminded Decker of his childhood, when his mother and grandfather used to take him up Coit Tower to look out across the Pacific. As a child he would stare out into the blue and imagine the heroic father he never knew waving from the bridge of a mighty warship, returning home from some secret and glorious mission.

Decker had been brought up in the Bay Area and had roots here. He may have neglected them, particularly his grandfather and the few old friends he still had from his college days at Berkeley before he left for Harvard and the all-consuming FBI, but they still existed. He was convinced that he was doing the right thing leaving the gray oppressive bureau and returning here to teach at Berkeley. Perhaps he would follow up his surprise meeting with Kathy Kerr. Yeah, right. All he needed now was Kathy Kerr back in his life just when he was getting himself together. Round-the-clock arguments and his world turned upside down.

Leaving the bridge and passing through Marin County, he glanced at the open files on the passenger seat of the Ford rental. A man's face stared out at him from a color photograph on the top of a pile of documents. The face was handsome with high cheekbones, green eyes, and lightly tanned skin. His thick silver hair was cut short and neatly styled. He looked like a powerful politician, an eminent doctor, or a charismatic captain of industry.

But Karl Axelman was none of these things. He was a killer who made Wayne Tice look like a choirboy.

Dubbed the Collector by the media, Axelman was still the only serial killer in American legal history to have been convicted and condemned to death without any trace of the bodies being found. A successful construction site foreman for thirty years, Axelman had been arrested seven years ago for the murders of at least twelve teenage girls over a period spanning decades.

Twelve neatly labeled boxes, giving each girl's full name, physical statistics, date, and place of abduction, were discovered in a concealed chamber built into a wall of his house in San Jose. Each box contained the clothing the girls had last worn, their personal effects, and an audiotape. On the tape Axelman could be heard giving each victim a minute to explain why she should be spared. All were forbidden to hesitate, repeat themselves, or cry while pleading for their lives. It would seem that all failed. None was seen again.

Decker hadn't been directly involved in the case, but he'd read the files and formed his own impression. Now in his mid-fifties, Axelman was still a master of control. He had been a highly organized killer who honed his technique over the years. His profile showed that he had probably broken the law most of his life, starting with indecent assaults, graduating to violent rapes and finally murders. The twelve teenage girls had been abducted over a twenty-year period, at roughly eighteen-month intervals. This told Decker that each abduction had been planned in meticulous detail, with the stalking and anticipation giving Axelman as much excitement as the eventual act itself. The fact that the bodies had never been found meant Axelman had stored them someplace where he could visit them again and again, thus enabling him to stave off his need to kill for long intervals.

Karl Axelman would have gone undetected too, if seven years ago his Jeep Cherokee hadn't been involved in a collision on the Bay Bridge. The California Highway Patrol had found playing on his deck a tape of one of the girls pleading for her life. Axelman evidently listened for pleasure to the tape, stacked alongside the Carpenters and Leonard Cohen, as he drove from his home to the construction site he was working on. Decker guessed it was one more trophy, along with the boxed belongings of each victim, that allowed him to relive his crimes and delay the need to kill again until he was fully sated.

After his arrest the FBI had searched his house and eventually found the twelve boxes. Decker's FBI colleagues in forensics couldn't have amassed a better mountain of evidence confirming Axelman's guilt, but despite every inducement, threat, and deal, Karl Axelman never told them where the bodies were. "Don't worry," he'd said with a chilling smile, "their bodies are fine. And they'll stay that way."

Even after being sentenced to death, he had shown no remorse or inclination to reveal any details about how they had died or what he had done with their bodies. Agents on at least three occasions in the past had interviewed him with no success.

So as the yellow walls of San Quentin Penitentiary came into view, Decker had few illusions about his chances. But this could be the bureau's last opportunity. Somehow over the last seven years Axelman had managed to postpone his date with the recently reinstated gas chamber, successfully appealing and being granted a stay of execution on several occasions. Decker checked the file. His date with destiny was now scheduled for tomorrow, Thursday, October 30. It was at least fifty-fifty he'd wriggle out of it again.

Parking his car in the visitors' lot, Decker considered how Axelman had asked for him by name probably because of his involvement in the Tice murders. It occasionally happened that way after a high-profile case. He took off his suit jacket and tie and rolled up his sleeves. The last thing he wanted to look like when interviewing a con on the row was a stiff G-man. He gathered his files together, put them in his case, and locked it in the trunk of the car. Then he collected his pad, pen, and tape recorder and walked toward the imposing entrance of the prison.

The recent security changes meant that San Quentin, like most state penitentiaries, had increased the number of guards. Decker had been here often in the past and recognized most of the men on the gate when he handed in his gun and showed his badge. No one bothered to ask him what he was here for; he was just waved through the metal detector and X-ray scanner. One guard, a tall black man in a neatly pressed uniform named Clarence Pitt, escorted him into the inner prison more out of habit than necessity. Decker knew exactly where he was going. He had requested the private visiting room he always used when interviewing cons.

"Watch the game, Decker?" Clarence Pitt asked as they walked past the adjustment center, where death row inmates were placed when they first arrived. He looked perplexed, as if something unjust and unfathomable had come to pass. "The Forty-niners got creamed *again*."

Decker laughed. As a kid he'd been an ardent fan. "What do you expect? When was the last time they won anything?"

Pitt shook his head and frowned. He looked genuinely upset. "You always gotta have hope," he said, and then fell into silence.

"Ain't that the truth," mumbled Decker, looking around him. He had never got over his hatred of these places, never got used to his deep discomfort whenever he visited them. There was a pervasive smell that tainted every prison he'd visited across the States, a bitter blend of institutional disinfectant, stale air, sweat, and despair. He looked down and studied his shoes as they neared the north segment of the prison where the green chimney of the gas chamber rose to belch its poisonous fumes into the sky. Decker's spirits lifted for a moment when he considered that this would be his last visit to death row.

Eventually they reached the private visiting room, and Pitt stood aside from the closed steel door. "He's waiting inside with his attorney. You know the drill. I'll be outside if you need me."

"Thanks, Clarence." In his mind he went over the key points he wanted to cover with Axelman and his strategy. Taking a deep breath, he ensured that he felt calm and in control. Then he opened the door.

Not much surprised him anymore. But the sight of Karl Axelman sitting manacled to the stainless steel table in the middle of the room shocked him so much that he broke one of his cardinal rules and allowed it to show on his face. What astonished him even more was the equally obvious shock on Axelman's face.

Decker immediately turned to Axelman's attorney to regain his composure. The lawyer introduced himself as Tad Rosenblum. He was a round man with a cherubic face and curly brown hair, graying at the temples.

"Special Agent Decker, I want to make it perfectly clear that my client has agreed to speak to you against my instructions. His execution date is scheduled for tomorrow, and an appeal is currently lodged with the governor. My client is in an extreme state of agitation verging on the irrational. If I feel that speaking to you makes his condition deteriorate any further, I will overrule Mr. Axelman and immediately stop this interview. Is that clear?"

Decker nodded slowly. He didn't bother to make it clear to Mr. Rosenblum that his client had asked to see him, not the other way around, or that if Decker felt Axelman was wasting his time, *he* would stop the interview. "Mr. Rosenblum, I was under the impression your client wanted to see me alone."

Rosenblum frowned, and Decker could see the lawyer's jaw muscles twitch. "I shall be outside."

Now that Decker felt calmer he turned back to Axelman, keeping his face devoid of expression. But it was difficult. Axelman no longer looked like his photograph. His groomed thick hair had fallen out in clumps, exposing pink scalp beneath. His skin was pitted with acne, and he clearly hadn't slept in an age. The man's eyes were bloodshot and puffy with dark shadows beneath them. But what unnerved Decker the most was the way those eyes stared at him. Axelman seemed mesmerized by him, studying him like some rare antique whose authenticity was in doubt.

Decker sat at the table facing the convicted killer. "Karl, my name is Luke Decker. I run the behavioral sciences unit at the FBI training academy in Quantico, Virginia. You asked to speak with me."

Axelman said nothing, just continued staring at him. Rosenblum was right. He didn't look rational. This wasn't the man Decker had read about. Axelman was supposed to be an iceman, an arrogant control freak who would pretend to tell him where the victims were buried and then at the last minute give Decker nothing and laugh in his face. That was what Decker had prepared for. But this man looked on the verge of a breakdown. Could the imminence of his execution be getting to him this time? Or was this an even more elaborate mind fuck? If so, it was a good one.

Decker smiled at the man as if he were a patient rather than a criminal. He kept his voice friendly and matter-of-fact. "Karl, is there anything you want to tell me? Anything you want to talk to me about?"

For a second Decker thought Axelman was going to say something. He leaned forward, and Decker instinctively copied his body language and leaned forward too. But then Axelman shook his head and let out a low moan. He seemed to be fighting some battle in his head. "I can't tell you," he whispered suddenly, holding his head in his hands.

Decker frowned. A battle was raging in his head too. His

experience told him that the man was screwing with him, doing what he'd done to three other agents before him. But Decker could also see that the man was patently troubled, physically and mentally. "Why can't you tell me?" Decker asked reasonably.

"I can't," Axelman shouted suddenly. "I thought I could. But I fuckin' can't. Not face-to-face." His body began to shake, and he seemed about to crush his head in his hands as if trying to make it disappear. From being unable to stop staring at Decker, Axelman now couldn't meet his eyes.

Decker rose slowly from the table. He had seen manipulative killers feign madness before, and many had done it brilliantly, but usually he could tell. This was different. He kept his voice calm and matter-of-fact. "If you have nothing to tell me, I may as well leave."

Axelman stood and pulled at his manacles, reaching for him. "No," he shouted in panic.

"Then talk to me. There's no point in my staying if you won't say anything."

"I can't," Axelman screamed at him, so loud that Decker heard the scrabble of the door being unlocked behind him. The man was demented or putting on a very good display. Either way Decker wasn't too disappointed that Axelman's protective lawyer was coming in to end the interview.

But his instinct told him to try one last time. Moving to the door, he saw the handle being turned from the outside. "I'm going now, Karl," he said calmly. "Just explain one thing before I go. Why couldn't you tell me? What's the problem here?"

Axelman slumped back into his chair defeated. As he did so, he said something so quiet and so outlandish that Decker assumed he had misheard it.

Decker stepped toward the murderer. "What? What was that?"

Axelman sat statue-still, his shoulders slumped, his head bowed. A droplet of sweat dripped off the tip of his nose and shattered on the table. Behind him Decker could hear the door opening, but before Rosenblum could enter, Decker grabbed the handle and pushed against the door with his body weight to keep it closed.

Then Axelman repeated what he had said.

Although the killer only whispered the four words, Decker heard each one as clearly as if it had been shouted into his ear: "I am your father."

4

ViroVector Solutions, Inc., Palo Alto, California.
Wednesday, October 29, 3:47 P.M.

Dr. Alice Prince was more preoccupied than usual. After adjusting her thick, round eyeglasses, she brushed back wiry black hair, streaked with gray. Her white lab coat had been buttoned incorrectly, making it appear as if her right shoulder was drooping. When she wandered through the reception lobby of ViroVector's vast dome and nodded at numerous members of her staff as she passed, a few of them stopped to tell their boss that her jacket was crooked. All did it with a respectful and affectionate smile as if this weren't the first time. To each one she gave a small smile and a thank-you and then moved on, leaving her buttons untouched. She had more important things on her mind. The project she had been working on for years was finally coming to fruition. But now that the theory would soon be a reality she could see all the small things that could unravel. In particular she was trying to remember exactly when Karl Axelman was meant to die.

Now fifty-one, Alice Prince had founded ViroVector Solutions in 1987, two days before her thirtieth birthday. Twenty-one years later her brainchild was already the world's third-largest biotech company and the most influential on the West Coast. Headquartered just south of Palo Alto between San Francisco and San Jose, its sprawling campus comprised the huge crystal dome, three separate hundred-yard production sheds, a helicopter landing pad, a sports complex, and a parking lot. Bordering a science park and the Bellevue Golf and Country Club, the perimeter was protected with a lightweight steel fence, linked to a series of sensitive scanners and alarms. The crystal dome, like the rest of the campus, was a so-called smart building, designed by the celebrated British architechnologist Sir Simon Canning. It resembled a visiting spaceship, particularly at night when the interior lights illuminated the predominantly glass structure. But everyone at ViroVector called it the Iceberg because the visible part of the building, which housed the commercial offices, administrative departments, and the supercomputer TITANIA, was a tiny part of the overall structure. The majority of it was underground, where the extensive warren of biocontainment laboratories was located.

It was to the underground laboratories that Dr. Alice Prince was heading now. After going through one of three doors off the dome's ground-floor reception hall, she walked down a long corridor, past a white door on her left. AUTHORIZED ENTRY ONLY was stamped above the acronym TITANIA. As she passed, the temperature in the corridor dropped slightly. The Cold Room housed ViroVector's vast protein-based biocomputer. TITANIA, an acronym for Total Information Technology and Neural Intelligence Analogue, was the artificially intelligent brain that controlled and coordinated all the smart buildings and most of ViroVector's corporate functions, from data capture and manipulation to production scheduling, project management, payroll, and security.

At the end of the corridor Alice stopped before a yellow door marked with a large black biohazard symbol. And when Alice placed her palm on the door sensors, it was TITANIA that recognized her DNA profile and ratified her Gold clearance to the biolab complex. Through the yellow door was a small vestibule with a computer terminal and a printer. Two white-coated female technicians greeted her, and she smiled back. She wished she had a better memory for names because she recognized their faces. From here she walked to another door, which again required TITANIA to check her identity before hissing open to reveal a transit station containing lockers and shower cubicles. She undressed and took a quick shower, then dressed in surgical greens and safety goggles. She now walked to one of two yellow elevators with large black biohazard symbols on the doors.

Inside the elevator there was only one button with a star on it. When she pressed it, the doors closed, and she felt the high-speed cabin descend fifty feet underground to the main complex. As the doors opened, the safety goggles shielded her eyes from the ultraviolet light in the screening corridor outside. The light was used to break down viruses. At the end of the corridor was an entry area that gave access to the underground system of five concentric circles forming ViroVector's biosafety laboratory complex.

The structure was built to exacting federal standards and could withstand an earthquake or a direct hit from any known warhead. This was intended less to protect the inhabitants than to ensure nothing inside escaped. The concentric circle design was based on the Russian model; each glass-walled airtight circle was kept at an increasingly lower air pressure toward the center. Any breach in the reinforced glass walls would suck air into and not out of the structure.

Each circle represented a staging post, reflecting the four classified levels of virus. Level one viruses, such as influenza, were stored and researched in the outer circle. Levels two and three viruses, including HIV and hepatitis, were in two circles closer to the center and required increased protective clothing and vaccinations. Level four viruses, so-called hot agents, such as Ebola and Marburg, with up to a 90 percent mortality rate, were housed in the penultimate area and required full biological suits. In the few institutions authorized to house these highly infectious agents, including the U.S. Army Research Institute of Infectious Diseases (USAMRIID) at Fort Detrick in Maryland and the Centers for Disease Control in Atlanta, there was no more dangerous area than the BioSafety Level 4 lab, the so-called Hot Zone.

But at ViroVector there was one more level of peril. The

central circle was a Level 5 facility. Ahead was an airtight door. "BioSafety Level 1," was printed on the glass in ten-inch-high red letters. Again she placed her palm over the DNA sensor and stepped through when the door opened. Walking down a glass corridor, she could see the Level 1 laboratory facilities to her left and right. They were busy but not overpopulated with white-coated virologists. Much of her viral work was now automated. In one corner on the right were the huge stainless steel refrigerators that housed ViroVector's library of bacteriophage samples. Alice Prince was particularly proud of her phage collection.

ViroVector owned the largest selection of phage specimens known to humankind. These quasi-viruses fed on bacteria, such as *Mycobacterium, Staphylococcus,* and *Enterococcus.* Each was bacterium-specific, feeding off a particular strain, mutating with it so the bacterium could never develop immunity, as it could to antibiotics. In the mid-nineties, at a time when the power of bacteriophage technology was discredited by the giant drug companies still trying to sell their increasingly ineffective antibiotics, Alice Prince had seen an opportunity.

Her company had bought access to the vast phage library in the Tbilisi Institute in Georgia, collected during the Soviet Communist era of central control. Having replicated and enlarged the collection, ViroVector now had a phage virus to kill most known bacteria. And since the year 2000 many Western hospitals, plagued by antibiotic-immune superbugs, such as methicillin-resistant *Staphylococcus aureus* and vancomycin-resistant *Enterococcus,* had been forced to use her company's products to sterilize their wards and operating rooms. Now airports and many train stations and seaports used ViroVector's bacteriophage air purifiers in their embarkation and disembarkation tunnels, as viral customs officers to reduce the risk of deadly bacteria moving around the world with their human hosts. The bacteriophage business had become ViroVector's major income stream, funding much of its growth.

Looking straight ahead, Alice made her way through the sealed doors leading to BioSafety Level 2 and then Level 3.

These labs were smaller, and many of the personnel wore masks. Leaving Level 3, she found herself in a decontamination and preparation area equipped with chemical decon showers, scrub stations, and another row of lockers. Alice walked to her locker and pulled out a blue Chemturion biological space suit with "Alice Prince" printed on the back. After checking it for tears, she suited up and then made her way to the BioSafety Level 4 door. Keeping her head still, she allowed the retina scanner to confirm her identity through the glass of her visor and then walked into a buffer chamber. Once the first door had closed the next opened, and she was finally in a glass corridor that passed through Level 4. She was now in the hot core of the biolab complex. To her right was a door to the Level 4 labs, and through the glass she could see scientists wearing suits similar to hers. To her left was another yellow elevator door. This led down two more levels to the extensively equipped BioSafety Level 4 hospital and the BioSafety Level 4 morgue below that. Both were rarely used, but every eventuality had to be covered.

Dr. Prince carried on to the heart of the biolab complex, to the door with "BioSafety Level 5" stamped on it in red. Standing for her retina to be scanned one final time, she waited for the door to open, allowing her access to what most scientists at ViroVector ironically called the Womb.

The Womb was one of the most perilous places on earth. Gleaming apparatus sat atop otherwise uncluttered worktops, and in one corner stood a six-foot-high Genescope, the black swanlike instrument that could decode an organism's entire genome from one body cell. The room looked harmless enough with its nonslip white floor tiles, spotless stainless steel tables, freezers, and walls of reinforced glass. But despite the reassuring cleanliness and hi-tech equipment, humans did not reign here. The virus did. And one pinprick in Prince's protective clothing could mean a short visit down to the BioSafety Level 4 hospital before she was transferred even lower to the BioSafety Level 4 morgue.

However, as soon as she entered the Womb and heard the door hiss closed behind her, Prince felt safer than when she was in the outside world. Usually she had an assistant with her, but today she wanted privacy, so she had the room to herself. This place was classified as BioSafety Level 5 because nature was not only studied in here but tampered with. And when one played God, there was always the risk of creating an even more deadly strain.

It was in the Womb that Prince and her team genetically engineered viruses and created new ones. Viruses are basically nonthinking capsules of genetic material wrapped in protein that exist to seek out hosts in order to reproduce themselves. When a virus finds a host with receptive cells, it enters one of those cells and, like a cuckoo taking over a sparrow's nest, usurps the genetic code already there, replacing it with its own. Then, when the cell containing the new viral DNA divides and replicates, the virus copies itself. Thus the virus spreads throughout the body.

This property made it ideal for delivering gene therapy, the technology of spreading modified genes throughout a human patient's damaged cells. By scooping out a virus's own genetic material, Prince and her team could render it harmless. They could then insert new therapeutic DNA into the virus and create a vector to target a diseased cancer cell or cystic fibrosis cell and reprogram the cell's damaged genes. Creating viral vectors was at the very heart of ViroVector's work. Alice Prince had founded her company by specializing in turning lethal viral killers into genetically engineered "magic bullets" to deliver some of the most spectacular cures in modern medicine. With viral vectors she could change a human's genes, correcting the genetic inheritance received at birth.

ViroVector had become successful by focusing on viral DNA. It rarely developed the therapeutic human genes, just the viral vector to target and deliver them to the patient. Prince and her team knew more about viruses than any organization on earth. Even the CDC in Atlanta and USAMRIID frequently consulted them for advice. And personnel were often exchanged among the different institutions to foster learning.

Alice Prince felt at peace here in this temple to science,

insulated from the stresses and worries of the outside world. When she put a lethal filovirus under the electron microscope and lost herself in its threadlike beauty, she could almost forget about losing Libby, her only daughter, ten years ago, or about the husband who had deserted her. Gazing at her glass library of viruses, she felt safe and in control, each vial a precious and powerful balm.

The vials in the refrigerator in front of her were slotted into trays, and each carried a small white computer-generated label with a bar code down one side. "Ebola filovirus (V. 3)" was typed on one vial, "HIV retrovirus hybrid" on another, "Adenovirus 5: gene therapy vector for sickle-cell anemia" on yet another.

At the bottom of the refrigerator a black rack contained twenty shorter, stubby vials. Each of these bore a label with a Pentagon-approved code. All contained viral vectors genetically engineered to counter known biological weapons. "BioShield #7" immunized against anthrax, and "BioShield #13" against most known rheovirus pathogens. ViroVector sold these vaccines to many of the world powers—friend and foe alike. Classified as medicines, they could bypass even the most stringent sanctions.

As she ran a gloved hand over the vials, the tinkling sound was to her the music of endless possibilities. Here in the Womb she could fundamentally change things, turn the bad into good. Create order out of chaos for the random world outside.

With a small sigh she shifted her attention to the job at hand. She walked to a small black safe in the corner beside the Genescope gene scanner. "LENICA 101" was written in big red letters across the front. Bending, she punched in the code on the electronic keypad, and the door opened. Inside the refrigerated interior was a tray of five vials, each the size of a large cigar. Two of them were of red glass, and three of green. The red vials were labeled "Conscience Vector (V. 1.0)" and "Conscience Vector (V. 1.9)." The three green vials bore the legends "Crime Zero (Phase 1—telomeres test)," "Crime Zero (Phase 2)," and "Crime Zero (Phase 3)."

She put the tray on a work surface next to one of the three

computer terminals and turned the red vials around in their slots so their bar codes were exposed. Then she took a computer wand from next to the monitor and scanned the bar codes of "Conscience Vector (V. 1.0)" and "Conscience Vector (V. 1.9)." As she did so, she watched the monitor to her left, checking the differences between the two vectors. She pressed "Print" so a hard copy would appear on the ground-level printer above. The differences between Version 1.0 and Version 1.9 were negligible, certainly not significant enough to merit troubling the Food and Drug Administration. She only hoped Dr. Kathy Kerr would agree.

She then turned to the green vials. These were even more important than the Project Conscience vectors. Kathy Kerr knew nothing about them. First she scanned "Crime Zero (Phase 1—telomeres test)." When she looked at the computer monitor and watched the project summary spreadsheet appear, she noted the six names with "San Quentin" typed above them. The five younger men had recent dates beside them—all different—plus a file number, referring to the autopsy findings. The same five had a tick in the far right column of the spreadsheet. So far all had met TITANIA's predicted timings. Only the sixth remained undated and unticked: Karl Axelman.

Alice Prince took a deep breath. She could see from the projected date in the left-hand column that Axelman was due anytime now. TITANIA had already brought forward the Phase 2 shipments to Iraq to meet the looming crisis. This was on the understanding that Phase 1 would be fine. They couldn't possibly go to Phase 3 if either 1 or 2 was compromised. To compound her concern, there was also the call she had received from the orphanage in Cartamena. It was probably only a scare, and she would hear back any moment. But it still made her nervous. Project Conscience was going to be difficult enough. Perhaps Crime Zero was too ambitious, too risky, whatever Madeline Naylor said.

A sudden beep made her heart lurch, and she instinctively checked her suit for tears. Then, realizing it was only the signal for the door opening, she breathed a sigh of relief and vowed to have the tone changed; it was too similar to the biosuit alarms. Turning around, she heard the hiss of the air-tight seals and watched the lab door to her left slowly open. She had expressly instructed her senior staff with Silver level access to the Womb that she wanted the place to her-self for the next hour.

Flustered, she switched off the computer and reached for the tray of colored vials. But before she could move them, a blue suit entered the Womb. When it turned, Alice saw Kathy Kerr's excited face smiling through the visor. Kerr glanced at the tray for a moment before Alice awkwardly stepped in front of it.

"Alice, I've just heard the news. Isn't it great?" Kathy said. Alice smiled but said nothing, letting Kathy continue. "The FDA have approved all the Conscience safety tests for Version nine. Now, at last, we can go ahead with efficacy tri-als on criminals. Isn't it brilliant?"

Alice Prince nodded. "Yes, yes, it's great," she said quickly, turning to put the tray back in the safe. The last per-son she wanted to see the vials was Kathy Kerr. She scolded herself for not including Kerr in her request for privacy. Kathy had Silver level clearance but was based down the road at Stanford University. "Look, Kathy, I'm busy now. And really I had planned to be alone."

Kathy's smile faded. She looked embarrassed. "Oh, I'm sorry, Alice. I didn't realize."

Alice closed the safe, heard the lock click, and then turned to Kathy. "That's OK. It's good news. Madeline Nay-lor's coming tomorrow. We'll celebrate then. OK?"

Kathy looked at her, obviously disappointed she wasn't more excited. "OK, Alice. See you tomorrow," she said qui-etly, and left.

As soon as the door closed behind her, the speakerphone beeped. "Dr. Prince, I have a call from Director Naylor for you," said a voice from the speaker by the door. "It's on a se-cure line."

"Thank you," she said.

"Alice, are you there? Can we speak?" said the booming voice of the FBI director. Alice could just imagine Madeline Naylor sitting in her office on the fifth floor of the Hoover

Building in Washington, her professionally manicured Chanel Rouge Noir nails drumming on her desk. It still amused Alice to think that the skinny twelve-year-old girl with shocking white hair and dark eyes whom she had known at school was now running the most powerful law enforcement agency in the world.

"Yes, I'm alone, Madeline. You still coming over?"

"Of course."

"Have you got my E-mail? We've got FDA approval to go ahead with Conscience."

"About goddamn time. Pamela was getting more than a little nervous, as you know. She's got a TV debate tonight and wants to tee up the Conscience policy announcement for this Friday. Still, better late than never."

Friday was only two days away. In less than forty-eight hours the first stage of their strategy would go public. Just enough time for the American voters and media to get excited, without giving Pamela's Republican opponents an opportunity to rally before the election next Tuesday.

"I'm still worried about Crime Zero, though," said Alice. "The BioShield vaccine's been dispatched early to Iraq because of the escalating crisis, but we have a potential issue at the orphanage, and the San Quentin experiment is looking tight. Perhaps we—"

"Stop worrying, Alice. That's why I'm calling. I've got news as well."

"Yes?"

"San Quentin. It's happened. Just as TITANIA predicted." Madeline's voice softened. "Relax about Crime Zero, Ali. Cartamena will prove to be a false alarm. The FDA Conscience approval was the big one. Well done. I'm due in a meeting about now. But I'll be over in a few hours."

"See you later," said Alice as the speaker went dead. Perhaps Madeline was right; she usually was. Gaining FDA approval to begin Conscience Phase 2 trials was vital for Pamela Weiss to go ahead with her preelection announcement. And it was looking as if it would be increasingly crucial to the election itself, given the latest opinion polls, which showed a strong Republican lead. As for the FDA approval to embark on efficacy trials, that was academic. Under the auspices of Project Conscience, Alice Prince and Madeline Naylor had been secretly testing behavior-modifying gene therapy on unsuspecting convicts for more than eight years now.

5

Dr. Victoria Váldez looked down at the small boy lying on
the gurney and released a sigh. Fernando, only thirteen, was
one of her favorites. Brave and cocky with a skinny body
and huge dark eyes, he had a gift for soccer and making her
laugh. He was far too young to have suffered a brain hemorrhage. She looked around the small, spotless clinic attached to the orphanage. His death was especially poignant
because it was so rare for a child to die here.

The Cartamena Orphanage for Young Boys, thirty miles
south of Mexico City, was fortunate. A large proportion of
its costs and all its medical expenses were funded by a little-
known charitable trust in the United States called Fresh
Start. The funding and resources had been provided for
some nine years on the understanding that there would be no
publicity. Váldez knew Fresh Start was a front for ViroVector Solutions in California, but if a large company wanted to
help young children without claiming the credit, she wasn't
complaining.

The great Dr. Alice Prince even visited from time to time
and selected certain children for her personal attention. And
if the children ever had any serious problems outside Dr.
Váldez's experience and training, then Dr. Prince and her
company provided more specialist care. No, Váldez thought

49

that she and the orphanage had much to be grateful for. The boys here were better cared for than in any institution she knew. In the last nine years she knew of only seven fatalities, remarkable here in Mexico. And those had been just as sudden and unexplained as Fernando's death had been. Some of his hair had fallen out recently, but that could have been vitamin deficiency. And the acne on his face was normal for a boy of his age. When he had gone to sleep last night, he had been fine, but today he was dead.

As a matter of procedure she had immediately called Fresh Start. It had asked to be notified of all deaths. She was put through eventually to Dr. Prince herself. Victoria told her that the boy had died of a suspected brain hemorrhage. At first Victoria was touched by Alice's apparent genuine concern but then was surprised to be asked only one question: Had Fernando reached puberty?

Nonplussed, Victoria already guessed the answer but said she would check after hanging up the phone. The orphanage cared for boys only until the age of puberty and then either sent them to other homes or found them jobs. The rules were strict, and Fresh Start insisted on them, but Victoria still thought Dr. Prince's question was strange. The boy was dead. What did it matter whether he could still stay at the orphanage or not?

Looking down at the naked corpse, she shook her head again. She walked to the wall, picked up the handset, and dialed the number Dr. Prince had given her. "Yes," she said in reply to the American's first question, "but only just."

Váldez frowned when she heard the sigh of relief. The response hardly seemed appropriate.

The Marina District, San Francisco, California.
6:47 P.M.

Luke Decker felt calmer when he pulled up outside his grandfather's tall Victorian house in the Marina in San Francisco. He had spent the last few hours driving aimlessly around the city. He almost called in on one of his old buddies from Berkeley, a journalist called Hank Butcher, who lived in Sausalito, just to take his mind off things.

He was still reeling at Axelman's claim. What the hell was he playing at? Decker had tried to challenge him afterward, but he'd begun screaming again and frozen up, so Rosenblum had stopped the interview.

Obviously it couldn't be true. Axelman was either demented or playing stupid mind games. Killing time before his killing time. But however much Decker tried to dismiss what he'd been told, the notion still stirred something deep and disturbing within him.

Eighteen months ago, when his mother had died, he had been working simultaneously on six particularly gruesome cases. He had been in Buffalo, New York, when his grandfather Matty Rheiman called to give him the news. Apparently his mother had died quickly, but her last words had been "I want to see my son before I die." It was only when he touched her cold face in the mortuary the next day that he realized how late he was. Decker had been so busy he hadn't made time to see her for almost nine months. He still wore the guilt like a cold vest.

His grandfather, a mild man, had reproached him at the time. "What's with you, Luke? Your mother needed you, yet you never visited. It's like you *prefer* to spend time chasing after your killers."

Matty had immediately apologized, but his words had struck home. The idea that he might *enjoy* inhabiting the minds of murderers terrified Decker. The notion that he empathized with the evil in others because he possessed it too was abhorrent. Combined with physical overwork and guilt, this thought had contributed to a breakdown. It had taken being institutionalized and more sessions than he cared to remember with the gentle Dr. Sarah Quirke at the Sanctuary to soothe his frazzled brain. Until then Decker had always believed there was a mental firewall between his own mind and the inflamed minds he hunted, that the evil he pursued in others was somehow separate from him.

When he was younger, he'd challenged his mother about his fascination with the darker side. But she had quickly reassured him, telling him that he was perfectly normal and that his father had been just like him. That was why Captain Richard Decker was such a good interrogator, his mother used to say. He knew the questions to ask the enemy because he could think like them.

But what if Richard Decker hadn't been his father? What if his inherited gift for understanding the darker side in others came from a more sinister source?

Even though he tried to dismiss these thoughts, they remained. He kept thinking of Wayne Tice and his family tree and remembering how he'd scoffed at Kathy's theory of inherited evil.

After getting out of the car, Decker approached the house. He wondered if he should have phoned ahead to let Matty know he was coming, but there was something almost child-like in his grandfather's enjoyment at seeing him when he least expected it. He seemed delighted that Decker had taken to dropping by since his mother's death, as if this house were still his home rather than some hotel where he needed to make reservations in advance. As he neared the front door, he heard the sound of the sweetest music coming from a room upstairs. Decker could picture his grandfather standing in the music room on the middle floor, violin on his shoulder; his gnarled fingers shaped by years of playing curled around the instrument. The large windows would be wide open, a breeze blowing in from the bay as if summoned by his playing.

Opening the front door, which was rarely locked, Decker entered the spacious hallway. Rhoda, the live-in house-keeper who looked after Matty, greeted him from the living room. She was a large woman with a larger smile and had been with Matty ever since his wife died twelve years ago.

"Luke, what a great surprise," she said, coming over to give him a hug. "He's upstairs," she whispered with a con-spiratorial wink. "Come, give me your things."

"Thanks, Rhoda. Good to see you."

Decker handed over his old tote bag and walked upstairs to the middle floor. The mahogany banisters had just been polished, and the smell took him back to his childhood. His mother and maternal grandparents had brought him up in this house. He had spent half his life here, and whenever he entered the front door, it felt like coming home. On the middle landing he walked to the spacious music room. A piano stood in the corner, alongside an empty open violin case. Luke's own battered saxophone leaned against a tall bookcase filled with tapes, compact discs, and sadly antiquated vinyl.

Photographs of his grandfather sat atop the piano next to an ancient metronome. Most of the pictures were taken at Davies Hall, where despite offers from the best orchestras in the world, he had played with his beloved San Francisco Symphony for most of his illustrious career. Other photographs showed Matty at the Hollywood Bowl, in London's Royal Albert Hall with Yehudi Menuhin, and of course the famous one of him embracing Isaac Stern onstage at Carnegie Hall. Beside them, slightly by itself, was a picture of a tall blond man and a petite dark woman, Richard and Rachel Decker, Luke's parents. The man was in naval uniform, and his hair was cut short, like Luke's.

Just as Luke had imagined, his grandfather stood by the large window facing out across the blue bay, violin tucked under his chin, his guide dog, Brutus, at his feet. He was shrunken and stooped with only whispers of hair on his head but Matty Rheiman still played as if his very survival depended on it. There was a time in his life when it had.

Decker's grandfather had spent his early teenage years during the Second World War at the Buchenwald concentration camp, where most of his family had been led in turn to the killing chambers. He had been blinded in the camp's experimental hospital by Nazi doctors' injecting blue dye into his brown pupils, trying to change their color and turn a Jew into an Aryan. Only his prodigious gift for the violin and the lessons invested in by his parents had saved him. The commandant's wife, Frau Ilse Koch, wanted a talented violinist to entertain guests at their villa in the camp. The fact that the scrawny Matty was only barely a teenager made him an additional curiosity.

"Hello, Gramps," Decker said, walking over to embrace

him. As he put his arm around Matty's frail shoulders, he realized how old he was, eighty-one in December.

The sound of music was replaced with a deep laugh as his grandfather turned, leveled dead eyes of brilliant unnatural blue on Decker, and smiled. "Hello, Luke." He placed his precious violin carefully down on the piano top. "Brutus, look who's here," he said as he returned Decker's embrace with both arms. Luke felt a warm, wet tongue graze across his hand as Brutus raised himself on two legs and began barking to join in with the greeting.

"Come, come, Luke. Sit down," said his grandfather, ushering him to the nearby sofa. "How long are you staying this time?"

Decker heard the pleasure in Matty's voice and was stricken by the brevity of his visit. "Just the night. Then I must get back to Quantico. But I'm thinking of moving back here, you know, Gramps."

"Really?" Matty said, in a way that meant "I think I've heard this before." "What, they've finally had enough of you in Virginia?"

"No, I'm thinking of leaving the bureau altogether." Decker told him about his offer at Berkeley and how he wanted to come back here to settle down and get his life in order.

"Well, that sounds like a good plan to me. And about time too," said Matty with a surprised grin. "You could stay here. It's your home after all."

Decker smiled. He suddenly had a compelling urge to ask him about Axelman's claim, to hear him laugh at it. But before he could say anything, the doorbell rang.

Matty's eyes lit up. "That'll be Joey. He's coming around for a violin lesson. Hey, we could all play together, Luke."

"Joey Barzini?" Decker groaned. "Come on, Gramps, you're not still schmoozing with that old hood?" Decker wanted to talk to his grandfather about Axelman, and instead Matty was giving a music lesson to a man reputed to head up one of the most powerful Mafia families on the West Coast. Decker knew about Barzini. His business—real estate and lots of it—was ostensibly legit, and he'd famously donated one million dollars a year to the San Francisco Symphony for the last decade or so. However, it was widely recognized by the great and the good that Barzini was still far from respectable.

But Matty had never cared much for the great and the good, and over the last few years the sixty-year-old Mafia man and the eighty-year-old concert violinist had become unlikely friends. Perhaps that was why Matty felt so relaxed about leaving his door and windows unlocked. Nobody with half a brain cell was going to burgle this place with a pal of Joey Barzini's living there.

"Why do you still see him, Gramps? And why do you invite him here? I don't like your dealing with crooks."

Matty frowned. "Because he's my friend and because he comes to visit. And just because he's from a criminal family, it doesn't mean he's a crook."

Decker couldn't argue with that.

"Matty, how are you?" a rich voice called from the stairs.

"I'm fine, Joey. Come on up."

Decker shook his head. "Have a good lesson, Gramps," he said. "I'm going to find a drink."

"Luke, don't go."

Decker rested a hand on his shoulder. "Gramps, I came to see you, not Joey Barzini. Don't worry. I'll be back later." Turning to leave, Decker wasn't really angry about his grandfather's consorting with Barzini. He wasn't even angry about not being able to talk about Axelman. In fact he was kind of relieved he could leave that particular sleeping dog undisturbed. If he was honest, he was angry with himself for being unable to shrug off Axelman's stupid words.

On the stairs he passed a huge man in a suit. The violin case he held looked like a toy in his hands. He had blue-black hair and the darkest eyes Decker had ever seen. Decker knew Barzini was about sixty, but the man looked little more than forty-five.

They acknowledged each other with a cautious smile, never having met face-to-face before. "Your grandfather's a remarkable man," was all Barzini said.

"That I know," said Decker. "Enjoy your lesson."

Outside, Decker breathed in the evening air and walked to his car. He was even free now to catch up with Kathy Kerr. But he quickly dismissed the thought. He would call Hank Butcher or whoever was around and have a few cold beers. He would feel better after that.

He didn't see the white BMW pull up and park outside Matty's house as he pulled away from the curb and drove downtown. And he certainly didn't see Axelman's lawyer, Tad Rosenblum, climb out and knock on Matty's front door. In his right hand he held an envelope addressed in a spidery handwritten scrawl to Special Agent Luke Decker.

6

"She didn't even seem excited when I told her the news," Dr. Kathy Kerr complained, taking another sip of her Earl Grey tea. "It's been almost nine years of damn hard work, and we've actually gained FDA approval to start Phase Two efficacy trials. We've proved that Vector Nine is safe on animal and now healthy human volunteers. Finally we can go ahead and see if Project Conscience actually *works* on violent criminals. But is the great Alice Prince excited? Is she, like hell?

"And she was pretty quick to put those vials back in that precious safe of hers when I came in. She may be brilliant, but at times she can be bloody paranoid."

Kathy looked at the face opposite hers and smiled. "You don't know what I'm talking about, do you, Rocky?"

As if to prove her correct, the large chimp cocked his head to one side and proceeded to scratch his chin. Then he turned back to the flickering portable TV on the step outside his pen, its extension power cable trailing back across the yard to the house.

The night air was cool as she sat on the stoop by Rocky's pen in her backyard on Mendoza Drive. Mendoza Drive was a grand name for the rough track. Her house was at the end surrounded by woods and fields. Her nearest neighbor was hundreds of yards away, and that was just as well considering how noisy Rocky could get.

At more than four feet tall Rocky was a massive chimpanzee. If he put his mind to it, he could easily tear a man apart. He had been one of the original primates on Project Conscience. In Kathy's laboratory at the Stanford Medical Research Center as many as eight apes used to be housed in the adjoining primate compound. But since the project had moved on to human volunteers three years ago, the apes had been found homes in local zoos and wildlife sanctuaries.

However, Rocky was too old, and after his contribution to her work she felt obliged to care for him. So under the instructions of a keeper from the Charles Paddock Zoo down in Atascadero she had built this enclosed ape house in the garden of her stucco house on Mendoza Drive. Rocky had been instrumental in testing her discovery of the seventeen genes that coded for aggressive violent behavior.

A normal chimp, he had been unusually violent when younger, almost killing one of the other apes. But ever since he had received one of the earliest somatic gene therapy serums taken from the genes of a smaller, gentler bonobo chimp, Rocky's behavior had changed markedly, prompting many of the developments on Project Conscience. The reformed bruiser was now violent only when he thought Kathy was in danger; otherwise he was as mild as the proverbial lamb.

She put her half-empty mug of tea down on the ground next to her mobile phone and briefcase. After the Tice hearing this morning she had returned to her laboratory on Pasteur Drive at Stanford University. Any thoughts of Luke Decker were quickly pushed from her mind when she received the fax from the Food and Drug Administration giving her approval to test her viral vector on criminal volunteers. Grinning from ear to ear, she had broken the news to her two research assistants, Frank Whittaker and Karen Stein, and the lab technicians. An impromptu party in the labs had followed. So when she had rushed off to ViroVector to share the good news with Alice Prince, she'd felt deflated by her less than enthusiastic reaction. Still, tonight's farewell drinks for her assistants, Frank and Karen, had doubled up as a celebration as well. Kathy had taken them and the lab technicians out for a meal before dropping Frank and Karen off at the San Francisco airport.

She didn't begrudge them their six-week field trip to the Democratic Republic of Congo; after all she had helped arrange the sponsorship from ViroVector. And even though the timing wasn't ideal, Alice Prince had arranged for two fully qualified scientists from ViroVector to stand in while they were away. It was just that Frank and Karen had been with her from the beginning and had become more than colleagues; they were her closest friends in California. Staring up at the clear night sky, Kathy saw an airplane pass overhead. In a few hours theirs would be doing the same.

Reaching into her briefcase, she pulled out the folder she had prepared for tomorrow's meeting with Alice Prince and Director Naylor. Just reading the title, "Project Conscience—Next Steps," gave her a thrill.

Would Project Conscience actually work? Alice Prince could be strange at times, but her work was brilliant, and Kathy had learned a huge amount from her in the last nine years at the cutting edge of gene therapy and viral vector technology. And although her other main sponsor, Madeline Naylor of the FBI, was paranoid about secrecy, at least she gave clear direction on the few occasions they met.

Kathy stood up and patted Rocky's arm through the wire of the pen. She picked up her briefcase, unlocked the door, and walked to the back of the pen, where she bent down to an old school trunk screwed to the wooden floor. After taking a key from her pocket, she unlocked the trunk and lifted the lid. She then reached into her briefcase, took out a computer disc and a copy of the folder she had prepared for her key meeting with Madeline Naylor tomorrow, and placed them in the trunk. She put the disc into a plastic case alongside the thirty or so discs already there and laid the folder on a pile of similar files.

Along with a few personal photos and artifacts that had only sentimental value the trunk contained copies of every major document, journal, and experiment marking the de-

velopment of Project Conscience. This was her personal
record of her life's work, proof of what she had done, regardless of whatever anyone else might claim or say in the
future. She regarded it as safe because no burglar would
think to look here, and if any did, he would hesitate about
disturbing Rocky.

In that trunk were recorded all the disappointments and
triumphs that had led to this moment. And in the early days
she and the team had experienced their fair share of scares.
There had been a marginal risk of her original serum's increasing the risk of testicular cancer in the test primates and
their first male born. Although the numbers had been small,
they had changed the calibration four times, fine-tuning
them in iterative steps, until any hint of the problem was removed. When other concerns, minor but possible, had come
to light, they had done the same. Nothing was left to chance,
and Kathy had been pleasantly surprised how keen her FBI
and ViroVector sponsors had been about her findings' being
thorough. "Don't cut any corners," Alice Prince had said
with that distant smile of hers. "Spend all the time and
money you need. Just make sure that when we go to the
FDA, we gain approval." That patience was rare and made
up for many of the other constraints.

Now nine versions later the team had developed a viral
vector that the FDA had deemed safe on normal human volunteers. Of course Kathy still had years of trials to go before
she could prove it actually worked on violent offenders, but
given how few real changes she'd had to make from her
original primate thesis to get here, she was confident. Plus
all the data she'd used from the genomes of violent criminals on the FBI DNA database had allowed her to fine-tune
the calibrations.

As Kathy left the pen and locked the door behind her, she
noticed a woman on the small TV screen. She stood behind
a lectern in a tailored navy blue suit that set off her trim figure. Governor Pamela Weiss was over fifty, but the camera
loved her. Her neat, lustrous bob of auburn hair contained
few silver streaks, and her exquisite bone structure had
fended off time better than any plastic surgeon's scalpel.

With her height and piercing blue eyes she seemed to look right out of the screen directly at Kathy. The woman had true charisma, and Kathy found herself sitting down on the stoop and turning the screen toward her and increasing the volume.

She had no real interest in politics, but since acquiring U.S. citizenship, she had become more aware of the upcoming election. She also got a kick out of seeing a woman run as the Democratic candidate with a chance of becoming the first ever female President. Not only was Pamela Weiss media-friendly, but she seemed to possess real integrity.

By contrast her opponent, the gray-haired, gray-suited Republican senator George Tilson, had the bland good looks of a soap star. But he was a general who had fought in Desert Storm eighteen years ago, and with the Iraq crisis looming he was leading in the opinion polls by thirteen points. Despite Weiss's appeal, the Republicans were on track to succeed the outgoing Democratic President, Bob Burbank, next Tuesday.

Kathy never watched live political debates because they were invariably boring set pieces of hollow rhetoric. But Weiss interested her. The candidates stood facing each other behind lecterns on an otherwise bare stage. A moderator, the famous news anchorman Doug Strather, stood between them and a large studio audience. The TV debate had obviously been going for some time, but according to the commentator, no particular points had been scored either way.

Doug Strather turned to the Republican candidate. "Senator Tilson, do you think the gender of the President of the United States of America is relevant?"

Tilson smiled at Weiss and then at the camera, as if to apologize for what was clearly in his view a dumb question. "Of course, in principle I have nothing against a woman becoming President of the United States. However, with the immediate threat of Iraq retaking Kuwait, China's ambitions expanding, and North Korea still far from settled, what the world needs now is strong, experienced leadership. I am not saying that my experience in the Gulf War makes me more qualified than Governor Weiss to stand for the highest office in the land, but there is an argument for saying that now is not the time for experiments."

Weiss shook her head. "But surely, Senator Tilson," she said, "now is not the time to let history repeat itself. Particularly not with the weapons of nuclear or biological self-destruction that humanity now has at its disposal. Yes, women may historically have had little experience of waging war, but that's because we rarely start them." She paused as the studio audience laughed. "As a general rule women are better known for promoting consensus than creating conflict. And frankly I still think there is no such thing as a good war or a bad peace. However, when necessary, women can use force to end wars. Margaret Thatcher, Britain's first female prime minister, demonstrated that when she led the British to a successful war in the Falkland Islands, thousands of miles from her country. She also stiffened our own President Bush's resolve when Iraq last invaded Kuwait before Desert Storm. And if you remember, the initially nervous George Bush was both a man and a Republican."

"So, Governor Weiss, as far as you're concerned, gender is irrelevant?" asked Strather.

"Of course it is. As Senator Tilson said, what America needs now is strong leadership. Not male leadership or female leadership or black leadership or white leadership, just *good* leadership. And if you really want to look at gender, you could argue that when the world is poised on the brink of war, the one person you *do* want in charge is a woman, particularly one who hates the very notion of armed conflict. The last candidate *I'd* vote for is an old warhorse with something to prove.

"As for experience in running the country, my eight years as governor of California must count for something. Certainly more than Senator Tilson can lay claim to. Don't forget I also have the full support of the current President as he nears the end of his second successful term. I intend to build on his administration's achievements through injecting new blood, both male and female."

"But the current administration's record is appalling," said Tilson. "Vice President Smith is a laughingstock; his comments on the UN and the recent sex scandals have destroyed his credibility and by association weakened that of the President. But of even more relevance is the issue of crime. Violent crime is soaring at an unprecedented rate across the nation. Surely Governor Weiss doesn't think that record is good enough to simply carry on the good work?"

"No, of course not, there's always room for improvement. Still, if you look at the crime figures in more depth, you would know that my own state of California is already showing the way forward. Violent crime is down, particularly in the trouble spots like South Central L.A."

"That is true, Governor Weiss," acknowledged Doug Strather. "Can you explain why California has bucked the trend over the last five years?"

Tilson cut in quickly. "It's clear to me that building more prisons and having a death penalty we are willing to enforce go a long way to cutting down crime. The sooner we as a nation get tougher on crime and *stay* tougher on crime, then the sooner this country will be safer for normal citizens like you and me."

Some of the audience clapped at this hollow rhetoric, but Weiss laughed and shook her head. "But that simply isn't true. Texas, which has a Republican governor and a zero tolerance program in every major city, is the execution capital of the Western world. Outside of Islamic countries no other administration has more draconian laws or carries them out with more vigor than Texas. Ten people a month are currently being executed there, and many other states aren't far behind. But it's not working. Texas has the second-highest crime rate after Michigan.

"Time and time again more prisons and death penalties have been proved to fail. We need to reduce the incidents of crime by influencing the small minority that commits them *before* they commit them. The Philadelphia study and countless others have shown that over seventy percent of the homicides, rapes, and aggravated assaults attributed to any group of men are committed by a hard core of only six percent. If we could target this six percent and stop them, we would significantly reduce crime. And apart from the obvi-

ous social benefits, there are huge financial ones. If we reduce violent crime by just one percent, we save the country
over one-point-two billion dollars. That must be worth
doing."

"But how do you do this? How do you reduce crime?"

The camera again focused on Weiss. "First of all, we must
stop simply viewing crime as an external enemy to be fought
and vanquished. Let's be clear on one thing: Violent crime is
almost the sole preserve of *male* criminals. In this country a
man is about nine times more likely as a woman to commit
murder, seventy-eight times more likely to commit forcible
rape, ten times as likely to commit armed robbery, and almost six times as likely to commit aggravated assault. Altogether, American men are almost ten times as likely as
women to commit violent crime. They account for over
ninety percent of all these crimes. And the majority of all
penal reform is devised and implemented by men. Therefore
they are fighting against themselves, and that's a fight no
one can win."

Kathy Kerr was mesmerized by the screen. Pamela Weiss
was citing her own research, voicing her own arguments for
tackling violent crime.

"Are you saying that being a woman makes you better
equipped to fight crime?" asked Strather on the TV.

"Of course not. My gender makes no difference. Certainly not when it comes to *fighting* crime. What I am saying is that perhaps 'fighting crime' is the wrong mind-set.
Perhaps it would be better to think of *treating* crime, diag-
nosing its real causes and, as with any health strategy, seeking prevention as well as a cure."

"Again how?"

"By looking at not just social factors but others as well.
By looking beyond sociology and turning to the harder sciences, such as biology and genetics."

Kathy Kerr couldn't believe it.

"But that's preposterous," scoffed Tilson. "Even the governor must have heard about the disastrous double Y chromosome study in the late 1960s. Back then scientists
believed that men with an extra Y chromosome were more

likely to be violent. But that was later entirely discredited. The only way to—"

"I know that particular study was discredited," Weiss cut in. "But we need proof rather than just theories. There have been no conclusive results proving that any of the conventional methods of preventing or punishing crime actually work. Indeed all the indications are that they fail—*miserably*. It's time for a change."

Doug Strather adjusted his glasses. "Governor Weiss, there's a lot of talk in the media about getting proof, *biological* proof of what causes violent crime, but are you saying that through your success in California—?"

"This is ridiculous," interrupted Tilson. "She is part of a defunct administration exhausted of ideas, trying any gimmick to retain power. First the Democrats play the feminist card, choosing a woman to run for President despite the threat to national security this may pose. Now they try to claim some responsibility for the *one single* state in an otherwise crime-riddled nation that has a half-decent record. It's preposterous, not to say downright dishonest. Unless she knows something specific about curing crime that the rest of us don't, then she should keep her counsel."

"Did you hear that, Governor Weiss?" said Strather, smiling. "I think you've been told to stop talking the talk and *walk* the walk. What do you say to that?"

At that moment the camera zoomed in on Pamela Weiss's face. Looking totally in control, she gave a wide, relaxed smile and said, "What I say is this: The election is less than a week away. Don't worry, I'll walk the walk before then. I can assure you of that."

Kathy turned from the TV and looked at Rocky. "Did you hear that?"

Rocky gave a bored snort and scratched his chest.

She reached for her mobile phone, wanting to talk to somebody. With Karen and Frank gone she considered calling Alice Prince but then remembered her less than enthusiastic reaction to the FDA approval and thought it best to wait until their meeting tomorrow. There was no way she would get hold of Director Naylor. She then thought of having a chat with her parents back in Scotland, but they were on holiday. Usually she would have gone with them, but because of the expected FDA approval, she had passed this year. Anyway the time difference ruled out a call to Britain, so that ruled out talking to her best friend in Edinburgh too. Suddenly she had an overwhelming impulse to ring the one person who had always disagreed with her work, to see what he thought of the Weiss announcement.

Reaching into her bag, she pulled out his card. But by the time she read it she realized how stupid an idea it was to call him. Shaking her head, she put the card back. It had been years, she reminded herself. Luke Decker and she lived separate lives now.

7

San Quentin Execution Chamber,
Thursday, October 30, 7:00 A.M.

The director of the FBI stood perfectly still in one of the two
soundproof viewing rooms looking into San Quentin's ren-
ovated execution chamber. At five feet ten Madeline Naylor
was two inches taller than the prison warden standing beside
her. She wore a well-cut charcoal gray pantsuit, which ac-
centuated her sinewy frame. Her shocking white hair was
pulled off her high forehead and tied behind her neck. Her
face was pale with the translucency of mother of pearl, and
she wore the minimum of mascara around her dark brown
eyes. The only color in her otherwise monochrome appearance was the liverish red of her thin lips.

Director Naylor had come here personally to persuade
herself that there would be no obstacles. She had arranged
the execution papers with the governor herself. Ensuring
that all appeals were quashed had been a formality for such
a notorious criminal so close to an election. She only wished
Alice Prince would hurry up and get here. She hated it when
anybody was late. And it was almost time.

To her sensitive nose this place reeked of sweat. Not the
healthy physical perspiration from running in sunshine or
playing innocent sport but the acrid emotional stench of
adrenaline and fear. Even Neil Tarrant, the warden standing
beside her, gave off the trace tang of nervous sweat through

his aftershave. She hated that smell; it signified man at his basest. And looking through the airtight porthole of reinforced glass into the small execution chamber only confirmed her prejudice.

She looked down the corridor, past the second viewing room, where relatives of the victims sat waiting for justice, to the guards dragging the convict toward the airtight capsule. She had rarely seen a man look so pale before. He didn't struggle or betray any emotion. But then, how could he?

"What a farce! What a goddamn farce!" The words the warden muttered under his breath were almost inaudible, but she heard them. The irony that Tarrant, a man who had unflinchingly overseen the deaths of tens, if not hundreds, of men in that steel airtight capsule, found this more shocking than what he usually sanctioned did not make her smile.

"It is necessary," Naylor told him as she watched the guards open the capsule and slump the man in the crude chair inside. "You do understand that, don't you? We have to bring it forward to break the pattern, to avoid drawing attention to the five other men. That would look bad for all of us." She paused. "Not least of all you."

Tarrant refused to look at her, just rubbed the dark stubble on his chin and shook his head. "This was a mistake. I hate it when someone else's mess becomes mine."

"But that's the point: The mess is yours now. You might not know everything, but after all these years you are involved. You understand that surely?"

Tarrant gave a sullen shrug, and Naylor's face hardened. She knew her strengths. Blessed with both a decisive mind and a will of adamantine rock, she had smashed through the glass ceiling in one of the most male-dominated arenas, shooting up the ranks of the great FBI, finally becoming its first female director eight years ago after a seven-year break as a federal prosecutor and district court judge. Madeline Francine Naylor was not about to let some sulky warden jeopardize everything. Her tone dropped in temperature when she spoke.

"Tarrant, you do of course realize that the presidential

election is only a week away? And that we—and when I say
we, I very much include *you*—have been involved in something that could have a direct effect on that result. Something that *all* of us have been working on successfully for
years. Several extremely powerful people have far too much
resting on this to see it fail. This mistake, as you call it, has
happened, and regardless of whose fault it may or may not
have been, it won't jeopardize our plans. No one, least of all
you, will be allowed to compromise what we are doing
when we are so tantalizingly close. It just won't happen. Is
that clear?"

The warden stared at her, nervously playing with his tie.
He looked scared now, and that pleased the director. Naylor
liked men to be afraid of her; it made them easier to control.
Tarrant nodded.

"Good," said Naylor as Alice Prince arrived, escorted by
a guard. "Could I have a moment alone with Dr. Prince
please?" The dismissal was absolute; she didn't even wait
for his agreement. Instead she turned to the door and
watched Alice Prince enter. As usual Alice was flustered,
apologizing to the departing warden for being late.

With her humble manner, shapeless navy skirt and jacket,
graying hair, and large glasses, her friend looked more like
a timid librarian or confused primary schoolteacher than one
of the great minds of modern science. Only Dr. Prince's cool
gray eyes betrayed the fierce intelligence behind the bland
facade and the passion that fueled it.

Madeline Naylor had known Alice Prince since they were
children. They had attended high school and later Vassar
College together. She regarded Alice Prince as a younger
sister and the closest thing she had to a family. Madeline felt
even closer to Alice than she did to Pamela Weiss, the friend
they had both met at Vassar who was the current governor of
California and next week was running for the highest office
in the land.

"Sorry I'm late, Madeline."

"It doesn't matter," she said, embracing her friend.
"Come and stand next to me. We've got this room to our-
selves, so we can talk." She smiled at Alice. "Don't be so

nervous. Everything's going to be OK. In all the years we've been together have I ever let us down?"

Alice smiled back. "No, I suppose not. It's just that as we come closer to Crime Zero, I worry about all the things that can go wrong, and it's becoming so—so . . . *real*. It frightens me, Madeline, and makes me think that perhaps—"

Naylor smiled. She knew how Alice hated getting too close to the practicalities of what they were doing. She gestured to the man being strapped into the chair in the airtight capsule. "Look, we're on schedule, aren't we?"

Alice nodded. "Yes. TITANIA was out by a few hours, but no more than with the younger convicts. It was obviously an accelerated test, but it verifies the principles of the Phase Three Crime Zero vector. And I've just heard that the orphanage scare was nothing."

"Excellent. Well then, once this unpleasantness is over, you can forget about Crime Zero and let TITANIA handle the phasing issues. Just concentrate on Project Conscience for now. I've blocked out most of today to deal with this. The immediate concern is to ensure that Pamela is happy with everything. Her campaign manager has given us only an hour today to brief her for Friday's announcement. So after we leave here, we'll go back to ViroVector and make sure everything's buttoned down before she arrives. How is Kathy Kerr? Will she keep quiet about the FDA compromise when she finds out about it?"

"Yes, I'm sure she won't be a problem."

Madeline Naylor nodded, but she felt less sure. "Have you isolated her as we agreed?"

"Yes, yes. Her two closest colleagues are on a field trip to Africa, and all relevant files have been moved to a different directory in TITANIA."

"How about hard copies?"

"I imagine she'll have those at Stanford."

"OK, Jackson's people should have already removed those."

William Jackson was an associate director based at FBI headquarters who reported directly to Naylor. A powerful African-American with high cheekbones, fierce eyes, and a distinctive nasal voice, Jackson ran a team of four special agents who helped her tie up loose ends and keep her abreast of any developments in the bureau she should be aware of. She regarded them as her law within the law.

"But, Madeline, is this really necessary? Kathy'll be fine. It's in her interests to cooperate."

"Perhaps." Naylor understood Alice's loyalty. It had been Kathy Kerr's thesis that had inspired Alice to get through her breakdown nine years ago after her daughter, Libby, had been abducted and Alice's spineless husband had deserted her "to rebuild my life" with his younger secretary. "Anyway, we're seeing Kathy before Pamela," Naylor said. "I can find out then how cooperative she's going to be. We can't afford any dissenting voices now."

Saying nothing, Alice gave an acquiescent nod and nervously fingered the unusual pendant on the silver chain around her neck. The size of a thumbnail, the glass teardrop mounted in platinum contained liquid, which moved as she touched it. Naylor shifted her attention back to the prisoner. The guards remained expressionless as they went about their routine task. Alice Prince looked away, her face pained by the spectacle.

But Naylor didn't turn away. She knew all about Karl Axelman; she had studied his files, both criminal and medical. He had no family, which is why he and the other five death row convicts had been selected for the Phase 1 Crime Zero trial. Most of Axelman's victims had been about sixteen, little older than Alice's daughter, Libby, when she'd disappeared ten years ago. Naylor was Libby's godmother, and she had taken it personally when the FBI—*her* FBI— couldn't find the child's abductor. They still didn't know who he was. For a time they'd thought it might be Axelman, but the absence of Libby's effects among his trophies made that unlikely.

Still, if a person deserved to die, then Karl Axelman did. Naylor was sure of it. But she wanted more than justice for men like him. She wanted punishment. Revenge. So she felt cheated when the door to the execution chamber was sealed and the warden in the other viewing room nodded twice, authorizing the release of the lethal gas pellet. Unlike his victims, the man being executed in front of her could feel no fear or pain.

Karl Axelman was already dead. He had died almost eleven hours ago.

Naylor gleaned some satisfaction from the way he had killed himself. Last night he had stuffed a sheet into his mouth to stifle his cries, and despite terrible self-inflicted injuries, the prison doctor estimated that Axelman had taken at least three hours to die from loss of blood. It was gratifying to know that far from being the error Tarrant thought it was, the manner and timing of Axelman's death had vindicated their plans.

Her only small concern was that a senior FBI agent had interviewed Axelman yesterday. She had asked Deputy Director McCloud to keep her informed of what Axelman might have revealed but on past evidence thought it was unlikely to be anything significant.

As Director Naylor watched the gas fill the chamber, she wished she could have witnessed Axelman's agony. Only what they had learned from his death, and what they still had planned, tempered her frustration. He was beyond their justice now. After all, only God could punish a dead man.

But there would be others, she consoled herself. There would be many others.

8

The Cold Room, ViroVector Solutions, Palo Alto.
Thursday, October 30, 9:11 A.M.

If TITANIA could have expressed an emotion, it would undoubtedly have been satisfaction as it updated the status on
both Project Conscience and Project Crime Zero.

TITANIA was housed in the Cold Room, a sterile room at
the heart of the ViroVector dome in Palo Alto. Embodied in
a twelve-foot steel and glass cube, it was protected in an air-
cooled jacket of white Kevlar. Air ducts blowing sterilized
eight-degree centigrade air emitted a slow rhythmic sound
as if TITANIA were breathing. Any service engineer entering this domain had to pass through an antistatic air shower
to remove dust, before donning white overalls, overshoes,
hair net, and face mask.

The supercomputer was born of the genetics age, when
the need to sequence the three-thousand-million-letter sentence of the human genome had spurred computer program-
mers and hardware designers on to greater heights. The
breakthrough came with the invention of the Genescope by
the Genius Corporation of Cambridge, Massachusetts, just
months before the last millennium ended. That revolution-
ary gene sequencer eschewed the use of electronic logic
gates in its processor, using the primitive photo-responsive
protein bacteriorhodopsin instead. This instantly multiplied
processing speeds a thousandfold within an industry that

until then had prided itself on doubling speeds every year. Of the ensuing new generation of "living" biosupercomputers, TITANIA was one of the most powerful.

TITANIA controlled a myriad of projects within ViroVector. Its programs included payroll, inventory control, smart building security and maintenance, the ordering of raw materials, production planning, and distribution. It also controlled the data flow of the company's ten Genescope gene sequencers. In its database were the DNA records of every ViroVector employee or associate plus the gene sequences of every known virus in existence and every genetically engineered viral vector ever worked on or produced by the company.

Both Conscience and Crime Zero were controlled by a program located in its Project Management suite of applications. These applications controlled the schedules and status reports on every project managed by the company. They were updated automatically with suggestions submitted to the human managers based on TITANIA's constant roaming of the information superhighway. Although physically based at ViroVector, TITANIA could be omnipresent in cyberspace. It drove a variety of search engines to probe and, if necessary, steal relevant data, and its mission was to learn everything and convert what it learned into usable information. It used this omniscience to maximize the success of each project's outcome, whether launching a new product, coping with imminent new legislation, or choosing a new menu for the staff cafeteria.

Currently a small section of its powerful neural net was focusing on the Crime Zero program, the most complex and secure system under its control.

First it noted the related Project Conscience inputs and data, although that project was almost complete. Conscience had always had two objectives as far as TITANIA was concerned. One was to act as a learning process to develop viral vectors for the infinitely more complex Crime Zero. The other was to help Pamela Weiss win the presidency—again vital for Crime Zero. Checking back over time, TITANIA noted the key dates for Project Conscience.

PROJECT CONSCIENCE MANAGEMENT
SUMMARY: 0900 hr,
10/30/2008

V.1 Criminal efficacy trial	02/10/2001
[non-FDA approved]	to present
V.9 Vector optimization complete	10/12/2004
V.9 FDA human safety trials commence	01/06/2005
V.9 FDA safety approval	10/29/2008

Democratic Crime Policy Statement	10/31/2008
Pamela Weiss elected Democratic president	11/04/2008

There was nothing more TITANIA could do. The Version 9 FDA approval lag had been suboptimal, but with the forthcoming policy statement this Friday and next Tuesday's election, Project Conscience had almost fulfilled its purpose. It could do no more to effect the outcome, merely record when it would happen. Next TITANIA checked Crime Zero:

PROJECT CRIME ZERO: MANAGEMENT
SUMMARY: 0900 hr,
10/30/2008

Phase 1: Telomere Trials

San Quentin patient trial commenced	09/02/2008
Final patient # SQ6 terminated	10/29/2008
Cartamena patient trial commenced	02/11/2005
Patient # C78 confirmed as postpubescent	10/30/2008

Phase 2: Controlled Trial

BioShield Batch # VV233456H dispatched	10/10/2008
Microchip confirmation of batch activation	10/23/2008

The Phase 1 telomere trials had been a complete success with the suicide of the sixth and final San Quentin patient less than twenty-four hours ago and the Cartamena incident proving to be an isolated false alarm. But the escalating crisis in Iraq had necessitated pulling forward the Phase 2 controlled trial before Phase 3 could confidently be launched. Interrogating its search engines, TITANIA scoured the Internet for feedback on what might be happening in Iraq. Knowing what it was looking for made its quest efficient.

One definition of intelligence is the ability to see patterns in apparently random data. If this was true, then TITANIA was a genius. Logging into hospital databases in Baghdad and Iraqi military systems, while at the same time piecing together apparently unrelated snippets of information from Reuters, CNN, the BBC, and the other syndicated news agencies on the World Wide Web, TITANIA continuously searched for the pattern to emerge. But it was still too early. The reports TITANIA was looking for would surface only in the next few days. Still, for the moment Phase 2 appeared to be active and on schedule.

Only now did TITANIA look at Phase 3, the most complex stage of all. This was much harder to predict.

Given that Phase 3 hadn't yet begun and Phase 2 was on track, the computer could only check the delivery and replacement schedules of the modified bacteriophage air purifiers at Heathrow Airport. Once it had confirmed these were in place, it kept its original forecast unchanged, putting the final outcome of Crime Zero still some three years away. That is, if nothing altered in the meantime.

As TITANIA compiled its Project Conscience and Project Crime Zero status reports for the two humans with Gold level clearance, the biocomputer's air-cooling ducts seemed to exhale more loudly for an instant. As if breathing a sigh of satisfaction.

9

Life was looking less than satisfactory for Luke Decker as
he drove toward San Quentin for the second time in two
days, with Axelman's letter on his mind.

This morning he had woken late in his old bedroom at
Matty's house. Cracking open his eyes the way he used to as
a kid, he'd watched the morning light reach impossibly long
fingers beneath the curtains and stretch across the polished
wooden floor toward his bed. For a brief moment he had felt
like a child again. Only when he rolled over did the dull
throb in his head remind him that he was a stupid adult who
had drunk one too many bottles of Budweiser with Hank
Butcher last night.

Butcher wrote mainly for magazines like *Vanity Fair* and
had a gift for tapping into the zeitgeist. He had made a name
for his witty pieces commenting on the main issues and per-
sonalities of the day. As always he'd been excellent company, knowing all the trivial gossip that rarely touched
Decker's life. He had managed to push thoughts of Axelman
from his mind.

But then over breakfast Matty had given Decker the
sealed letter delivered by Axelman's lawyer, and the doubts
had come flooding back. Decker had read Axelman's handwritten confession with growing horror, and Matty had

sensed his shock. But when Matty asked what was wrong, Decker refused to elaborate. What Axelman had written about Decker's mother and father was so preposterous, so poisonous that he couldn't tell or indeed *ask* Matty about it. Not until he had to.

The letter had been clever because only half of it related to him, explaining why Axelman couldn't talk to Decker yesterday and detailing why he believed he was Decker's father. The other half contained the revelation Axelman wouldn't give yesterday—namely, the general whereabouts of the twelve girls he had abducted. To complicate matters, Axelman had also confessed to murdering a thirteenth victim and indicated that this girl's parents unwittingly knew the exact location of all the bodies.

It was these final revelations that meant Decker couldn't just crumple up the poisonous letter and throw it away. He was professionally obliged to acknowledge this information and check it out and then share it with the rest of the FBI. But Decker didn't want Axelman's sick little joke made public in the bureau yet. Not until he'd made more sense of what currently lacked any semblance of sense at all.

His first thought had been to go to the San Francisco FBI field office and use the computer to check out the facts on the thirteenth victim. But then he'd remembered that although Rosenblum had lodged yet another appeal, Axelman's execution date was scheduled for today. So he had rushed to San Quentin.

Squinting in the bright light, Decker parked his rental car in the visitors' parking lot. As he killed the ignition, his cell phone rang. He picked up and heard the deputy director on the line. "Spook, it's Bill McCloud. I hear the Tice hearing went well yesterday."

"He's not going to be able to kill anyone else, Bill, if that's what you mean."

"That'll do for me."

Decker liked Deputy Director Bill McCloud. The laid-back Texan was a healthy foil to the chilly absolutism of Director Naylor. McCloud had once worked in the behavioral sciences unit and campaigned hard to maintain its budget and status within the bureau, which is why he couldn't afford to lose Decker and had refused to accept his resignation.

"How did your meeting with Axelman go? Her man Jackson told Director Naylor about it. And for some reason she's taken an interest in what you found out." McCloud always called Assistant Director William Jackson her man Jackson. Jackson had no real role that Decker could make out except spying for Director Naylor and carrying out her dirty work. He was universally hated and feared within the bureau. "Perhaps she values your famed psychological powers after all."

Decker hesitated, feeling the letter in his jacket.

"I assume you struck out with him, nothing new, huh?" said McCloud before Decker could say anything. McCloud threw the words at him, a rhetorical question that required no response. So Decker didn't supply one. "Don't feel bad about it, Spook. That guy was cold, one of the worst. Didn't even know the meaning of the word 'remorse.' "

"You're using the past tense, Bill. I thought he had an appeal."

"Canceled by the governor. He was executed a few hours ago. So, anyway, where are you now?"

Decker took a deep breath and sat back in the car seat. With Axelman dead there was only one way of proving what he'd claimed. Plus he had an overwhelming urge to see him again. "Look, Bill, I need to check a couple of things out for a day or two."

McCloud sighed, and when he spoke again, he sounded suspicious. "You're not still sniffing around Berkeley, are you, Spook? The bureau needs you, boy. Don't you forget that."

Decker wasn't going to be drawn on that issue now. "Bill, I'll keep in touch via our field office here," he said, and hung up. He quickly called Quantico to warn his team that he'd be away for a couple of days. He put the phone away, got out of the car, and walked toward the prison gates, mentally ticking off the little he knew.

Axelman was a classic sociopath, controlled, self-centered, and vain. He was incapable of showing any empathy for his victim's pain or remorse for his actions. He had killed twelve girls and delighted in keeping the whereabouts of their bodies a secret. Every psychological test showed that Axelman had no real fear of death or punishment.

Yet yesterday he had looked like a physical wreck. He had acted completely out of character, hysterical with guilt and shame. And last night Axelman had arranged through his lawyer to deliver a sealed letter to Decker, a letter containing personal details of why he had chosen to confess to Decker and a full confession indicating where the twelve bodies were buried—plus the existence of a thirteenth body.

Now the man was dead, and the answers died with him.

Decker felt torn as he approached the guards' window by the main door. The professional in him calmly tried to figure out how a man incapable of remorse could suddenly become so consumed by guilt that he confessed all. But on a personal level Decker ruminated on Axelman's outlandish paternity claim. It was no longer enough that Axelman was unable to prove he was Decker's father. Decker now had to *disprove* it.

Clarence Pitt was one of the guards manning the gate. He looked bored and smiled when he saw Decker. "Hey, Decker, what are you doing back here? This place is becoming like FBI central. Had the big boss herself in earlier."

"Director Naylor was here? Do you know why?"

"Nope. But I guess it had something to do with watching that Axelman guy meet his maker."

Decker frowned but said nothing. It was hardly usual for the FBI director to attend the execution of a killer.

"That's what I'm here for, Clarence. I need to see Axelman's body."

Pitt checked a computer screen to his right and screwed up his face in a pained grimace. "The Axelman stiff's been flagged. That means the warden wants it left alone. You got authorization?"

"Come on, Clarence, don't make me go through all the paperwork. I just want to look at the body. I saw him yesterday when he was alive. What harm can it do if I see him today when he's dead? Five minutes is all."

Pitt scowled for a bit longer, then pulled out a form from his desk and handed it to Decker. "Sign this, and then if anyone asks questions, it's your butt that gets kicked."

Pitt handed over his post to another guard and led Decker through the entire length of the prison to the hospital building. The only sounds Decker heard as he followed Pitt down four flights of steps and walked along the white tiled corridor to the morgue were the occasional shouts of far-off human voices, the click-clack of heels on the tiled floor, and the whispered rustle of Pitt's starched uniform.

Turning through an arch, the guard pointed at a pair of swinging doors. "This is it," he said, pushing them back. As he did so, Decker was hit by a wave of cool air reeking of chemicals. Inside was a large white room. The floor and the lower two thirds of the wall were tiled. Two stainless steel autopsy tables dominated the middle of the room, and an unoccupied gurney stood on one side. Along the far wall were three basins. Part of the left wall was made up of stainless steel drawers. A skinny guy in a soiled white coat stood by the drawers mopping the floor. Walking over to him, Pitt introduced Decker. "Steve, this here is Special Agent Decker. He's from the FBI. He needs to see the Axelman stiff." Pitt left him then, telling Decker he'd be back in exactly five minutes.

With the casualness of a clerk locating frozen peas in a grocery store, Steve wandered over to the row of stainless steel drawers and pulled out number seven. Extended to its full length, the drawer acted as a table, displaying its contents. The body lay on its back, a sheet loosely draped over it.

Steve picked up a tag next to the corpse's head, then read in a bored voice, "Executed on Thursday, October thirtieth, at seven twenty-three A.M. Cause of death: asphyxiation from gas." Steve checked his watch. "I got to go clean up a few things. What else you need to know?"

Decker continued to stare at the contours of the shrouded corpse below him. "Nothing."

"OK, I'll leave you to it. But you better hurry. This one's on a fast track for cremation pretty soon."

As the sound of the man's footsteps receded, Decker tried to maintain some professional detachment. Taking a deep breath, he pulled the sheet back off the head.

Luke had seen many corpses in his life, but rarely one so white before. The man's face had the pasty bluish pallor of soft cheese. Luke examined Axelman's face more closely, trying to see any likeness in the features. The more he looked, the more he imagined his own features reflected there, the high cheekbones, the wide forehead. He reached forward to open one eyelid, revealing a cloudy iris as green as his own. Then he pulled the sheet back farther and reached for one of the hands, comparing his with the cold digits curled on the slab. There was only one way to be certain.

With careful fingers he plucked three hairs from the dead man's head, checking that each follicle was still intact. He stared at the bare patches of scalp, amazed how much hair the man had lost since his recent file photograph. Placing the hairs in a small plastic evidence bag, Decker again studied Axelman's face, this time staring at the unusually pale, acne-pitted skin. It was as white as the victims he had examined in the past who had bled to death.

Suddenly wishing his task over, he pulled the sheet off the body. At first he couldn't see the wound, because it was detectable only by what had been removed. Grimacing, he moved down the drawer and examined the jagged, torn flesh beneath the gray penis lying inert on the man's left thigh.

The scrotum was missing, severed by what must have been a dull blade. By the look of the wound Decker guessed it had been done before the execution. But it was still recent, and there were flakes of congealed blood on the hairs of Axelman's inner thigh. Peering more closely, he studied the angle and nature of the purple cuts and the surrounding bruises.

Decker straightened then and tried to mimic the cutting action required to make such a rough laceration. It wouldn't be the first time a convict had been castrated in jail by vindictive or vengeful inmates. But Decker couldn't see how any other inmates could have reached him on the row. He didn't believe the guards would have done this either. And however Decker tried, he couldn't get the required angle to duplicate the wound. Then, with an insight that chilled his blood, he mimed one more series of movements, and the angle of the ripped cuts tallied perfectly.

Karl Axelman had inflicted this on himself.

It was incomprehensible and went way beyond mind games. Why had a serial killer notorious for his lack of remorse castrated himself? What could have motivated Axelman to do this?

Hearing footsteps approaching, Decker quelled his feelings of disgust and reached out to pick two small flakes of blood off Axelman's inner thigh. The hair follicles would be enough for the paternity test, but blood could tell him much more. His fingers brushed the corpse's flesh, and the cold, waxy texture sent a shudder through him. Quickly he placed the flakes of blood in the evidence bag with the hair and put the bag in his pocket.

When Steve returned, Decker asked him about the wound. The morgue attendant gave an uninterested shrug and pulled the sheet back over Axelman's face. "That's the way he was when he came down here. You'd be surprised what happens to folks before they go to the chamber. I just deal with 'em after they come out."

"How often do they come down with their balls cut off?"

"Not often enough in my opinion," said Steve, looking suspiciously at Decker. It was a look Decker had seen on the faces of countless witnesses. It said: "I'm not involved in any of this shit and don't want to be. So stop asking your fool questions." Then Steve smiled a thin "fuck you" smile. "The warden's coming down soon to authorize the body for cremation and possible autopsy. You can ask him about what happened to his balls if you like."

Decker smiled. "That's OK." The last thing he wanted now was to have to explain to the warden what he was doing here. He had got what he came for. "Thanks for your help. I've seen enough."

After a nervous Pitt had walked him back to the main entrance, Decker strolled over to his rental car and tried to collect his thoughts. Something very weird was going on, but he didn't know what it was. For the time being he would focus on the one thing that really mattered: checking the validity of Axelman's letter—particularly Axelman's claim to be his father and the revelations on the whereabouts of the bodies, including a thirteenth victim.

Holding the transparent evidence bag up to the light, Decker studied the flakes of blood and three hairs. Then he pulled another evidence bag out of his jacket pocket and plucked two hairs from his own head. Ensuring that the roots were intact, he placed them in the empty bag. Placing each bag in separate pockets, he thought of what to do next.

He needed to ensure the test was done discreetly. And he couldn't involve anybody in the bureau. He only had one option, someone who was trustworthy and nearby. The thought of involving her made him squirm inside.

He reached for his wallet. After a small search he soon found what he was looking for. Checking the address on the card, he climbed into his car. He had no choice. He had to ask for her help. But that didn't make him feel any better.

He just knew that Kathy Kerr would regard his sudden dependence on her genetic wizardry as some kind of moral victory.

Al Taji Camp, Baghdad, Iraq.
The Same Day, 4:17 P.M.

In the Baghdad barracks of the Northern Corps of the Elite Republican Guard, Dr. Uday Aziz was worried. The more he looked at the corpse sprawled on the barrack room bunk, the more he couldn't escape the conclusion that this wasn't good. This wasn't good at all.

Aziz stroked his thick mustache and studied Colonel Ali Saadi standing opposite him. The colonel was a squat, powerful man with a massive stomach and thick eyebrows untroubled by interruption. He was glaring angrily at the corpse. For a moment Aziz thought he was going to kick the dead soldier.

"This is the fourth in two days," Aziz said softly, looking at Private Jaafar Hammadi's medical file, trying to find some reason why a perfectly fit twenty-four-year-old should have had a brain hemorrhage. "That's if you ignore the suicides and the Khatib shooting."

"I don't understand it," the colonel said. "He hadn't complained of being ill to any of his immediate superiors."

"Was he under any particular strain?"

"He'd been training hard for his transfer south, but no harder than the other men."

Aziz scratched his head and studied the corpse again. Apart from the acne and the recent hair loss there was hardly anything remarkable. After the first unusual death two days ago, Dr. Aziz had ordered standard postmortems on the corpses. Most either had died of brain hemorrhages or had been suicides. All had been physically in excellent condition with no history of mental problems. However, their blood tests had all revealed similar abnormalities. These abnormalities pointed to one possible explanation—particularly given the hair loss and acne—but he would need to make more tests. "We need to find out what's happening," he mused as if talking to himself.

"You're damn right we do," said the colonel. "You need to make it top priority. We've managed to keep it quiet for now, but morale is suffering, and people are talking. If this gets any worse and the rais hears of it so close to a possible offensive, he will demand an explanation."

"I understand." Aziz returned to stroking his mustache. The suicides and the shooting couldn't be blamed on him, but the others could. Why did this have to happen now? In the past his job as senior military doctor had been comfortable. The army, particularly the Republican Guard, was well fed and re-sourced. And apart from the obvious risks of war the health of the men wasn't an issue. But over the last few months Aziz had been working all hours in a bureaucratic role, preparing for the rais's planned offensive on Kuwait, organizing field hospital contingencies and the vaccination of hundreds of thousands of troops. And now, already with more problems than he could handle, he was being confronted by this . . . *annoyance*.

"Are you sure these men haven't been taking any unauthorized medication?"

"Well, I haven't authorized any if that's what you mean," said the colonel with an angry frown. "What sort of medication are you talking about anyway?"

Aziz studied him closely, trying to decide if he was telling the truth. It wouldn't be the first time officers had tested drugs on troops to improve their combat capabilities, especially so close to an offensive. Aziz shrugged, still looking at the colonel. "I'm talking about anabolic steroids. You know? The drugs some athletes take to improve their performance."

The colonel shook his head in disbelief. "You think these men have been taking steroids? And that's why they're dead?"

"I don't know yet," Aziz said, closing the corpse's staring, bloodshot eyes. "But I'm going to find out."

10

Stanford University, Stanford, California.
Thursday, October 30, 12:53 P.M.

Kathy Kerr checked and double-checked her proposal. She didn't want any last-minute obstacles.

All morning she had been preparing for her meeting with Madeline Naylor and Alice Prince. Pacing around the small private office in her lab at Stanford University, she reread the recommendations she had made for taking Project Conscience forward. However she looked at them, she was sure each one stacked up. The funding budgets were realistic; the timings were ambitious but achievable. Then she turned to the one thousand prison inmates she'd selected from the FBI DNA database of convicted violent criminals. As she registered each name, she tried to memorize their files, double guessing any objections Madeline Naylor might have for using them.

She also made a mental note to ask about Pamela Weiss's TV debate last night and whether Dr. Prince or Director Naylor knew anything about Weiss's apparent plans to use biology and genetics to treat crime.

Sitting at her desk, Kathy watched the two lab technicians clearing the incubators and loading soiled petri dishes and beakers into the autoclave. No one else was present. Frank and Karen's replacements would arrive next week; that was just as well because until the forthcoming procedure had been agreed to, there wasn't that much to do.

When a minute later the main doors to the lab suddenly swung open, Kathy was startled. In that split second she thought that the director of the FBI and Dr. Alice Prince had arrived early and she thanked God she was ready.

But she wasn't ready because the visitor wasn't Madeline Naylor or Alice Prince.

When the tall blond man tentatively walked into the main lab, she saw one of the lab technicians talk with him and then point to her office. Kathy could only stand and stare through the blind as the man strode through the laboratory and knocked on her door.

"Come in," she said, suddenly wishing she'd worn her contacts in to work today rather than her old eyeglasses.

The door opened, and Luke Decker walked in. He seemed nervous, his eyes wary above a tight smile. "Hi, Kathy. I hope you don't mind my popping in unannounced?"

She smiled. "No, not at all."

"Impressive setup," he said, indicating the laboratory.

"Thanks," she said, putting her proposals for the forthcoming meeting down on the table. "So what brings you to this neck of the woods?"

Luke's face became more serious as he turned and closed the door. "Well, to be honest, I need a favor, a discreet favor. Do you have a minute?"

Kathy's curiosity was piqued. "Sure, I've got Director Naylor arriving in about half an hour, but I'm OK until then."

At the mention of the FBI director Luke frowned. "Sounds important."

"It is. We've just got FDA approval for a big project we're working on, and she's coming around to discuss next steps."

"That's great," he said. "Congratulations." But he was still frowning.

"What's the matter?" Kathy asked.

"Let's just say that I don't want what I'm going to discuss to become bureau business just yet."

Kathy nodded. Genuinely intrigued, she was studying Decker now. "Don't worry, my lips are sealed. So, what do you need?"

Decker paused. He seemed to be weighing how much to tell her. Reaching into his jacket pocket, he pulled out a small plastic bag. Then out of a side pocket he pulled out another one. "Well," he said, lifting the first bag, "I need to compare the DNA of the hair in this bag with what's in this one."

"How do you mean, compare?"

He opened the first bag, revealing three gray hairs and two flakes of dried blood. "I want to know if there's a relationship between them both."

She narrowed her eyes. "Relationship, as in family relationship? Brother-sister, father-daughter, that kind of thing?"

"Exactly."

Kathy took the bag and peered at the hairs and flakes of dark blood, then placed it carefully on her desk. Then she took the other bag and looked at the two blond hairs there. "You're not going to tell me what this is about, are you?"

"Not unless you make me. No."

She could see from Decker's face that he disliked asking for her help, that he was somehow endorsing her belief that understanding genes was at the root of understanding everything. For a fleeting moment she felt an irresistible urge to draw attention to his sudden dependence on the very technology he had openly derided in the past. She needed him to realize the significance of what he was requesting and recognize that the work she had dedicated her life to had meaning. "OK, I'll give it a go."

"How long will it take?" he asked, checking his watch. Now that he had told her, he seemed anxious to leave.

"How long? Well, in the old days we had to use the dot blot technique, or RFLP analysis, to isolate the sections of DNA that highlight the genetic relationship between individuals. You'd be lucky to get the results in two weeks."

His face fell.

She pointed at the black swanlike Genescope in the main laboratory and picked up the first bag. "But with that thing out there we can read all ninety thousand or so of the genes in the samples in here and compare them with those in the other bag in a fraction of that time. Leave it with me, and give me a call in a couple of hours. I should have a definite result by then."

Decker nodded, and in his face she could see both relief and dread. "Thanks, Kathy, I appreciate it."

"Are you sure, Luke? You don't look like you want to know the answer at all."

He shrugged and flashed a deceptively casual smile. "Let's just say I need to know."

At one-thirty precisely Director Naylor and Alice Prince arrived.

Moments earlier Kathy Kerr had given the lab technicians both batches of Decker's mystery samples to scan through the Genescope gene sequencer and analyze for any relationship. She couldn't help wondering why he had asked her to conduct the scans and why he was so eager to avoid the FBI. But for now she focused on her visitors.

Smart in a charcoal pantsuit, her white hair immaculate, the usually stern director was smiling. Dr. Prince wore a shapeless navy jacket and skirt and seemed strangely nervous.

Within the opening minutes, in the privacy of Kathy's office, Alice Prince told her that the FBI and ViroVector were increasing Kathy's funding by a further five million dollars a year. This money would be deposited as a lump sum in a special project account to use at her sole discretion. "Naturally," Naylor said with a grin, "you would be expected to fund your personal salary—as much as you deem appropriate—out of this additional grant."

Kathy was dumbstruck. Her current grant was already more than enough to continue her work within the tight budgets she set herself especially since ViroVector subsidized much of her lab equipment costs at Stanford anyway. But with additional funding she could recruit more people. Speed up the whole program.

"I don't know what to say. It's very generous. In fact it's much more than I need."

"Nonsense," said Naylor. "The first rule about seeking

grants is that you can never have too much funding." She smiled again, the skin creasing beneath her dark eyes, lips stretching over strong teeth. Kathy had rarely seen her smile before, and it seemed unnatural, more unnerving than her usual stern expression.

"Anyway," said Naylor, rising from her seat at the small circular conference table and moving close to where Kathy sat, bending over her, "you deserve the additional funding, and we want you to realize how much we appreciate all you have achieved."

Flattered but slightly embarrassed, Kathy reached for her notes in the middle of the table. "Well, thank you, I'm very grateful. But what I most want to gain is your agreement on the next steps for the project." She waited for Naylor to re-take her seat and then handed her and Alice a folder each.

Kathy opened her proposal. "As well as outline the next steps, rationale, budget breakdowns, objectives, and timings, this proposal contains a list of all the subjects I'd like to test Conscience Version Nine on—subject to their approval. And of course yours."

Neither Alice nor Naylor said anything for a moment; Naylor didn't even look at the papers Kathy had given her.

Then Alice Prince cocked her head to one side and appeared to study a spot just above Kathy's head. "What would you say if I told you we could reduce the next eight to ten years of your research?"

Kathy didn't understand. She looked from Alice to Naylor. "What do you mean? Accelerate the tests on criminals?"

Naylor nodded slowly, her smile gone. Unblinking, she stared at Kathy, a snake watching its prey.

Kathy shrugged. "Well, that would be great if it didn't compromise the results. Accelerate it by how much?"

There was a pause as the dark eyes studied her even more closely. Kathy had the distinct impression she was being tested, judged on her reaction. "Let's say we wouldn't so much accelerate the trials," said Naylor, "as *bypass* them."

"But we have to do tests. To make sure it works."

"Not if they've already been conducted," said Alice.

"But that's impossible; that would have taken years."

A nod as the director's thin lips twitched into a smaller smile, which didn't reach her eyes. "Eight years, in fact."

Kathy stared at Naylor, searching for the teasing irony. "Come on, Director, I don't understand. Tell me you're kidding."

But the director of the FBI was no longer smiling.

Kathy put a hand over her mouth and looked at Alice, but she was looking down at the table. "You've been conducting secret trials on our work—on *my* work?"

"It's not quite as simple as that," said Naylor. "Without our knowledge a group of overzealous senior FBI officers and ViroVector scientists found out about Conscience and began a secret unauthorized trial. Naturally all the people involved will be severely disciplined. But the point is, their trials worked."

For some seconds Kathy's disbelief numbed her to any other feelings. Then, as she realized that this was serious, her anger surfaced. She pushed her chair away from the table and paced around the office. "But who are these people? Why weren't they discovered earlier?"

Naylor sat coolly in her seat. Prince squirmed in hers.

"It doesn't matter now," said Naylor, "but, Kathy, you must be aware of the improved crime figures in California."

Kathy was so furious she could feel her nails digging into her palms. Of course she was aware of the state's improved crime figures. The news and current affairs shows were full of theories to explain them, especially now that the governor credited with them was running for President.

"Well," continued Naylor, "they are a direct result of tests conducted on violent criminals using your theories on gene manipulation." Naylor held up Kathy's proposal. "The people who did this test have done nothing different from what you planned. Indeed some of the criminals on your list have already been given the treatment. In one way you could argue that it's good news; your theories have been proved to work. You've been saved ten years."

Kathy reached across and snatched her proposal document from Naylor. "Well, this was a bloody waste of time, wasn't it? My team and I worked our butts off for nothing.

And how the hell could the tests have started eight years ago? The safe Version Nine serum approved by the FDA was developed only four years ago."

Naylor paused and gave a small sigh.

Kathy felt sick as she understood. She could see her life's work, the hours of dedication and sacrifice wasted, the whole of her research discredited and put back decades. "Good God!" she shouted. "They used the original serum, didn't they? Christ, I bet the subjects weren't even volunteers."

"No, they weren't. But you could argue that after the crimes they had committed they weren't given any choice about going to jail or death row either. The criminal subjects might not have been aware of the tests, but almost all have benefited. Kathy, consider one thing. No one has been harmed by the treatment. Some sixteen thousand convicts have been tested, and not only does it work, but it's safe."

"How the hell do you know? The effects could manifest themselves years into the future. God, our own research indicated that testicular and prostate cancers could be caused and accelerated by the early vectors. Not just in the subjects themselves but their children too. Male babies born with testicular cancer could be—"

Alice Prince shook her head. Her voice was almost pleading. "Kathy, I saw your early reports. Causation was never proved. I've looked into it."

"How can you say that, Alice? You know it was."

"OK, OK. But the percentage risk was minute. Come on, Kathy, the difference between the early vectors and the final Version Nine is negligible."

"Negligible? What gives you the right to say that?"

Alice looked flustered and looked toward Naylor. She had always hated conflict.

"Why don't you wait outside, Alice?" said Director Naylor. "Let me handle this."

Alice paused, and then with a look of shame and relief on her face she stood up and walked out.

Without missing a beat Naylor continued. "Kathy, the negligible differences are vital for gaining official FDA approval, I grant you, but hardly necessary to be safe. Kathy, the money and lives that have already been saved by doing what these people did more than offset any minute risk involved. And after Pamela's preelection announcement all future treatments will use the FDA-approved Version Nine anyway."

"What announcement?" said Kathy. She couldn't believe this.

"This Friday, Pamela Weiss—"

Kathy stopped her pacing. "Is that what Weiss was talking about on yesterday's TV debate?"

Naylor nodded. "Yes, and that's what we want to talk to you about. Once we learned that the unauthorized tests worked and your Version Nine had received full FDA approval we decided to use the crisis to the project's advantage. A scandal could push Conscience back decades, but a brave visionary announcement that seizes the opportunity might not only save the project but actually accelerate its acceptance.

"So with the full support of President Burbank, Pamela Weiss will take responsibility for the successful results of the criminal tests, putting an end to all the speculation about the positive California crime figures. She will also announce a proposed policy to treat all convicted violent criminals across the nation with your FDA-approved version of Conscience. She will tell the American people that if they elect her, she can guarantee to reduce crime across the country. What's more, Kathy, Alice, who is just as horrified about the unauthorized trials as you are, suggested you share full credit for the successful tests.

"Think about it, Kathy. You'll be famous. A Nobel Prize isn't out of the question. But more important, with the full political power of the presidency behind it, you will see your life's dream of a cure for crime realized sooner than you could have imagined. Not just in this country but worldwide. However, it's important that no one is left in any doubt that the tests conducted over the last few years were done with the FDA-approved vector. Although we know the trials were safe, we have to be seen to have known all along. Pamela

Weiss must appear as a bold visionary taking calculated risks, not as irresponsible or dangerous."

This was unbelievable. Kathy walked back to her desk and leaned against it. "But she *is* being irresponsible and dangerous."

For the first time Naylor looked angry. "No, she *isn't*. The future President still isn't aware of the minor differences between Version One and Version Nine. As far as Pamela Weiss knows, the FDA approved what was tested in the unauthorized trials. And that's the way it has to stay."

"You can't do this to me. It's completely unethical. You want me to lie about my life's work?"

"No, of course not. This whole project is based on your life's work. We just need you to see the bigger picture and make the most of the opportunity. This irresponsible test threatened to ruin the credibility of everything you worked for. But this way you can use it to your advantage to make the world a better place. How can that be a bad thing?"

Kathy sat on the desk and shook her head. Minutes ago her future had been bright and challenging, but most important of all, it had been her own. Now all her dreams were being ripped from her. "But it's a lie. I'm not sure I can go through with it."

"Come on, Kathy, you have to be pragmatic to protect your ideals. The choice is simple. You can embrace what has happened and make the world a better place. Or you can denounce it, merely because some petty rules were broken, and a tiny percentage of convicted violent criminals were *possibly* exposed to a *negligible* risk of disease. If you do the first, you will achieve everything you've ever dreamed of, including the realization of your vision of a gentler world. If you do the second, then you will destroy any hope of your vision becoming a reality."

"But it's still wrong. Don't you see that?" Kathy said, her mouth dry with anger. "You want me to commit a crime to promote something that's supposed to stop it."

Naylor stood slowly and spoke calmly and forcefully. "What's done is done. The question now is, what do we do next? Do we build on your work or destroy it? Think about it. This is important. I need to know your decision by six o'clock tonight. Is that clear?"

Kathy said nothing for a moment. Her head ached with the unfairness of it all. If she kept her integrity, she would compromise her life's work, perhaps destroy it. But if she compromised her integrity, she would see her dreams realized in a fantastically short space of time. It was a deal with the devil.

"Six o'clock. Is that clear?" Madeline said again, her face impassive as she opened the door to leave.

"No, it's bloody not," said Kathy eventually. "Nothing's clear anymore."

Alice Prince squirmed inside as she waited in her car in the parking lot. She felt like a coward for walking out, but she was secretly glad to let Madeline deal with Kathy. Alice knew she owed Kathy so much. It made it difficult to lie to her. But Madeline didn't care. She was fearless.

Alice could remember the first day she met Madeline as clearly as if it were yesterday. She had arrived at St. Joseph's School in Baddington, in upstate New York, the oddest-looking girl Alice had ever seen.

Madeline was only thirteen when the principal introduced her to Alice's class, halfway through the fall semester. She had the whitest hair Alice had ever seen in an aggressive spiky cut and dark, defiant eyes that stared out of her long face. All the other kids laughed at Madeline because she looked so odd and because she lived with her grandmother, Mad Mrs. Preston, the stern old lady who lived in the rambling old house on Oxford Street, not two houses from Alice's family.

No one knew then that Madeline was staying with her grandmother only because her own mother had abandoned her when she was a toddler and her policeman father had been shot dead in front of her two weeks earlier, the shock of which had turned her hair white. Instead they teased and bullied her. Alice was glad at first because it took the heat off her.

But when the two biggest boys in the class, the Tyndale

twins, picked on Madeline in the yard, Alice felt sorry for her. At least until Madeline turned on them like a wildcat, scratching them and punching them, not stopping until the boys limped off. Afterward, Alice picked up the bag and books the boys had knocked out of Madeline's hands and returned them to her. "Hi, I'm Alice," she said. "So, what's it like living at Mad Mrs. Preston's? Is it true she's got dead bodies buried under the floorboards?"

Brushing herself off, Madeline shrugged. "I don't know," she said. "Let's go take a look."

Alice still loved Madeline's fearlessness and was still frightened of her. She only hoped she wouldn't do anything to Kathy.

Striding into the sunlight of the Stanford University parking lot, Director Naylor wasn't too disappointed with the meeting. In a perverse way the fact that Kathy Kerr had been so openly combative pleased her. It made her decision easier.

Naylor had lied about who was responsible for the criminal tests on Project Conscience, to probe Kerr's true feelings. She had feigned innocence of the unauthorized tests to convince Kerr they were on the same side and were both forced to make the best of the situation. But Kerr hadn't bought the pragmatic approach. She was opposed on a matter of principle. Naylor had learned that when it came to compromises, people with principles could never be trusted. Whatever she said at six o'clock tonight Kerr was too much of a risk. Not only would she jeopardize Conscience, but she could also raise doubts in Pamela Weiss's mind when Crime Zero was activated. Kerr had to be taken out of the mix. Fast.

Approaching her official car, she saw Alice Prince sitting in the backseat of her Mercedes, her driver sitting obediently in front. As soon as Alice saw her, she got out of the car and came over to her.

"How did it go?" Alice asked.

"You heard her. Kerr isn't listening."

"Really?"

"Don't feel bad about it, Ali. I gave her every chance, but she's adamant."

"Are you sure?"

"As sure as I can be."

"So what do we do?"

"Don't worry, I'll handle it."

A note of panic appeared in Alice's voice. "You aren't going to hurt her, are you?"

"No, of course not," said Naylor. "I'll just make sure she's put somewhere safe until after the election. It's nothing for you to worry about." She looked around the parking lot, searching for Jackson. He should have arrived by now. "It'll look like she's gone away for a short vacation. It's all arranged."

There was a pause. "If it's the only way." Alice looked unhappy but resigned.

"It is, Ali. Trust me, it is. Anyway, we'd better get ready for our meeting with Pamela. I'll see you there."

As Naylor walked back to her official car, two agents, classic G-men in their dark suits and short haircuts, stepped out. The taller agent opened the door for her. But before she stepped in, she watched two other cars enter the lot and park next to each other a short distance away. The first was a gray Chrysler. A powerful black man with a handsome face and fierce eyes sat in the passenger seat, a weasel-faced agent at the wheel. The second car was identical and contained three men.

That was one of the things she most liked about Associate Director William Jackson; he was always exactly where she wanted him to be. Jackson had been with her for years. His team were all highly motivated agents who had faced disciplinary charges in the past that, if pursued, would have landed them in jail for a long time. Naylor had used her influence to lose the charges, and they were now unquestioningly loyal to her. Through the buffer of Jackson they kept her informed of what was happening within the bureau and sorted out any local difficulties without there being any trace back to her.

Jackson and his men didn't leave the cars.

"Banion, get me a phone," she said to the agent holding the car door open for her.

As soon as Naylor was seated in the car and the door closed behind her, a handset was passed to her. She dialed a number. Across the lot she saw William Jackson pick up his cell phone.

"Jackson," he said in a deep, distinctive nasal voice.

"I want you personally to handle this," she said. "Don't forget, only Dr. Peters is to know about it. Don't involve anyone else there." She paused, leveling her gaze at the fierce eyes across the lot. "And, Jackson, don't disappoint me."

11

Sitting at one of the desks provided for visiting agents, Luke Decker tried to keep his mind off Kathy Kerr's test. Instead he placed his laptop computer into the docking station provided and proceeded to check out the thirteenth victim mentioned in Axelman's letter.

First of all he reread part of the relevant section:

> . . . This last girl, the thirteenth, recognized the place I left all the girls. She told me her parents took her to play near there. The tree that covers the entrance to my tunnels was just one of many, but she called it a name. She told me she and her mom called it the Snake Tree. It's in a large forest near their home. Contact the girl's parents; they will know the place. That's where you will find the bodies—all thirteen. That's where I kept them safe.
>
> I don't want you to go straight to the bodies. I want you to approach the parents of this last victim. Please make my peace with them. I will die soon, and only now do I realize what I have done. The knowledge is killing me, but the one thing I cling to is that my evil produced something good. I produced you. Perhaps as my son you can help me find peace by helping me make amends for my crimes. . . .

Decker dropped the letter, an unclean thing, onto the desk. He hated the very notion of somehow helping Axelman find redemption. Going back to his computer, Decker used slow movements of the mouse to run a search on the FBI case files database, entering the victim's name and abduction date given in the letter. As the files were retrieved, he printed them out on the printer by his desk, favoring the lowest-tech option available.

He pulled the four-page document from the printer and scanned the text. It confirmed that a girl of the same name had been abducted at the time given in Axelman's letter and that her body had never been found. But her disappearance would almost certainly have been reported in the newspapers, so that proved nothing. Decker could visit the girl's family and ask about the tree. But if this was a hoax by Axelman, a clever, cruel attempt to inflict more pain after his death, then Decker wanted no part of it. Instead he read all the available details about the victim and her family and studied the photographic images in the case file. One of the saddest consequences of Decker's work was that whenever he walked down a street and saw a young girl or woman, he unconsciously graded her for risk, instinctively knowing signs of vulnerability. Clothing, age, looks, makeup, bearing, and personality all played their part. Knowing the victim was as important as knowing the killer. The girl in the file photographs was high risk for a person like Axelman. She looked young, pretty, and innocent. It was possible Axelman was telling the truth about his thirteenth victim. But why weren't her personal effects in one of the boxes found in his house?

Decker now used the mouse to move the cursor over the Internet icon and clicked twice. After keying in his America Online password, he used a search engine to enter the area where the thirteenth victim's family still lived. In seconds he was looking at a list of possible data sources. He clicked on one: the Los Altos Verdes Community website. The home page was decorated with a stunning picture of soaring trees in a forest. A forest not unlike the one described in Axelman's letter.

**Los Altos Verdes, San Bruno Mountains,
San Francisco Bay Area.
One Hour Later**

Eight miles from Palo Alto, Luke Decker stood by the rental
Ford in a clearing overlooking one of several multimillion-
dollar houses that studded the wooded estate of Los Altos
Verdes.

From the website he had learned that some thirty years
ago these luxury houses had been built over what was once
a vast private zoo. Despite the beautiful natural setting, the
zoo had fallen on hard times, and eventually the owners had
sold out to a real estate company that built ten prime properties on the site, using the existing terrain and replanting
new trees. It was a magical place, but the prospect of visiting the house below gave Decker no pleasure. It belonged to
the family of the thirteenth victim.

Taking a deep breath, he looked up the hill to the towering trees that lined the denim blue sky. The website had
made no mention of any Snake Tree, and if it did exist, then
it had to be a name known only to the victim's family. Scanning the oaks, firs, and bay trees, Decker knew he would
never find it without their help—if Axelman had been telling
the truth.

Telling the truth.

Just the notion that Axelman was telling the truth about
anything in his letter was chilling.

Checking his watch, he wandered back to the car and picked
his cell phone off the driver seat. He punched in Kathy's number and waited for her to pick up. His heart was pumping so
hard he was sure the whispering forest could hear it.

The phone rang five times before it was picked up. With
each ring he braced himself for the news.

"Kathy Kerr." Her voice sounded strained.

"Kathy, hi, it's Luke. I was wondering if you had the results yet." There was a pause. "Kathy? Are you there?"

"Sorry, Luke. Yes, I'm here." But she sounded distant as
if her mind were elsewhere. "Yes, yes, the samples. I'll just
get them. I'm sure they're ready by now."

Her apparent diffidence only made him feel worse. She sounded more focused when she came back on the line. He could hear her fingers tapping on a keyboard. "Luke, hi, I'm now in front of the Genescope. I'm scanning for the top line results and—"

"Yes? What is it?"

"Hang on, let me just double-check something."

He could hear surprise in her voice. If his heart had been beating fast before, it was racing now, a gallop of anticipation. "Well?"

"Luke, is this official?" She sounded guarded.

"What do you mean?"

"The samples in one of the bags you gave me have thrown up a virtual match with a subject on the FBI DNA database. A killer on death row. What's going on here, Luke?"

"Kathy, trust me. You don't want to know. Just tell me. Is there a relationship between the samples?"

"Luke, there's something very weird here—"

"I know that," he almost shouted down the phone. "Is there a goddamn relationship or not?"

A heavy sigh was followed by a long pause. For a heart-wrenching second he thought she was going to hang up. When she spoke again, her voice was calm but strained. "Yes." She seemed unwilling to reveal the results. "According to the Genescope, the samples are from the same family. Father and son."

Decker's knees buckled, and he leaned against the car. On the phone he could hear her fingers tapping on a keyboard. "But, Luke," she was saying, her voice insistent, "there's something really strange here. We need to talk urgently."

He was no longer listening. He had hung up, turned the phone off, and thrown it in the car as if it were somehow contaminated. But the phone wasn't contaminated. He was. His stomach contracted, and he dry-heaved. The words on the letter in his hand swam before his eyes, taunting him.

I asked to see you, because for some reason I suddenly feel real bad about all the things I've done. I thought if I told you—my son—you could help me put things right. But when I saw you today, I couldn't tell you to your face. You looked just like my father. He was a strict man, a religious man, and I felt kind of ashamed.

I've guessed you were my son for months. Ever since I saw your picture in the *Examiner* after saving some girl in a graveyard. Your face in the picture looked exactly like one of my father when he was about your age. And I remembered the name. I've got a good memory, too good a memory. I wish I could forget all the things I've done. I raped a woman once near Union Square in San Francisco at about the time that fits with your age. I know her name because her husband tried to help her. He was the only man I've ever killed. According to the papers, he was a Captain Decker in the U.S. Navy, but they never said anything about the woman being raped. . . .

Decker sat on the ground, his back against the car, taking deep breaths. When he looked up, the tall treetops seemed to dance around him, a giddying carousel in the clear sky. Not only was he Axelman's son, but Axelman had killed the man Decker had worshiped as his father all his life. Decker felt his very being called into question. Every constant on which he had based his assumptions of who he was, what he did, and his place in the wider world had been irrevocably destroyed. Even the validity of his work was suddenly doubtful. If Kathy Kerr and Director Naylor were right and humans were little more than their genes, then what did that make him?

Standing up, he replaced the letter in his inside pocket and looked down at the house below. A chill formed in his gut and then spread throughout his body. He got in the car and glanced at the brand-new spade and flashlight he had bought on his way out here, sitting ominously on the rear seat.

He gunned the engine into life and turned the Ford around. Looking into the rearview mirror, he saw two green eyes staring back at him, judging him. And for a second those eyes weren't his at all, but Karl Axelman's.

12

Stanford University, Stanford.
Thursday, October 30, 3:12 P.M.

In her laboratory at Stanford University Kathy Kerr sat staring at the Genescope monitor in a state of shock. What the hell was Luke Decker up to?

After her meeting with Madeline Naylor, Kathy had been so furious she'd been unable to concentrate on anything else. But when she calmed down a little, she'd tried to think through the consequences. What would she really achieve by exposing the unauthorized criminal trials? Apart from undermining the credibility of the Version 9 serum she *had* gained approval for. Not to mention the personal damage she would cause herself. However hard she protested her innocence, she would undoubtedly be tarnished solely by her involvement with Project Conscience. She could kiss good-bye any dreams she might have of fulfilling her ambition of treating violent crime.

But what she saw on-screen in front of her eclipsed these concerns, making them seem academic by comparison. As she studied the DNA profile from the blood flake samples Luke had brought in the first evidence bag and compared it with the matching profile on the FBI DNA database, her anger turned to ice.

The genome of the convicted killer called Karl Axelman had subtly changed.

Switching to voice control, she instructed the Genescope to search Axelman's DNA in chromosome 1. As the lights blinked on the neck of the black swan, there was a grumbling noise, and then its mellifluous male voice said, "Subject's 5-HT1Dα receptor gene is instructing boosted serotonin production. Three hundred percent higher than normal levels."

Kathy took a deep breath. "Go to chromosome nine."

The monitor shifted out of focus and then back, revealing a multicolored double helix. Beside the colored image was a table showing codons of triple letters: *CGA AGT TGA*. Each codon represented an amino acid, and the order of amino acids determined the genes, which in turn instructed the production of proteins. Part of the multicolored double helix was highlighted, and a battery of codons showing the code at that particular part of the DNA strand scrolled down the screen.

"Genetic abnormality present," said the honeyed voice. "The dopamine β-hydroxylase gene instructing boosted production of dopamine. In excess of four hundred percent typical levels. Effect exacerbated by similar boosting of dopamine receptor genes."

When Kathy asked the Genescope to search out all similarly boosted genes throughout Axelman's genome, she discovered that the changes centered on the seventeen key genes her work had been focusing on. Karl Axelman had received gene therapy to modify his behavior. But it wasn't Kathy's Conscience Version 9 therapy. In fact it didn't look like therapy at all.

Kathy's FDA-approved Version 9 serum was a genetically engineered viral vector that carried control genes to reduce excessive aggression and increase appropriate emotional inhibitors to violence. It did this by reducing a patient's key drivers of aggression, including the dopamine receptor, noradrenaline receptor, and testosterone genes, and boosting impulsive behavior inhibitors, such as the 5-HT1Dα serotonin gene.

But Axelman's modified profile indicated that *all* his hormones and neurotransmitters had been boosted to intolerable levels. Far from harmonizing and calming him, this gene therapy would have made Karl Axelman implode, on the one hand, boosting his aggressive impulses to unprecedented levels, while burdening him with huge emotional anxiety and guilt. She had never seen levels this high before, not even half as high. It was like pushing a foot down on a Ferrari's gas pedal, revving it to the limit, while at the same time pushing your other foot down hard on the brake pedal. Eventually something had to give.

She went into the Genescope's PACT menu and chose T for "threats." "What are the implications of these genetic changes?" she asked.

"Subject's original genome shows no other major defects. Eighty-seven percent probability of prostate cancer in his late eighties but otherwise healthy. Realigned genome indicates intolerable levels of stress and anxiety. Subject's life expectancy reduced to days. Projected causes of death: brain hemorrhage, heart attack, or positive choice."

"What do you mean, positive choice?"

"Suicide," the soft voice said.

Kathy's hands were shaking as the implications began to sink in. Had Axelman been treated in the unauthorized criminal tests? He was certainly a prime candidate. Suddenly this looked bigger than just a cover-up over FDA approvals.

She reached for the phone and tried to call Luke, but his phone was switched off. Shit, she really needed to talk to him about this. Perhaps he knew what was going on here? Was this why he was so paranoid about going through authorized channels and involving the FBI labs?

She inserted a Hi-Data Storage Zip disc into the base of the Genescope and made a copy of Karl Axelman's genome from the DNA database and another of his modified genome from the blood samples Decker had brought in. Given how sensitive these data were, she wanted to keep them safe.

She took the disc out of the Genescope, walked across the main lab, past her two lab assistants busy emptying the autoclave, and retreated into the relative privacy of her office. Having closed the door behind her, she rushed to her desk, turned on the computer, and moved the cursor to the folders holding all historical Conscience files. She wanted to check if she'd overlooked anything in the original viral vector that might have caused Axelman's fatal genetic mutation. Moving the cursor, she clicked on the directory folder marked "FDA Approval: Clinical Trials History."

A message appeared over the folder: "This file has been moved to a different directory. Please seek authorization."

Only hours ago she had had open access to these data, to *her* data. An irrational paranoid thought rose in her consciousness, but she quelled it. Nervously she looked out of her office at the technicians in the laboratory. She didn't know any of them well enough to trust. Christ, if only Karen and Frank were still here and not somewhere in the middle of the Congo.

Still keeping calm, she walked back into the laboratory, to the two large filing cabinets by her office. Although most of the data were stored electronically, a number of the text-based reports and completed approval applications were stored as hard copy as well. Opening the middle drawer on the left cabinet, she immediately spied the blue folder marked "Project Conscience Trials." It seemed significantly thinner than she remembered it. The paranoid thought nagged at her now. With trembling fingers she opened the folder. Seeing the batch of files on the FDA-approved Version 9 vector, she breathed a sigh of relief and admonished herself for being so foolish. But then she looked for documentation on the original serum, the one used in the unauthorized trials. There was no trace of it at all.

The paranoia returned with a rush. What the hell was going on? Someone was shutting her out, isolating her.

She turned to one of the laboratory technicians stacking up clean culture bottles by the autoclave. "Warren, do you know what happened to these files?"

He put the bottles down and shook his head. "Nope, I haven't touched any of them in days."

She looked at him for a moment. Had he or one of the other technicians taken the files under orders from Director Naylor to ensure she didn't rock the boat? Or had men come in the night and removed them? A shiver ran through her.

This was getting way out of hand. "No problem," she said, "I must have left them at home."

As casually as she could she strolled back to her office and sat at her desk. Something that she didn't understand was happening. And after her less than constructive meeting with Director Naylor, she didn't know whom to turn to. That included Alice Prince. There was only one person who might be able to shine some light on this, someone whom, despite whatever else she felt about him, she still trusted.

She quickly scribbled a note to Decker. When she was finished, she pulled a small brown envelope from a pile by her desk and placed the note and the Axelman disc inside it. She addressed the envelope to him at Matty Rheiman's house in the Marina in San Francisco, at the address Decker had written on the back of his card. Finally she stuck a stamp on the envelope, checked that she wasn't being watched through the glass window of her office, and discreetly placed the envelope into the deep pocket of her white lab coat.

She walked out of her office through the laboratory to the swinging doors that led to the corridor outside and made her way to the rest rooms. When she reached them, she doubled back and cut through the biology section to the reception area of the Medical Research Center. Here she smiled at the woman at the main desk, strolled as nonchalantly as possible toward the two large mailboxes attached to the wall, and as surreptitiously as she could palmed the envelope out of her pocket and into one of the slots as she passed. Now, regardless of what was going on, at least this piece of evidence was safe, even if she and all her computer files were searched.

Back in her office she picked up her handbag and took out a well-thumbed road map of San Francisco. If she couldn't phone Luke, then after going home to pick up a couple of things, she would drive to his grandfather's place and wait for him there. She quickly pinpointed Matty Rheiman's street on the map and put it back in her bag. After taking off her lab coat, she picked up her laptop and handbag and left her office.

Out in the parking lot she climbed into her old Volkswagen, started the car, and left the campus. Kathy began to feel better as she left Palo Alto. Turning into Mendoza Drive, she passed a gray Chrysler parked off the road near one of her neighbors and saw her house ahead. Its cheerful white stucco facade made her reconsider whether she was overreacting. After parking the car, Kathy picked up her cell phone and dialed Luke's number again. This time she left a message on his voice mail. Explaining her fears, she told him that she was going over to his grandfather's house now and that they urgently needed to talk. Just saying her concerns aloud helped put them into some kind of perspective. She jumped out of the car and ran across the green lawn to the ornate Mexican-style wooden door. Even as she put her keys in the lock of her home, she felt calmer.

But as Kathy Kerr opened the door to her house, she would undoubtedly have felt less calm if she had seen the three men step out of the Chrysler parked two hundred yards back. Or seen the second identical Chrysler pull up beside it, a weasel-faced man at the wheel. The calmness left her altogether when she entered her house and confronted the dark face and fierce eyes staring at her. She almost stopped breathing.

She froze on the spot as the man pointed his gun at her with one hand, while wielding a hypodermic in his other. Her own right hand was in her bag dropping the house keys. Trying to keep her voice calm, she asked, "What do you want?" Her fingers reached for the top left-hand button on the cell phone and pressed it.

"Just to keep you safe and silent for a while," the man said in a deep, nasal voice.

She couldn't believe this. Despite her fear, she felt anger. "Why?" she shouted. "This is something to do with Project Conscience, isn't it?"

The man smiled at that. "All I've been told is that you're overstressed and are likely to say things you may regret." He moved closer. "We're going to take you somewhere you can calm down, somewhere you can have peace and quiet."

"Keep that damn needle away from me, you bastard," she

shouted, backing out the front door. But three men blocked her path. Two held her while the first man approached with the syringe. The fourth man covered her mouth with a cloth that smelled of stale water. Struggling as hard as she could, she felt a sharp prick as the needle entered her arm. All the time she kept her hand in the bag, her finger on the redial button of the cell phone, hoping it had called Decker's number, a silent cry for help to a man who wasn't there.

13

Smart Suite, ViroVector, Palo Alto.
Thursday, October 30, 3:12 P.M.

Returned from the meeting with Kathy Kerr, Dr. Alice Prince felt calmer viewing the data with Madeline Naylor on the presentation screens in ViroVector's Smart Suite. The large interface room was directly adjacent to TITANIA's carefully controlled chamber. It was populated with the usual equipment, such as monitors, printers, microphones, speakers, and keyboards, allowing TITANIA to communicate in every possible way with its human colleagues.

There was also a long conference table and five workstations. At the back of the room were four small monitors, each showing quickly shifting views of the ViroVector complex as seen through the series of sixty closed-circuit security cameras TITANIA controlled around the campus. But these were peripheral to the two main display media.

The first was the screen wall dividing the Smart Suite from TITANIA's Cold Room. The fifteen-by-ten-foot liquid crystal display was currently running through a series of projection charts on Project Conscience in anticipation of Governor Weiss's arrival.

The second was the hologram floor pad at the head of the conference table. Using leading-edge laser hologram imaging technology from KREE8 Industries in San Jose, TITANIA could holo-project virtually anything over the pad, making the projected 3-D "object" appear at such high definition that to all intents and purposes it existed in the room. On display now was a rotating double helix of DNA showing the 5-HT1Dα receptor gene on chromosome 1, which instructed for the production in the human brain of serotonin, the neurotransmitter that controlled impulsive behavior.

Two identical hard copy briefing packs lay on the table in the places set for Pamela Weiss and her campaign adviser, Todd Sullivan. The black-bound document was labeled "Project Conscience—Scientific Data and Crime Statistics."

"Everything seems to be in order," said Madeline Naylor, checking her watch. "Pamela should be here any moment now."

Alice thought she'd try it one last time. "Perhaps we should tell Pamela about the FDA findings, explain why the differences don't really matter? She'll understand."

Madeline raised an eyebrow and flashed that look of hers, both bullying and protective. It was the same look she had used on an icy pond more than forty years ago, when as children they had witnessed an act that still bound them together in an invisible web of guilt and dependency.

"Come on, Alice," Madeline said patiently. "We've agreed on this already. That's why it was so important to get Kathy Kerr organized. Pamela can't be told anything that might compromise her. She must believe that the original Conscience vector used in the criminal trials was exactly the same as the later FDA-approved version. And on no account must she know anything about Crime Zero. She can't be told about the San Quentin deaths and suicides. As far as she's concerned, they were normal executions to which she signed the papers. She wouldn't understand. Not as we do. Come on, Alice, we're doing this for Libby, and all the Libbys in the world."

Alice Prince looked into Madeline's dark eyes and, despite her doubts, knew Madeline was right. She had always been the stronger one, always able to make the tough decisions.

Just then the phone beside her rang. Alice picked it up. "Dr. Prince," said the voice on the line, "Governor Weiss has arrived."

Pamela Weiss had left most of her election entourage behind. This was a private meeting to discuss delicate matters. So her campaign manager and would-be chief of staff, Todd Sullivan, had adroitly slipped her away like a reclusive rock star from the huddled press battalions and shuttled her down to ViroVector by helicopter.

"We've got fifty-nine minutes before Governor Weiss has to leave for Los Angeles" were Sullivan's first words as Alice Prince greeted them in the foyer and escorted them to the Smart Suite. Two Secret Service men in dark suits and glasses followed behind and stationed themselves outside the closed door. They neither acknowledged nor spoke to the two FBI agents already standing there to escort Director Naylor.

"Relax, will you, Todd?" said Weiss, embracing Alice and Madeline with the same affection as they had shown since college.

Sullivan seemed vaguely discomfited by the obvious closeness of the three women and sat down. He was a lean man of forty-eight with dark hair and a neat face, remarkable only for a small scar on his chin.

When everyone had been offered coffee and drinks, Alice adjusted her eyeglasses and began. "The first thing to say is, we've got FDA approval. So Friday's announcement can go ahead as planned."

"Excellent." Pamela beamed.

Sullivan looked relieved. "We really need this announcement. The national crime figures are scaring voters, and we're seen as too soft. Iraq isn't doing us any favors either."

"And it looks as if it's going to get worse," said Madeline. "I was talking to Mike Clanton at Langley yesterday. His people believe that the Iraqis have definitely got the bioweapon they're bragging about. Probably paying some rogue scientist from Russia. The CIA reckons there's a real danger they'll use it if we stop them from retaking Kuwait."

Pamela Weiss was nodding in agreement. "And although the polls say the people want to vote for us," she said, "it's the same old story: They don't believe a woman has the toughness and vision to handle either Iraq or the crime rate. So anything we can do to change their minds is vital."

"Oh, I think this will help change their minds," said Alice, pressing the console on the desk in front of her. Suddenly the lights dimmed, and all the monitors on the screen wall went dead except for the largest screen in the center. "Project Conscience" appeared across the top in white letters, and below it the line "A *Proven* Treatment for Crime."

"On the table you'll each find a bound briefing pack we'll be supplying to the press, complete with computer discs, slide show presentations, and summaries. In the front you'll find the crime stats and results from the Project Conscience field tests. In the back you'll find all the details of the formulations and scientific data, including all the preclinical and safety information. The first section should reassure you that Conscience works, and the second that it is completely safe. At the beginning of each section you'll find the summary pages. I suggest you look at those now while Madeline and I go through the presentation."

Alice sat down and gestured to Naylor. "Madeline will take you through the stats, and then I'll take over for the scientific findings. If either of you are unclear about anything, just holler, OK?"

Sullivan and Weiss nodded as Naylor stood and walked to the screen.

"To recap," Madeline Naylor said in her low, professional voice, "every year for the past eight years, two thousand prisoners convicted of a cross section of violent crime have been selected from Folsom, San Quentin, and the other major penal institutions in California. Under the pretense of a flu inoculation, this sample population was unwittingly injected with noninfectious stem cell gene therapy, the Conscience viral vector. Over the last eight years we have amassed and been tracking a total of some sixteen thousand treated men. This tracking has been done with the assistance of four senior members of the bureau, all of whom report directly to a person on my staff. None of them has any knowledge of the treatments or the project's overall objectives." As Naylor spoke, the screen shifted, showing charts and slides that demonstrated her points.

"Since we started the trials, two percent of the treated subjects have since been executed, one percent have died of natural causes, and twenty-one percent are still incarcerated. But even this twenty-four percent performed well in aggression studies, showing significantly reduced testosterone levels and increased frontal lobe activity. More important, of the remaining seventy-six percent who were released, only a tiny percentage has reoffended. Recidivism is down to less than ten percent, against a norm of over sixty. And their repeat crimes tend to be minor felonies.

"But the most interesting finding is that not only have the individuals benefited, but so have the communities to which they returned. Genetic and environmental factors appear to become inextricably entwined, one influencing the other. Watts in South Central Los Angeles is the best example of this." The screen shifted to show black-and-white TV coverage of the Watts riots in 1965; Alice could clearly see the skeletal Watts Towers towering above the mayhem.

The screen shifted to show a color view of the same scene five years ago. The place was relatively quiet, but it still looked run-down with graffiti and boarded-up shops.

The last screen change revealed the same scene taken a week previously. It looked similar except that freshly painted, thriving storefronts had replaced the boarded-up windows daubed in graffiti. And people were walking down the street as if pursuing their normal business.

To Alice the differences were subtle, but the overall contrast was striking.

"You can't see much from this footage," said Naylor, "but when you go there on Friday to make your announcement, you'll notice the difference. And more important, so will the voters. The clincher, though, is that the overall crime rate in the test state of California has defied the national trend of escalating crime. Homicides are down fifteen percent, assaults down five percent, robberies down eighteen percent, rapes down twenty-five percent.

"Furthermore, from a financial point of view, the results are just as dramatic. If the positive trend in California is maintained, the state will reap hundreds of millions of dollars from keeping crime off the streets. More people at work plus fewer jail, policing, hospital, and urban rebuilding costs will all contribute. Each percentage point drop in violent crime as a whole releases over thirty million dollars. On a national basis a conservative estimate puts the savings at over two billion—*per year.*"

As Alice Prince listened to Madeline Naylor's steady, authoritative voice recite the facts Alice knew by heart, her mind drifted back in time to Vassar College, where she and Madeline had first met the glamorous Pamela Weiss.

Vassar was a revelation. Madeline with her tall, powerful physique excelled at sports and soon became a key player on the college track and field team. For the first time in her life she was not only accepted but also admired. Alice found she was similarly nurtured. Her teachers recognized her intellect and pushed her hard. Socially, Madeline and Alice still kept to themselves.

Alice didn't want to go to the party at West Point Military Academy, but everyone was going and some of the women from Madeline's team had space in their van. The party was in full swing when they arrived, and both of them hated it. It was packed with students drinking, dancing, and making out. Alice couldn't see the point of it. The music was so loud she couldn't even talk to anyone.

Then she saw the woman standing in a quieter corner encircled by people hanging on her words. Amid the hellish chaos there was this radiant, poised creature holding court. She was laughing and drinking, but she was in control. Everyone was drawn to her as to some brilliant sun, rotating in her orbit like lesser planets needing her light and warmth. Seeing her made Alice yearn to be one of those planets, to belong. Turning to Madeline, she saw that she was equally enthralled.

An hour later, after drinking too much and talking to

Madeline's teammates, Alice and Madeline went outside to walk in the grounds, waiting for the other women to take them back to Vassar. It was a dark night with the moon making only brief appearances from behind the clouds, so they stayed close to the main buildings and the well-lit paths.

They heard the commotion before they saw it. The sound of a struggle came from the bushes at the dark end of the grounds. At first Alice thought it was an animal. Then she heard the scream. Madeline immediately ran toward the noise, and Alice followed behind. In the shadows she saw two men holding a woman down; one had his hand over her mouth, and the other was pulling up her dress. An open bottle of Jack Daniel's lay on its side, spilling its contents on the soil, its smell heavy in the warm air. Bile rose in Alice's throat, and her left leg began to tremble. The woman was struggling, but the men were too strong. Suddenly the moon broke through, and Alice saw that it was the beautiful woman who had been holding court only an hour before. Her blue eyes were angry more than scared, and her courage helped Alice find hers.

Alice began to shout for help as she saw Madeline run up to the man who was covering the woman's mouth. Madeline made no noise; she just steadied herself for a moment and kicked the man as hard as she could in the face. She was wearing spiked heels, and Alice heard the man's nose break. Like a ballerina, Madeline turned then and kneed the stunned second man in the temple, rolling him over. Alice reached for the woman and pulled her up. But Madeline wasn't finished. Her face was white with rage; her eyes were as dark and cold as midnight lakes. Methodically, she stood over the two dazed men and proceeded to kick them in the genitals until Alice and the woman pulled her back.

Both men were charged, and one had to have a crushed testicle removed. That single act of saving Pamela Weiss from rape opened up a whole new world for Alice and Madeline. Pamela Weiss had connections and friendships that made Alice and Madeline popular simply for being her friend. Madeline in particular blossomed at that time. She idolized Pamela and learned from her social ease, acquiring a public poise that Alice could never emulate.

Alice never understood why the gilded Pamela became their friend just because they had helped her once. It was almost as if Pamela felt guilty for all her privilege and found others like herself too shallow. She was from a powerful banking family and never tired of listening to Madeline and Alice's accounts of their childhood experiences. She seemed to be ashamed of the fact that both her parents were alive, wealthy, and happily married and loved her. As if it had starved her of a perspective on the world and disqualified her from being taken seriously as someone who wanted to make a difference.

"Alice, do you agree that it's empirically proved that the gene treatment calms violent men?" Pamela Weiss said, reading through the briefing pack notes.

Alice sat forward in her chair, looking at Pamela, Madeline, and Todd Sullivan, quickly regaining her bearings. "Absolutely. The overall benefits will still take time to come through, but the proof that it works is irrefutable. These data are more than enough to make your announcement."

"And we're sure safety isn't an issue?" asked Pamela, turning to the back of the briefing pack.

Alice smiled. "Pam, we've been testing the treatment over the last eight years with no ill effects at all. We've just undergone successful safety trials on human volunteers. The FDA have approved these and given us their blessing to go to the next step of efficacy trials. For good measure we've also shown Conscience Version Nine to the National Institutes of Health and got their approval too. This means that as far as the two most stringent bodies in the United States are concerned, the treatment won't harm anyone. And since our secret tests already prove its efficacy, we are in an unassailable position. Any concern over the timing of the premature criminal trials will be forgotten once everyone realizes this. I've spoken to Calvin Briggs at the FDA and asked a few hypothetical questions. Basically, for all its bureaucracy, the FDA is there to facilitate progress, not to stop it. As long as the treatment is *safe* and it *works,* that is all it and anyone else care about."

"Don't forget," added Madeline, "with all the press interest in California's improved crime figures you and Bob Burbank are going to be seen as heroes, visionaries. And let's face it, Pamela, our guinea pigs weren't children or defenseless old ladies. They were violent criminals, hated and feared by society."

Pamela leaned forward in her chair. "So, Ali, the treatment we used is the same as the one approved by the FDA?"

Alice paused and caught Madeline's eye. Madeline just gave the smallest nod. Alice disliked lying to Pamela, but she had no choice. "Yes," she replied. Alice smiled then, allowing her genuine excitement to shine through. "Trust me, Pamela," she said, "Project Conscience is both safe and effective. Politically, scientifically, socially, and morally you have every reason to make your announcement."

Pamela Weiss smiled but said nothing for a moment. She looked down at her notes, then up at Madeline, and finally back to Alice. Her clear blue eyes rested on each of them for some seconds. Alice thought she was going to ask one of her difficult questions. For a horrible moment she wondered if Pamela had somehow found out about Crime Zero or the San Quentin deaths. But she needn't have worried. A beaming smile suddenly lit up Pamela's face. "Well done," she said. "We've all taken some risks, I know, but I promise that if I become President—"

"You mean *when* you become President," corrected Todd Sullivan with a smile.

Pamela laughed. "Then I will make sure we realize this vision of a gentler society, a society with a conscience."

Todd Sullivan stood up. "Sorry about this, but we're going to have to run."

"I'll see you both at the dinner tonight in L.A. with Bob Burbank," said Pamela. "It's a celebration of the Conscience announcement tomorrow and a chance for me to brief the President on the latest. It's going to be a good evening."

14

Alice Prince loved the way the afternoon sun filtered through the tall branches of the surrounding trees, dappling the grass and earth of the broad forest clearing. This was a private enchanted place full of happy memories. She often came here, only a brisk fifteen-minute walk away from home, with her two golden Labradors. She liked to smell the sweet air, watch the sun move over the swaying treetops in the valley below, and be alone with her thoughts.

After the meeting at ViroVector with Pamela Weiss she had been driven the eight miles home. She'd gone straight out into the garden and called the dogs, put on their leashes, and walked them over here for a quick walk before taking the company Gulfstream to LAX and dinner with Pamela and the President.

Alice wished that they could have persuaded Kathy to see their point of view. In many ways their objectives were the same. Alice admired the fact that Kathy had stood up to Madeline. But she was frightened that Madeline would do more than just keep Kathy quiet until the election. She knew how far Madeline could go. Alice loved her friend, but Madeline was never happy with doing only what was necessary. She always had to go further.

Alice sat on a tree stump in the middle of the thirty-yard

clearing and tilted her face to the sun, enjoying the warmth on her skin. Around her she could hear the trees whispering in the breeze and the dogs barking as they played together. If she closed her eyes, she could even hear Libby's voice.

Alice used to come here often with Libby. Her husband, John, and Madeline would sometimes come too. Even Pamela Weiss had come once or twice with her husband, Alan, and their three boys.

After Vassar College Pamela had become a successful lawyer in the Los Angeles district attorney's office and then married one of the partners of the law firm she most often opposed in court. Her marriage had remained strong, and she now had three sons; the youngest, thirteen-year-old Sam, was Alice's godson. Pamela's husband, Alan, was one of the few men Alice was genuinely fond of.

Madeline, who had also gone on to study law before joining the FBI, married next—despite her increasingly obvious ambivalence toward men. She said it would be good for her career, and she wanted children. Unsurprisingly the marriage failed, and there were no kids. Still, divorce aided her real marriage, the one to the FBI, which blossomed spectacularly.

Alice's marriage had been a disaster. After a Ph.D. at Stanford and a spell with GeneCell Industries she started up ViroVector. It was then that she met John Prince, and at first he seemed to live up to his name, especially compared with her father. She soon learned that John was far from being a prince, but he did contribute to the single most wonderful thing in her life, Libby.

Even now, if Alice squeezed her eyes shut and listened hard to the wind, she could hear Libby's laughter in the clearing from happier times.

Of course she was no longer there. Plucked away as if she had never even been here.

As Alice sat there, she allowed her mind to fold in on itself. The present no longer existed, only the past and the future. An acid pain burned in her chest, the anger and grief as intense as when Libby was first taken. What had the monster done with her? How had she died? If only Alice knew these answers, she could bury her daughter and grieve for her properly.

But her anger and grief were no longer impotent. Madeline had seen to that. Soon no other Libby would ever again fall prey to the evil that stalked every street in the land.

Suddenly the warmth left Alice's face, and through her closed eyelids she could tell the sun had disappeared behind a cloud. The dogs barked. She shivered involuntarily and opened her eyes.

Then she saw the tall man standing at the edge of the clearing, his car parked on the dirt track. He was looking directly at her.

She looked so peaceful sitting in the sun that he was loath to disturb her. But Luke Decker's course was set. He had no choice but to carry this through to its conclusion. Dr. Alice Prince was the mother of Axelman's thirteenth victim, and to find where the bodies were buried, he had to ask her the location of the Snake Tree.

He had driven to Dr. Prince's house, but she was out. After some persuasion her maid said she was walking the dogs and had given him directions. He had come straight here.

Prince looked the way she did in the case file photographs, older but otherwise unchanged. She wore flat shoes, a pleated skirt, and a navy cardigan over her cream blouse. She didn't look like the founder of a major multinational corporation. Just over five feet tall, she had a moon-shaped face, short black hair streaked with gray, and thick, round eyeglasses. Her small mouth seemed pinched into a permanent frown. She wore no jewelry except for an unusual teardrop amulet around her neck. Only her gray eyes flecked with gold made her stand out. They scrutinized Decker with a ferocious, unblinking intellect.

He walked toward her, introduced himself, and showed his badge. "Dr. Prince, my name is Special Agent Luke Decker. I run the FBI's behavioral sciences unit, which specializes in serial crimes. I wish to talk to you about your daughter, Libby."

Her shoulders slumped momentarily, and the pain in her eyes told Decker more about her damaged psyche than any record of her divorce or breakdown in the FBI case file. Time didn't always heal. Alice Prince was still a devastated woman. She stood up and folded her arms in a defensive gesture, barely looking at Decker's badge; instead she kept her eyes locked on his face. For a moment they both stood in silence, listening to the wind blowing in the trees.

"If you prefer, we can talk back at your house," he said.

She didn't appear to have heard him. "Have you found Libby?" she asked.

"Not yet, but I believe I know who was responsible for her murder. With your help I might be able to locate her body."

"Who killed her?"

"A man named Karl Axelman."

"Karl Axelman?" she repeated, her face frowning in disbelief. She said his name as if she were familiar with it. Her right hand moved to the unusual teardrop amulet around her neck, stroking it like a worry bead. She suddenly seemed miles away, her eyes peering off into space at some scene Decker would never see. "How can I help you find where Libby was buried?" she asked him, her voice barely above a whisper.

"As you may be aware, Axelman committed a number of other similar crimes. Something we believe your daughter said to him could identify the resting place of all his victims."

"What? What did Libby say to him?"

"Apparently Axelman gained access to his victims' resting place through an entrance near a tree your daughter called the Snake Tree. Does that mean anything to you?"

Prince's eyes suddenly misted over, and she smiled, the saddest smile Luke had ever seen. "Yes, yes, I know the Snake Tree."

Decker's mouth felt dry. "If you can tell me the location, I'll get it checked out."

Alice Prince gazed at him for some seconds in silence, before suddenly turning away. At first he thought she might be collecting herself, stopping herself from crying. Then she pointed to the other end of the clearing, toward the setting sun. "See the big oak. That's the Snake Tree. That's the tree Libby always used to climb."

Squinting into the dying light, he looked at a silhouetted clump of trees. Slightly by itself was a vast gnarled oak, which looked much older than the trees around it. It had low branches and a thick trunk. Around the base some of the roots were exposed and seemed to coil around the trunk like slumbering serpents.

"Thank you," he said. "I'll get the place checked over. If we find anything, we'll inform you immediately."

She opened her mouth as if to protest, but then said nothing.

"Can I give you a lift home?" he asked. "Can I call anyone for you?"

"No," she said, leashing her dogs. "I prefer to walk. I want to be alone."

Alice Prince was numb as she walked her dogs out of the clearing to the path that led back home. It seemed wrong somehow. She was sure she ought to feel hysterical relief or grief or something. But she could feel nothing. There was a cold void in her soul that robbed her of all sensation, as though she'd just put her hand under a tap of scalding water and were awaiting the pain.

When Agent Decker had told her about Libby, she had been less shocked than she expected. Over the last ten years she had been subconsciously preparing for this day. But the news about Karl Axelman had been a blow to the stomach. She had thought it could be he, as indeed had the FBI. But since none of Libby's effects were among the killer's trophies, it was deemed unlikely. It seemed ironic now that she'd unwittingly used Axelman as one of the guinea pigs to verify TITANIA's projections on Crime Zero.

Axelman's abduction of Libby had been the catalyst for both Conscience and Crime Zero.

When Libby was taken, Alice's husband, John, deserted Alice for a woman he had been secretly seeing for years.

After this betrayal Alice collapsed and was admitted to an upstate sanatorium. Madeline and Pamela visited often, vowing to do everything in their power to help. Alice took great comfort from them, but her science had saved her sanity.

Making them bring the papers and books she required to the sanatorium, she devoured everything she could find on the topic, believing that if she could discover the answer, then she would repair her fractured mind. Just as she was about to give up, she read an article in *Nature* published by a Ph.D. student from Harvard named Kathryn Kerr. It was an ingenious theoretical model based on primates, and like an epiphany, a sacred message from God, it made sense of everything. It was to be her salvation.

Within weeks she was back at ViroVector Solutions. Taking Kathy Kerr's detailed theories, Alice used her expertise with viral vectors to put them into practice, not only to diagnose violent behavior but modify it. Most science is built on failure and disappointment, but Kathy's theories on gene calibration were rigorously thought through and extremely well documented. Within months of leaving the sanatorium Alice lured Kathy Kerr to Stanford University and, using her expertise on gene calibration, developed a genetically engineered retrovirus that successfully modified chimpanzee genes. Within another three months, without Kerr's knowledge, Alice perfected a viral vector that she was convinced could deliver Kerr's control genes into man.

She laid out her plan to Madeline and Pamela when they next met. If they really wanted to help, as they had vowed to do, then she had found a way to stop crimes like Libby's abduction from happening again. But she would need to conduct criminal tests. And to do this without FDA approval, she would need the backing of her now powerful friends.

Dr. Kerr wasn't told about the criminal trials yet; instead she was given the brief of following the usual painstaking stages of preclinical screenings, primate studies, and human volunteer trials to gain FDA endorsement that the treatment was safe. Once she had done this and won approval, and assuming their secret efficacy trials on criminals had worked, they could go public. The FDA approval would vindicate conducting human experiments years before they should have.

Pamela, who was then being groomed to be the new governor of California, had been difficult to convince. But in time she came aboard, especially when she realized how political correctness and the notoriously conservative FDA were stifling research into this area. Some black civil rights groups even protested against conducting research on black males because they claimed the findings would be used to reinforce white prejudices. Even though these fears were completely unfounded, the National Institutes of Health avoided using black subjects, making any broad-based research meaningless. Pamela eventually realized secret trials would not only speed things up but also get them started. She even approached the new U.S. President, Bob Burbank, and, using her formidable powers of persuasion, gained his broad agreement that curing crime was a good idea. Making no commitments, Burbank made it easier for them to cut through red tape and keep the project secret, while always maintaining a distance should anything go wrong.

But it was Madeline who had taken the project to the next level. She had been even more excited about it than Alice. In fact her initial reaction was that Conscience didn't go far enough. Over the following months she slowly convinced Alice of the controversial but shockingly logical next step of Crime Zero.

Turning back to the clearing, Alice saw Decker standing motionless in the slanting sunlight, staring at the Snake Tree. No doubt he would call his colleagues soon, and then they would conduct the search. She felt compelled to stay, even though she knew he wouldn't allow her to. She was desperate to find the body. The nightmare of "not knowing" had poisoned the past ten years.

After strolling farther on, she paused behind a bank of bushes and watched Decker walk back to his car. To her surprise he didn't get in and drive off or reach for a phone. Instead he opened the back door and pulled out a spade and a flashlight.

She watched Decker carry the spade on his broad shoulders and switch on the flashlight. Wielding the flashlight like a sword, he cut through the encroaching shadows and moved toward the Snake Tree, its massive trunk silhouetted against the sun.

15

The Snake Tree.
Thursday, October 30, 5:47 P.M.

Luke Decker was embarked on a course of action from which he could not deviate. Yet as he approached the looming tree with its serpentine roots, he couldn't remember such fear. A band of steel tightened around his chest, and a film of sweat covered his skin. In his time he had faced all manner of killers, but physical danger had never affected him—not in the way psychological danger could. Not like now, when he couldn't escape the bizarre notion that somehow he was returning to the scene of his own crimes.

After Decker's breakdown, Sarah Quirke, the FBI shrink at the Sanctuary, had warned him not to inhabit the minds of the killers he hunted so completely, particularly when working simultaneously on a number of traumatic cases. "If you play with too many fires, one of them's bound to burn you," she'd said. He'd always believed he could handle it. Entering a killer's mind didn't mean he had to bring something of him back with him.

Now as he sat down on the roots of the large tree and tried to think the way the killer might have done, he wasn't so convinced. This time the killer had been his own flesh and blood. He was walking in his father's shoes, and he shuddered at the thought of how snug the fit might be.

He began to compile a mental profile from what he re-

membered out of Karl Axelman's files. The teenage girls
had been abducted over a twenty-year period, with at least
eighteen months between each one. This meant that the ab-
ductions had been planned in meticulous detail, with the
stalking and anticipation giving Axelman as much excitement as the eventual act itself. It also told Luke that Axelman had done something with the bodies that allowed him
to visit them again and again, thus enabling him to stave off
his need to kill for long periods. It was likely therefore that
the bodies had somehow been preserved. Since Axelman
was a hoarder, he would have wanted to keep all the bodies
intact, not just the most recent kills. That required space, a
lot of space.

Decker looked around him and then studied the huge
Snake Tree. He stood up and moved around the trunk, tapping the bark for clues, testing for any hollow sounds. Nothing.

It was unlikely that Axelman would have squirreled the
bodies in the trunk of the tree; they would have rotted too
fast, and wild animals and insects would have eaten them.
But in his time Decker had seen stranger hoarding sites.

It was far more likely that Axelman had buried the bodies, perhaps in protective wrapping to prevent the ingress of
worms and other predators. But he needed access to them.
This place was remote, but people did come here. Axelman
would have had to have some means of viewing the corpses
without fear of being disturbed. Just the thought of discovery would have seriously inhibited his fantasies and cur-
tailed his enjoyment.

But then Axelman had been a builder. He would have
known how to construct some kind of storage facility that he
could easily enter and exit without the entrance's being discovered. Decker could only guess at why Axelman had chosen this particular site.

Stepping over the gnarled roots, Decker moved closer
into the base of the tree and studied the vast trunk. It was at
least eight feet in diameter. From one angle the base of the
tree resembled an upside-down Y, as if the tree stood on two
squat legs. Walking farther around the trunk, to the side that

still caught the last rays of sun, he noticed an area of earth, three feet square, partially sheltered under the low crotch of the two legs. He jabbed the earth with his spade, and the impact jarred his shoulder.

Moving in closer, he scraped away the scrubby grass, leaf litter, and topsoil, revealing dark wood. More roots, he thought, before scraping away a wider area. Gradually he uncovered more wood, until there was a flat platform a yard square. His heart beat faster; the wood was too regular to be natural. Then his spade hit something metallic, and in the dying sunlight he saw a glint of dulled brass. Throwing the spade to the ground, he dropped to his knees and began to brush away the damp dirt from the center of the panel, revealing a brass hand ring lying flat in a brass well. He gripped the ring and pulled it upright, forming a handle. Then he stood and tugged the ring as hard as he could. There was a groan and a creak from the damp wood, and then the panel hinged upward, a trapdoor opening to the underworld.

Grimacing at the stale air that emanated from the hole, Decker reached for the flashlight and shone it down into the dank darkness. To his surprise there was a timber-lined hole that went down about ten feet; an iron ladder was attached to one side. The timber was green with damp, but there was no sign of rot, and the workmanship was impressive.

He found a stick to wedge the trapdoor open, took the flashlight in one hand, and eased himself into the hole. He tested the ladder with his right foot and, when he was convinced it was firm, made his way down into the darkness. At the bottom of the ladder a tunnel gently sloped away from him and away from the tree. The ceiling and walls were made from interlocking beams, and the floor had a matted surface that stopped him from slipping. Every ten yards or so there were perforated panels in the ceiling that looked like ventilation ducts. There was a smell of damp earth and decay.

Tentatively he walked forward into the blackness, his feet testing each step before he trusted his full weight to it. All the time he sought out telltale cracks in the ceiling with his flashlight. But aside from the occasional creak and groan the tunnel appeared robust. Then, after some twenty yards, he turned a bend and came to an abrupt dead end. Using the flashlight, he saw that to his right there were broad concrete steps, leading deeper down. To his left the wall was a square plug of cement, as if the passage to an earlier entrance had been filled in. The wall on each side of the concrete steps was no longer timber but brown tiles caked with mold.

Decker suddenly understood why Axelman had chosen this place. It was part of the old zoo, which had been bull-dozed over thirty years ago to make the exclusive estate where Alice Prince lived. Evidently not all of the zoo had been destroyed. The underground sections that didn't inter-fere with the foundations of the new houses were simply sealed and returned to nature, with new trees planted on top. Axelman had built the wooden tunnel to gain unauthorized access to the sealed area.

The smell coming from the base of the concrete steps was different, no longer earth but something else, a chemical smell Decker recognized but couldn't place. He had en-countered it only recently but couldn't remember exactly where. The flashlight shook in his hand as he gradually walked down the steps. He tried to tell himself it was the damp and the cold, but it wasn't.

The beam of the flashlight reflected off a rusting steel sign screwed onto the tiles: REPTILE HOUSE AND AQUARIUM. At the base of the stairs, discarded on the floor, was another sign. Dented and buckled, it was barely legible. CAROLAN CONSTRUCTION was painted in black letters. Axelman must have worked on this area thirty years ago and earmarked it for his own private use. It couldn't have been that difficult to seal the area, as he was contracted to do by his employers, while at the same time making plans for his secret tunnel.

Decker came to a junction in the brown tiled maze. A faded arrow marked AQUARIUM pointed right, and a virtually invisible arrow with illegible markings pointed left. The chemical smell, now so strong it made his eyes water and stung the back of his throat, was coming from the right, from the aquarium. He took a handkerchief from his pocket and tied it over his nose and mouth. Suddenly he remembered where he had last encountered that smell: the morgue of San Quentin. With leaden legs he began to walk toward its source.

A few yards into the aquarium section he realized that the flashlight beam in front of him had narrowed. He must have twisted the end of the Maglite when tying the handkerchief around his face. He quickly adjusted the flashlight, and as the beam broadened, he realized that the corridor had narrowed dramatically, each wall now less than an arm's length away. He also realized that the claustrophobic walls were no longer tiled but smooth.

As smooth as glass.

A chill ran down his spine, and the skin prickled on the back of his neck.

As if chancing upon some slumbering beast, he slowly lowered the beam onto the floor in front of his feet, highlighting the mold-stained tiles. Then, gripping the Maglite white knuckle–tight, he carefully inched the flashlight to his right. Where the floor met the wall there was a strip of chrome and above that a thick black band of rubber. The rubber was a seal, and the smooth reflective material making up the rest of the wall was a plate of thick glass. Moving along the base of the glass, he saw a typed label. It didn't identify the species of some rare fish or carry notes on its preferred diet and geographical origin. There was simply a name, a date, and a location.

"Mandy James. April 7, 1979. Sausalito."

Decker could hardly breathe, his chest was so tight and the smell so noxious. He remembered the girl's name from the Axelman case files. She had been one of his earliest victims, and her belongings had been found in a box at his house in San Jose. On autopilot Decker moved the flashlight upward, its beam shining through the glass into the greenish, clear liquid beyond.

The first thing he saw in the ghostly green light was Mandy James's foot, a rope attached to her right ankle, anchoring her to a heavy rock on the base of the tank. Moving the light farther upward, he saw the rest of her naked body, floating perfectly preserved in the formaldehyde.

Pressing a hand to his mouth, he switched the light off; he couldn't bear to see the girl's face. He turned away and stood in the dark, leaning with his forehead pressed against the opposite wall, forcing down the rising bile in his throat. Gradually he regained control and straightened up. Not daring to turn around, he switched the flashlight back on.

In that instant his blood ran cold. Staring out at him was a face so heartbreakingly beautiful and so wide-eyed with terror that he could only scream and run. Disoriented in his panic, he ran as fast as he could down the dark corridor. As he ran, the beam of his flashlight flailed wildly, cutting through the darkness, to reveal the horrific tableaux on both sides of him. An avenue of glass formaldehyde tanks, each containing the perfectly preserved body of a young woman. Typed names and contorted faces, names and faces he remembered from the files, were intermittently thrown up in the beams of light.

Only when he reached a tiled wall on his left did he realize that he had run the wrong way. Standing panting in the dark, focusing on the tiles, he capped a hand over his mouth and took deep breaths of his own exhaled carbon dioxide. Gradually his heart slowed. To find the exit, he would again have to run the grisly gauntlet of bodies in the dark. He looked around for an alternative.

Turning slowly to the opposite wall of the corridor, he saw that it was also tiled. A red kerosene can sat on the floor, and halfway up the wall he noticed a box with a red button and lever protruding from the front. Calming himself, he steadied the flashlight and read the bold red letters above the top. FUEL-POWERED GENERATOR. TO START: PUSH BUTTON AND HOLD FOR TEN SECONDS BEFORE PULLING LEVER. Taking a deep breath, he followed the instructions and after two attempts heard a motor starting up. Suddenly the protective darkness was gone, and the full horror of his surroundings was illuminated by a row of lamps along the ceiling of the corridor, a light shining out from each tank. But at least in the light he could prepare himself for the sights around him.

He was in the middle of Axelman's horrific collection. To his right, toward the exit, there were ten tanks, five on each side. Each contained one of the abducted girls, in chrono-logical order of abduction. To his left there were a further ten tanks, but only three were full. The other seven were no doubt reserved for subsequent acquisitions. Keeping his eyes straight ahead, he walked past the last pair of victims to the final occupied tank. On the tiled floor in front of it was a cardboard box similar to those found in Axelman's house, and in it were a set of moldy clothes, some sneakers, and a pair of thick eyeglasses. There was also an audiotape with a name scribbled on it. He now knew why Karl Axelman had never been a suspect for Libby Prince's abduction. All her personal effects were here.

With terrifying clarity Decker could see what had happened.

Unlike the others in this macabre gallery, Libby Prince's abduction hadn't been planned. Visiting his trophies one fateful day, Karl Axelman had probably seen her wandering one of the nearby lanes and abducted her on impulse. Eventually he planned to take her effects to his house in San Jose but had been caught before he had been able to do so.

Bending to his knees, Decker studied the pitiful personal effects laid out neatly in the box, finding them as hard to look at as the body suspended in liquid to his left. Ever since he could remember, Decker believed that each man made his own choices, that a man's life should be judged at its end, by what he had done. Not at its beginning, by what he had been born with. To Decker, free will was everything; without it there was no point in living.

But now, as he willed himself to look at Libby Prince, he felt less sure. He had steeled himself against seeing the remains of his father's victims, preparing to view them as bones or body parts, not as the humans they once were. But seeing this innocent girl floating suspended in the tank made that impossible. Seeing her beautiful face frozen into a silent scream, forever young and forever in pain, he couldn't help feeling the sins of his father crushing down on him. Whatever he did he was tainted forever. Anything he did could never remove that stain from his soul. His career had been based on the premise that a man's capacity for good or evil was shaped by a host of influences throughout his life. But he didn't know anymore.

Perhaps his knack for tracking down evil in others stemmed from some genetic "gift" he had received from his biological father. Perhaps it did take a thief to catch a thief.

He was lost in his thoughts when the sound of echoing footsteps made him suddenly turn his head. Then he heard the scream.

16

When Kathy Kerr awoke, any sense of time and place had been taken from her. Her mind kept somersaulting, playing tricks on itself as if all sanity had fled. She could see a man's dark face coming toward her with a gun and a needle, yet she knew her eyes were still closed. There was a pumping in her ears, which she slowly recognized as the sound of her own racing heart. Her mouth was tinder dry.

What had happened to her? What *was happening* to her? Why couldn't she think straight or remember anything?

And why couldn't she move her arms?

She opened her eyes and stared up at a bare bulb of head-splitting brightness. Groaning, she closed her eyelids again, desperately trying to orient herself. She recognized a smell from her past. An underlying tang of human sweat masked by disinfectant and fresh paint: the smell of hospitals or prisons.

Trying to move her hands again, she realized her arms were strapped to her body, as if hugging herself. But when she peered down her body and saw the straitjacket, she drew no comfort from its embrace.

Kathy was breathing more quickly, close to panic. She had no idea at all where she was or how long she had been here. She had never felt more alone or abandoned in her entire life.

Rolling away from the bright light above her, she gradually forced her eyelids open and waited for her blurred sight to focus on the surrounding area. She saw that she was lying in a featureless cube, every surface—wall, ceiling, and floor—an identical off-white. Pushing her head against the floor, she felt it give beneath her. This was a nightmare. She was in a padded cell.

Inhaling deeply, she slowly tried to order her fractured thoughts. She remembered her angry conversation with Madeline Naylor about the unauthorized criminal trials, the terrifying revelation of Karl Axelman's lethal gene therapy, the missing files, and the shock of opening her apartment door to be confronted by the man with the gun and syringe.

Calming herself, she told herself that she must have been drugged and then brought here to keep her out of the way and discredit her. No doubt Madeline Naylor and Alice Prince and whoever else was involved had already prepared a credible story to explain that their brilliant young scientist had been taken to the hospital for the sake of her mental health.

She tried to remember what her kidnapper had said before injecting her, something about taking her somewhere quiet to recover for a few days. Did that mean until the election, so she couldn't jeopardize Pamela Weiss's precious announcement? Kathy took momentary solace from regaining her memory, but as her awareness increased, so did the realization that her predicament was hopeless.

She thought of shouting for help, but her mouth was dry, and the cell would undoubtedly be soundproofed. She was lying stranded on the soft floor, and a suffocating heaviness and helplessness descended on her.

As she lay there, her mind questioned why she had started working on curing violent crime in the first place.

It was during her early teens at school in England that her study of Cesare Lombroso, a nineteenth-century Italian physician, had first put the idea into her head that a person's violent nature could be explained scientifically. From his research on criminals Lombroso believed that certain primitive instincts resurfaced from time to time in "modern" humans and could be identified in the structures of their facial features. For example, sexual offenders could be identi-

fied by their full lips, and murderers by their sloping fore-
heads.

Even then Kathy had known Lombroso's theory of
phrenology was nonsense. But as simplistic as Lombroso's
ideas were, they opened her mind to the possibility that violent crime was *caused* and that guilt was in our natural
makeup. To her way of thinking, there had to be a reason for
everything.

It was when her younger brother, Mark, suddenly committed suicide in her last year at school that her curiosity developed into a crusade. Unknown to anyone, he had been
suffering since childhood from the mental illness called
obsessive-compulsive disorder. In his mind he was convinced
that he had murdered people even though he had done nothing of the kind. He secretly wandered the streets at night in
search of his mutilated victims. He was convinced he would
find them if he only looked hard enough, checking repeat-
edly, even though he knew at a rational level that his anxiety
and guilt were ridiculous.

If she'd known, she could have helped him. Drugs existed
to moderate the serotonin in his brain and treat his symptoms. After his death the whole concept of guilt obsessed
her. Why did some people have too much and others have
none? She was convinced it was genetic. And if these genes
could be identified and eventually modified, then senseless
violence and senseless guilt could become a thing of the
past.

Now her dream had become a nightmare.

Suddenly she heard the lock turn, and as the door opened,
she saw a pair of black shoes enter and walk toward her.
Looking up, squinting against the bright light, she saw a tall
man in a white coat.

"How are we feeling?" he asked, not unkindly.

"Who are you? Where am I?"

He stooped down toward her, and she could see he had
gray, curly hair and round glasses. "Come, come. So many
questions."

"I shouldn't be here. You must let me out."

"On the contrary, we can't possibly let you out. Although

I must say you must have done something very wrong for me to have to give you this."

She looked up and saw that he was holding a syringe and tried to roll away. "No, no more drugs. Just let me talk to someone."

But the man was smiling now, humoring her. "Oh, we can't allow that. That's why you're here. Let me just give you this, and it'll help take all your unpleasant memories away." He held the stainless steel syringe up to the light and tapped it twice. She could see a bead of liquid form at the tip of the hypodermic needle and dribble down the side. "Don't worry, the first few injections don't do any lasting damage." He spoke in a calm, helpful voice as if informing her of the weather forecast. "They merely prepare you for the fourth one, which I'm afraid does have more long-term effects. I understand you have a history of mental illness in your family. Your brother, I believe?"

"But why?" she screamed. "Why?"

"I'm afraid I don't know that. But whatever you did or saw, I'm afraid that the time for regrets is over. I think you should sleep now. Everything always seems less confusing after a little sleep."

She panicked now, screaming for help as loud as she could. When he knelt beside her, she tried to struggle, but the straitjacket was too tight.

"Relax, there's nothing you can do about it. So, try not to worry yourself," he said, easily holding her still and injecting her arm.

But she refused to stop struggling. Awake, she could at least think, but as she felt the drug work on her, she knew that even this freedom was being denied her.

In her despair, fighting to maintain consciousness, one fragile thought, like the flicker of a distant flame in the darkness, gave her hope: that Luke Decker had somehow heard her improvised phone message and would know how to do something about it.

Alice Prince screamed only when she saw the other girls. As soon as she saw Libby, she stopped.

She had waited as long as she could before following Decker down here. She had always thought that nothing could be worse than the nightmares in which she had witnessed Libby endure every conceivable horror. But now, as Alice stared at the glass tank two feet ahead of her, she realized that she had been wrong. No nightmare could be as bad as this. Raising her hand, she placed it against her daughter's palm, pressed flat against the cold glass.

Decker's voice was gentle when he spoke. "Dr. Prince, you shouldn't be here. Come, let me take you out of this place."

Pushing him away, she walked closer to the glass, both hands flat against the glazed wall of Libby's grave. "Of course I should be here. I should have been here years ago. I should have been here to save my daughter from a monster."

"Come," he said softly, directing her away from the cold glass, carefully guiding her down the avenue of grisly exhibits to the exit.

"But why?" she demanded, her voice brittle. "Just tell me that."

"I can't. I don't know."

But she wasn't asking about what happened to Libby. "Tell me, Special Agent Decker, why did Karl Axelman tell you about this? Why did the killer tell *you?*"

His green eyes were pained when he turned and met her gaze. Pale and tired, he looked like a broken man. "Because he was my father," he said.

17

Director Naylor didn't know what enraged her more, the fact that she hadn't been informed about Axelman's revelations to Decker or that Decker had let Alice Prince into the chamber of horrors.

Naylor was supposed to have been in Los Angeles with Alice Prince attending the campaign dinner for President Bob Burbank and candidate Pamela Weiss on the eve of the Project Conscience announcement tomorrow. But just as the bureau jet was about to take off for LAX, the call had come through from George Raoul, the special agent in charge of the San Francisco office, telling her that Decker had found Axelman's stash of bodies. Raoul had told her because Dr. Prince was involved and had asked for her.

After rushing back to see Alice Prince, who was now sedated at home, she had viewed the chilling exhibits and then commandeered the SAC's office in the San Francisco field office.

She sat at Raoul's desk, looking at Special Agent Luke Decker. To her left, on the video conferencing screen, Deputy Director Bill McCloud looked on tiredly. His craggy face frowned as he scratched his hair. It was midnight in Washington.

"Why the hell didn't you pass on what Axelman told

142

you?" she interrogated Decker. "On my instructions Deputy
Director McCloud expressly asked if you had received any
new information before Axelman's execution. Yet you said
nothing. Axelman may have claimed to be your father, but
that's no excuse. You're the head of a major unit and should
know better. That's why we have procedures, damnit: to
avoid the complications of personal involvement. Did Axelman tell you anything else?"

She waited, but Decker said nothing. He looked beat:
dark rings under his green eyes, his blond hair spattered with
mud, and his face pale. She pressed on. "Decker, are you
going to talk to me, or am I just going to have to suspend
you on the spot? Alice Prince, a very good friend of mine, is
now sedated after seeing her daughter's corpse. For that
alone I would happily kick you out of the bureau. But for
some reason, McCloud here's been begging me to save your
sorry soul. He says that we need you, but frankly I don't believe him. Your record's good, but if you can't fit in with my
bureau, then you're out of here. Do you understand that?"

Again she waited, and again Decker remained silent. She
was as surprised as she was annoyed. On the occasions in
the past when they had met, they had always sparred. She
didn't like him and thought the psychological mumbo
jumbo he practiced in the behavioral sciences unit was ob-
solete. But she had always grudgingly admired Decker's in-
dependence of spirit and the fact that he got results. Now he
looked drained of all passion or care. She wanted to know
what else Axelman might have told him or if Decker's
famed powers of observation had gleaned something suspicious about Axelman's behavior before he died. But any
concerns that Decker's mind might expose Crime Zero
seemed groundless.

As if to prove her right, Decker slowly reached into his
mud-encrusted jacket and pulled out his badge. "You don't
need to suspend me. I resign." He said it with no anger or
emotion, as if he were reading lines.

McCloud spoke then. He shook his head on the video
screen. "Hey, Spook, don't be so hasty. Just go home. Get
some rest. And think it over. OK?"

McCloud turned to her. "Director, surely it would be better to discuss this later when everything's calmed down somewhat. We can get everything into perspective then. Decide things away from the heat of the moment." McCloud looked at her, pleading. Decker didn't seem to care either way.

Naylor stared at Decker. He stared back. "You're fired," she said. "Now get out."

As soon as Decker and McCloud had gone, the phone rang. "I have Governor Weiss for you," said a voice.

"How is Ali?" was the first question Pamela asked.

"She's back home now, sedated, but she's bearing up better than might be expected. In a perverse way she says it's helped. At least she can now bury Libby and grieve for her, knowing she's finally at peace. And you know Ali; she's stronger than she looks. She even made me tell you to use this as added ammunition in your announcement. I doubt she'll make it tomorrow, but I'll still be there."

"Can I speak to her?"

"Pam, I'd let her sleep for now. I'm staying over at her place tonight. I'll tell her you called. She'll appreciate it, I know."

"So what happened exactly?"

Naylor told her the bare bones, including what she herself had seen in Axelman's gruesome exhibition chamber. "It's sick, Pam, but don't worry about it. Focus on the announcement tomorrow. It's exactly this kind of crime that Project Conscience's designed to end."

"OK, but give my love to Ali for me."

"Of course I will. Good luck tomorrow. I'll see you there."

Feeling tired, Naylor checked her watch. It was after nine, and today had been a full day. Tomorrow was important too. She looked forward to a glass of Jack Daniel's and a bath before hitting the sack. But first she had one more call to make. She put the desk phone to her ear and punched in the numbers.

"Jackson," said a deep, nasal voice. She could hear from the background noise that he was in a bar. Involuntarily she licked her lips.

"How is everything?"

"Fine, Director Naylor."

"Did you give her the injection?"

"Yes, and everything's been arranged. We delivered her a few hours ago. Dr. Peters handled it. No one else was involved. And the doc confirmed that he knows exactly what to do."

Madeline nodded into the phone. Dr. Peters had too much at stake to be unreliable. If she revealed just a portion of the abuse she knew he had been involved in, he would spend the next decade or so in jail, and when he got out, the only medicine he'd be allowed to practice would be opening a pack of Tylenol.

"Anything else?" asked Jackson.

"No, that's fine for now. Good night."

With that Naylor replaced the phone and stood away from the desk. As she left the office and made her way out of the building, she thought again of the horrors she had seen that afternoon.

The timing was advantageous, though. Crime Zero was approaching the critical stage, and seeing Libby and the other dead girls would have hardened Alice Prince's resolve to see it through to the end. After all, Axelman might be gone, but there were countless others like him still walking the earth.

18

**The Marina District, San Francisco,
Later That Night**

Pulling up outside his grandfather's house, Decker was grateful that neither Barzini nor any of Matty Rheiman's other friends appeared to be visiting. Emotionally drained, Decker was desperate to talk to his grandfather alone.

Inside the house Matty gave him a delighted hug. "Luke, what a surprise. I didn't know you were still in town."

"It's been quite a day, Gramps. And there are a couple of things I need to talk to you about."

Within seconds of hearing his voice Matty sat him down in the living room. "Luke, what's up?"

Feeling like a child, Decker let everything flow from him. He unburdened himself of all the fears and doubts he had felt over the last few days: Axelman's letter describing how he had raped his mother and murdered his father; the results of the DNA test; his discovery of Axelman's grisly collection of preserved corpses.

When he finished, Decker took a deep breath and asked his grandfather to tell him everything he knew. The old man sat silently for a while, just gently patting Decker's arm, before speaking of his daughter's ordeal.

"It was an awful night. Your mother was having a drink with friends downtown. Richard was away on Navy business, but he had agreed to meet up with her for a meal in town on his return. The police say her assailant must have been watching her all night because her friends had only just left her where Rachel and Richard had agreed to meet when she was attacked."

Decker's stomach churned. His mother had been a pretty, petite woman. She must have looked vulnerable and child-like to Axelman.

"According to the police, she was attacked from behind and knocked unconscious. He dragged her into an alley. Then Richard arrived, and when he couldn't find your mother on the corner where they'd agreed to meet, he must have started calling her name. From what the police think the killer ran out of the alleyway and called your father over, saying that a woman had been attacked and needed help. Richard probably ran to your mother then. While he bent over her and tried to revive her, the killer stabbed him five times in the back. Then he ran off."

"Did he rape my mother before my father—before her husband . . . began calling her?" Correcting himself brought bile rushing to his throat.

"Yes," said Matty in a soft voice. "And the man was never found."

Decker groaned and shook his head. If the crime had happened a decade later, the police could have used DNA fingerprinting to help catch Axelman. "What happened then?"

"Your mother was beside herself with grief. They had been married less than a year, and Rachel had even converted to the Catholic faith for Richard. He was her world. When she discovered she was pregnant, she wouldn't have an abortion. Not only was it against her faith, but she felt sure the child would be Richard's. She was convinced that something good had come out of something bad."

"She never suspected that I might have been the rapist's child?" Decker asked.

Matty shrugged, and the ancient face that expressed so much suffering creased in compassion. "She may have, but she never talked about it to me. Anyway, what difference did it make? You were her child, and no parent could have loved a son more." Matty placed his right hand on Luke's face and with feather-light fingers described the contours of his features. "I don't know what this Axelman looked like, but I can tell you that you resemble Richard so closely I can feel his face in front of me now. He was a good man, and although you never met him, his memory and your mother taught you who you are. Whatever science says, he was your real father as far as all that's important is concerned. And don't forget you've got your mother's genes too. They were good people, Luke, and you're a good man."

Decker held his head in his hands, his temples throbbing with exhaustion, desperately wanting to believe Matty's words of reassurance.

"Anyway," said his grandfather, patting him on the shoulder, "I regard you as my son as much as my grandson. I helped bring you up. And I couldn't be more proud of you."

Friday, October 31, 1:51 P.M.

It wasn't until the next day that Decker's mind began to focus on other anomalies relating to the Axelman case. He had been so obsessed with the paternity claim that he had pushed everything else to the back of his mind. But now the questions came forward, demanding attention. And Decker encouraged the distraction they offered.

Why had the cold, remorseless Axelman not only revealed where his victims' bodies were buried but also castrated himself? Why had his physical appearance changed so radically, so quickly?

Something had to have happened to him. He wouldn't have done or accepted these things naturally. They were totally against his personality. And why was Director Naylor so interested—over and above her friendship with Dr. Alice Prince?

It was these questions that Decker mulled over as he sat in front of the TV with a bottle of Michelob. Rhoda was fussing about the house, and Matty sat quietly with Decker in the corner of the drawing room reading a braille book.

Clicking the remote to escape the blanket coverage of

Karl Axelman and his victims, Luke felt almost grateful to see the faces of Governor Pamela Weiss and President Bob Burbank smile out from the screen. They stood behind a lectern bearing the presidential crest at the foot of the Watts Towers in South Central Los Angeles, the crime capital of the West Coast. A crowd gathered around them, along with a battery of media. Decker even recognized the rake-thin curly-haired figure of Hank Butcher in the press pack. The TV commentator promised a "groundbreaking announcement in the war against crime."

Bob Burbank without hesitation introduced Pamela Weiss as the next President of the United States. He praised her record as governor of California, particularly when it came to cracking crime.

Decker took a sip of cold beer and listened numbly to the rhetoric as Pamela Weiss began her announcement.

"Last night we all learned of the true horror of the notorious Karl Axelman's crimes. What you might not know is that the recently executed killer's last victim was the daughter of Dr. Alice Prince, a close personal friend of mine." Decker groaned and almost switched channels immediately, but he was curious. At the same time Matty looked up, his fingers pausing on the Braille page he was scanning.

"Sadly Karl Axelman is hardly unique. Although he has been executed, there are many other Axelmans at large. Violent crime in this country is an epidemic. Murders are up over ten percent nationally, rape by even more. Armed robberies and assaults are increasing so rapidly our overstretched police forces have to prioritize which crimes they deal with first, if at all.

"Aside from the incalculable human costs of violent crime the financial cost runs into billions. A drop of just one percentage point in violent crime would free up almost one and a quarter billion dollars a year to invest in health care and other more necessary areas.

"But this isn't a political point. Crime is a social cancer that has riddled society throughout history. For all the rhetoric and well-meaning schemes that have been attempted, no society has yet found a real solution to stopping the few malignant individuals who corrupt the rest of the social body. And unfortunately for Dr. Prince and the other victims of Axelman's crimes we can't undo what he did. Or indeed the victims of the countless other crimes. But I believe we can—we *must*—ensure that these crimes don't happen again. That is what we have been trying to do here in California."

Decker stared at the TV openmouthed. Pamela Weiss was going to claim credit for the California crime figures. To do that, she would have to explain something that had baffled police chiefs, sociologists, and media pundits for the last three years.

"Eight years ago with the backing of a visionary President, senior-level support from the FBI, and the involvement of Dr. Alice Prince we engaged on a bold project." The camera panned from Weiss and President Burbank to the right of the small podium, where Luke could see Director Naylor standing motionless and unsmiling. "A project designed not to fight crime but to treat it, to reawaken the good in all of us. We called this initiative Project Conscience. And it's Project Conscience that is behind California's improved crime figures."

As she said this, Pamela Weiss's confident face filled the screen. Luke was sitting forward in his seat now, his full attention on the TV. In the corner Matty was listening no less intently, his book forgotten.

"All men possess genes that make them more or less predisposed to commit violent crime. And over the last eight years we have proved that fact beyond any doubt. Through modifying the genes of some sixteen thousand convicted violent male offenders in California we have been able to improve their behavior, achieving the reduced crime figures that have dominated the domestic headlines over the last few years."

Pamela Weiss stopped and gestured with her hand, taking in the surrounding area. "Just look at the regenerated area around Watts Towers where the President and I are now standing. Once a symbol of all that was bad about our inner cities, it now represents a soaring example of improvement and hope through Project Conscience. And let me reassure you that the gene therapy that yielded these results has been rigorously checked and approved by the FDA as completely safe."

Decker sat stunned on the couch, as the camera panned around the regenerated shopfronts and houses of Watts. This had to be the project Kathy was working on, the one based on her original thesis back at Harvard and the one she had the meeting about with Naylor yesterday.

"I understand that many of you will have concerns about this bold decision to test a radical therapy outside normal channels. But hard crime requires hard choices. Of course there were risks, but the risks of doing nothing were far greater. Crime has become so entrenched that we believed drastic action was required—not political rhetoric or posturing but hard, decisive deeds.

"This project wasn't undertaken lightly. Rigorous research involving the best available minds was conducted over a period spanning almost a decade. This research was conducted on the most intractable violent criminals who have already forfeited their right to live in normal society. The results show that far from being inhumane, punishing their old life, we have given them a new one.

"I believe in free will. It is my firm conviction that genes only predispose us to behave in a certain way by virtue of our hormones and the chemicals in our brains; ultimately we *consciously decide* what we do. We must still all take full responsibility for our actions. But this therapy stacks the odds in favor of a subject's being better able to cope with inappropriate aggressive responses. It reawakens his conscience, allowing him to decide to walk away from a senseless fight, avoid initiating a brutal attack, or curb his base urge to rape a defenseless woman.

"Let me share a vision with you, a vision for America: With this therapy violent men will be freed to channel their energies into more productive areas that benefit society, rather than undermine it. Imagine such a society where all convicted criminals are given this treatment, where the majority of offenders can rediscover their better selves. Creating a more productive, tolerant, kinder world. Imagine it. A kinder, stronger America. Your America."

Weiss raised her right hand and pointed directly at the camera. "I tell you now, if I am elected President on Tuesday, I will make this dream into a reality."

Decker watched as Pamela Weiss paused for a moment, staring at the camera with just the right look of concern and warmth. She was doing this thing and making it plausible, even commendable. The beer suddenly tasted sour in his mouth.

"Don't they ever learn?" shouted Matty suddenly.

Luke whipped around at the sound of his angry voice. He had never seen his mild grandfather so enraged before. His face was red, the veins standing out on his temple. "What's wrong, Gramps?"

"What's wrong? You've just heard what that woman's been saying and you ask me what's wrong? They are judging people by their genes and trying to change them."

Decker found it hard to match Matty's anger. "They're only going to give the drug to convicted criminals."

"But that's just the start. First they give this drug to change the genes of criminals. Then they decide to give it to those young people who perhaps have genes they don't like, *before* they have done anything wrong. Because they *might* do something wrong. Soon they will separate those with good genes from those with bad, ignoring the fact that people *choose* to do evil. I remember when the Nazis first began to separate *us*. They made us wear the Star of David on our jackets so that they could tell who we were. Not humans. Not people like them. But Jews. Luke, we are more than our genes. You are more than your genes. Hasn't anybody learned anything?"

"But this is different, Gramps."

"Is it? What if they decide that you have the genes of Karl Axelman in you and are therefore a potential criminal who should be 'treated'?"

Decker couldn't answer that. He put the beer down on the table beside him.

"Yes, my fellow Americans, with the support of President

Burbank I have taken risks and challenged conventional procedures. But I firmly believe that what America needs now more than ever is a leader. Someone who will serve the people, not by slavishly *following* changing opinions but by taking tough decisions and *leading* them to a better, more peaceful tomorrow. If you share this vision, then vote for me on Tuesday so that together we can reawaken the conscience of America."

Even before Weiss finished uttering the last syllable of her speech, the crowd on TV erupted in applause. Decker turned to watch his grandfather shaking his head in disbelief. At that moment the door opened and Rhoda walked into the room. "Luke," she said handing him a brown envelope, "this came in the mail for you."

"Thanks."

Tearing open the buff envelope, he found a computer disc and a scribbled note inside. To his surprise it was from Kathy Kerr:

Luke, we've got to talk.

The samples in one of the bags you gave me match the DNA profile of a killer on the FBI database, Karl Axelman. Except there are some subtle, lethal differences, which might be connected to my work on a project called Conscience.

What's going on, Luke? You must suspect something; otherwise you wouldn't have asked me to analyze the samples instead of using the FBI labs. I've enclosed a computer disc for safekeeping. It includes a copy of Karl Axelman's original genome and his modified one taken from the samples in your evidence bag. But don't worry, I should be seeing you before you receive this. I guess this is just a precaution.

We really need to talk. This is scary.

Kathy

Decker frowned as he read the note, unsure what to make of it. He picked up the disc and placed it on the coffee table. She said she would be here before the disc. But she wasn't. She also said that Axelman's genes had been changed.

Could that explain his physical appearance, the hair loss, and the acne? Could it explain his sudden remorse and radically different personality? Did it also explain why Director Naylor had been so interested in what Decker might or might not have found out from Axelman?

He looked up again at the TV to the closing shots of the Watts rally. Pamela Weiss stood triumphant, arms raised. FBI Director Naylor stood close to her, staring out across the crowds, a look of cool satisfaction on her face. Had Axelman been one of the criminals tested in the unauthorized Conscience trials and had something gone wrong? Something that had been covered up?

"What is it, Luke?" Matty asked.

"I'm not sure yet," he said. He rose from the couch, went for his jacket, and retrieved his wallet. When he got Kathy's card, he picked up the phone and dialed her number at Stanford. But there was no answer. Then he reached into his jacket pocket and pulled out his cell phone. He had kept it turned off since he'd last spoken with her. Perhaps she'd left him a message.

Sitting forward on the couch, he replayed the messages. Matty rose from his chair and came to sit next to him. Kathy had left a message, but it sounded much the same as her scribbled note. Apart from a couple of old messages from the bureau, there was only one other voice mail and that had such poor sound quality Luke almost dismissed it.

"Play that again," said Matty suddenly, his head cocked to one side as if listening to a musical instrument. "Can you turn it up? I heard voices. One sounded frightened."

Luke turned up the volume and held his ear closer to the phone. Matty was right. A woman's voice was audible now. It was muffled, but Luke knew it was Kathy's. "What do you want?" she said, her normally soft Scottish lilt brittle with shock.

"Just to keep you safe and silent for a while," said a distinctive nasal male voice Decker also recognized but couldn't place.

"Why?" Kathy shouted. "This is something to do with Project Conscience, isn't it?"

Decker heard the man again. "All I've been told is that you're overstressed and are likely to say things you may regret. We're going to take you somewhere you can calm down, somewhere you can have peace and quiet." He was sure he'd heard that voice before.

There were sounds of interference or a scuffle.

"Keep that damn needle away from me, you bastard."

The message stopped then as it reached the end of recording time, but Decker had heard enough.

"Is she a friend of yours?" asked Matty.

"Not exactly," Decker replied, still trying to place the voice. Then he thought of Director Naylor, and he knew whom the nasal voice belonged to. It was someone who kept his nose stuck up the FBI director's ass: Assistant Director William Jackson, Naylor's senior Rottweiler in the bureau. Madeline Naylor had to be behind Kathy's abduction; Jackson wouldn't scratch his own balls without clearance from her. But why did Naylor want Kathy Kerr out of the way? It must be serious for Jackson to get personally involved and not just leave it to his goons.

Kathy was right; they did need to talk. Holding the phone up to his ear, Decker played the message back again, this time listening to exactly what Jackson said: "... *take you somewhere you can calm down, somewhere you can have peace and quiet.*"

Decker's first thought was a bureau safe house. He scanned his memory, remembering all the ones he knew near San Francisco. They were definitely options, but even safe houses were manned and maintained. Naylor would want as few people as possible to know about Kathy's abduction. But it had to be near San Francisco; a long journey would risk discovery. Where was there a discreet institution, controlled by the bureau, that could accommodate an individual in secrecy? Somewhere that guaranteed peace and quiet?

Suddenly it came to him. The perfect place. Filled with dark memories, Decker pressed a preset number on the phone and waited for the dial tone. The phone line clicked in his ear, and he heard a polite, professional voice greet him.

"Hello," he replied, "my name is Special Agent Luke Decker. You should have me on your books. I need an urgent appointment."

"What are you going to do?" asked Matty.

Decker shrugged with a casualness he didn't feel. "Find her and get her out, of course."

19

"As far as I'm aware, no one's been admitted in the last three days. Certainly not to the secure wing, Luke."

Dr. Sarah Quirke spoke softly with the trace of a Welsh accent as she sat at her desk in the main building of the Sanctuary. She was a petite woman in her late forties, with auburn hair and a round face; her kind eyes frowned with concern behind elegant spectacles. Behind her, half the wall of the office was a vast picture window through which Decker could see the distant purple haze of the High Sierra etched against a faultless blue sky. Sunlight flooded through the glass, highlighting the copper in Dr. Quirke's hair and bathing the wooden desk and chairs in a warm, honeyed light. His sessions with Dr. Quirke in her office were the only positive memories Decker had of his four-week stay here after his mother died.

"Luke, what's this all about? I came in on a Saturday only because you said you needed an urgent checkup although in my opinion, you're saner than most of the doctors here. But all you seem interested in are patient admissions to the secure rooms. You know full well that this is an FBI-funded retreat for agents with stress-related difficulties. We deal in counseling and therapy for temporary mental disturbances and dependencies, *not* insanity. We have only two secure

157

rooms, and those are for short-term emergencies. It's rare for them to be used at all. So tell me, Luke, what exactly are you after?"

Decker sat back in his chair and rubbed his temples. He didn't like coming back here, and it wasn't just because of the memories. If, as he suspected, Kathy had been abducted and was being held in the Sanctuary, then somebody very senior had to be involved, and that meant Decker was exposing himself just by being here. He had approached Dr. Quirke only because he trusted her absolutely. "Sarah, you probably know me as well as anyone, so please don't be alarmed. Something very strange is going on that I need to investigate. But the last thing I want to do is involve you. Trust me, it's safer this way. All I want to know is, have you a record of all the inmates and their rooms?"

Quirke frowned. It was clear that although his trust of her was absolute, it wasn't entirely reciprocated.

"I don't want to know any names," he told her. "I just want to know if there's *anybody* in the secure wing."

She paused for a while longer and then gave a small nod. "All right," she said, looking at the computer screen on her desk as she tapped on the keyboard. "I've got all the patients on my screen, and as I said, no one new has come in over the last three days. As for the secure rooms in the garden wing, they haven't been used for three and a half months. The last time was when a patient became violent and had to be restrained overnight in room A."

"So as far as you are concerned, there's nobody in any of the rooms now?"

"Correct."

"Who physically checks them?"

"No one really, because they're usually empty. Dr. Peters checks them occasionally."

Decker nodded, remembering the gray-haired doctor. They had never met, but Decker had often seen him around the place when he stayed here, and he knew the doctor's reputation. Peters was more an administrator than a medic. He was a drab career man who worked for the FBI first and the patients second. "Does he still manage the place, making sure it escapes the bureau budget cuts?"

She gave a small smile. "Yes."

"But you have access to the secure wing as well, don't you?"

"Well, like most of the senior doctors here, I have keys. I can easily check the rooms. Or I can call Dr. Peters. As I said, he's probably seen them most recently."

Decker raised a hand. "No, don't do that. If I'm right, I don't want to involve you or Dr. Peters in this. Just let me see inside the rooms by myself. No one need know I've even been here, and if the rooms are empty, no harm's been done. Please, Sarah, help me. If I'm being paranoid, I promise I really will book myself in for a checkup." He smiled at her but could see she was taking him very seriously.

After a brief pause she opened a drawer in her desk and reached for a bunch of keys. "Perhaps I should come with you," she said.

Luke was tempted for a moment, but then he thought of Jackson and Naylor. He couldn't endanger one of the few people who had genuinely helped him in his life. "Trust me, just give me the keys to the rooms, tell me when the secure wing will be quietest, and tell no one of my visit here. No one at all even if they ask you directly."

Dr. Sarah Quirke frowned again and then handed over three keys. "The large key gets you into the wing; the two smaller ones open each of the two rooms. Go now; the wing should be deserted."

Decker took the keys and thanked her.

"I don't know what this is all about," she said as he left her office, "but I hope to God you don't find anyone there."

He jangled the keys in his hand and smiled back at her. "I hope to God I do."

It came to Kathy Kerr in her drugged sleep. Madeline Naylor and Alice Prince's terrible objective guessed by Kathy's subconscious made no sense, but that hardly mattered. What mattered was that it flouted every reason she had embarked on Project Conscience for in the first place. This made her cry out aloud in her sleep, so loudly that she woke herself up.

As she came to full consciousness, she became immediately aware of a raging thirst, her tongue so swollen she could hardly swallow. Her arms ached from being strapped in the jacket, and she needed to urinate. So she felt relief as much as fear when she heard the key turn in the lock. Rolling over, she opened her eyes and saw the pair of black shoes enter the cell.

"Water," she croaked. "I need water." Still groggy with drugs, she closed her eyes and waited, too exhausted to struggle, hoping she wasn't going to be injected again. "I need to pee as well."

Bending to her level, the man with curly gray hair adjusted his round eyeglasses and smiled his kindly smile. In his right hand he held a bottle of liquid. It had a teat like a baby's milk bottle. "Drink this. It'll quench your thirst. It's rich in vitamins and minerals. I'll feed you some solids later. As for peeing, you're wearing diapers, so please just go ahead. You'll be changed when you're next sedated."

"I'm not a bloody baby," she croaked, stoking her anger in the face of exhaustion. "I demand to speak to someone. You can't keep me here."

"Come, come," he said in his condescending voice. "Don't overexcite yourself. Just drink." Kneeling down, he raised her head and laid it on his lap. Then he placed the drinking bottle in her mouth. The liquid was cool and tasted of orange Gatorade. She briefly tried not to drink, to exercise the only control she had, but she was so dehydrated she couldn't stop herself from sucking on the teat, gulping down as much as she could.

As she drank, she felt him bend over her, so near that his coat brushed her face. To control her claustrophobia, she closed her eyes and tried to ignore his suffocating closeness. Then she felt his hand move to her left breast and start to probe its contours through the fabric of the jacket.

The narrow tiled corridor leading to the secure wing was enough to bring the memories back. A glimpse of the small confined rooms on either side of him made Decker quicken his step. Just being in a place like this and contemplating the possibility of losing control of his mind set his pulse beating faster.

When he had been a patient here, he had been terrified of his obsession with hunting down the evil in others, scared it was an addiction, which somehow indicated he was evil himself. He hadn't even seen his mother in the nine months before she died because he had been so busy tracking down criminals.

Now the fears came flooding back. This time there was a firmer basis for them. He *knew* he possessed the seed of evil in him.

Banishing these thoughts to the back of his mind, Decker pushed through a set of fire doors to the secure wing ahead, trying to focus all his thoughts on one aim: finding Kathy Kerr and getting her out.

At first she couldn't believe he was touching her breast with any sexual intent. But when Kathy heard the catch in the man's breathing and felt him push his crotch against her cheek, she spit out the bottle teat. "What the hell are you doing?"

"Relax," he said soothingly, smiling down at her as if humoring a troublesome patient. Beads of sweat had formed on his forehead below his gray curly fringe. His eyes, magnified behind the round glasses, had a glazed look that sent a cold rush of fear through her abdomen. He put down the bottle and began to stroke her face, rubbing his fingers around her mouth, tracing the line of her lips. She could taste salt on his skin as he moved his fingers over her slick lower lip. She tried to bite him, but his fingers slowly traced the moistness of her lips, barely touching her gums. Totally helpless, she could feel her chest tighten in panic. Especially when his hand moved to his crotch and began to unzip his pants. This couldn't be happening, she thought. Only a few hours ago she had been on the verge of embarking on the final stage of her life's work. Now she was here in this hell. She struggled as the man began maneuvering her head. Out of the corner of her eye she could see him pull his penis out and begin to rub it.

"I'm warning you. I'll bite anything that comes near me," she shouted.

This seemed to excite him more as he tried to maneuver himself over her face. As his breathing increased, so did her panic and desperation. "Relax," he said. "In a few days you won't remember any of this. You won't remember anything at all."

She closed her eyes and gritted her teeth. Then suddenly his heavy breathing stopped, and from the door behind her she heard a sound that made her gasp with relief.

"Dr. Peters? What-the-fuck-are-you-doing?" Crisply controlled, Decker's words were still thick with anger. She tried to twist around to see him, but he was already moving into the room and pulling her tormentor to his feet. Looking up, she saw Decker hold the man with his left hand and punch him hard in the face with his right. It was an easy, powerful movement the way a professional golfer swings a club. The blow was followed by the satisfying sound of breaking eyeglass frames and a hoarse groan. As Peters crumpled, Decker pumped his knee up into the man's groin. Peters doubled over, holding both hands over his open zipper, his face white. Kathy felt such rage she wanted Decker to hit him again and again, but he didn't; he just let Peters collapse, squirming, to the floor next to her. As he lay there, Decker gestured toward Kathy and barked, "I've been sent by Assistant Director Jackson, on direct orders of Director Naylor, to take her to a new location." Decker's face was expressionless, but his green eyes burned with rage. "I'm supposed to deliver her unharmed. So I hope you haven't hurt her. Because if you have, I'll be coming back."

"No, I've done nothing," the man whimpered, moving his hands from his groin to his smashed nose.

"Then get out of here and leave me to my job."

"But I haven't given her all the injections yet. Director Naylor told me I was meant to hold her here for at least four more days."

"Well, the plans have changed. If you want to check, you

can call Jackson or the director. But Jesus Christ, you'll piss me off if you do, and I'll tell them what you've been doing. Now get the hell out of my sight, you sick fuck. I don't want to see you again before I leave this shit hole." With that Decker hauled the man to his feet and threw him out of the cell. Decker waited for a moment, listening to Peters scurry off, before he bent down and silently unbuckled Kathy's jacket.

The hands that had just demolished her tormentor were now infinitely gentle as they rolled her body and began untying her arms from around her body. He focused on the straps and knots, careful not to hurt her as he undid them. All the time she stared at him, terrified he might not be real. As soon as the jacket felt loose, his strong fingers were massaging her arms, pulling her up. "You came," she said, still not believing it. "You found me."

"Of course I came," he said, his face breaking into a grin. "I want to, I *need* to know what the hell's going on."

"We've got to stop them, Luke," she said. "Something terrible is happening."

"I kinda gathered that," he said, supporting her as her legs gave way. "I know about Project Conscience and their trying to cover up the mistake over Axelman."

"It's worse than that," she said, trying to think straight, realizing what little sense her revelation made. "Axelman's death might have been more than a mistake. I think it was a test for something else, something far worse than Conscience."

"What do you mean?"

Before she answered him, Kathy again questioned the insight that had come in her drugged sleep. Surely they weren't prepared to go that far, she thought.

"Luke, I don't think they want to treat violent criminals at all," she said. "I think they want to kill them."

Part 2

The Peace Plague

20

The New Military Hospital, Baghdad, Iraq.
Monday, November 3, 1:07 A.M.

Dr. Uday Aziz knew time was running out. Over the last
week the elite Republican Guard had suffered eighteen cases
of suicide and sixteen lethal brain hemorrhages. And every
indication pointed to the fact that this was just the beginning. All the deceased had been supremely fit, mentally sta-
ble soldiers under the age of twenty-five.

Three days ago the furious Iraqi president had demanded
through his generals that Aziz and his team uncover what lay
behind the problem. The rais would not countenance any
delay of the planned offensive on Kuwait to retake Iraq's old
province and reclaim the rich oil reserves. The loss of face
was unthinkable. Moreover, after tomorrow's U.S. elections
there would be a lame- duck administration in power, making it an ideal time to invade. Aziz knew he had to find the
source of the problem and identify the solution as soon as
possible or risk joining the ever-growing list of deaths.

But it wasn't the rais's threats that drove Aziz as he sat in
his office on the top floor of the drab brown stone building
that made up the main wing of the New Military Hospital.
Tapping away at his laptop, trying to complete his report for
presentation to the generals tomorrow afternoon, Aziz was
desperate to solve the riddle for more personal reasons. He
had never been emotionally involved in his work as a doc-

tor, seeing it more as a comfortable lucrative job than a vo-
cation. Now, for reasons he didn't understand, Aziz felt an
almost intolerable responsibility for the deaths, as if he were
in some way guilty of them. As each new case was recorded,
Aziz knew the only way he could ease this crushing burden
was to find a cure.

A desk lamp was the single light in an otherwise dark office. It was after one in the morning, and for the last four
days he hadn't returned home to his wife and two children
or slept for more than a couple of hours at a time. Over that
period he had returned to the first recorded incident two
weeks ago and studied the autopsies and relevant tests: a
twenty-one-year-old called Salah Khatib who had been shot
for refusing to shoot four deserters. Aziz had then charted
each subsequent suicide or brain hemorrhage, recording
every link between Khatib and the others.

Khatib's urine had yielded the first clue. It and the other
victims' had contained an exceptionally high level of androgens, hence Aziz's initial belief that they were suffering
from steroid abuse. The hair loss and acne plus pronounced
testicular atrophy in many of the men had seemed to confirm
this. Suicide was also a known risk of steroid abuse.

But the blood told another story. It confirmed the andro-
gen levels, but it also contained massive amounts of the enzyme monoamine oxidase. MAO is a marker for the level of
neurotransmitters in the brain, particularly the inhibiting
transmitter serotonin.

Aziz then conducted a full DNA scan on Khatib's blood,
using one of the two Genescopes in the military hospital.
These expensive gene sequencers were two of only three in
the whole of Iraq. The third was in a private medical bunker
below the main presidential palace two miles north of Baghdad.

Comparing the DNA profile in Khatib's military records
with the DNA profile in the blood taken from his corpse,
Aziz found a subtle but significant difference. Seventeen of
Khatib's genes had been modified by the addition of a series
of control sequences, sequences that were not present in the
original genome recorded in his military records and cer-

tainly not present in the standard human genome. At first
Aziz had been at a loss to understand why this should be the
case. Then he had checked if Khatib had received any gene-
modifying drugs in the last few weeks. In the man's records
among the battery of jabs and inoculations every soldier received, Aziz noted one DNA vaccine, the standard Bio-
Shield injection given to any soldier about to go into combat
to immunize him against biological weapons, particularly
those used by Iraq, allowing the weapons to be used in battle without harming its own troops. Despite the numerous
wrangles with the UNSCOM inspection teams, it was common knowledge that the rais had secretly developed a powerful biowarfare capability. It was this that allowed the Iraqi
president to consider defying the U.S.-led UN Security
Council and invade Kuwait again.

But the BioShield viral vector wouldn't change the particular genes that had been modified in Khatib's genome.
The BioShield vaccine merely modified stem cell DNA, im-
munizing the body to most of the standard threats while
making the cells receptive to more specialized booster vaccines designed to counter the ingress of newer bioweapons.
But Khatib had only received the standard BioShield vaccine and no boosters. Even if he had, they wouldn't have had
this effect on his genome. Something had subverted Khatib's
genes in a way that killed him.

Looking at the other suicide and brain hemorrhage victims, Aziz's team discovered that they shared the same
anomalies in the key seventeen genes. Studying these genes
and understanding how they boosted aggression hormones,
fuel neurotransmitters, and inhibition neurotransmitters had
convinced Aziz that they were the cause of the problem, but
how and why had they been changed?

He had also checked with Yevgenia Krotova, the Russian
scientist who headed Iraq's biological warfare capability.
According to her team, not all the deceased had received the
BioShield DNA vaccine, and many of those who had were
given it years ago. How could it be the source? Especially as
all the batches of vaccine his team and hers had subse-
quently checked revealed nothing unusual. What was the

link? If only he had been a more committed doctor, he might now be able to explain this. He might be able to prevent more men from dying.

Pausing from writing his report, he rubbed the painful spots on his chin and picked up a small blue cardboard carton from beside the laptop. He had studied medicine at University College London two decades ago and could easily read the Western lettering on the pen-size carton. The text told him nothing he didn't already know, but as he stared at the carton, four dark hairs fell on the keyboard of his laptop computer. Instinctively he scratched his scalp. A cold tremor ran through him as he watched the dark strands fall like fur off a molting dog.

Suddenly everything was as clear as ice.

The source of the epidemic wasn't in *all* the BioShield serums at all, only in a few, perhaps in just *one* random corrupted sample. That was why his team hadn't found anything in its batch checks. It would take only one person infected by a rogue viral vector if the vector hadn't been attenuated, rendered noninfectious. That person would then spread it to all the people he came into direct contact with, starting a chain of infection.

Which included him.

With a trembling hand Aziz began to type on the laptop, rewriting parts of the report. He had to record what he had discovered and alert his team and Yevgenia Krotova. Khatib was probably the index patient and had been infecting others before he died. With the close quarters in which the army lived, it could decimate the troops within weeks, if not days. His team had to search their stocks for any other corrupted samples of vaccine and analyze them to find a cure. He must also tell the generals about what happened, tell them to call off the advance. Yes, he thought, as he typed feverishly, suddenly painfully aware of all those soldiers going to war, perhaps he could avert the conflict and save all those lives too.

Sweat streamed down his forehead, and he felt so tired he wanted to sleep. But he couldn't rest; he had too much to do.

When he suddenly stopped typing fifty-eight minutes later, he wept in frustration. His left hand lay limp on the keyboard, refusing to obey his instructions. Then the whole left side of his body went numb. A tight band of steel tightened around his forehead. He could only gasp as he tried to focus on the screen in front of him.

"Oh, no," he groaned. "No." But the brain hemorrhage wouldn't abate, and when it struck, the seizure was so massive Aziz felt pain for only fractions of a second. Disturbing half the contents of his desk as he fell backward in the chair, he pulled the laptop with him, closing it down. His body was lifeless by the time his head and the laptop struck the cold hard floor, deleting the report.

Next to the doctor's face, inches from his open unseeing eyes, lay the blue carton of the BioShield vaccine. Under the BioShield brand name was the manufacturer's logo, a target made up of rings of chromosomes, with an arrow in the shape of a double helix hitting the nucleus in the center. "Targeting a better future" was the tag line next to the company name and address: "ViroVector Solutions, Inc. Palo Alto, California. USA."

The Marina District, San Francisco,
The Same Day, 4:37 P.M.

"I feel like I'm going mad. All the signs point to a bigger picture than Conscience, but I can't believe it. Whatever's going on, we can't just let them get away with it," Kathy Kerr said, sipping at her tea, in the living room of Matty Rheiman's house.

Matty Rheiman sat listening quietly in the corner while Decker paced around the room. "Do we have a choice?" Decker said, bending to the coffee table and pushing the pile of photographs toward her. He picked a picture from the top and handed it to her. "Look, I've been to your house on Mendoza Drive twice now. Jackson's people are crawling all over it. They're probably waiting until after the election, just to make sure anyone who comes looking for you doesn't cause a fuss. They don't give a damn who sees them either. Which means they don't know you've escaped yet. But it also means they think they're above the law. And they're probably right."

Kathy Kerr looked at one of the photographs Decker had taken of her house. It showed three men, looking relaxed, leaning against a gray Chrysler parked beside her front door. She recognized all of them. They had been with Assistant Director Jackson when she'd been taken. Another photograph showed them going into her house. Going inside *her* home as if it belonged to them.

"Jackson hasn't been around," said Decker. "He's probably trying to distance himself now. He's pretty senior within the bureau, and he's probably back in Washington. I bet his rogue agents don't even know Director Naylor's involved— not directly anyway."

"But we've got to do something, Luke."

"What?" Decker's voice rose in exasperation. "Kathy, it's your word and mine against the director of the FBI, the head of a major biotech company, and the future President of the United States. I've just been fired from the bureau. Shit, after Weiss's 'Conscience Against Crime' announcement the polls are putting her in the lead—a long, long way. The press loves her. The police love her. *Everyone* loves Pamela Weiss and her miracle cure for crime. And sooner or later Naylor and her cronies are going to find out that you escaped from the Sanctuary and come looking for you. They don't know I'm linked to you yet, but you should get away."

Kathy clenched her jaw but said nothing.

Almost two days had elapsed since Decker had rescued her from the Sanctuary and taken her back to his grandfather's house in the Marina. All of Saturday night and most of Sunday she had slept fitfully through drug-induced nightmares while Decker watched over her. By Sunday afternoon she had felt strong enough to talk, and that evening they had shared their discoveries.

Using Decker's overspecified but underused FBI-issue Toshiba laptop, she had reexamined the changes in Karl Axelman's genome from the disc she'd posted to Decker and used his FBI access codes to probe other suspicious deaths at San Quentin.

She probably owed Decker her life, but if she expected him to share her outrage and be totally sympathetic to her plight, she was disappointed. After they'd pieced together all they knew, Decker shook his head and gave her a weary look as if to say, "What did you expect?" Project Conscience had been her dream ever since their arguments at Harvard, so why was she complaining now, just because the methods weren't entirely ethical?

"Luke, if nothing else, we've got to find out what they're really up to."

"Isn't it obvious what they're up to? Face it, Naylor and Prince took your idea and used you to dupe the FDA. They screwed up with Axelman and the others at San Quentin or maybe they didn't. And because they didn't want Conscience to be compromised, they covered everything up and put you away. It's as simple as that. I want to see them pay, and I'm pissed at what they did to you. But you're out now, and perhaps you should just walk away."

Kathy looked at Decker long and hard. "Shit, there was a time when you'd have turned over every stone if you felt a crime had been committed. Don't you care anymore?"

"Of course I care. I'm just being realistic. Let's say we did get into your house and got to your trunk in Rambo's pen—"

She frowned. "*Rocky*'s pen. The chimp's name is Rocky."

"OK, Rocky's pen. Let's say we did get out all your discs and files, what would that prove?"

She sighed. God, she'd been through all this already. "It would prove that Conscience was based on false data. That the original vector used on unsuspecting convicts wasn't the Version Nine vector approved by the FDA."

Decker shook his head. Kathy could see the muscles working on his jaw. "OK, but who's going to *care*? Look, everyone now *wants* this miracle cure for crime *you* helped create. And since all future treatments will be done using your safe Version Nine, who gives a shit that violent cons were given potentially unsafe stuff?"

His voice rose in volume. "Christ, Kathy, apart from the fact that you were kidnapped, why do *you* care? This is your dream. I've got reason to be pissed off. I've never believed in all this 'genes means everything' shit. I've spent my whole working life hunting down killers and rapists based on the notion that the way they think and behave is based on their past. I've done a pretty good job of it too. But now I discover that my own daddy was a particularly unpleasant serial rapist and murderer. And according to this brave-new Genes "R" Us world of yours, I'm suddenly no better than the scum I've hunted down."

He lowered his voice and turned away from her. "Kathy, I've always hated the whole fascist notion of genetic prede-termination, but this is what you wanted: an ordered society where unpleasant variables are canceled out. So don't ac-cuse me of not caring."

Kathy bit her lip. Matty was still sitting quietly in the cor-ner of the room, his dead eyes leveled at her. She had the un-settling impression that he could see not only her but also what she was thinking.

"Luke, that's not fair," said Matty quietly. "Hear her out. I don't agree with Kathy's ideas either, but I'm sure her mo-tives are good. Kathy didn't want this, did you?"

"No, of course not. Certainly not like this. Luke, I can un-derstand why you're angry, but I'm angry too. And I want to try to stop them. Look at Axelman's death! The disc I sent you shows that his genome was altered, and any scientist with half a brain cell can plug the disc into a Genescope and it'll tell them how lethal the alterations were. Axelman wasn't corrected to make him behave better. The corrections killed him."

"But he would have died anyway. He was on death row. And if it was just an accident, who really cares?"

"But that's the whole point. I don't think it was an acci-dent. Trust me, I know a bit about viral vectors; I had a good teacher. What killed Axelman and the others at San Quentin was too well designed to be an accidental mutation. Some-thing very strange is going on. I don't know what, but it's more than Conscience. I'm sure of it."

Decker sighed and turned toward her. His eyes searched hers, as if seeing her for the first time. She could see his analytical mind working, weighing the implications of what she was saying.

"You can't do nothing, Luke," said Matty simply.

"Gramps, I'm sorry, but would you please stay out of this?" He turned back to Kathy. "You're really sure this was no accident?"

She paused. "Pretty damn sure. Yes."

"Sure enough to risk your life trying to prove it?"

She swallowed hard and took a deep breath. "This was my life, so I guess so, yes."

Decker kept staring at her for a moment and then gave a small nod. She looked vulnerable wearing his baggy sweater and rolled-up jeans, especially with her ruffled dark hair and pale skin. But there was steel in her eyes.

During the last few days he had watched her sleeping form toss and turn, jettisoning the drugs injected into her system. He had been consumed with anger that the director of his FBI could have justified this and whatever else she had sanctioned in the name of fighting crime.

He was also incensed with Kathy for being so naive. She seemed to think that everything in the big bad world could be smoothed as neatly as variables in one of her experiments, that people, especially senior people, obeyed set rules and laws. But his anger was outweighed by a real fear for her, knowing that if Naylor's people got hold of her again, they would have no choice: They would kill her.

He didn't believe in her conspiracy theory, but the cover-up was real enough. And he did want to get to the bottom of this. He hated the whole idea of Conscience, and his continually churning mind couldn't help throwing up anomalies. Kathy wouldn't have blown the whistle on the FDA scam. She would have been pissed off initially, but after calming down, she wouldn't have risked her life's work. Naylor and Prince must have known that, so kidnapping Kathy and potentially murdering her did seem excessive. Also, Alice Prince didn't seem like a person who would willingly allow Kathy, someone she knew and trusted, to be hurt—not of her own volition anyway. The San Quentin deaths weren't a factor either. As far as Naylor was concerned, no one—least of all Kathy—knew about those. The bodies had been officially executed and then cremated.

Still, Decker couldn't see how Kathy's life was worth the futile goal of thwarting a project she herself had initiated. However, he realized that if he refused to help her, she would go it alone and wouldn't last five minutes. Plus Matty had been fussing over her the last two days, telling him how something had to be done to stop this.

"Let's say you could prove all this, and that's a big assumption because I bet Naylor and Prince have already got plans to discredit you, then who would you tell?"

"Pamela Weiss."

"What makes you think she isn't involved?" he asked. It didn't fit with his impression of her. But he wouldn't bet on Weiss's not being involved.

"Because when Naylor and I argued about this, she insisted that Weiss knew nothing. She seemed furious at even the idea of her finding out. I'm telling you, we've got to get to Weiss." Kathy stabbed her finger into one of the photographs. It showed her house viewed from the rear. The top of Rocky's pen was just visible over the fence of the backyard. "And to make her believe us, we've got to get the evidence that proves her friends are deceiving her."

"I assume Rambo." Decker corrected himself again. "I mean, *Rocky* can be noisy. And he'll get pretty excited when he sees you?"

"Yes," said Kathy. "He'll make some noise." Her face fell. "Are you saying we can't get to the trunk until the men have gone?"

"Not if we don't want to be found out."

"Shit."

Then Decker smiled as an idea came to him. "But that doesn't mean we can't start stirring things up before we get all the evidence. We've got the Axelman disc, and you know what's in the trunk, yes?"

"Yes."

"And you reckon Pamela Weiss should be informed of what we know as soon as possible?"

"Of course, but how? There's no way I can get to her, and even if I could, Naylor would get to me first."

"You're right," said Decker, reaching for the phone, switching it onto speaker. He dialed a number he knew by heart. "So we need a go-between. Someone with access to the great and the good."

Kathy gave him a quizzical look, but he didn't say anything. Matty smiled as if he'd already guessed what Luke was going to do. The phone rang five times before the familiar voice of his old Berkeley buddy picked up. "Hank Butcher," the journalist said, his voice filling the room. He sounded harried.

"Hank, hi, it's Luke. Do you remember the other night when you said that you were tiring of just doing profiles and witty stories and wanted to get your teeth into something big? What did you call it, a real Pulitzer prizewinner?"

Butcher laughed. "Yeah, buddy, isn't beer great? Hey, Luke, now isn't a great time, OK? You might not realize it, but one of the most historic elections in American history is taking place tomorrow. This Project Conscience announcement has changed everything. I've even got myself invited to a celebration party on Thursday, assuming Weiss wins and becomes our first female President. Frankly I don't think any story of yours is going to cut it right now."

"What if I said my story involves the star of that historic celebration bash you're going to on Thursday?"

"Oh, yeah?"

Decker looked over at Kathy, who was now nodding her understanding. "How about an exclusive on Weiss's Project Conscience announcement from the scientist behind the original idea?"

Hank gave a dismissive snort. "You mean, Alice Prince?"

"No, the person she got the idea from."

"Go on."

"And what if I told you that Project Conscience wasn't all it seemed?"

"Meaning?"

"There's a huge cover-up under way, including abducting

the scientist behind the project, deceiving the FDA, and covering up deaths related to the Conscience treatment?"

"Luke, this is on the level, right?"

"Yup."

"I assume you've got evidence?"

"Let's just say I've got enough for you to ask our future President some pretty searching questions. And there's more evidence coming." Decker could almost hear Hank's mind working, preparing his Pulitzer Prize acceptance speech. "So, Hank, do you want an exclusive or not? Of course, if you're not interested, I can call someone—"

"Cut the crap, Luke." Hank interrupted with a short laugh. "You have my undivided attention. Tell me more."

21

As the United States of America awoke to the news that it
had elected its first female President, TITANIA was not surprised. It had planned for Pamela Weiss's victory and based
many of its far-reaching projections on its coming to pass.

TITANIA had had no vote to cast in yesterday's election,
but since it never slept, it had been busy all night raiding the
computer-controlled electronic ballot boxes, counting up the
results. TITANIA knew within a matter of hours that Pamela
Weiss had won with the biggest landslide victory since Reagan's in 1984. The reason for TITANIA's lack of surprise
was that this victory represented yet another domino falling
in a sequence it had long predicted.

As always, a small proportion of its vast neural net was
focusing on Crime Zero, continually updating progress on
the differing phases and fine-tuning its predictive sequences.
Phase 1 was now complete, as was the related Project Conscience. The supercomputer needed to check how Phase 2
was developing. Its progress against predicted action standards was vital to the launch of Phase 3. Interrogating its
search engines, TITANIA scoured the Internet for feedback
on Iraq.

Logging on to hospital databases in Baghdad and military
systems while at the same time piecing together apparently

179

unrelated snippets of information from Reuters, CNN, the BBC, and the other syndicated news agencies on the World Wide Web, TITANIA soon found the pattern it was looking for.

The above-average number of deaths on the computers at the military hospital in Baghdad, all males below twenty-five with suspected brain hemorrhages, and isolated reports of an unexplained rash of suicides within the armed forces of Iraq told TITANIA all it needed to know. The Iraqi military was fast becoming an amplification zone, and the reports were increasing in number. TITANIA would continue to monitor these reports, feeding the findings into its predictive model. But for the moment Phase 2 appeared to be on schedule.

Only now did it look at Phase 3, the most complex stage of all. First of all, it interrogated the control computer at the target airports, ensuring that the radioactivated bacteriophage filters were in stock, waiting for its command. Only then did it rerun its predictive sequences.

Phase 2 employed an infectious vector that was transmitted by touch. But Phase 3 was transmitted via the respiratory system. It was airborne, and therefore, once launched, the spread would be much faster and much harder to predict.

Using earlier test data, TITANIA knew how fast the Crime Zero Phase 3 viral vector incubated within the human body. It could also predict the spread of the viral vector through a population by extrapolating the spread characteristics of past airborne pandemic plagues, particularly the Spanish flu epidemic of 1918–1919, which had killed almost fifty million, and the more recent Chinese flu outbreaks of 1957 and 1961. Using this base model and continually checking empirical data on the World Wide Web, TITANIA was able to give a real-time prediction for when Crime Zero met its final objective of Time Zero.

Its original forecast was more or less unchanged, putting Time Zero still some three years away. If nothing changed and the human entity, Madeline Naylor, carried out her next task, then TITANIA had only to launch Phase 3 at the designated time and wait for the final dominoes to fall.

As TITANIA E-mailed its Crime Zero status report to

Prince and Naylor, it had no conception of the morality of
what it was doing, only that it was technically possible and
increasingly inevitable.

The White House, Washington, D.C.
Thursday, November 6, Noon

Director Naylor hated being kissed. At social functions she
always tried to avoid the European affectation of greeting
people with a kiss on each cheek—air or otherwise. A hand-
shake sufficed. But at the White House champagne reception Bob Burbank held in the magnificent East Room
Madeline allowed herself to be kissed. She even maneu-
vered her face so that the President's lips momentarily
brushed against hers. As she did so, Alice Prince looked on,
a nervous frown of fascinated horror on her face.

The grand room with its Bohemian crystal chandeliers
and floor of Fontainebleau parquetry was filled with the
party faithful who had helped Pamela Weiss win. Campaign
advisers, secretaries, canvassers, and a few journalists min-
gled and congratulated one another as liveried waiters fer-
ried around endless trays of canapés and champagne.

Naylor stood with Alice Prince and Pamela Weiss, talking
with Bob Burbank, as his wife, Nora, chatted with Pamela
Weiss's husband, Alan, and Todd Sullivan, Weiss's campaign organizer.

The President was all charm and bonhomie, beaming his
Gregory Peck smile at Prince and then Naylor. "So since
you guys are the real heroes in winning this election, can
you tell a simple country boy like me *how* Conscience actually works?"

"Don't ask me," said Naylor with a smile, resisting the
urge to wipe her lips. The President was no country boy, and
he was only laying on this charm offensive because Project
Conscience had made him look good, a visionary President
assured of his place in the history books. But that was OK.
Bob Burbank's charm offensive had already allowed her to
achieve what she had come here for.

She turned to Alice, who now appeared to be coming to terms with the shock of seeing Libby. The funeral had been two days ago, and she already seemed calmer. She had been typically reluctant about today, though, forcing Naylor to remind her of their plans. "It's the science that makes Conscience work," she said, smiling at Alice.

"Well?" Burbank said, turning to Alice. "Can you explain it to me?"

Alice looked at her and then back at the President. "Vectors, Mr. President."

"Vectors?"

"Yes, viral vectors," said Alice nervously, clearly annoyed Naylor had focused the spotlight on her. "You see, Mr. President, Project Conscience is all about getting the right control sequence into the right cells, and to do that, I must create the right virus. Like a cross between a parcel and a cruise missile, a viral vector can target and deliver any DNA I insert into it. Viral vectors are gene changers. With them I can alter the very essence of what a person was born with."

Burbank took a sip of his champagne. "How targeted can they be?"

"Well, with the right engineering I can create a virus that will target a particular cross section of humanity, or a particular person, or even a particular type of cell."

"You mean, it will ignore any other target and hit only what it's supposed to? Like a smart bomb?"

"That's the idea."

"I wish we could be as precise in solving the Iraq crisis."

At that moment the tone changed. The escalating problem with Iraq was casting a shadow over the celebrations.

"Yes, what's the latest?" asked Alice Prince.

Burbank shrugged, and Naylor fancied she saw relief in his eyes. As if he were glad to pass on this particular baton to his successor in the new year. "Well, we're doing everything we can. I only hope he's going to see reason. But as you know, Iraqi troops are still gathering north of the thirty-second parallel."

"Surely he realizes that if his troops cross that line, for

whatever reason, then the coalition allies will stop them?" asked Alice.

Burbank nodded. "Oh, yes. French and British carriers as well as our own are already on standby in the gulf. Troops and fighter planes are also on alert in Saudi, Kuwait, and Turkey. We're ready for him, but he doesn't appear to care."

"Why?" asked Alice.

"He's warned that he'll view any attempts to thwart his repossession of what he calls the Iraqi province of Kuwait as extreme provocation and will unleash an 'appropriate response.'"

"But he hasn't got nuclear weapons, has he?"

"No, not yet. Not nuclear. But we believe his biological capability is pretty awesome. Despite all our inspections, our intel suggests he's got something special up his sleeve."

"And if the Iraqi president does launch anything?" Alice asked.

Burbank frowned. "Then the allies under the U.S. will have little choice but to escalate to nuclear weapons, razing Baghdad to the ground."

Naylor turned to Pamela Weiss and could see that this very real scenario filled her with dread. Becoming the first ever woman President was fine, but becoming the first to launch a nuclear warhead in anger was not.

As if to reinforce the urgency of the situation, a tall African-American in dress uniform appeared beside Burbank. General Linus Cleaver was the chairman of the Joint Chiefs of Staff. "Mr. President, can I have a word, please?"

No sooner had Burbank turned away than he turned back again to lean toward Weiss. Speaking to his successor, he kept his smile fixed and his voice low, but Naylor heard him. "I'm sorry to break up the party, but something's just come up involving Iraq. I've arranged a briefing in the conference room. I think you should be there. We need to keep a united front during the handover. I suggest we meet in the Oval Office in ten minutes."

Naylor watched Weiss clench her jaw. "Thanks, Bob, I'll be there."

Burbank smiled once more before walking back toward

the chairman of the Joint Chiefs. With him Alice recognized Secretary of State Jack Manon and Defense Secretary Dick Foley.

"You OK, Pamela?" asked Alice.

"Yup. But it looks like I'm not going to get much of a honeymoon period. I'll see you guys later."

"Good luck," said Naylor, watching her say good-bye to her family, then walk toward the door in the direction of the Oval Office. As Weiss neared the door, Naylor saw a compact sandy-haired man in a dark suit appear from the throng and shadow her. Naylor knew it was Toshack, the Secret Service agent assigned to organize her protection. She didn't like him. He never showed her fear, only politeness. And since he was Secret Service, she had no authority over him.

Then, just as Weiss reached the door, a rake-thin man with curly hair suddenly stepped out in front of her and extended his hand. Toshack tensed but held back. Everyone here had been vetted and searched. Weiss shook the man's hand, but she kept on walking, clearly not intending to stop. He smiled at her and appeared to be congratulating her.

"Who is that?" Alice Prince asked Naylor.

Squinting her eyes, Naylor stared for a while, then gave a small nod. "I think it's a journalist. You know? He does all those pieces for *Vanity Fair.* Interviewed Pamela about three years ago, when she was being launched as a major contender for the White House. It was a big piece in all the magazines at the time. Did her a lot of good. Hank . . . er, Butcher, I think."

Suddenly Weiss stopped in her tracks, her face no longer smiling. Butcher was saying something, and Weiss was listening intently. Then Pamela darted a quick look in Naylor and Prince's direction before shaking her head at the journalist and pointing to her watch. After exchanging a few more words, the journalist pulled an envelope out of his jacket and handed it to her. Then they shook hands, and Butcher left. Weiss quickly looked in the envelope, then called Toshack over. She said something to him before leaving the room.

"I wonder what's going on," Alice said to Naylor. "She doesn't look too pleased."

To Naylor's surprise, Toshack approached them. The agent was courteous but unsmiling as he addressed them. "Excuse me, Dr. Prince, Director Naylor, but Governor Weiss requests that you meet her tonight to discuss an urgent matter relating to Project Conscience. Eight o'clock at your offices, Director Naylor?"

"Fine," said Naylor with a tight smile. Next to her Alice was fingering her pendant nervously.

"She also has a question for you," said the agent, his face impassive.

"Oh, yes?" said Naylor. "And what's that?"

"Who is Dr. Kathy Kerr?"

22

The Mandrake Hotel, Washington, D.C.
Thursday, November 6, 1:17 P.M.

Hank Butcher felt pretty pleased with himself as he walked to his rental car in the underground garage beneath the new Mandrake Hotel, where he had stayed last night. The evidence Decker had given him about irregularities on Project Conscience had been enough to challenge the President-elect, and she had appeared suitably shocked. With more evidence to come, he was sure there was a huge story here.

His story.

This could dwarf Watergate and the Lewinsky affairs of the last century. Moreover, if he handled it well, he could be credited with blowing the first ever female presidency wide open—*before* she was even inaugurated.

He blew onto his hands. The temperature had dropped dramatically since election day. Washington was in the grip of a cold snap, and snow was forecast. After getting into his car, Butcher opened his briefcase and checked his airline ticket. His American Airlines flight from Reagan National to San Francisco left in one and a half hours.

He pulled out his cell phone and pressed a preset button. Decker's phone was turned off, so he left a voice mail. "Luke, hi, it's Hank. I've spoken to Weiss. She put on a pretty good show of looking shocked. I'd even go so far as to say she knows nothing about this. Let me know when you've got the rest of the stuff. I should be back home tonight."

Just then a figure entered the deserted underground lot. A tall woman in a thick winter coat. Although he recognized the face, he couldn't believe it. She was so rarely alone. Her entourage usually accompanied her. She stopped and checked her watch as if annoyed that whoever was supposed to be picking her up hadn't arrived. She must have had a clandestine meeting at the Mandrake. It wouldn't be the first time deals had been struck in the discreet hotel. She had probably arranged to be picked up down here so as to avoid prying eyes.

Butcher had thought of approaching her at the White House reception earlier but wanted to get a response from the President-elect first. Also, Decker had warned him to leave her alone until they knew more. But this was a heaven-sent opportunity. He opened his door.

"Director Naylor?"

Turning to face him, she looked startled and wary. "Yes?"

"The name's Hank Butcher. I saw you at the White House reception. Can I ask you a few questions?"

She gave him a withering glare. "You can do what you like. But I doubt I shall answer them. I'm in a hurry." She checked her watch again and turned away from him toward the exit sign.

He left his car. "C'mon, Director. It'll take only a few moments. I need to ask you about Project Conscience. I was going to ask you at the White House, but I wanted to get a comment from Pamela Weiss first."

"I'm sorry, but like I said, I'm in a hurry. I have to get to National." She pulled a cell phone out of her pocket with her gloved hand.

"No, don't call for your car. I'm going to the airport too. Let me give you a lift there. We can talk on the way, OK?"

"I don't think so."

Butcher gave her a sly smile. "What if I told you I know all about the cover-ups on Project Conscience? And that I'm going to get all the evidence I need to blow it right open. Do you still refuse to talk to me?"

Naylor's eyes narrowed, and he saw shock on her face. "What if I told you that you've been misinformed by people who wish to sabotage the most significant initiative against crime since DNA fingerprinting?"

Butcher opened the passenger door of his car. "I'd say you might be right. But I'd need to know more about your side of the story. The President-elect was too busy to give me an immediate response; perhaps you might like to instead."

Naylor hesitated for a moment and then let out a defeated sigh. "OK," she said eventually. "Let me tell my agents where I'll be." She put the cell phone to her thin lips and left a curt message. "But, Mr. Butcher," she said after she hung up, "what I'm going to tell you is off the record. And I'm telling you only so you understand this initiative mustn't be sabotaged."

"Fine, whatever you say," he said as she got into the car.

By the time they reached the Potomac it had begun to snow. As Butcher asked his questions, he ignored the large flakes falling from the sky. "So tell me about Dr. Kerr. She's made some serious allegations."

"Look, Dr. Kerr's brilliant, and the origin of Conscience undeniably comes from her work. But over the last six or so years she has been acting more and more unstable. Her work hasn't been a success, and most of the recent step changes on the project have come from Alice Prince, not her. Kathy's been feeling very insecure about her role in a project that she still regards as hers.

"Alice Prince offered to share the credit, but Kathy wanted a ridiculous financial reward and full credit or she would trash it. Naturally we can't allow a project as important as this to be held for ransom by one person—however much she's contributed. So we accepted her resignation, and now it appears she's trying to discredit the whole process."

Ahead, the sprawl of the airport rose through the thickening blizzard. Butcher peered through the windshield. "She claims you had her put away. Put in some mental asylum."

Naylor laughed at that. "What proof do you have for all

this nonsense? I thought you were supposed to be a responsible journalist."

"It isn't just Kathy Kerr who claims you put her in an asylum. I've got another witness."

"Oh, yes? Who?"

"I'm not telling you that," he said. "Not yet anyway."

"Look, Mr. Butcher, there's no way anyone can corroborate a story that didn't happen unless he's lying. I asked for proof, not hearsay."

"I'm expecting more proof anytime now," he said. "Dr. Kerr says she's got records going back ten years or so."

They were heading for the main terminal building and the rental car dropoff points. He turned to ask her where she wanted to be dropped off when Director Naylor calmly reached into her jacket and in one fluid motion pulled out a gun and pressed it into his crotch. "Mr. Butcher, please take the turn for the long-term car lot. If you do not do exactly as I say, I will pull the trigger." The pistol was pushed hard into his balls, but for a good second or two he didn't react. His brain simply couldn't believe that this was happening.

Butcher exhaled suddenly, and Director Naylor watched in satisfaction as his grin faded and his face paled.

It hadn't been easy to make her prey think he was the predator. But she had no choice. She couldn't get one of her minions to handle Butcher because she needed to know what he knew. And she needed to do it quickly and discreetly.

Immediately after Toshack had asked about Kathy Kerr, Naylor had been on the phone to Jackson. Kerr had been delivered to Dr. Peters as agreed. Naylor hadn't been able to contact Peters, but he wouldn't have released Kathy. He had too much at stake. She had to find out who had got her out and why. Just the thought of Kerr's shooting off her self-righteous mouth to Weiss made her squirm. This had to be stamped out fast.

It had taken Director Naylor just two phone calls to discover where Hank Butcher was staying in Washington. She learned that he had checked out of the recently opened Mandrake Hotel this morning and had a reserved American Airlines seat to San Francisco from Reagan National Airport at four forty-six this afternoon. But his rental car was still parked under the hotel.

After a brief talk with Prince to sort out what they were going to tell Weiss tonight, she had taken a taxi to the Mandrake, then waited. Once Butcher spotted her, the rest had been easy.

Now *she* could interview *him*.

"What are you doing?" he demanded, his voice at least an octave higher than before. "You can't possibly hope to get away with this. I'm a journalist, for chrissakes."

"Be quiet and drive to the long-term parking lot."

It was now so white outside she couldn't see more than a few yards ahead. Butcher kept pleading with her as he drove through the automatic barriers and followed her instructions to the middle of the vast lot, parking eventually in a space surrounded by hundreds of increasingly snow-blanketed cars. His face had a greenish cast and was covered in a film of sweat when he switched off the ignition and turned to her. She could tell from his eyes that he was close to panic. Good.

"Hand me the keys."

He took the keys from the ignition and gave them to her. "What do you want?" he asked.

"Who got Kerr out of the Sanctuary?"

"I can't tell you that. I promised him I wouldn't. I've got to protect my sources."

She pushed her gun further into his groin until he grimaced in pain. "I'd think about protecting more than your sources right now, if I were you. Trust me, Mr. Butcher, unless you tell me what I need to know, I will shoot you and feel justified in doing so. We are embarked upon something that is vital to the future success of our species, something far too important to allow a couple of individuals to hijack it."

Butcher looked really scared now. "But if I tell you, how do I know you won't kill me anyway?"

"God, you journalists always ask questions. You don't know. But I assure you that if you don't tell me, you'll beg me to kill you."

She stared into his eyes and cocked the gun.

"OK, OK, I'll tell you. His name's Luke Decker; he contacted me by phone."

"Decker? As in Special Agent Luke Decker? Jesus."

"Yeah. He told me about getting Dr. Kerr out of the Sanctuary and how you'd deceived the FDA. Also how Axelman was possibly a mistake you wanted covered up. Or something else."

"Did he tell you what this something else might be?"

"No, he said Dr. Kerr's got some suspicions but nothing concrete. That's what I was asking Pamela Weiss about at the reception, but she seemed completely in the dark."

Naylor smiled at that. "Oh, she is, Mr. Butcher, she is. And that's exactly how it's going to stay. Would you please get out of the car now?"

A look of relief and then renewed fear crossed his face. "Why? What are you going to do with me?"

"Mr. Butcher, get out of the car, or I will shoot you where you sit. If you run or shout for help, I will shoot you dead. In this blizzard no one will see or hear you anyway."

Once they were out of the car she steered him to the back. "Open the trunk."

Shivering with terror and the sub-zero temperature, he did as she asked. There was a small case and a laptop inside. Otherwise it was empty.

"Get in the trunk."

"But it's freezing."

"Now! Or I will shoot you."

For a moment she thought he was going to struggle, but then he sat on the bumper, allowing her to push him into the trunk. Butcher lay there trembling, his eyes staring up at her though his eyeglasses, pleading with her.

"Let me leave you with two points of consolation," she said to him. "One, you aren't dying much sooner than you would have anyway. Two, you got off light compared with what I'm going to do with Dr. Kathy Kerr and Special Agent Luke Decker." With that she fired one perfectly placed bullet into Butcher's forehead and closed the trunk.

After checking she was still unseen in the vast snow-

swept lot, she retrieved a Swiss Army knife from her inside pocket and unscrewed the rear and front plates from
the rental car. She swapped the rear one with a Saab's
plate ten cars down and the front plate with a similar one
on a Chevy's two rows back. The whole process took her
twelve minutes, but it ensured that Hank Butcher's rental
car and therefore his body wouldn't be found for weeks,
especially if the weather stayed cold. By then it wouldn't
matter.

Walking toward the courtesy bus shelter, she turned to
watch her footsteps disappear in the falling snow. Despite
her reservations about exposing herself, there was something satisfying about doing a job personally and doing it
well. It took her back to her early days as an agent, when
she'd finished in the top percentile in her class at the Quantico FBI academy and helped bust two murder cases in her
first six months, receiving a bullet in her left leg and right
shoulder for her troubles. She certainly felt no remorse for
what she had done. It was necessary, and in the long run the
morality of the deed would cease to be relevant. In the courtesy bus shelter she reached for her cell phone and dialed
Assistant Director Jackson's number.

"Jackson," she ordered when he picked up, "find Dr. Peters and get rid of him. He allowed our guest to escape. Then
find Luke Decker. Dr. Kerr will be with him."

"Decker?"

"Yes, the same Decker who beats you every year at the
Quantico shooting meet. Find them both and bring them to
me. Naturally no one in the bureau except your people must
know about this. Understand?"

"Yes, but what if I can't bring them to you alive?"

Naylor looked up as the courtesy bus approached through
the snow. She checked her watch, calculating that she could
get a cab from the terminal building in plenty of time to ren-
dezvous with Alice Prince before their meeting with Pamela
Weiss.

"Director," said the voice on the phone, "if I have to, can
I kill them?"

Madeline Naylor looked back across the rows of cars, already unable to identify which contained the rapidly cooling corpse of Hank Butcher. "Of course you can, Jackson. You can do whatever you like. Just make damn sure you get them."

23

The presidential palace in Babylon, one hundred kilometers
south of Baghdad, was one of more than fifty built since the
1990 war. Its unrestrained opulence seemed obscene in a
land where continuing international sanctions meant many
people lived in poverty. The rais and his family now owned
over eighty such residences, including the older palaces,
around the country.

Standing in one of the military planning rooms, Dr. Yevgenia Krotova shifted the weight of her heavy frame from
one foot to the other and stared at the six silent television
screens on the far wall, each showing a different cable channel. These flickering images of the modern world contrasted
sharply with the palace's old-world splendor: the marble pillars, the thick rugs, the gilt high-backed chairs facing the
screens, and the alabaster water fountains visible in the
floodlit courtyard beyond the tall, arched windows.

The ostentatious show of wealth didn't shock Yevgenia
Krotova. After she had sold her soul to the devil, nothing
shocked her anymore. Ten years ago she had been deputy director of Russia's State Research Center of Virology and
Biotechnology in Koltsovo, helping run its illegal germ warfare program. But Russia was poor and unable to maintain
even the meager salary she was paid. Iraq had outbid both

Iran and North Korea to purchase her expertise—and whatever secrets she could bring with her.

One freezing night in January 1998 Yevgenia had decamped with her husband and three daughters, and for the last decade she had headed Iraq's formidable biological warfare program. She was paid more money than she could ever use and had a good life, but she was a guarded prisoner, a bought possession of the rais. She was forbidden to leave the country, and her family would always be watched. Dr. Krotova never allowed herself to question her decision, though. Regret served no purpose.

But now she was in trouble. Aziz had died before he could explain the escalating deaths in the Republican Guard, and because he had involved her in his investigations, she had been summoned to the palace to supply answers. Any sadness she may have felt for Aziz's death was more than countered by frustration. She had been left to explain the unexplainable to the three generals? Why couldn't Aziz at least have left a few clues before he died? The only consolation was that the generals, not the rais himself, were here.

After greeting the generals, she stood in the middle of the room. It was late, and she felt tired. She wanted to sit down, but they didn't invite her to join them on one of the comfortable-looking high-backed chairs surrounding the long table. Instead they left her standing and proceeded to interrogate her. Frowning, she tried to ignore the screens flickering over the generals' shoulders and concentrate on their questions.

"Dr. Krotova, do you or do you not know what the cause is?" General Akram was the tallest of the three men. His eyes searched her face as he spoke, his voice brusque. Ostensibly Akram had overall responsibility for medical matters in the army, although the man was an idiot who was given the role only because of his distant blood relationship to the rais.

"Not exactly, but I'm convinced Dr. Aziz was close. He thought it was steroid abuse at first, but now he has died with the same symptoms, which implies that whatever killed the men is infectious."

"Infectious?" asked General Rashani, a short, bald man

with glasses. He sounded incredulous. "But these men have been dying of brain hemorrhages and committing suicide. How could that be infectious?"

"That's what Aziz was trying to confirm. It might be a complex virus or a prion or else something entirely new that changed the men's DNA and brain chemistry. Aziz was writing up his work on the night he died, and I tried to recover his report, but his computer was damaged, and most had been deleted. However, from the fragments we salvaged from his hard drive, I think he may have found something."

"But you don't know the cause or how to cure it?"

"Not yet. My people are reviewing all the tests Aziz's team conducted on the patients, and we are currently conducting detailed autopsies on the men's brains to shed more light on the pathology. But we need more time."

"You haven't got more time. *We* haven't got more time. We await the rais's order to march on Kuwait at any moment."

"But you can't wage a military campaign until we know more. This phenomenon is no longer confined to the Al Taji camp. At least a hundred men are now dead, and the rate is increasing. We need to check how widespread this epidemic has become and contain it. If you don't, you will lose even more men."

"In war men always die," said General Akram. "Unless you can explain what's wrong, we shall proceed as planned. If it's noninfectious, then there's no problem. And if it is, then at least they can serve a purpose before they die."

"But that's—" she started to say before the third general gave her a dark look.

"This is not open to debate," he said.

Yevgenia bit her lip, framing a more positive response. It was dangerous to anger them any more than she had done already. Before she could say anything else, she heard a loud voice speaking in English. The three generals swiveled around to face the wall of televisions, and Yevgenia realized that the volume had been increased on the top right-hand screen. The channel was CNN, and the voice she could hear was that of the U.S. President. He was standing in front of a podium, and at the bottom of the screen was a subtitle that read: "Bob Burbank Live from the White House." Behind him were four men and a woman. One of the men was in uniform. The President had been speaking for some minutes when Yevgenia, who spoke English well, picked up what he was saying.

"I hope and pray that the president of Iraq sees reason and doesn't cross the thirty-second parallel. But if he does, then the coalition allies are committed to crush his offensive. He must understand that we will execute this ruthlessly and decisively because we firmly believe that to delay would only encourage him further. We have the conventional force in place to destroy his army, and we will employ that force *immediately* if one Iraqi boot, tank, or plane crosses that line in the sand."

As the U.S. President spoke, his face was pale and his eyes looked tired. His face worried Yevgenia; he had the look of a man telling an awful truth. "We are aware that the Iraqi president has promised to retaliate with unconventional weapons, but we will not appease him. We *cannot* appease him. The very last thing we want to do is start a conflict, let alone escalate one. But he must be in no doubt that if he raises the stakes one notch, we will have no choice but to end this decisively. The game of bluff and counterbluff he has been playing with the UN for the last eighteen years has come to an end. There is no more patience."

President Burbank seemed to sway on his feet, and as he did so, he wiped beads of sweat from his brow. At first Yevgenia thought that the man was affected by the import of what he was saying, but then she realized that it was more than that. He looked ill. "As I speak, the president of Iraq controls the greatest destructive force we have ever seen. His actions will determine whether this nuclear response remains unused or whether it is unleashed on him and his country." Burbank paused and looked into the camera, his face haggard. "I hope he chooses his actions wisely."

When he finished, there was a hush—not only in the palace but also in the White House briefing room on camera. Yevgenia looked at the generals and could see them craning

over the backs of their chairs staring at the screen. Then, just
as the journalists began asking their questions, the most
unimaginable scene unfolded before her eyes: Bob Burbank
clutched his chest, reached for the podium as his knees
buckled, and collapsed to the floor. There was a second of
shocked silence; then the screen went mad. Secret Service
men in black glasses formed a circle around the man. Journalists left their seats to rush forward, and the President's
aides stood around in panic.

The camera suddenly focused on one of the men who had
been standing behind the President. A tall, thin man identified by an excited commentator as Vice President Smith, he
looked shellshocked, paralyzed by terror. "I'm sure somebody will take control of this awful situation soon," said the
CNN commentator more out of hope than knowledge. But
Yevgenia could see from his stricken face that the Vice President was not going to be that someone.

At that moment there was a thumping noise, and the camera shifted back to the podium. The woman who had been
standing behind the President was now tapping her hand on
the microphone, her eyes looking straight at the camera, her
gaze unflinching. She was a striking-looking woman with a
thick bob of auburn hair streaked with silver. Her face was
open and strong, and although she was clearly in as much
shock as anybody else was, she was not debilitated by it.

"Please resume your seats. This briefing isn't yet over,"
she said. Her voice wasn't loud, but the tone was so calm
and clear it cut through the collective panic, stopping everyone and making all turn to her. Gradually the journalists returned to their seats, and a semblance of order was restored
as the Secret Service men and two paramedics lifted the
President and removed him from the room. One man, who
looked like a doctor, came over and whispered something in
the woman's ear, and her chest heaved as she took in this
new information.

"My name is Pamela Weiss. I am the President-elect of
the United States of America. I have just been informed that
what you have witnessed was a heart attack. The President,
Bob Burbank, is now being rushed to the hospital, where he

will receive the very best medical care. A full bulletin will be issued as soon as his condition is known."

For the briefest of moments she paused and glanced behind her at the Vice President, who still stood frozen to the spot, his eyes dead with shock. Pamela Weiss cleared her throat, and Yevgenia could see her steeling herself. She couldn't help admiring the woman as she continued, "I'm sure that all the country's thoughts and prayers are with the President and his family at this moment. But let no one be unclear, friend or foe. This changes nothing. The U.S. and UN position on Iraq is unambiguous. The President's words stand."

The volume faded then, leaving just the silent screen. Yevgenia wondered who had the controls. But all the generals stood silently taking in what they had just witnessed, their hands loose by their sides.

Suddenly one of the high-backed chairs at the large table in front of her swiveled around, revealing the rais in full military uniform. In his right hand he held a TV remote. His thick black hair and mustache were still unnaturally devoid of gray, and his jowls heavy. As was his wont he had been listening in on her meeting, trying to hear what she really thought.

"We definitely can't delay now, Dr. Krotova," he said in a delighted voice. "We have the wonderful weapon you made me, and we have this opportunity." His face was smiling as he stared at her, though she knew that his smile stemmed from what he had seen on TV, not from what he had heard her say to the generals. "General Akram," he said, not taking his eyes off her, "you and the others will organize for the invasion to begin as discussed. The timing is perfect. Whatever the Weiss woman says, the Americans will be distracted.

"Come," he said, beckoning to Yevgenia with the remote as if controlling her.

Nervous, she walked past the generals and stood in front of him. Smiling, he beckoned her to come closer until she was bending down; his thick mustache almost scratched the skin of her cheek. His breath smelled of stale cigars. "Find out what is killing these soldiers," he whispered, "or I will kill you and all your family." The smile didn't leave his face as he spoke, but she believed every word he said.

24

Waiting outside Kathy Kerr's isolated house on Mendoza Drive, neither Kathy Kerr nor Luke Decker was aware of events on Capitol Hill. Their only concern was to steal into her house unnoticed.

"They've gone," said Decker, getting back into the car after checking out Kathy's house for the third time in the last hour. "But we still shouldn't stick around when we go in. They're soon gonna find out you've escaped. Five minutes, like we agreed. No more."

Kathy Kerr nodded her agreement as she sat silently in the passenger seat of the rental Ford Taurus.

He turned to her. "You sure you want to go through with this?"

"Yes," she said, staring at her house. It looked the same as before, but now the white facade, which she had always viewed with such affection, seemed sinister, as if concealing some threat behind its darkened windows. In her mind's eye she could see Jackson, armed with a gun and syringe, waiting behind the front door, like the last time. "You're sure no one's waiting inside?"

"As I can be," said Decker. "I've checked the whole place. There's no one there. You've got no security alarms or lights I should be aware of, have you?"

She shook her head. "Nope. Before we go in, should we call your journalist friend again to see if he's heard anything more from Pamela Weiss yet?"

Decker shrugged and dialed the cell phone resting on the dash. The phone rang in the car, and then Hank Butcher's voice mail kicked in. Decker hung up. There was no point leaving another message.

"Shit," she said, "why doesn't he turn his phone back on?"

"Don't worry, we know from his message that Pamela Weiss probably isn't involved. And she's not likely to get back to him until she's checked things out herself. Hank isn't shy. He'll call back if he gets any response. When he does, he'll want the rest of your precious evidence." Decker smiled at her, his eyes glinting in the half-light. "Ready?"

She took a deep breath, picked up the empty canvas bag she had brought with her, and opened the car door. "Let's go."

She took the spare key from under the right plant pot and opened the front door. The house was silent, but apart from a vague mustiness in the air there was nothing different about the place. It was as if the last few days had been nothing more than a bad dream. Feeling her way through the darkened rooms, she led Decker to the back of the house and the yard beyond.

As soon as she stepped into the yard, Rocky began to screech with excitement. In the moonlight she could see him standing by the wire mesh of the large wooden pen. His teeth shone white as he grinned madly at her, delighted to see her. She ran to the door, released the bar and latch, and walked in. He jumped on her, chattering and screeching, almost knocking her over as he hugged her. Decker moved to support her, and Rocky suddenly turned on him, baring his fangs.

"No, Rocky," she said quickly, stroking Decker's face. "He's not hurting me. He's a friend." Decker froze and didn't move while Rocky sniffed him suspiciously. Then Rocky reached out a long hand and roughly prodded his shoulder. It was a grudging gesture done more for her benefit than Decker's, but it signaled that the ape accepted him.

Kathy checked the store of food in the automatic dispenser at the far end of the pen and could see it was almost exhausted, as was the tank of drinking water beside it. The pen was in need of cleaning, but otherwise Rocky seemed unaffected by his recent neglect. Once she was reassured on this point, Kathy went to a tire hanging from a tree in the middle of the pen. Reaching into the bottom of the tire, she felt for a ridge of duct tape and pulled it off. Attached to the tape was a key.

Then she walked over to the trunk, unlocked the padlock, and raised a lid. She felt a rush of relief when she saw her files and personal memorabilia inside. All untouched. All safe. She reached for her canvas bag. "It's all here," she said.

Decker checked his watch as he stood guard. "Great, now hurry up."

"Don't worry, it'll take only a moment. I'll just get a few of Rocky's things; then we can go."

"Rocky's things? Why?"

She busied herself sifting through her journals, taking all the important ones, and putting them in the bag. She picked up the complete selection of computer discs and stacked them in too. "Well, we can't leave him here."

Decker shook his head in exasperation. "Why the hell not?" he demanded. "He's big enough and ugly enough to look after himself. For Christ's sake, Kathy, he's not the one in trouble; you are. Where the hell are you going to keep him?"

"I know somebody in a zoo down at Atascadero who'll take care of him until all this blows over. Come on," Kathy said casually, picking up the bag. "Let's go."

Decker frowned but said nothing as the three walked out of Rocky's pen, past the tall Douglas fir, toward the house. She smiled up at the dark sky bejeweled with stars as Rocky walked beside her, his hand in hers. She had begun to feel hopeful for the first time in days when suddenly Rocky let go of her hand and disappeared into the dark. Turning in surprise, she saw Decker drop the bag of discs and files and launch himself at her. He pushed her to the ground, and rolled her behind the fir tree.

Then she heard them as well, two men coming out of the house, whispering to each other. One of them raised something in his hand, and the whole yard was bathed in light so bright she could only look down at the ground. Three yards beyond the shelter of the large tree trunk, the bag of files was illuminated in the blinding light, its contents spilling onto the grass.

"Shit," said Decker beside her, pushing her tight against the trunk. "What the hell are they doing back here?"

"I don't know," she said in shock, as if he actually expected her to know the answer.

"Rambo was a great help, wasn't he?" spit Decker.

"Rocky." She corrected him automatically. The light was now shining directly on the tree they were hiding behind.

Decker scowled and retrieved a gun from his shoulder holster. "More like Bambi if you ask me."

"I told you, he's no longer violent."

"I wouldn't sound so goddamned proud if I were you. Right now we could do with some good old-fashioned aggression."

She heard the men walk toward the open bag of evidence and pick it up. It was frustrating, but there was nothing she or Decker could do about it. The light was so brilliant that if they moved a fraction beyond the protection of the tree, they would be not only blinded but starkly visible too. "I told you," she hissed. "Rocky gets aggressive now only when I'm under threat."

Decker turned and gave her a wry grin, which despite the circumstances made her smile. "Kathy, I don't know about you and Bambi, but I've been under threat before, and trust me, this qualifies."

Suddenly the spit of a silenced gun cut through the night, and she felt the thudding impact of a bullet hit the tree. Then a man's voice said, "Come out, or we'll come and get you."

25

"Madeline, this is getting out of hand. Perhaps we should slow down, look at what we're doing." Alice Prince adjusted her glasses and toyed with her pendant.

The FBI director sat back in her chair and drummed her fingers on the desk. They were alone in Naylor's office on the fifth floor of the Hoover Building on Pennsylvania Avenue. It was an oppressive masculine room. Dark wood paneling covered the lead-lined walls designed to thwart electronic surveillance devices. Photographs of famous predecessors lined the walls. But the most striking feature was the obsessive neatness of everything in the office. The piles of reading were stacked so perfectly that not one book or leaf of paper protruded. Even the pads and pencils on Naylor's desk were in regimented lines. But then even as a child she had exerted extreme control over her environment, even more than Alice had. "Relax, will you, Alice? Everything is under control."

Alice Prince rose from the small conference table and paced around the room. Everything wasn't under control. Most important, she wasn't under control. She was used to planning projects like Conscience and Crime Zero at an academic level but generally left the operational aspects to others. Madeline Naylor had murdered two men today, and she had participated.

Even though Madeline had administered the kiss of death to Burbank, Alice felt a direct responsibility for killing the President. After all, she had genetically engineered the viral vector Madeline had smeared on her lips, had created it to target the heart cells of a particular individual, the President, matching that man's unique DNA sequence, seeking out any fatal flaw it found there, bringing it forward in time. Harmless to any other human, Madeline's kiss had been fatal to Bob Burbank.

It had served its purpose. Citing the constitutional amendment of 2002, both the Senate and House had sworn Pamela in as President two hours ago, effectively bringing forward her inauguration. The Vice President had expressed no objection.

But Madeline had killed the journalist too. Just for asking the wrong questions. Kathy Kerr was now also on the loose, and she was probably the only person on earth with comparable knowledge of viral vectors. If anyone had the technical talent and experience to stop Crime Zero, it was Dr. Kerr.

As far as Alice was concerned, things were far from under control. "Perhaps we should cancel Crime Zero. Just stick with Conscience. There's still time."

Madeline Naylor sat forward and shook her head. "Stop worrying. You know that Crime Zero is the only long-term option. We've discussed this already, and you know the arguments better than I do. Everything is going to be OK. Kathy Kerr isn't going to be a problem. Look, Pamela's going to be arriving any moment now. I'll explain everything after she's gone. Just stick with what we agreed to say. No more. No less. OK?"

Alice sat down and released a huge sigh.

"C'mon, Ali, you know I'm right. Haven't I always been right in the past? Think of Libby. Think of the future. Think of our vision. Just focus on the benefits—for everyone. OK?"

The phone rang, and Madeline picked it up. She listened for a second, then looked up, her dark eyes willing Alice's collusion. "She's here."

*   *   *

The recently sworn-in President threw two sheets of paper on the table. "I've got ten minutes. Tell me what the hell's going on. I've got enough on my plate without worrying about Conscience. The last thing I need now is some journalist raising questions about the very project that got me elected."

Pamela Weiss was dressed in black, and her face was pale with stress.

"Pamela, we can explain any concerns you have," said Madeline coolly. She sipped a glass of mineral water and looked completely unfazed by Pamela's anger.

"OK, this journalist Hank Butcher has given me this list of issues and questions to respond to before he goes public with new evidence." Pamela slapped her hand on the papers she had just flung onto the table. "I'll go through them for you. First of all, who the hell's Dr. Kathy Kerr? She claims that Project Conscience is little more than a test before it moves on to something more drastic, which apparently involves *killing* criminals with dangerous genes rather than curing them. This of course would be preposterous except that apparently there have been some deaths at San Quentin caused by a mutation of your vector."

Pamela straightened and walked around the table with her arms crossed, the fingers of her right hand drumming on her left arm. She wasn't just angry, Alice realized now; she was hurt too.

"And that's not all," said Pamela through gritted teeth. "She also claims that the serum we secretly tested on criminals is actually different from the one that gained FDA approval. And that you had her committed to a mental asylum so she couldn't expose this 'conspiracy.' "

Alice fingered the teardrop amulet around her neck and breathed deeply. Madeline was staring right at her. "Well, let's start with Dr. Kathy Kerr," Alice said. "I may have mentioned her before. She's a British-born scientist, and it was her initial project on curbing aggression in male primates that gave me the idea for Conscience. I recruited her nine years ago to head up one of the research teams, and she has been working for me ever since. She is brilliant but unbalanced. Apart from her original work she has contributed little over the last few years, and she's bitter. When we gained FDA approval for a serum she played no part in developing, she became defensive and angry. I promised her shared credit, but she refused."

Alice felt uncomfortable with the lies, but they were what was required. Madeline had said so.

Pamela frowned. "So what are you saying? That she invented these claims out of spite?"

"Mainly, yes."

Pamela's frown deepened. "Mainly? You mean, some of them are true? What about the San Quentin deaths? A whole list of symptoms is on this sheet of paper, symptoms that end up with either suicide or a brain hemorrhage."

"That did happen, yes."

"What!"

"But it was a mistake."

"A mistake? That's not what Kerr told Hank Butcher. It's no goddamn wonder he thinks our endgame is killing violent criminals. How did it happen?"

Alice adjusted her glasses. "Well, those men received corrupted samples. It was a one-time occurrence. A routine check highlighted the bad batch, and we managed to stop it before it was sent out to any more test subjects. The fatal samples had nothing to do with the proper serum we tested on the others. Somehow the batch was tampered with."

"Tampered with?"

"We can't prove anything. But when we checked all our procedures, the only weak link was the involvement of Kathy Kerr. She has access to most of the ViroVector facilities, and she has the knowledge. It would appear now that she has been disaffected for some time, and perhaps she sabotaged the batch to subvert the project. Luckily we discovered it before the problem became more widespread."

"But what about Axelman, Alice? It could look like you tried to kill him in revenge for Libby."

Madeline stepped in before Alice could reply. "Alice didn't know Axelman was responsible until after he had

been executed. That was entirely coincidental. And before
you ask, Pamela," she added, "yes, we did cover their deaths
up. There was nothing we could do about them. They were
on death row anyway, and any scandal would only have
jeopardized the success of Conscience and your election.
Right or wrong, whatever we did we did for you because we
wanted to protect you. The country needs you as President,
and it needs Project Conscience. Nothing we did was intended to betray you. We are your most loyal friends. We
would never intentionally hurt you. You have to believe
that."

Pamela stared at them, thinking through what they were
saying. She looked so tired and beleaguered Alice could tell
she wanted to believe them in order to focus on other more
important issues. "What if the journalist can prove Axelman's DNA was changed?"

"It doesn't matter," said Madeline emphatically. "His
scare story about intentionally killing criminals doesn't
stack up. There have been sixteen thousand men treated over
the last eight or so years, and all are fine. Plus Axelman's
body has been cremated along with the other five in San
Quentin. So no further proof can be found as to *why* their
DNA changed. More to the point, Axelman was a killer. He
had no family, nor did the others. Even if the journalist could
get all the proof in the world, no one would care. This Kathy
Kerr has obviously done some digging and is using whatever
she found to cause trouble. But she has no real proof of anything."

Pamela rubbed her temples. "But what about the FDA-
approved serum? Kerr claims it was developed only four
years ago, long after you started unauthorized trials on criminals. Are the serums different?"

Alice shrugged. "Again, strictly speaking, yes. There are
minute differences, but nothing important. Certainly nothing
to trouble the FDA."

Pamela sat down and held her head in her hands. "Then
why the hell didn't you gain FDA approval for the one we
did test?"

"Because we improved it. There were some minor concerns with the original serum, involving possible side effects."

"Such as?"

Alice paused, and Pamela leaned forward, waiting. "There was a low-level risk of causing testicular and prostate cancer," said Alice.

"Cancer?" Pamela almost shouted the word. "The treatment we tested, the treatment that won me the election gives men cancer?"

"No, it doesn't. There is merely a very low risk that it might, so low it's hardly statistically significant. But we thought it best to iron out even this risk. So we developed an improved serum, which we tested on healthy human volunteers to gain FDA approval. That vector is Version Nine. Naturally all subsequent treatments will use this new vector."

Pamela struggled to remain calm. "So you lied to the FDA? And you lied to me?"

Madeline Naylor shook her head. "Pamela, you're missing the point. We have tested over sixteen thousand men, and all have benefited. Some risks needed to be taken; otherwise the whole project would have collapsed. Perhaps we should have been more open with you, but I decided against it because if we told you, it would compromise your position."

"Well, I'm compromised now."

"No, you're not. If the journalist had anything concrete, he would have used it. Kathy Kerr is simply stirring things up for reasons of her own. She is a bitter woman with a family history of mental instability. She has no real proof, and frankly, even if she did, it wouldn't matter now. The public and the media have bought into your vision of a crime-free future. They want it to work. Pedantic quibbling about the finer points of how one genetic vaccine differs from another won't change anything. The fact is, in the future all criminals will be treated by a Food and Drug Administration–approved vaccine that works. That's all anyone cares about. The journalist doesn't have a story. Trust me on this."

Pamela looked down at the sheet of paper, clearly wrestling with the issues. Alice could see she was weakening. "Still, what we did was wrong."

Madeline set her jaw. "*You* did nothing wrong. We did. But if you want to come clean and resign, go ahead. Throw away the chance of the millennium to cure one of the main scourges of society. I'll resign too, if you like, but it would be pointless. Yes, we did a few small wrongs, but we achieved a far greater good."

"What about Kathy Kerr's claim that you authorized her abduction and held her in an FBI mental facility to keep her quiet?"

Madeline snorted and clapped her hands together. "Well, that just proves she's making trouble. A mental asylum sounds like the perfect place for her, but I didn't put her in one. Pamela, frankly you have more important things to worry about than some deranged scientist with a grudge and a journalist trying to win a Pulitzer. Ignore them. I'm sorry if we hurt you by not telling you everything, but this is exactly why we didn't. Let us handle these minor annoyances, while you prevent Iraq from starting World War Three."

Before Pamela had time to answer, a cell phone on the table rang. Alice picked it up and listened. "Yes, Special Agent Toshack, the President is here. Yes, she will be with you in five minutes. Thank you." She smiled and put the phone down. "Well, Madam President, your Secret Service detail is waiting to escort you to the Pentagon."

Pamela stood then, and Alice rose from her seat to embrace her. "Please, Pam," said Alice, "always remember that we are your friends. If you can rely on no one else, you can rely on us."

"The way I see it, Pam," said Madeline Naylor, moving to hug her tightly in sinewy arms, "is that you have embarked on a great journey and it is our job to keep you from falling. I for one will do anything to stop that from happening. Anything."

Pamela studied them both for a moment, then gave a small nod and a smile. She seemed satisfied, even touched.

"Just tell me one thing before I go. What are you going to do about Kathy Kerr? She sounds like a real loose cannon."

Madeline laughed at that. "Don't worry about it, Pamela. She isn't your problem. She's ours. We'll talk to her."

Alice watched Pamela leave, escorted by two Secret Service agents. It appeared that their performance had allayed Pamela's fears, but Kathy Kerr was still most definitely a problem.

After the President had left, Alice silently reviewed the meeting. Madeline seemed to be doing the same. Alice checked her watch. She had arranged for the company jet to fly her back to San Francisco in an hour's time.

"Do you think she believes us?" Alice asked, preparing to leave.

Madeline nodded. "Yes, because she has no proof. And because she wants to."

"But what do we do about Kathy?"

Madeline smiled and lay back in her chair, putting her hands behind her head like a man. Her dark eyes glowed, and she looked surprisingly confident. "Well, Hank Butcher told me that Dr. Peters let her escape. And Jackson called me just before Pamela arrived to say that Dr. Peters has now been punished—permanently. Jackson's hot on Kathy's trail. He's pretty sure he knows where to find her. He knows who helped her get out."

"Who?"

Madeline paused and raised her left eyebrow. "Luke Decker."

Alice felt something hard and cold contract in her stomach. The last time Alice had seen Decker was when he led her out of that macabre gallery of death his father had consigned her daughter to. "So that's how Kathy found out about Axelman?"

"Yes, it seems they knew each other from way back. Anyway, it doesn't matter now. Jackson's people are specialists in this area."

Leading her out of the office, Madeline said, "By the way, did you read TITANIA's latest E-mail? Everything's in place. Now that we've got rid of Burbank we just have to sit and wait. As for Kathy Kerr and Luke Decker, they won't be standing much longer. Much bigger dominoes than they have fallen already."

In the black limousine driving her to the Pentagon, President Weiss reached into her coat and retrieved Hank Butcher's list of questions and the computer disc he had given her. She handed the disc to Toshack, the head of her Secret Service detail. He was a broad-shouldered man of medium height. He had sandy hair and a dimple in his chin, which made him look as if he were always just about to smile. But he rarely did.

"I need you to get this disc to Major General Allardyce at USAMRIID. Tell him I want a full analysis done. I also need you to check out someone called Dr. Kathy Kerr. Don't involve any other agencies. How soon can you get me some answers?"

"How soon do you want them?"

"Yesterday."

"That shouldn't be a problem, Madam President."

26

As he pushed Kathy Kerr closer to the trunk of the tree, Luke Decker's guts churned with frustration. He was trapped. Checking the magazine of his SIG pistol, he wondered if he could reach around the tree and shoot out the light. He doubted it. To judge from the intensity of the dazzle, it was an FBI-issue handheld Maglite. Fitted with a two-thousand-watt bulb and a two-inch-diameter reflector, it could send out an adjustable beam so searing it bleached night, blinding the naked eye to anything, including the source. It was the flashlight equivalent of a power water hose.

"I suggest you come out from behind that tree," said the voice with the light. "If we have to come and get you, we can't guarantee your safety."

"Yeah, right," grunted Decker. "Like our safety is their big concern." He looked to his left and, shielding his eyes, could just make out Rocky's pen but not much else. All he knew with absolute certainty was that the voice wasn't Jackson's. Since Jackson would almost certainly have done all the talking, he probably wasn't here. But there would still be at least two of his cronies here. And that was enough. One only had to hold the light while the other circled.

"Kathy," he said as calmly as he could, "keep your eyes

214

peeled behind us—for anyone coming around to cut us off. Use the beam's light to see any shadow or movement."

To her credit, although Kathy's eyes were wide with fear, she was calm. "What are you going to do?" she asked.

"No fucking idea, but whatever it is, I'd better do it quick." Taking a deep breath, he considered his options. But there was only one: to roll around the right of the tree and fire at the voice. He probably wouldn't hit anything, but at least it should make the man move the damn flashlight, and then Kathy could make a run for it. He guessed they would hesitate before shooting Kathy here. Even the director of the FBI would find it difficult to explain shooting Kathy Kerr in her own yard without a good reason. He, on the other hand, was going to shoot at whomever he damn well could. "Kathy," he said, not looking at her, "when I start firing, run to the left and get the hell out of here."

"But what about you?"

"For chrissakes, just this once, don't argue with me."

He heard her start to protest, then sigh. "OK."

Tensing his muscles, he gripped the gun in both hands and was just about to roll around the tree and let off as many of the seventeen slugs in the SIG's magazine as possible when he heard a fierce roar and a bloodcurdling scream.

The intense light suddenly faltered, and Luke heard the spitting thud of a silenced gun being fired. The flashlight beam now began to flail about madly, describing arcs of light in the night sky like some frenetic laser show. In the stroboscopic chaos Decker could just make out a man wrestling with a ferocious beast. A second man was sprinting toward them, training his gun on the two figures dancing their frenzied jig. The man with the gun was obviously scared of hitting his screaming partner. Not waiting another second, Decker grabbed Kathy by the arm and dragged her to her feet.

"Come on," he shouted. "Let's go."

"What about the evidence?"

Decker yanked her arm, pulling her behind him. "Forget it. Run."

"But we can't leave Rocky!"

Just then the screaming stopped, and the flashlight flew through the air and landed on the ground in front of them. Its beam pointed away, and in his rush Decker almost missed the fact that the flashlight was still held in a human hand attached to a severed arm. He jumped over it and grimaced. "I wouldn't worry about Rocky," he said, pulling Kathy past the debris, hoping she hadn't seen it. "I think he can look after himself."

But Decker knew he was mistaken when he heard the hiss of two silenced shots. Rocky groaned once and then fell silent. The sound of his body falling to the ground was unmistakable. "Come on," Decker shouted, dragging Kathy through the French windows into the house.

Outside the front of the house they passed the Chrysler of Jackson's men. After firing four silenced bullets into the two front tires, Decker ran to the rental, clambered in, and waited for Kathy to climb into the passenger seat. Calmly he placed the key in the ignition and gunned the motor. As Decker turned his car around and accelerated down Mendoza Drive, he glanced in the rearview mirror and saw a figure emerge from the house and raise his arms into the firing position. Suddenly Decker felt a cold feeling in the pit of his stomach. But it wasn't the shots that worried him. It was the fact that the attacker would have seen his car and now could easily trace the rental to him.

What if his involvement had already been discovered? The fact that he would be in danger didn't bother him. The novelty of that had long worn off. But he wasn't worried about himself.

This was getting out of hand. Way out of hand.

He turned to Kathy beside him. She looked pale. "We've got to hurry," he said, and pressed his foot down on the gas.

Kathy Kerr swallowed the bile in her mouth as they sped on Route 101 toward the lights of downtown San Francisco. The evidence they needed, their only hope of proving the allegations, was back at her house.

She didn't notice another gray Chrysler speeding past in the opposite direction. Every car she did see seemed to contain smiling people, living normal, unworried lives, oblivious of how hers had changed.

As they passed the sign to the airport, she turned to Decker, but he kept his face straight ahead. He drove as fast as he could, but it seemed he wasn't fleeing *from* their pursuers so much as rushing *to* somewhere. Decker slapped his hand on the steering wheel. "Shit, shit, shit. How could I be so goddamned stupid?"

"What?"

"If they find out about me, they'll use Matty to get to us. We've got to get him somewhere safe as fast as possible."

Realizing what he was saying put their situation into perspective for Kathy. This wasn't only about stopping Madeline Naylor and Alice Prince anymore. Perhaps Luke had been right when he said that she should have just walked away. What had she achieved by staying—except to put those who had helped her in danger?

In the city Decker took South Van Ness Avenue toward the Marina. They passed Pacific Heights and then turned onto Broadway. Driving in silence, Kathy saw Decker's frown deepen and his eyes narrow as they pulled up outside Matty's Victorian house. The front door was wide open; the windows were dark.

Decker curbed the car and killed the engine. His voice was hushed when he spoke. "Gramps always leaves at least one light on," he said. "And even he doesn't leave the front door wide open. Kathy, wait here while I check inside." He jumped out, ran up the steps, and disappeared into the house.

Ignoring his request, Kathy opened her door and more cautiously followed Decker inside. Inside, she clicked on the hall switch, but nothing happened. It was as if all the lights had been fused. Gradually her eyes adjusted to the gloom, using the moonlight and illumination from the streetlamps filtering in through the windows to make out her surroundings. To her left the dining room was a wreck. Drawers had been pulled out, their contents strewn over the table and floor. Chairs had been upended, and the upholstery ripped out. To her right through the open double doors of the TV room she could make out similar carnage. This either was a burglary or meant to look like one. But if this was the work of Jackson and his men, how could they have found out about Decker and Matty so quickly?

"Gramps? Where are you?" Decker's voice came from the next-floor landing. Kathy went up the stairs after him. Before she got to the top, she heard Decker call his grandfather again, but this time it was less a question than a cry of disbelief.

At the top of the stairs Kathy ran to her left, to the music room that overlooked the bay. There was something on the landing ahead of her. Looking down, she saw it was Matty's golden Labrador, Brutus. His tongue hung out of his mouth; his eyes were wide open and glassy. Two red holes punctured the glossy fur of his neck. A shiver ran through her. The bastards had shot a goddamn guide dog. Stepping around Brutus, she saw that the door to the music room was open, as were the large French windows looking out onto the balcony and the bay beyond. A brisk breeze was blowing into the room, seeming to carry the moonlight in with it. Light streamed through the open windows, forming a ghostly trapezium on the rug. The rest of the room was in shadow, but she could see the debris: photographs knocked off the piano; a violin thrown to the floor, the metronome shattered beside it.

In the moonlight in the center of the rug she saw Decker crouching down, tears of silver on his cheeks. He cradled his grandfather in his arms, studying the man's hands. When Decker spoke, his words were so choked that she had to put her hands to her mouth, to stop herself from crying out. With her horror came fresh guilt. They had done this to find her.

"They broke his fucking fingers," Decker said, turning to her, his eyes almost luminous in the light. "Even the goddamned Nazis didn't do that to him."

He gripped his grandfather tighter to him, trying to contain the grief and fury welling up inside him.

Acid guilt seared through him when he thought of how this brave old man had suffered and died alone, trying to protect him, this man who had already endured and given so much. Jackson must have uncovered his involvement with Kathy's escape and then sent one car to check on her house while he had come here. But how had Jackson found out about him? Dr. Peters couldn't have told him; Peters didn't know who he was. And they couldn't have traced his car this quickly. The only answer that made sense was that Hank Butcher had talked.

Decker's rage and guilt were nothing compared with his feeling of loss. He wanted to scream it out loud. Without Matty he felt cast adrift, anchorless in a fickle sea, his compass gone, and with it a lifeline to his own decency. Matty was the antidote to the knowledge that Axelman's blood ran in his veins; just knowing he was descended from him gave Decker hope.

But now Matty was dead.

Looking down on his lined face, Decker closed the staring blue eyes. He stroked Matty's smooth scalp and vowed that he would avenge him, make some sense of his death.

He heard Kathy kneel close beside him and felt her arms move around his shoulders. "I'm so sorry, Luke," she whispered in a small voice. Her soft hands moved to his neck, caressing him with the same gentleness with which he stroked his grandfather. "If you hadn't helped me, perhaps this would never have happened."

"But it has happened," he said. He turned and looked at her; the hurt in her eyes. "Kathy, you were right. This has to be about more than just Conscience. We've got to find out what they're really doing, and we've got to stop them. I couldn't stand it if Matty died for nothing—"

Then he heard the sound. Decker froze, and he could tell from Kathy's sharp intake of breath that she had heard it too.

A footstep. No more than a yard or two behind them.

Then a man's voice, deep and smooth. "You'll need help" was all it said.

Swiveling around, Decker saw an enormous figure step out of the shadows and tower over him. Two other men stood behind the figure. It took Decker a moment to recognize the blue-black hair and strong patrician nose of Joey Barzini. The man knelt, but he was so tall he still appeared to be standing. In the moonlight his clear blue eyes were moist and his chin was set in a determined cast as he looked at Matty's crumpled body. Like a father tentatively touching his firstborn, he reached across and gently inspected Matty's broken fingers. Decker watched the big man wince and shake his head. "My friend, my friend, what have they done to you?" he whispered. Then he turned to Decker, his voice suddenly harsh. "Your grandfather called earlier and told me you were in some kind of serious trouble. He explained the problem, and I said I'd come around tonight to see if I could help." He paused. "I wish I'd come earlier."

Joey Barzini looked at Kathy and then back to Decker. "The only way I can help Matty now is by helping you two. Come with me. I need to know more about what's going on." The man paused for a moment, and Decker considered what he really knew about him. Although Barzini was supposed to be legitimate, his list of friends and family read like a who's who of organized crime. Still, his grandfather liked and rated him as highly as anybody, highly enough to call Barzini for help when he and Kathy were in trouble. If Barzini was good enough for Matty, he was certainly good enough for him.

"Luke," Barzini said, as if reading distrust in his look, "I know from Matty how you feel about my family connections. I'm often not too proud of them myself." Suddenly his noble face creased into a smile, a momentary flash of gleaming white teeth. "But trust me, at times they have their uses."

27

FBI Director Naylor was annoyed that a group of them had somehow escaped detection. She pulled the trigger and then moved on. It infuriated her that however fast she killed them, they always came back. She could never totally eradicate them.

Brandishing her insecticide spray like a pistol, she patrolled the neat rows of yucca plants, African violets, and rare orchids in the conservatory garden of her house in the exclusive Washington suburb of Alexandria. Above the glass roof of the climatically controlled room a frigid moon looked down from a cloud-riddled sky. The interior garden was effectively another room of her house, adjoining the spacious living room. Entirely made of glass, it allowed her almost total control over everything that grew there.

When she was finally satisfied everything was as it should be, she opened the inner door to the living room, poured herself a glass of Jack Daniel's, and lay back on the recliner by the large TV in the corner. Two walls were taken up with a large stone fireplace and the entrance to the conservatory. A third was covered from floor to ceiling with books covering every theme, particularly history and gardening. And the fourth was similarly bedecked with tapes and compact discs.

Naylor had showered and wore a blue robe, her long

white hair flowing loosely to her shoulders. Her pale face devoid of makeup looked almost translucent, like paper-thin mother-of-pearl. She pointed the remote at the multimedia system. As the music of Wagner filled the room, her mind traveled with it, away from the responsibilities of office, away from Crime Zero, Kathy Kerr, and Luke Decker to a kinder, more peaceful place.

According to TITANIA, everything was in order; so Naylor convinced herself for now that she could do no more. She would retire soon and set the alarm for six o'clock; she needed only a few hours' sleep.

As always when she wanted to relax, Naylor thought of the garden and protecting her beloved plants. As she allowed her mind to wander, she went back to her fourteenth birthday and Alice's gift.

Apart from Alice, Madeline has no friends at school. Most of the other kids regard her aggressive manner and white, spiky hair as too weird or too frightening. So it's not surprising that on her fourteenth birthday she receives no presents and cards. Especially as it falls on a Saturday.

But she's not unhappy. Her grandmother Mrs. Preston is pretty cool really. The old woman forbids her to invite any boys around and won't allow men into the house, saying they're "different" and can't be trusted. But Madeline doesn't mind that at all, and her grandmother lets Alice come around. On her birthday the old woman makes Madeline a special breakfast of strawberries and cream with a glass of chocolate milk.

It's June, and the sun's shining. After breakfast Madeline goes out into the garden. Her grandmother's house is a rambling mansion, and Madeline loves exploring all the old rooms, but the best parts are the gardens. They're so big that Madeline is allowed to have a small walled section all of her own. Here she can plant and do what she likes. She's put up a sign on the rickety gate forbidding entry. Even her grandmother knocks before entering when she brings her cold lemonade and stale Oreos.

On her birthday Madeline tends her flowers and pulls out

her weeds as usual. She has created a strictly ordered world with regimented beds and weed-free paths. Rows of sunflowers stand to attention next to manicured marigolds. But today, as with most days, much of her time is spent killing the ants infesting the pathways and beds. This is the one place where she can banish everything she hates in the world outside. Here she can pretend that the bad men who killed her father will be punished and that the mother who left her will return. Here she can control everything.

But the invading ants keep wrecking the fantasy. Whatever she does, whatever she tries, she can't get rid of them. The beds are pockmarked with holes she's dug trying to find their nests. And in each corner of the square walled garden there is an empty mayonnaise jar full of dead ants. The jars are intended to act as a deterrent to the others, but they seem only to intensify the problem. However fast she kills them, the faster they return.

"Madeline, Madeline," calls a small, excited voice from over the wall. "Are you there?"

"Yeah, come over."

Alice's backyard is on the other side of the far wall. She often climbs over to play in Madeline's secret garden. Watching her friend scrabble awkwardly over the wall makes Madeline laugh.

"Don't laugh or I won't give you your present," warns Alice as she falls onto the earth by the sunflowers. Her glasses are crooked on her nose, and despite the warm weather, she wears a long-sleeved dress.

"Present?" Despite herself, Madeline can't help feeling excited. "You got me a present?"

"Only a little one." Alice looks at the holes in the ground. "But it's a good one." She reaches into her bag, and as she does, one of her long sleeves rides up and Madeline sees a purple and yellow bruise on her forearm. It is so livid Madeline can see the finger marks where a large hand has squeezed her arm.

"Who did that to you?" she asks. She doesn't need to ask what it is. Madeline's own father had hit her enough times to teach her about bruises.

Alice gives a flustered shake of her head and quickly pulls the sleeve down. "It's nothing."

"Was it your dad?" probes Madeline. Alice's father is a respected doctor, but this doesn't surprise Madeline. Her dad was a respected cop, and he still beat her. She feels angry for her friend but also a small stab of satisfaction. She's always envied Alice's having a perfect mom and a dad, so it makes her feel closer to her knowing that her dad's bad too. "Does he hit you a lot?"

But Alice won't be drawn out. "Do you want your present or not?"

Madeline drops the matter but stores it away. "Yeah, sure."

When Alice pulls the tiny parcel out of the bag and puts it in her hand, Madeline's initial reaction is disappointment. The blue paper-wrapped tube is smaller than one of her fingers. "Open it," says Alice, nervously straightening her glasses. "I hope you like it."

Madeline peels off the blue paper and reveals a tiny bottle. It looks like one she's seen her grandmother use for her eyedrops.

Madeline opens it and smells it. "Maple syrup?" She starts to squeeze a drop on her finger so she can taste it, but Alice screams at her, "Don't eat it. You mustn't eat it."

"Why not? What is it?"

Alice takes it from her and bends down near a line of ants at the bottom of the wall. She removes a leaf from one of the sunflower stalks, places it on the floor in the path of the ants, then drops one bead of syrup from the small bottle on the leaf. "Watch," she says.

Madeline sees how at first the ants walk around the drop and then some start to circle the syrup and feed off it. "Is it poison?" she asks, delighted.

"It's better than just poison."

The feeding ants move on after a moment and continue in line, making way for other ants to feed on the droplet. "So, what does it do?"

"Well," says Alice with a frown, "according to the stuff I've read, the maple syrup and chemicals I mixed together should attract the ants to make them eat it. Then, when they go back to their nest, they will puke up what they've eaten for the queen ants to feed on. The chemicals should kill the queens before they lay any eggs. The base poison is trichlorfon, but I've added some refinements. It's slow-acting, so it doesn't kill just the ants that eat it but the whole nest as well. And you don't have to dig up anything; the ants do the work for you."

Madeline is so impressed and delighted she laughs for joy. "Awesome. You made it yourself?"

"Oh, yes. It wasn't very difficult. Dad had some stuff in his shed, and the school labs had everything else. It should get rid of your ant problem, though, completely."

Beep-beep-beep.

The insistent tone of the speakerphone by the TV interrupted Naylor's reverie. The volume automatically lowered on the laser disc, and a soft feminine voice issued from the speakers: "You have an override phone message on the multimedia system. Please pick up."

Naylor thought for a moment, regaining her bearings, resenting the intrusion into the dome of self-reflection she had built for herself. Reaching for the phone, she was still thinking back to how in a matter of weeks Alice's magic potion had eradicated virtually every single ant from her garden.

"Madeline, it's Bill McCloud. I'm in the incident room at headquarters looking at the satellite screen. You might want to come in and see this. I think Iraq is about to invade Kuwait."

FBI Headquarters.
Washington, D.C. 3:07 A.M.

Half an hour later Director Naylor was in the FBI incident room on the ground floor of the Hoover Building on Pennsylvania Avenue, looking at an eight-foot-by-five-foot screen. To her right was Deputy Director Bill McCloud. He looked even more grizzled than usual. Three other senior bureau officials sat around the table in the dimly lit room. A flask of strong coffee sat on a hot plate by the door, and its aroma filled the air.

"They're going to goddamn do it," McCloud said, rubbing his steel gray eyes. His normally laid-back Texan drawl was tense.

"Looks like it," Naylor said, staring at the screen. She tried to sound calm, but it was difficult. According to TITANIA, this shouldn't be happening. "Are all national contingencies in place?"

"Absolutely," said Associate Deputy Director Ray Tate, a short, barrel-chested man who ran the investigations section of the bureau. "We've updated our lists of Iraqi sympathizers. The key threats are under surveillance and can be pulled in at a moment's notice. All major terrorist targets across the country are on full alert."

Naylor nodded silently and kept her eyes on the screen. The picture she was seeing was a feed from CNN, which was as good as any government satellite surveillance. In the top right-hand corner the gold CNN logo looked faint against the pale background. At first the overall image meant nothing to her, thousands of dark shapes moving over a light yellow backdrop. It looked like a microscope picture of diseased cells spreading across an organism.

"Do you want to hear the CNN commentary?" one of the agents asked behind her.

"Yes," she said, not wanting to engage in conversation, her eyes riveted to the screen.

"This is incredible," said a male commentator in a British accent. "Using our access to the Kamagachi high-resolution satellite, we are able to bring you what might prove to be the first-ever live pictures of a war starting. You are watching history in the making. As I speak, our engineers are trying to increase the magnification still further. It's a clear day in Iraq, and soon we should be able to make out each individual tank. They are now less than twelve miles from the thirty-second parallel. And I don't need to remind anyone watching how eight years ago that line in the sand moved from being simply a no-fly area to a no-go area for any Iraqi military personnel. If the Republican Guard cross that line into southern Iraq, they will be declaring their intent to invade Kuwait. Once that happens, and it looks like it will, then the United Nations coalition forces led by the United States will be forced to act."

Naylor sat forward in her chair. At least this vindicated the decision to target the Iraqi Army as the amplification zone for the Phase 2 launch of Crime Zero. Not only had that nation shown itself to be the most belligerent, but it was also an excellent "real world" test before giving final sanction to the Phase 3 rollout. They had even pulled Phase 2 forward because of the Iraq crisis. However, now it looked as if they hadn't pulled it forward far enough. This shouldn't be happening. Not a war. Not after this much time had elapsed.

Taking a deep drink of black coffee, she watched as the screen faded and then returned at a higher magnification. She could now clearly discern the contours of the sand and the markings on individual tanks, thousands of them moving across the arid plain in ordered rows. She could even make out the helmets of the commanders protruding from the gun turrets. She wondered if Alice was watching this. Pamela certainly would be, probably in the War Room deep below the Pentagon.

"President Weiss and other world leaders have confirmed that the UN forces will attack Iraq's tanks and destroy them if they cross the line," continued the reporter. "The question on everyone's lips is, What will the Iraqi president do next? Reports suggest he has at least ten warheads loaded with a new doomsday virus aimed at selected sites around the world, each one ready to be launched if his troops are stopped from reclaiming what he regards as the Iraqi province of Kuwait and all its oil.

"But if Iraq unleashes biological weapons, then the coalition allies have pledged to mount a nuclear strike against Baghdad. This is surely a baptism of fire for Pamela Weiss, the new American President. If there are any who still question whether a woman has the necessary resolve to fight a war, their questions may soon be answered."

As the satellite camera panned across the expanse of desert, the screen mottled with the dark shapes of the machines of war. Perhaps TITANIA was wrong, she thought. Perhaps the computer's projections were off by a day or two, and she was watching the Last War unfold before her.

Staring at all those troops, she was reminded of the ancient historian Herodotus' account of the Persian emperor Xerxes watching his vast army march across the Hellespont into Greece. As he watched them, the emperor had wept. When asked why, Xerxes had replied that he was weeping for all the thousands of men he could see before him because in one hundred years not one would be alive.

Dry-eyed, Naylor sipped her coffee. Only a man could feel such sentiment watching other men about to engage in barbaric war. She knew that all those on the screen, and all the others they represented, would be dead in a fraction of that time. But she felt no sadness, no remorse.

On the screen some of the tanks appeared to be breaking ranks; then the camera angle widened, and the picture shifted back to lower magnification. A red superimposed line suddenly appeared on the screen. Although miles away, it seemed impossibly close to the approaching swarm of ordered black dots. Naylor could imagine Weiss in the War Room along with her advisers, making decisions, thinking that *she* held the future in her hands.

As Naylor squinted at the screen, the ordered phalanx of dots now appeared to be breaking up. Some even seemed to be stopping. But because she was willing them to stop, she couldn't be sure she wasn't just imagining it.

"They are less than ten miles from the thirty-second parallel," continued the commentator, his voice increasing in pitch. "The red line indicates the barrier they must not cross. Wait! Something is happening."

And it was, although for a time Naylor couldn't determine what. Sitting forward, clenching her coffee cup, she watched the tanks slow and then stop.

"Increase the damn magnification," said McCloud beside her.

As if in answer to his command the screen shifted again to such a high level of resolution that Naylor could almost see individual faces. But still nothing seemed to be happening.

"The world is on tenterhooks," announced the commentator. "What are they going to do? Are they waiting for the final command to advance?"

Gradually the ordered pattern began to dissolve into apparent chaos. Some of the tanks were turning around. So were many of the troop carriers. Soldiers in the stationary trucks were jumping out, throwing down their guns, and walking away.

"Jeez," said McCloud softly, "what the fuck's happening here?"

Naylor just stared, willing it to continue.

"If I weren't seeing this with my own eyes, I wouldn't believe it," said the commentator. "Scores of tanks and troops are turning around. Many are throwing their weapons down and just walking back into the desert. It appears that fellow officers and soldiers are forcibly trying to obstruct them. But short of shooting them, which many are now doing, they are helpless to stop them. What is incomprehensible is that the apparent deserters—and there are thousands—are not retaliating. They are simply turning their backs and walking away.

"In over twenty years of reporting on conflicts from around the world, I have never seen anything like this. As the deserters' numbers continue to swell, the rest of the tanks are now turning back as well. It appears as if at the eleventh hour, on the very brink of war, Armageddon has been averted."

The men in the room with Naylor burst into spontaneous applause.

A surge of euphoric vindication swelled in Naylor's chest. TITANIA had been right, its projections perfect. A potential nuclear war had been averted. Mankind had been saved from the mindless aggression of men.

She could imagine the rest of the world, including Weiss,

breathing a huge sigh of relief. Surely after seeing that display, even she might begin to understand the merits of what they were trying to do. Crime Zero was finally happening, and the future was beginning to look brighter.

28

Sipping her red wine and picking at a plate of steaming tagliatelle, Kathy Kerr couldn't relax. The guilt she felt corroded her stomach, but she forced herself to eat because she needed the focus and strength. She couldn't escape the conclusion that this was somehow all her fault.

She sat with Luke Decker and Joey Barzini around a plain stripped wood kitchen table. For a man of Barzini's obvious wealth the large beautiful house in Tiburon was first and foremost a family home. Pictures showing his five—now adult—children at various stages of development were dotted around the large kitchen. But despite the warmth of the place, she still felt on edge, and she could tell Decker did too. There were obviously servants here, but Kathy hadn't seen any yet. Carmela, Barzini's wife, had made the pasta and was now preparing their rooms.

Decker quietly sipped his wine and left his food untouched. He still appeared to be in shock after leaving Barzini's men to handle the police and ensure his grandfather's body was properly taken care of. Barzini had concocted a story of how he had been visiting his friend Matty when he found the body, keeping Decker and Kathy out of it. A limousine had swept the three of them across the Golden Gate Bridge to Tiburon.

When they arrived at his house, Barzini told them that the President had died and Pamela Weiss had been sworn in. Neither of them had really been able to digest the information in the aftershock of the evening's events. Now, just after midnight, Decker looked as exhausted as Kathy felt. But despite Barzini's pleas for them to rest, she and Decker insisted they resolve what was to be done before retiring.

"Start from the beginning and tell me everything," said Barzini, nursing an oversize cup of espresso.

Still unsure whether to trust this huge man, Kathy looked at Decker. Decker returned her look and shrugged, as if in concession.

So for the next fifteen minutes she outlined Project Conscience and the subsequent events to Barzini. She told him about Decker's DNA test and how this had alerted her to Axelman and other death row prisoners in San Quentin receiving lethal gene therapy similar to Conscience. She recounted her abduction by Madeline Naylor's people and her rescue from the Sanctuary by Decker.

She then explained about Decker's contacting the journalist Hank Butcher, using him to pass the evidence to Pamela Weiss and how their evening had unraveled.

"And that's where you were tonight, getting the evidence?" Barzini asked.

"Yes," said Decker quietly. "While Matty was being killed. And we didn't even get it."

"How important was this evidence?" asked Barzini. "What did it really prove?"

"That the unauthorized Conscience criminal trials used a potentially unsafe vector," said Kathy.

Barzini frowned. "Even though the final vector they were proposing to use in the future was FDA-approved?"

"Yes."

Barzini looked puzzled. "Let me get this straight. These people's unauthorized tests had risked the health of a few hardened criminals in order to develop a different but better FDA-approved cure that would help radically reduce violent crime. If this had got out before the election, I could understand its being embarrassing. But now that Conscience is accepted and Weiss is in power, why should they care who knows this? They could easily rationalize it. They certainly don't need to kill people to keep it quiet. Not anymore."

"But the Axelman discs prove that their tests have killed at least one person," said Kathy.

Barzini shook his head. "Surely they could say it was an accident, a mistake. And again the unfortunate casualty was death row scum. The benefits of their work far outweigh any harm. Why kill Matty to get to you? Why kill anyone now? There must be another reason."

Kathy sighed then. "But that's the point. I can *prove* that they intended to kill Axelman. I understand how complex it is to create the viral vector that did this and how close it is to the more benign Conscience. That is why they can't let me alone. They are planning something, and they are worried I might jeopardize their plans."

Decker leaned forward. "The question is what those plans are. Once we know that and can prove it then we can stop them."

Barzini slowly sipped his espresso. "What do you *think* they're planning?"

Kathy shrugged. "Well, I thought they were trying to kill criminals, but Luke doesn't believe that's politically feasible. Still, I can't think of a better hypothesis. Perhaps it's just Category A prisoners they're targeting. It would save money if the worst criminals in prison quietly fell ill and died. And thinning the prison population would be much easier to keep quiet. As far as the voting public is concerned, they don't give a damn about what goes on in a high-security prison. What's out of sight is out of mind. And if taxes fall, who's going to complain?"

Decker frowned. "It doesn't sound right to me, but I can't think of a better theory. All I know is that they killed Matty because of it, and I want to find out what it is and stop it. Come on, Kathy, you've worked with these people. Where would they keep proof of a secret project?"

Kathy Kerr thought for a moment. "I don't know. I've had

pretty good access to ViroVector, but I haven't come across anything. Christ, I didn't even know about their secret trials on Conscience."

"Can't you think of anything suspicious!" said Decker. "I don't know. Documents, that kind of thing."

"The information must be kept somewhere!" said Barzini, warming to the theme. "Could Dr. Prince have it locked away in her office? Perhaps in a safe?"

It was the word "safe" that did it. Kathy suddenly remembered the last time she had seen Alice Prince at ViroVector. It had been in the Womb just after she had been told about the FDA approval. When Alice had tried to shield her tray of precious vials before hurriedly placing them back in her safe, Kathy had assumed it was her usual paranoia. Prince's refrigerated strongbox had always been a standard feature in the Womb, somewhere for her pet projects, and no one, least of all Kathy, had ever paid it much heed.

She rose from the table and went to the small pile of belongings they had taken from Matty's home. She picked the laptop and cell phone off the top and brought them back to the table. She plugged the laptop modem into the cell phone, she logged on to the main menu of ViroVector's network manager, and clicked on to the access authorization schedule. She let out a small "yes" of satisfaction. Her hunch had been correct. Her name was still there with a silver key beside it. Alice and Madeline had been so confident she was going to be out of the way that they hadn't bothered to tell TITANIA to deny her physical access to the buildings.

"Have you found something?" asked Luke.

"Well, I know one place we can look."

"Yes?" said Barzini.

"In the storage fridges at ViroVector all samples are tagged with an electronic bar code. When a computer laser wand is waved over this code, it automatically opens a file in the main computer, regardless of who's waving the wand. That file contains all the technical data on the sample and a summary of project objectives and background. It makes it easy for scientists working in difficult conditions to get quick access."

Decker nodded, renewed fire in his eyes. "The bar code gives you the project background and the formula specs for each sample? And there's no other code you need to access this?"

"No, but you do have to get hold of the sample and run TITANIA's computer wand over it. You see, the vials I'm thinking about are already in a very secure place."

Barzini smiled. "No place is completely secure."

"This comes pretty close. It's in a safe in a BioSafety Level Five lab called the Womb. Believe me, it's not as comfortable as it sounds."

Briefly she told them about the Womb: its security measures, the protective clothing procedure, the contamination risks, and the vials in the locked steel safe she had seen Alice Prince closing when she was last there. "I reckon I can still get in because they haven't wiped me off the security register. TITANIA controls all security with cameras, alarms, and steel barriers. The locks are DNA-coded, but my profile appears to still be active. Once inside, though, I'll need help breaking into the safe. And help getting stuff out."

"Don't worry about the safe," said Barzini. "If you describe it or give me a model name, I can probably find someone who'll rig up something to help you."

Kathy thought for a moment. "It's black, about waist-high, with a large silver dial on the front. And it's refrigerated. There's a brand name in big red letters across the top of the door. Something like Lemka, with a number after it. One hundred and one, I think."

Barzini nodded his head. "Big red letters? Refrigerated? Sounds like a Lenica One Zero One. Swiss. Very good, but not impregnable with a correctly set-up quantum pulse box."

"What?" asked Kathy.

"Don't worry, it's an electronic code breaker," explained Decker. "We'll go into that later. But if we find anything, what do we take out as evidence? Surely everything will be contaminated."

Kathy had thought of this already. "We take out only information, nothing else." She turned to Barzini. "Have you got a pencil and paper?"

He passed her a pen. "Use your napkin."

Quickly she sketched an elevation view of the main dome, showing the concentric circles of the underground BioSafety laboratory complex drilling down to the hospital and morgue beneath it. "Much of the action at ViroVector happens underground. Apparently there are safety tunnels leading to and from the lab complex but only Gold clearance employees know the codes to the airtight doors. We'll have to use the ground-floor entrance of the main dome to enter the lab complex."

She pointed at the center of the underground lab complex on the napkin. "I'll go down to the Womb here. Assuming Joey can tell me how to get into the safe and I find something, then I'll be able to scan it." She pointed to the ground-floor level of the dome. "But, Luke, I'll need you to wait up in the anteroom above the complex. There's a terminal and a printer here. The terminal can be used to transfer data onto a hi-data digital disc and the printer to generate hard copy. You turn on the printer and insert a blank disc into the terminal. I then send topline data from the Womb terminal to the printer and copy the detailed stuff to the blank disc. It's standard practice to get info out of the Womb, avoiding contamination."

Decker nodded. "OK, but how do we get in and out without being spotted or challenged?"

"Well, with Silver clearance I can sign one other person in as long as he submits to a DNA scan. But we've still got to—"

"Hey, hey, hey. That's enough for tonight," said Barzini, standing up and raising his two huge hands. "You know what you're after and where you think it is. That's great. Now it's time for you both to get some sleep. Let me make a few calls, and by tomorrow morning I should have some people to help you with surveillance, transport, and equipment. They'll know the best way to get in and out of the campus, and they'll supply a pulse box and safe for you to practice on." Barzini smiled. "These people are very good at what they do, but I must stress they have nothing to do with me." His smile broadened. "Sadly not all of my family is as law-abiding as I am."

29

The Oval Office, Washington, D.C.
Friday, November 7, 9:30 A.M.

First came relief and euphoria, then concern and finally fear. The administration ran through the extremes of emotions on the morning after the dramatic Iraqi retreat. The concern and fear came later, though, when Pamela Weiss received more information.

The secretary of defense and the secretary of state were tired but smiling when they accompanied the uniformed chairman of the Joint Chiefs of Staff into the Oval Office at nine-thirty that morning. The usually sober trio had an almost discernible spring in their gaits; they were men who had received a stay of execution.

At first the Iraqi volte-face seemed inexplicable. The first reports of a mystery epidemic ravaging the Iraqi Army arrived via the CIA and Britain's MI5 at eleven that morning. Again the initial reaction was positive. The nation was a known belligerent, and therefore anything that affected its military capabilities was regarded as beneficial. Such infections were common on military bases where troops lived in close proximity to one another.

At one-forty in the afternoon sketchy intelligence reported that the mystery illness was more serious than the usual epidemics, that it led to either suicide or brain hemorrhage and appeared to be already spreading to the civilian

238

population. Another report claimed that all sufferers had been men.

The fact that the epidemic, if that's what it was, wasn't understood and that it was spreading caused the President and her advisers grave concern for the wider implications. It was immediately agreed by the UN and the World Health Organization that all of Iraq's borders, which were already strictly patrolled, should be sealed, allowing no one in or out. The country was effectively to be put into quarantine.

But it was the symptoms the more detailed reports were outlining that gave cause for greater worry. Reaching into a drawer in the impressive desk that dominated the Oval Office, President Weiss pulled out two sheets of typed paper. She frowned when she read the second page. After asking her advisers to leave the office for a moment, she reached for the secure phone and began dialing a number she knew by heart. Then she paused for a second before deciding against it.

It was a minute past 2:00 P.M. in Washington, therefore just 11:00 A.M. in San Francisco. She dialed one of the two numbers at the bottom of the sheet of paper. When she received no reply, she tried the second number, hoping it might be his office. A woman answered.

"I'm sorry," the woman said, not even asking who was calling. "I'm Mr. Butcher's personal assistant, and I was expecting him to return from Washington last night, but for some reason he missed his flight. I'm expecting him to turn up or call in at any moment. I apologize, but it's very unusual for him not to tell me of his whereabouts. Can I take a message? I'm sure he'll get back to you as soon as he can."

"No, that's fine," said the President, her face pale. "I'll call later." She took a deep breath and asked the White House operator to put her through to Fort Detrick in Maryland. "This is the President. I need to speak to the commander immediately."

Within seconds Major General Thomas Allardyce, M.D., of the U.S. Army Research Institute of Infectious Diseases, was on the line. "Hello, Madam President, I assume you're calling about the computer disc Agent Toshack brought me."

"Yes, I hope you've still told no one else about it, not even

within USAMRIID." She drawled the abbreviation phoneti-
cally, "you sam rid."

"Of course not."

"What can you tell me?"

"Well, it contains two copies of an individual's genome.
Except they're not exact copies. The second contains subtle
changes in seventeen of the genes."

"What would those subtle changes do?"

"Well, quite a lot."

"Such as?"

Listening to his answer, Weiss stared down at her desk,
comparing his report with the two sheets of typed paper that
Hank Butcher had given her with the disc. When the doctor
finished, she asked him one more question and then thanked
him and hung up.

For a long while she sat in silence, trying to marshal both
her thoughts and feelings. Finally she came to a decision and
pressed a button on the desk summoning the head of her security detail.

Special Agent Mark Toshack entered the room. He held a
file in his hand. Without saying anything, he passed it to her.
Opening it, she scanned the photograph and notes. It only
confirmed her thoughts. "Thank you, Mark," she said. "Now
I would like you to do something else for me. Again I want
you to use only Secret Service personnel, and I need you to
do it fast."

**Overlooking the ViroVector Campus, Palo Alto.
Noon.**

"Well, if you want my advice, I wouldn't do it. The first rule
of this business is you don't go into a rathole. You always
make sure you've got a way out. And this Womb sounds like
the mother of all ratholes."

Decker groaned and took the binoculars from Barzini's
cousin Frankie Danza and trained them on the main dome of
ViroVector. "Thanks, but that's not really the kind of advice
we're after."

Luke Decker and Kathy Kerr sat inside Frankie's Mercedes van on a raised part of the main road overlooking the ViroVector campus. The other two men with Frankie hadn't volunteered their names, and their faces didn't invite further questions.

The irony of Decker's current situation didn't really register. It was probably one of the less weird things that had occurred to him over the last few days. Working with the opposition was only part of it. Earlier this morning, after Joey Barzini had made a few vague introductions, Frankie and his men had taken him and Kathy to a warehouse near Fisherman's Wharf. There the two nameless men had given Kathy a pulse box and taught her how to use it on a safe similar to the one in the Womb. Throughout the three-hour session their conversation never once strayed outside the narrow confines of the task in hand.

And now Frankie Danza, a whip-thin guy with nervous hands, no hair, and a Camel cigarette surgically attached to his lower lip, was trying to explain the problems involved getting into and out of smart buildings.

Frankie's van was parked next to an imposing blue sign with "White Heat Science Park" written in letters three feet high. The park of the same name, a cluster of small high-tech start-up companies, comprised the only buildings adjoining the relatively isolated ViroVector site. A large man-made lake and the eleventh hole of the Bellevue Golf and Country Club bordered its other perimeters.

The campus itself was an emerald blanket of manicured lawns and perfectly proportioned trees, interrupted only by a few tennis courts, a helicopter site, parking lots, and large production warehouses. The most striking feature was the crystal dome sitting like a vast alien moon in the center of the site.

A lightweight steel fence encircled the campus, and on the road there was a gateway. All around the perimeter and at key locations on the campus, high up on twenty-foot steep poles, Decker could see what looked like sensors and closed-circuit TV cameras.

"Getting in ain't the problem," said Frankie, "especially if

Kathy's got the clearance. The guardian computer don't question you or give you no trouble if your clearance is OK. But it'll watch you, and sometimes it'll splash your face up on the monitors inside the dome. And if this Dr. Prince is inside and sees you, then you're in deep shit. But you can wear headgear to disguise yourself. The other risk is being eyeballed in the flesh. But again, if you go late in the day, you can minimize that.

"Your big problem is that there's only one way out. And if you don't leave in time, that computer mother's gonna close you down. And if Dr. Prince catches you on one of the monitors while you're in the Womb and sets off the alarms, kaboom, you're history.

"A guy I knew did a bank job in Hong Kong. A brand-new grade A smart building overlooking Kowloon Harbor. He got in easy, outsmarted the computer, fooled all the sensors. Got right into the vault. Even tripped the time lock codes with a quantum code breaker. Then, when the team was in the heart of the vault, the computer closed 'em down. Two-foot-thick steel doors shut 'em in, then sucked all the air out. Game over. They were found the next day: a pile of stiffs. That's what smart buildings do. They let you check in, but they don't never let you check out."

"Thanks for the encouragement," said Kathy. "Any ideas?"

"Well, if you gotta go in, the only real advice is timing. From what you've told me, the whole place closes down to all personnel except Gold clearance at ten. That means you must be out by ten. If you're inside the dome, the computer will seal you in. Even if you're outside, it'll get you. Those flimsy fences around the campus are like the computer's skin. If you try to break through it, it'll feel you and send a few thousand volts your way. So, rule number one: You *gotta* be off campus by ten.

"Rule number two: Go in as late as you can to avoid most of the working suits. When do most people leave the site?"

Kathy shrugged. "Most are out by seven. Few, if any, people work after that. It's virtually unheard of to go into the Womb after six. It's not the place to be when you're tired and prone to making mistakes."

Frankie nodded. "Rule number three: Give yourself enough time. This is the hardest rule to stick to because no one knows what enough means. How long you need to get your stuff? Give yourself at least a half hour to get into the safe."

Kathy thought for a moment. "I've got to get into the space suits beforehand and then go through the decon showers when I come out. Assuming we find a sample of something, it shouldn't take more than ten minutes to scan the file and for Luke to copy it to disc in the anteroom above. I'd say we need an hour, tops."

Frankie nodded. "Give yourself two. That means we drop you off outside the main gates at eight. And we pick you up before ten. In the meantime you better get some more practice with the pulse box. And then you better start praying no one catches you in the Womb. It sounds like an awful easy place to die."

ViroVector Solutions. 7:59 P.M.

By eight most of the ViroVector offices were empty, but the tireless TITANIA was still at work. The biocomputer's electronic receptors scoured the World Wide Web, monitoring any data even remotely related to Crime Zero, continually informing its neural net of any relevant information. Its air ducts breathed with precise regularity as it absorbed much of the same information President Weiss had received from her intelligence sources.

TITANIA had no moral compass against which to evaluate the escalating deaths it was recording. It could only objectively compare the deaths and their causes with its predictions. The death of Bob Burbank and the swearing in of President Weiss were logged, as were the Iraqi retreat and the spreading epidemic. TITANIA calculated that more than nine thousand humans had died as a consequence of Crime Zero within Iraq and that the rate was increasing, all in the expected demographic groups.

These figures elicited no concern from TITANIA, unlike from the President of the United States.

Similarly TITANIA felt or raised no alarm when at a more basic level of artificial cognition it registered the activation of one of the DNA scanners allowing entrance onto the campus. Like a human's subconscious, TITANIA's base operating system controlling ViroVector's security noted that the genome taken from the palm of the human hand pressed against the sensor matched one on file. Since that genome possessed Silver clearance and the second unauthorized person acceded to a DNA scan, TITANIA simply allowed the two entrants access without troubling its higher-level consciousness, in the same way that a human's subconscious automatically regulates breathing, only alerting the conscious mind when it perceives a problem.

Its eyes, however, followed the two entrants, watching their every move.

30

"Please place your palm against the sensor," said the voice at the main gate of ViroVector. Decker did what he was told, but he was disconcerted by the fact that the gate wasn't manned. Not by a human anyway.

The tall guard in the gatehouse was a lifelike hologram, his face a composite of leading male film stars. It was standing above a KREE8 Version 6 holopad, according to the sticker on the window. "Is he meant to scare off people or welcome them?" Decker whispered to Kathy.

Kathy shrugged and removed her palm from the sensor where his was now being read. She looked nervous, and he didn't blame her. "Don't worry about it. He's just there to impress you with how technologically advanced ViroVector is."

"It's working," he said, feeling a slight heat under his palm as the sensor peeled a microscopic layer off his skin, scanning his DNA. Suddenly a rush of irrational panic hit him, wondering if the scanner would somehow be able to identify Axelman's genes in his DNA and bar him access.

"Welcome, Dr. Kerr," said the hologram after Decker's palm had been read. "Please state your guest's full name."

"Luke Decker." She spoke into a small microphone on the wall of the guardhouse.

"Thank you, Dr. Kerr."

Suddenly the large gates slid silently open, and they were in.

He briefly turned around and saw the lights of Frankie Danza's van a hundred yards farther up the road. It had brought Decker and Kathy here an hour ago. In that time they had sat in the van, watching the last stragglers leave for home, and waited the final half hour while no ViroVector employees had left. The parking lot was empty, and the whole place appeared deserted. At eight precisely they had approached the gates, trusting Kathy's clearance was still live. It was a gamble, and now they were inside. But as Frankie had said, that was the easy part.

As Decker followed Kathy toward the large dome, which glowed in the evening gloom like some implacable space-ship, he felt the sting of hundreds of invisible eyes watching him.

"There shouldn't be anyone here," said Kathy as they neared the steps that led up to the entrance. "But if there is, just smile." Ahead he could see a pair of thick glass double doors. The name ViroVector was etched into both of them. Looking in, Decker was relieved to see that apart from two people talking intensely by the rest rooms the reception lobby was empty.

"To open the door, put your hands on the sensor again," said Kathy.

"Does every door have these damn sensors?"

"Yup. TITANIA likes to know where everyone is."

"Great," said Decker as he placed his hand on the steel pad.

He turned as they were both in the foyer to see a set of car headlights pierce the darkness of the parking lot. A limousine drove past the dome. It could have been his nervousness, but he was sure he saw the white hair of Director Naylor in the passenger seat.

"Shit," he said.

Kathy had seen her too. "Don't think about it. Let's go," she said, clutching her bag. She led him through a door at the end of the foyer, which opened out on to a long corridor.

At the end was a yellow door with a black biohazard symbol. "Be quiet," she whispered as they walked past a steel silver door with "TITANIA Smart Suite" written on it in black. A dull hum could be heard from within.

When they reached the yellow biohazard doors, their palms were read once more. As the door opened, Decker could see before him a white sterile environment, totally devoid of warmth or color. And just as the door closed behind him, sealing in the air, he was sure he heard the door to the Smart Suite opening.

But it wasn't the door to the Smart Suite Decker had heard. It was the sound of TITANIA thinking.

The Smart Suite was humming with activity. The main display media, the fifteen-by-ten-foot screen wall and the KREE8 hologram floor pad at the head of the conference table, were in use. At the rear of the room, four small monitors were showing quickly shifting views of the ViroVector complex as seen through TITANIA's sixty closed-circuit security cameras dotted around the campus.

The hologram being displayed on the pad was a five-foot-in-diameter, three-dimensional globe rotating slowly a yard off the ground. The definition of the hologram was so precise that the silver globe looked solid, as though made of real metal. Each country, its border demarcated by thin black tracing, was layered with three colored strata forming population mountains like a topographical three-dimensional map—red, green, and blue—graphically demonstrating the demographic breakdown of each country. Unlike the static colors in the rest of the world, the red in Iraq pulsed with light as if alive.

When a country was simply touched by a fingertip, the layers of color separated to display a percentage figure and an absolute number, showing the importance and size of that demographic group in the particular country. The absolute numbers were constantly changing, reflecting births and deaths collated from the numerous data sources on the World Wide Web. As did the rising total world population

number shown on the screen wall. The last number stood at
6,567,987,601.

There beneath the population counter was a cryptic legend, indicating what each color represented. Red was labeled "target," green, "carrier," and blue, "corrected."
Beside each color was a number counter giving a total for
that segment.

As she stood alone in the room, Alice Prince's eyes
were sparkling with excitement while she watched the
globe, its iridescent colors reflected in the thick glass of
her spectacles. After witnessing the Iraqi turnabout last
night, she felt born again. World War III had been averted,
and the doubts she may have had had ceased to trouble
her. Crime Zero was a just project, and it was going to
work. Phase 2 was performing so well it looked certain
that they would be able to launch Phase 3 within days.
And the vision was so much cleaner and clearer when seen
in its clinical entirety, far from the confusion of face-to-
face human realities.

TITANIA began to run its Global Predictive Sequence for
Phase 3.

At the top of the screen wall a time line appeared, showing today as time zero and then counting off the months and
years as they elapsed in the simulated sequence.

The colored layers started pulsing in each chosen index
country for Phase 3. But no sooner had the epicenters been
illuminated than black parabolic arcs, simulating air, sea,
and land travel, spread across the globe like the legs of a
malevolent spider. Within days on the time line all the color
segments in most of the so-called first world were pulsing.
Only the remoter regions of the Amazon and Patagonia in
South America, Antarctica, and central Africa as well as the
more distant islands north of New Zealand remained unaffected.

Within ten days in the major countries the red band of
color representing the "target" stopped pulsing and began to
glow. The other countries soon followed, and within weeks
90 percent of the red sections on the globe were aglow and
therefore in decline. In one month every single country had

been touched in one way or another. On the main screen wall the rising number in the counter beside the red legend slowed to 2,408,876,654 and then began to fall. Within two and a half months the figure had dropped by almost 300,000,000, within six months the decline had doubled, and within a year the figure had dropped by more than 1,250,000,000. After thirty-six months and three days all traces of red in the world had disappeared.

There were only two color strata left on the depleted population mountains: green and blue, "carrier" and "corrected."

The total number on the population counter had reduced by almost 2,500,000,000 humans in three years, fifty times that of the great influenza pandemic of 1918.

The time line moved forward another twenty years, and the counter gradually began to climb once more with new strata of differing shades of blue adding to the rising population mountains in each country.

The silver globe was now dominated by calming blues and green. The angry rash of red was effectively extinct.

As TITANIA laid out their vision like the onslaught of the inevitable, Alice felt she was seeing something sacred, a purging flood she had played her part in unleashing.

So transfixed was she by the globe that she hadn't even registered Madeline Naylor entering the room.

"It's beautiful, isn't it, Ali?" said Madeline.

"Unstoppable," said Alice with a sigh.

"There's just one small thing we need to make this perfect," said Madeline.

"What now?"

"Decker and Kerr still aren't out of the way. Jackson's working on it but—"

"It doesn't matter now, does it?" said Alice, staring at the shimmering globe and the New Eden it represented.

"I suppose not," said Madeline. "I just wish I knew where they were."

Ironically she only had to have asked TITANIA and the biocomputer would have told her exactly Luke Decker and Kathy Kerr's location. Or had she looked behind her at the four screens continually monitoring the entire campus, she might have even snatched a hurried glimpse of a figure in a blue Chemturion biological space suit entering the Womb.

31

As the glass doors of the Womb hissed closed behind her,
the first beads of sweat prickled on Kathy Kerr's skin within
the rubberized suit. Entering the campus, she had felt nervous but in control. And even seeing Director Naylor had
spurred her on rather than paralyzed her. But now, here in
the Womb, she could feel herself tensing, only the sound of
her breathing for company. This time was different from the
many previous visits.

The clock above the door indicated 2032. TITANIA was
to close down the Womb at 2130. Including the essential
half hour to undergo the decontamination procedures, Kathy
had to make her exit before the computer closed down the
whole compound at 2200 hours: Fifty-eight minutes to use
the pulse box, open the safe, find what she was looking for,
and capture the data on the computer and printer upstairs,
where Decker should be waiting. It didn't seem enough. The
prospect of another scientist's entering the biolab complex
in the meantime was beyond contemplation. If anyone did,
she would be helpless.

Taking a deep breath, she walked past the first bank of refrigerators to the corner where the waist-high black safe sat.
On the front was a flap about the size of a paperback book

covering the electronic keypad. It was as she remembered it and looked reassuringly like the Lenica 101 she had practiced on, but she couldn't be sure.

On the workstation beside Alice Prince's safe was a computer VDU. Kathy powered it up and opened the link with the terminal on the ground floor above, where Decker waited with a new box of blank discs ready to copy whatever data she found.

The keyboard was twice the normal size with large flat keys covered in a sterile plastic sleeve. With her unwieldy gloved fingers she jabbed out a message:

I'm in and have found the safe. Are you set up with discs and the printer?

There was a heart-stopping pause.

Everything looking good up here. Good luck.

She looked down at the slim chrome slab the size of a checkbook resting on her left palm: the pulse box—and the key to the whole operation. Exploiting nuclear magnetic resonance and liquid molecules, the quantum code breaker used qubits, which, unlike classical binary bits, could exist simultaneously in multiple states, allowing it to decipher each element of a code in parallel time rather than sequentially. It was fast and efficient, but was it enough? Studying its liquid crystal display and the two silk-thin wires trailing out one end like wispy antennae, she recalled the procedure. Using the magnetic pad on the back of the quantum pulse box, she anchored it above the safe's electronic keypad. Once she was satisfied it was secure, and with Frankie's words in mind—"If you drop this thing, it's history"—she carefully taped the spring-hinged plastic keypad cover back on itself, revealing the keys. Then she took the two trailing wires in her fingers and searched for the two tiny holes in the top edge of the keypad. "After a bit of practice it should be easy," she'd been told.

But it hadn't been easy in practice, and it wasn't easy

now. At first she couldn't even find the holes, and when she did, she almost gave up in frustration. The protective gloves she wore were even thicker than the ones she'd been using before. They had been designed to give as much movement as possible, but inserting the two silk-thin wires into minute holes obviously hadn't been on the usage spec.

"Relax and take your time," she told herself. But time was the one thing she couldn't afford. Maintaining composure, she straightened out the inch-long wires with one hand, aligning them with the two holes. If they met any resistance at all, they began to bend and she had to ease them in at a painstaking pace. It was vital that they connect with the inner electronics. Frankie's guys had taught her how to "jiggle" them, as they put it, gently vibrating the wires until they found a way into the opening. But jiggling required sensitive fingers, and her gloves didn't allow her that luxury.

She could feel perspiration on her brow as she concentrated on her task. She wanted to rip off her helmet and wipe the sweat away but had to blink through the droplets. She lost count of the number of times both wires were in the holes before one became snagged and she had to start all over again. Finally, twenty-six minutes later, her arms aching with the effort, she heard a beep, and the pulse box burst into life. The liquid crystal display began racing through numbers as it simultaneously searched for every character constituting the code.

Kathy immediately turned to the computer terminal and plucked the wand from its bracket. She ran it over a bar code on one of the vials in the main refrigerator to check if it was functioning. Instantly the screen displayed a contents menu offering the genetic composition of the vial's contents, its history of clinical trials, and topline rationale and objectives. Satisfied, she replaced it and waited for the pulse box to do its work.

It only took five and a half minutes for the chrome code breaker to work its magic and show six characters illuminated on the LCD: 666%£5. Carefully she extended a gloved finger and punched out the characters on the safe's electronic keypad. Silently the door opened.

                    I'm in,

she typed on the computer, checking the time. She had a little more than half an hour to copy what she needed. It
should be enough. She removed a tray of cigar-size colored
vials, rested them on the work surface by the terminal, and
began to read their labels. The two red vials were marked
"Conscience," so she ignored those, but two words on the
three green vial labels made the hairs stand up on the back
of her neck.

   "Crime Zero."

   In what way was each of the three vials different? To ex-
tract all the evidence, she would have to capture the data on
each one. Suddenly the remaining twenty-seven minutes
didn't seem long at all.

   She typed,

   Think project is called Crime Zero. You need to stand by
   with two more discs. At least three vials, all might be vital.
   Do we have enough time for three?

Decker responded immediately.

                    Hope so.

   Kathy picked up the vial marked "Crime Zero Vector
(Phase 1)" and ran the wand over the bar code.

   Not bothering to scan what was on the screen, she immediately clicked on the copy icon, selecting the disc drive on
the computer upstairs.

   The file was large. The clock symbol at the bottom of the
screen was moving painfully slowly, indicating it would take
seven minutes to download. Assuming the other two were as
big, she would be lucky to get them all out before TITANIA
closed down the Womb. She looked at the two other terminals in the Womb, but there was only one computer next to
Decker, and she could only copy each disc sequentially.

   While she waited, she removed the quantum pulse box,
extracted the wires from the safe, and searched for a place to

conceal it. She couldn't take it out of the Womb now that it had become contaminated, but its presence would alert someone, particularly Alice Prince, that she had been in here. Eventually she dropped it into a sample tray, closed the lid, and then placed the tray at the back of the lowest shelf of the largest refrigerator.

By the time she had finished and returned to the computer screen the Crime Zero Phase 1 vector file had been copied. Eighteen minutes remained.

Ready for disc 2?

she typed to Luke.

Ready.

Barely pausing, she picked up the vial labeled "Crime Zero Vector (Phase 2)" and waved the wand over it. As soon as the screen registered that the file had been opened, she copied it upstairs to Luke. Again she checked the clock at the bottom of the screen. This file transfer would take eight minutes. There would be virtually no time for the third phase.

Fearing that time was slipping away, she decided to scan the last Crime Zero vial on a second terminal to check its contents. She switched on the terminal by the Genescope.

At that moment a soft feminine voice interrupted her. "The time is now twenty-one-fifteen. The BioSafety Level Five and Level Four facilities will be closing in exactly fifteen minutes. If you have not yet done so, you should clear the workstations and prepare to leave. The ViroVector Campus will be sealed at exactly twenty-two hours."

Kathy glanced at the screen where Crime Zero Phase 2 was being copied: more than three minutes to go. With one eye on the digital clock above the door of the Womb she turned to the data on the second terminal.

Scrolling to Crime Zero Phase 3 technical specifications, she speed-read the summary. Words and phrases jumped out at her: "engineered influenza vector . . . chimera . . . respi-

ratory transmission . . . Y chromosome trigger . . . Project
Conscience control genes . . . hormonal imbalance . . .
telomeres-determined time release." Each word or phrase
was innocuous on its own, but the cumulative implications
were terrifying.

Her heart beating like the wings of a trapped bird, Kathy
quickly scrolled to the summary objectives. What she read
there was so outlandish it made her gasp. Yet what shocked
her most was that at an entirely amoral, scientific level it made
perverse sense. With horrible clarity Kathy realized that
Crime Zero represented her life's work taken to its ultimate
extreme. In part she had to take some perverse responsibility
for what Alice Prince and Madeline Naylor were doing.

A deeper chill clutched at her heart.

Or for what they may have *already* done.

"You now have ten minutes exactly before the Level Five
and Four facilities will be closed down," informed the soft
feminine voice.

Kathy took a deep breath and rushed over to the first monitor.

Ready for third disc?

she typed.

No time. Get out of there.

Decker typed back.

Make time. Explain later.

Kathy typed.

It's your call. Third disc ready. Hurry!

Decker's response was instantaneous.

She rushed back to the second terminal, selected Decker's
disc drive, then pressed "Copy." She wouldn't have more

than a few seconds after the copying was complete if she wanted to switch off the terminals before leaving. No one must know that she'd been here.

Keeping her eye on the main clock, Kathy quickly put the vials back in their tray, careful to replace them as they had been, before returning them to the safe.

"The Biohazard Level Four and Five laboratories will be closing in exactly five minutes."

GET OUT!

she read on the screen from Luke.

But she still had to hide any trace of her intrusion.

Four minutes.

If Naylor or Prince knew, they might activate Phase 3 prematurely. If they hadn't done so already. She slammed the safe shut.

Three minutes.

She raced back to the large refrigerator and checked that the pulse box was concealed as discreetly as possible.

Two minutes.

She closed down the first terminal and checked that everything was as she had found it.

One minute.

Come on, she shouted at the screen of the second terminal, willing it to finish.

Then, suddenly, it was done. She turned off the terminal and walked as fast as her suit allowed her to the door, pressed the open button, and exited the Womb.

The airtight doors hissed shut behind her with forty-three seconds to spare.

"The Womb is now closed," said the disembodied feminine voice. "The ViroVector main gates will be sealed in half an hour. This site will close at twenty-two hundred hours. If you have not yet done so, please prepare to leave."

"OK. OK. I heard you," Decker said aloud, assuming Kathy had got out of the Womb in time. No alarm had sounded. Yet.

He stood in the sterile white vestibule next to the single computer and printer. To his left was the door leading to the transit station into which Kathy had disappeared to descend to the biohazard labs and the Womb. To his right was the main exit leading to the corridor and the foyer beyond.

After extracting the third disc out of the computer, Decker labeled it and placed it with the others in the tote bag beside him. He then switched off the terminal and sat on the desk. He could do nothing but wait. Every few seconds he looked toward the main exit, expecting someone to come walking in.

He checked his watch. Kathy still had to pass through the decontamination showers and change out of her suit before they could leave this technological nightmare. And they had to leave soon.

As he waited, he wondered why Kathy had insisted on risking getting locked into the Womb in order to copy the third vial of Crime Zero. Surely two were enough.

"Let's go," said Kathy, suddenly bursting through the doors of the transit room.

Picking up the tote bag, Decker rose from his chair and made for the door. "We've got about twelve minutes. Let's get the hell out of here."

In the corridor they ran past the Smart Suite and the Cold Room to the foyer. Outside the dome the campus was as quiet as before.

At the main gates Decker put his hands on the scanner and began to feel better only when the gates opened for them. Seconds later Frankie Danza's van appeared and pulled up by the gates, its broad tires screeching on the tarmac.

Breathing a sigh of relief, he walked up to the driver's tinted window, Kathy in step beside him. He opened the door and froze.

It wasn't Frankie Danza in the seat. Not that Decker really noticed, because the gun barrel staring him in the face held his attention.

"Drop the bag! Now!" said the man in the driver's seat, pressing the barrel against Decker's forehead.

32

"The Peace Plague" was how the media dubbed the epidemic raging through the ranks of the Iraqi Army. Some U.S. and British tabloid newspapers even claimed that it was a good thing, a divine curse sent to blight the warmongers.

The morning following Thursday's Iraqi retreat the World Health Organization, with the full backing of the UN Security Council, had endorsed and enforced the quarantine of Iraq. Every country bordering that nation, terrified the mystery plague might spread to it, applied the quarantine rigidly. Already deaths were being put at over thirty thousand with more Iraqis—military and civilian alike—being stricken by the hour. So far few, if any, women or children had been affected.

The World Health Organization, Médecins sans Frontiers, and the Red Cross immediately dispatched specially equipped teams to try to understand the nature of the mystery epidemic and offer advice on containment strategies. Even the U.S. Army had released a team from the Epidemic Intelligence Service based at the Centers for Disease Control in Atlanta. Within a matter of hours Iraq had been transformed in the eyes of the world from dangerous bully to needy cripple.

By Friday early findings were suggesting that the disease affected the patient's hormone levels and brain chemistry. It was speculatively hoped that the plague was not airborne, that it could at least be contained if ruthless measures were applied and adhered to.

Isolated reports began to surface that even the hitherto ruthless Iraqi president had expressed remorse to the Kurdish leaders for past atrocities and sent apologies to Kuwait for his aggressive stance. At first these acts, they were indeed true, were seen as a cynical means to ingratiate himself with his enemies at a time when Iraq was collapsing. But increasingly they were seen as proof that he had also succumbed to the Peace Plague.

Against a backdrop of rising hysteria the press besieged the White House, demanding a statement from the new President. Some reporters from the more sensationalist press asked if this plague had been intentional, a brilliant preemptive strike by the new administration. Inspired by the success of Project Conscience, a biological solution to crime, was the Peace Plague the next step: a biological solution to war?

These claims were strenuously denied by President Weiss, who stressed that she took the Iraq plague seriously and Baghdad was being offered America's full support. She claimed that whatever their differences, humanity must always unite against its common enemy, disease.

Surprisingly few of the national journalists asked if the Peace Plague could spread to North America? If so, how soon could it get here?

That was one question Pamela Weiss was unable to answer.

Saturday, November 8. Morning

Kathy Kerr was made to wear the blindfold for hours. The plane had been flying for at least four, perhaps more. The dull roar of the engines and the nylon wrist binders increased her sense of isolation. The cabin smelled of cheap cologne and of commercial airliner rest rooms. But this wasn't a commercial airliner. That much she knew.

There were at least two other men in the cabin with them, but she didn't know where they were sitting. She took some comfort from knowing Decker was three seats to her left. They had hardly talked since they had been bundled into the van and then onto the plane. She had only just enough time to whisper the basics of Crime Zero, what she knew about Phase 3 anyway. They hadn't talked since. There was nothing to say.

A wave of hopelessness washed over her. The project was so huge, so outlandish that alerting the authorities suddenly seemed irrelevant. Decker had been right. She should have gone home when she'd had the chance. Just because she had helped start this nightmare didn't mean she could ever stop it. This was global, inevitable, and final.

As Decker tried to make himself comfortable in the seat, he failed to understand why they were still alive. If what Kathy had told him about Crime Zero was true, they should be dead already. Naylor would have to assume that they too knew about the project and make the necessary arrangements to kill them.

Decker shook his head. It didn't make sense. Alice Prince was damaged and therefore probably not naturally vindictive. Her involvement in Crime Zero was almost certainly fueled by idealistic fantasies, which denied the realities of the human costs. The dominant partner in this was Naylor. Instinctively he knew she always had been.

So why were they alive?

When he heard the undercarriage drop and felt the plane coming in to land, he guessed he would soon find out.

As the plane eased to a stop, Decker was bundled outside into the cold and transferred with Kathy to another van. While it sped off, their blindfolds were removed, and Decker studied the two men sitting with them in the windowless rear cabin. His tote bag containing the discs was at the feet of the shorter one with sandy hair. Typical agents, dark suits and impenetrable manner. But he didn't recognize either of them.

Decker assembled the facts. The plane had been government or military, and the ease with which the van had met it on the airport tarmac confirmed that they had landed at no ordinary commercial airport.

At least on the ground there was a chance of escape.

Decker smiled wearily at Kathy. She looked pale and tired, but she smiled back.

Decker turned then to the shorter agent. From his relaxed body language he looked like the leader. "Do you know what's on those discs you took from us?"

The man's face remained impassive as if he hadn't heard the question. Decker spoke again, calmly as if to an ally. "Don't you even *want* to know what's on the discs?" he said, feeling the anger build inside him. "You should, because it'll involve you two sooner than you think. Doesn't that bother you just a little?"

Still, the man said nothing.

Decker prided himself on keeping control, on using reason to solve most things, but now he allowed the hurt and anger of the last few days to build. As his rage and frustration peaked, the van came to a sudden stop, and he made his move.

There was no plan, no coolly timed stratagem, only an opportunist explosion of vented energy. As the van engine died, both his captors visibly relaxed and looked toward the driver's cabin. At that moment Decker leaped forward and using his bound hands as a club brought them down on the side of the larger man's head, felling him to the floor of the van. Extending the same fluid movement, he swung his clasped hand to his right in a double-handed tennis backhand, smashing back against the smaller man's jaw and catapulting his head against the side of the van. His knuckles burned with pain as he felt one pop with the impact. "Grab his gun," Decker shouted, feeding off the adrenaline surging through him.

Kathy bent and scrabbled through the felled man's clothes and came up with a black revolver. Decker did the same with the other man, who, still conscious, lay sprawled against the side of the van, clutching his head. He also picked up the tote bag lying next to his feet and kicked it toward the van doors. He paused for a moment, considering how to unlock them, when suddenly they opened.

Raising his gun, he leveled it at a small group of outlines silhouetted against the night sky. An imposing female figure stepped forward. She was flanked by four men, their guns drawn and pointing directly at him.

"Oh, my God," said Kathy behind him.

Decker's jaw dropped. What was she doing here?

"What the hell is going on here?" The woman's voice was firm and commanding. Looking first at Kathy and then at Decker, she peered beyond him to the sandy-haired man groggily rising to his feet. "Special Agent Toshack, what happened?" the woman demanded. She looked tired and pale, but her manner indicated total control. "I told you to bring them to me, not fight with them."

Stunned, Decker turned and watched the man stumble to his fallen colleague, who was also beginning to stir. Toshack rubbed his chin and gave Decker a rueful grin. "I think Special Agent Decker here had his own ideas about that. And he's got a pretty good way of expressing them."

"How's Brown?" she demanded.

The man checked his groaning partner. "He'll live."

The woman shook her head in disgust and then, ignoring Decker's gun, extended an open hand toward Kathy. "Welcome to Fort Detrick, Dr. Kerr. Now that I've ascertained we're both on the same side I'm very pleased to meet you. I'm Pamela Weiss."

Kathy shook her hand in dumb silence.

Weiss then turned to Decker and gestured to the tote bag at his feet. "Special Agent Decker, are you going to shoot me? Because if you're not, can I have whatever it is you took from ViroVector?"

Decker didn't move for a second, still trying to work out whose side she was on. Finally he lowered his gun and picked up the bag, holding it close to him. "I think we all want to see what's on these discs, Madam President."

33

Two senior ViroVector scientists discovered the chrome electronic gadget in the Womb on Friday morning. Working on a deadline to develop a viral vector for Alzheimer's disease, they had been incensed to find that part of their allocated refrigerator space had been annexed.

When they complained to Alice Prince, her initial reaction had been annoyance. The last thing she needed was a petty dispute about lab resources. But when no one could identify the chrome box or knew how it had got there, her irritation changed to concern.

She donned her biological space suit and entered the Womb to examine the box, which had apparently been concealed in a tray at the base of one of the refrigerators. She interrogated TITANIA, which informed her that only authorized personnel had entered the Womb in the last few days. As a matter of course TITANIA listed all entrants to the biolab suite and the Womb. Scanning the list on the monitor, Alice gasped when she saw Kathy Kerr's name, and she was shocked to learn that she and Luke Decker had entered last night. It was impossible. Both Alice and Madeline had actually been on-site. But then she remembered that she hadn't canceled Kathy's Silver clearance; Madeline had said it wasn't necessary. As far as TITANIA was concerned,

Kathy Kerr was still authorized to come and go as she pleased.

With a beating heart Alice moved to the safe and punched in the code on the electronic keypad. Opening the door, she peered in and pulled out the tray, checking the tamper-evident caps on the vials. Everything appeared as it had been. Then she picked up one of the Crime Zero vials and ran a computer wand over it. Looking at the nearest monitor, she saw the project menu appear. In the bottom right-hand corner were the time and date of the last scan: 2116 on November 7. Yesterday.

Alice moved back to the speakerphone and with a heavy heart prepared to tell Madeline Naylor.

Heathrow Airport, London.
The Same Day, 2:12 P.M.

Heathrow has always been among the world's busiest airports. In 2005, when the first phase of Terminal 5 opened, it became the undisputed number one. A town in its own right, the complex employed more than one hundred thousand people and processed almost eighty million passengers a year.

Amid the Saturday afternoon throng of people, no one was even aware that three of the embarkation and disembarkation tunnels had been closed for two hours. Passengers were diverted to other departure gates, and the disruption was minimal. Few paid any heed to the two men in blue overalls entering the closed departure gates with a cart of white cardboard boxes, each bearing the same brand name as the one stamped on the back of their overalls, Air-Shield Industries. At the base of the carton was a small line of blue type to denote that AirShield Industries was a subsidiary of ViroVector Solutions, Palo Alto, California.

It was a routine task. The computer had informed the operatives that certain cartridges were exhausted and had itemized the exact serial number of the replacement from the inventory. They were doing what they were told. Neither of them considered questioning the task. They had no way of knowing the consequences of their actions.

The departure gate ahead was deserted, and the display that usually showed the flight number and destination now flashed "Closed for Maintenance." Like most major airports, Heathrow used bacteriophage air purifiers on its embarkation and disembarkation tunnels. Passengers were largely unaware of being sterilized by the bacteria-destroying phage as they left or boarded the plane. Only a slight breeze perfumed with a fresh soapy fragrance made them even notice the phage-rich air. The process was simply accepted as a sensible precaution.

Stepping through the deserted passport and ticket control, past the empty rows of seats for waiting passengers, the maintenance men entered a service hatch marked "Authorized Staff Only," leading down to a series of interconnecting walkways beneath each tunnel to access the individual phage purifier cartridges. Once inside, the men left their cart at the top of the steps and walked down to a lower level with a carton each. Ahead was a long chrome corridor with rows of airtight doors to their left. Each door was numbered, corresponding with the individual departure gate above.

Using a key, the first man watched door number 28 slide open, revealing a crawl space beneath the bacteriophage air tunnel. The second man walked on to the adjacent gate. Crouched down, the first man made his way into the small inspection chamber and quickly located the two-foot square flue of the air purification system protruding from the ceiling. He removed the grille from the flue to reveal a red button marked "Seal" and a green light. Beside the button was a lever that released from its bracket the cylindrical magazine of six vials, each containing a distinct bacterium-specific bacteriophage.

Pressing the button, he watched the airtight door slide shut behind him. When the green light changed to red, indicating that no new air was entering or leaving the tunnel, the man checked the number on the carton, opened it, removed the replacement cartridge, and placed it on the floor.

He then reached up and pulled the lever, freeing the mag-

azine already in place. Carefully checking that there was no
breakage, he removed the magazine and placed it in the
empty carton. As always he briefly examined the cylindrical
cluster of six glass vials and was surprised that most of them
seemed at least half full. He didn't question it; he only op-
erated on the computer's instructions.

Without a second thought he quickly inserted the replacement cartridge into the purifier. There was no difference between the two canisters. Any slight change in color in one of
the vials didn't interest him. It wasn't his job. He also ignored the fact that there was a minute high-power radio an-
tenna in one corner of the casing. After replacing the grille
on the flue, he picked up his carton and left the crawl space.
Another task completed.

Once he used to tell himself that his job was important because he helped protect people's health, but now he didn't
care about what he did. It paid the mortgage.

He might have cared today if he'd known that ten maintenance men just like him and his partner, in five other airports across the globe, had unwittingly helped change the
world forever.

34

USAMRIID, Fort Detrick, Maryland.
Saturday, November 8, 12:23 P.M.

"You've all seen the topline data from the discs Dr. Kerr and Special Agent Decker took from ViroVector. We know from the Phase Three disc that remote activation is planned in the very near future. So we have to assume and plan for the worst.

"Plus we need a full strategy for attacking the Iraq Phase Two epidemic with contingencies should it leak. No one here should stand on ceremony or rank. Say what you think. And if we need anybody else on the team, for God's sake get them on board now. This is a National Security Directive Seven. It doesn't get more serious than this."

President Weiss looked drawn as she addressed the task force gathered around the table in the main conference room. Kathy understood why the President was taking such a personal interest in this. If *she* felt bad about Alice Prince and Madeline Naylor's using her work on Project Conscience to develop and test their abomination, then Weiss must be devastated. They were her trusted friends. Project Conscience had helped elect her. And now Alice Prince and Madeline Naylor had turned what she thought was their shared dream into a nightmare.

Kathy had since learned that the alarming similarity between Axelman's symptoms and those of the Peace Plague in Iraq had galvanized Weiss into sending Toshack in search of her. Armed with a faculty photograph from Stanford, Toshack and his men had tailed the FBI director, believing she would lead them to her. Last night, after following Director Naylor to the ViroVector campus, they had challenged and neutralized the men in Frankie Danza's van, parked a short distance up the road from them, and waited for Luke and Kathy to emerge.

Since arriving three hours ago, Kathy and Decker had time only for a meal, a scan of the discs, and some hasty introductions. Now Kathy sat back and scanned the table. Next to Decker sat the President of the United States of America, along with six other people trying to make sense of madness.

The large black man in uniform on Weiss's right was General Linus Cleaver, the chairman of the Joint Chiefs of Staff. To his right was a square-jawed man also in uniform. Major General Thomas Allardyce, M.D., was the commander of USAMRIID, although he asked everyone to call him Tom. Next to him was a thin-faced woman with long dark hair and quick, intelligent eyes. Dr. Sharon Bibb ran the Epidemic Investigation Service at the CDC in Atlanta. Beside her was Assistant Director Bill McCloud of the FBI. A tall, lean man with a buzz cut and a southern drawl, he had relevant experience with the bureau's Hazardous Materials Response Unit. He and Luke knew each other already. The other two men were Todd Sullivan, Pamela Weiss's new chief of staff, and Jack Bloom, who headed the Doomsday Committee. Part of the National Security Agency, the Doomsday Committee existed solely to brainstorm the bleakest of disaster scenarios and lay down plans should they arise. The very fact that he was here was implicitly terrifying.

Major General Allardyce spoke first, indicating the deck of charts in front of each of them that summarized the discs' contents. "I suggest we make sure we all understand the full implications of Crime Zero before we assign responsibilities and agree on the next steps. Kathy, since you're the closest to this, would you summarize the three phases as you see them?"

Glancing at the charts in front of her, Kathy briefly out-lined the Project Conscience background. She could see Pamela Weiss grimace as she explained how Alice Prince and Madeline Naylor had used Kathy's research on Conscience to develop a gender-specific vector.

Kathy sipped at her glass of water. "Phase One was a test on six prisoners at San Quentin, including Karl Axelman. They inserted the modified genes into an attenuated viral vector, which inserted itself into the stem cells of the patient. This meant that the treatment—if I can call it that—affected only the person it was injected into. The vector targeted the cells in the hypothalamus in the brain and the testes. The new genetic instructions boosted all hormone and neuro-transmitter levels to literally mind-blowing proportions, on the one hand, stimulating their aggression while at the same time racking them with suicidal guilt. The main aim of that phase was to check that the treatment would first render the patient incapable of violent deeds and then kill him in a given time frame."

"Given time frame?" asked Todd Sullivan, the President's chief of staff.

"If the vector and the modified genes within it were engi-neered correctly, the patient's age at death could be geneti-cally predetermined."

"How?" asked Dr. Bibb as she checked her charts. "By using the length of the telomeres?"

"Exactly."

"What are telomeres?" asked General Cleaver.

Kathy looked at Sharon Bibb to see if she wanted to an-swer, but she smiled as if to give Kathy the floor. "They are the protective tips on the ends of chromosomes, like those on the end of shoelaces. As we get older, our cells divide and the telomeres erode. If the virus is so engineered, it could recognize a host's age by their length. You must understand that Alice Prince has an incredible array of vectors. She can do almost whatever she wants.

"Phase Two was intended to move from an isolated test to a real-life situation. They chose a belligerent nation because they wanted to show the power of their vision, I guess to impress people that they could stop war. After all, what greater violent crime is there?"

"I think they particularly wanted to impress you, Madam President," said Decker quietly.

Pamela Weiss frowned but said nothing.

Kathy continued. "The disc clearly shows that they used a single corrupted sample of BioShield vaccine to start the infection. Iraq, like most military powers, is a client of ViroVector's. It would have ordered a supply of DNA vaccines to protect its troops, and it wouldn't be hard for Alice Prince to instruct TITANIA, the computer that runs ViroVector, to insert one corrupted sample in the batch sent to them. Unlike Phase One, this vector is infectious. It's a hand-to-mouth agent, passed on by contact."

"But why didn't they use a more infectious vector right off?" asked Jack Bloom.

"I think they needed to ensure it could be contained if it misbehaved," Kathy replied. "Iraq is effectively a trial of the treatment on a larger scale, both in terms of who it affects and, as important, who it *doesn't*. This vector is designed to *infect* everyone, whereas the DNA modifier within the vector is designed to *affect* only men. Alice Prince and Madeline Naylor wanted to make sure that their smart assassin killed only what it was aimed at."

"According to our intelligence, that's happening," said General Cleaver. "It appears that no children or women in Iraq have caught the disease yet."

Kathy nodded and chewed her lip. "They've probably caught it; they're just carrying it without any symptoms. The brilliance of the Crime Zero vector is that it targets only what it's meant to, but it uses everyone as a carrier. Ebola and Marburg burn out because most often their victims die before they can pass it on. Crime Zero isn't like that. Phase Two lives on; there's no end zone."

"But how the hell are they coordinating all this?" asked McCloud, the FBI man. "Pandemic plagues are nightmares to contain. How do they expect to get one to do their bidding?"

"Through TITANIA, ViroVector's supercomputer," said

Kathy. "Alice Prince and Madeline Naylor are the composers. But TITANIA is almost certainly the conductor, orchestrating everything, monitoring each phase before moving on to the next one. And the last phase is the really clever one. Phase Three is the killer."

Kathy flicked through the deck of charts in front of her, her hands trembling as she came to the last charts. "The Phase Three vector overrules everything that went before. If a person has been exposed to Phase Two, Phase Three will overwrite any genetic changes with its own. This vector is a piece of genius. Like Phase Two, it infects everyone but affects only some of the population. And even those effects differ according to the age of the victim. This combines the best of Conscience and the worst of Crime Zero. It's frighteningly clever."

"Explain," said Weiss.

"OK. First of all, this vector is designed to infect females of all ages but not give them any symptoms. They carry the viral vector in the cells lining their respiratory tract and can pass it on, but they remain healthy save for a mild cough. This means the virus won't burn itself out. With male children under the age of puberty their genome actually changes but only in the way that the Conscience vector modified genes. It won't kill them. Infected prepubescent boys have their genes recalibrated to make them less prone to violence regardless of their natural predisposition. It will also affect their germ cells. This means that they will pass on these modifications to any children they sire. But they're lucky compared with any male over puberty who becomes infected."

She paused for breath.

"As with the Phase Two vector, every postpubescent male who catches the Phase Three virus will first be rendered emotionally incapable of committing violent acts and then will die. But with this virus, guided by the telomeres on a target's chromosomes, the timing of death will be determined by the victim's age. Essentially the young will die first. Postpubescent men under about twenty-five will die in a few months. The last to go will be the older men, those who are the least violent and have the most knowledge to pass on. They will die in about three years. The other key thing about this vector is that it is based on the influenza virus, which means it's spread through respiratory aerosol. It's airborne. Just breathing in the vector can infect a person. With modern air travel it'll spread around the globe in twenty-four hours."

There was a moment of silence. Then Sharon Bibb spoke. Her voice had the monotone of someone in shock. "Can I just put this into context? The greatest pandemic to date occurred in 1918 after the First World War. Influenza spread like wildfire throughout Asia, America, and an already exhausted Europe. We all know that millions of men died in World War One, but that number was dwarfed by the fifty million who died of Spanish flu. Twenty million died in India alone. But this would make even those figures seem small. If Phase Three got out, almost two and a half billion people would die over three years."

"All men," added Decker. "You can't fault the logic. Violent criminals cause violent crimes. Violent criminals are men. So no more men equals no more violent crime. Only females and boys with modified genes would remain on the planet. Violent crime, wars, and all acts of senseless violence wiped out at a stroke, by one enormous act of violence. Within a few decades a new stock of peaceful males would grow up, and violent men would just be a memory." He let out a deep sigh. "You can't say it lacks vision. And, President Weiss, I think they've chosen you as part of that vision."

Pamela Weiss turned to Luke, a look of horror on her face. "In that case can I make them see sense?"

After he had listened to the others discuss the three phases of Crime Zero, it became increasingly obvious to Luke Decker what role the President was meant to play in Madeline Naylor and Alice Prince's brave new world.

Project Conscience wasn't just a precursor to Crime Zero. It had also been a means to get her elected. Although Prince and Naylor planned to stagger the deaths over three years, the logistical implications alone would still be enormous. They needed someone strong and female in charge to provide continuity and prevent the world and particularly the United States from sliding into chaos when the mass deaths began.

"Why haven't Prince and Naylor been arrested yet?" asked Jack Bloom of the Doomsday Committee.

"Because the third disc doesn't say how or where the airborne virus is going to be set off," said Deputy Director McCloud. "For all we know, they could have numerous devices geared up to go. What we do know is that according to the strict timing plans on the disc, Phase Three isn't due to be released for at least a few more days. Director Naylor is one smart woman. We've got her and Alice Prince under surveillance, but I don't want to jump them until we're sure how to handle them."

Bloom frowned. "But they could be releasing it now. Surely the risks of taking them in and neutralizing them are less than letting them run free."

Decker shook his head. "I think Bill's right. The only thing in our favor at the moment is that Naylor and Prince don't know that we know. They aren't in any hurry, and that's to our advantage. They don't see themselves as terrorists or psychopaths, but more as physicians curing a great disease. They've planned this meticulously and won't have any knee-jerk reactions unless we force them to. They don't want to destroy the world; they want to save it. They think. they're the good guys."

"So what do you suggest we do?" asked Weiss. "Just wait until they save the world?"

Decker smiled. "No, Madam President, I think *you* should talk with them face-to-face. They're partly doing this for you, and they want you to help them. Don't alert them before the meeting that you know anything. Use the pretext of the Peace Plague to call a meeting with them both. Appeal to them as friends. Focus on Alice Prince; make her realize the human cost of what she is doing. She's the weak link. My guess is that Naylor is committed to this, and you won't move her. From what I know Prince likes the concept of

Crime Zero but shies away from the real implications. Is she particularly fond of any of your family?"

Weiss blanched. "My third son, Sam, is her godson."

Decker nodded. "How old is he?"

"He's over puberty if that's what you mean. Thirteen." Weiss took a deep breath. "He would be one of the first to go."

Decker nodded again. "Use that. Show her your pain. Make Alice relate your potential loss to the loss of her daughter, Libby. Make her realize in no uncertain terms that she would be murdering your child as brutally as Axelman murdered hers. If Alice connects, she might help us control Naylor and stop the genie before it gets out of the bottle. She might even help with the Peace Plague."

Weiss's face was expressionless, as if frozen. "I'll meet them both at ViroVector," she said.

"Good idea," said Allardyce. "We could cordon off the campus, containing them and any hot agents they might have on-site. Then regardless of how your meeting goes, we'll have them in custody."

Sharon Bibb tapped her fingers on the table. "That's all fine and dandy. But surely we've got to assume the worst. We've got to work on a vaccine for the Peace Plague and Phase Three in case it gets out."

Allardyce nodded. "The problem is that these are extremely complex recombinant viral vectors. Most of my people don't have that kind of specific experience. Not to find a solution fast anyway. This has taken Prince years to develop. We have, what, a few months?"

Bibb sighed in agreement. "The same at Atlanta. We tend to specialize in combating naturally occurring emerging viruses."

There was a pause as all eyes looked to Kathy.

"Kathy, how long have *you* worked in this particular area?" asked the President.

Kathy nervously ruffled her hair, and Luke could see her shoulders sag as if suddenly laden down with a heavy burden. "Almost ten years."

"With Alice Prince?" asked Sharon Bibb.

Kathy nodded.

"And Crime Zero is based on your work?" said Allardyce, nodding slowly.

"Yes, I'm afraid it is," Kathy whispered.

Pamela Weiss leaned forward then and looked straight at Kathy. "I want you to lead the task force looking for a vaccine. Would you do that? Can you do that?"

Luke watched as Kathy hesitated and then gave a small nod.

The President then turned to Sharon Bibb and Allardyce. "You will supply Dr. Kerr with all the personnel and resources she needs."

Both nodded.

"Where shall we base the main BioSafety lab?" asked Bibb. "Atlanta or here at USAMRIID?"

"I'd personally prefer to work somewhere I know," said Kathy, "and somewhere where there's a large library of relevant samples at hand. How about ViroVector? The Womb there is the most advanced virology lab I've ever used."

Allardyce gave a resigned shrug. "Well, we would be effectively commandeering the site after the President's meeting with Alice and Naylor, so taking control isn't an issue. And it's got a slammer, hasn't it?"

"Yes and a submarine," said Kathy.

"What the hell's a slammer?" asked Todd Sullivan.

"A BioSafety Level Four hospital," said Allardyce.

"And a submarine?"

"A BioSafety Level Four morgue," said Kathy.

There was a short silence.

"OK," said Weiss, "that's agreed. Let's move on." She turned to Jack Bloom. "What contingencies are in place if it all goes down the drain?"

Bloom pushed a strand of black hair off his forehead and pulled a sheet of paper from an attaché case beside him. Decker could see that the sheet was made of flash paper. One whisper of flame, and it would disappear in a puff of smoke. "Naturally this information doesn't go outside this room. We must plan for the worst-case scenario but present the best case to the media and the public. Panic must be avoided at all costs. Every exercise conducted by any agency in this or any other country involving the spread of an airborne pathogen has shown that once the population panics, the shit hits the fan.

"This applies internationally as well. We tell no other world leader the full story about Phase Three until we are sure it has been released. The golden rule is we give people information only if they can do something positive with it.

"So first of all, the cover story is the Peace Plague in Iraq. We are helping seek a vaccine while at the same time taking precautions in the extremely unlikely event that it spreads beyond those borders. These precautions will not be specified, but if they are discovered, we will just put them down to extreme caution.

"Let's start with the bleakest scenario. Fifty-five mass graves have been prepared across the nation, at least one in every state. These have been around for decades, and the largest can hold up to fifty thousand. Most of these are disused mine shafts, quarries, and natural caves, but the current capacity won't cover our little problem. So we are already seeking more sites." He looked up and gave a humorless grin. "At least Director Naylor and Dr. Prince, our two angels of death, allowed time for the dying to bury the dead.

"Next, the key personnel list, including everyone vital to maintaining the nation's basic infrastructure, has been updated. All those on it have been allocated space in quarantined accommodation. Again, our angels of death have thought this through as well. If we ensure that women are trained to undertake all vital tasks, then disruption can be kept to a minimum even if the worst happens."

Bloom paused and looked around the table at their pale faces. "Oh, it's not all bad, not yet at any rate," he said dryly, giving a sardonic smile. "On a more positive note there are numerous contingencies in place to contain this thing and stop it from causing any damage." He turned to McCloud. "Bill, do you want to run us through what the bureau's got?"

McCloud leaned forward, his hands clasped on the table. "Basically it's all the standard stuff, but there's lots of it. On the operation side we've got a squad of Hostage Rescue

Team trained ninjas on standby in every major city equipped with full body armor, Racal biosuits, and Envirochem sprays. Similar squads will be deployed to secure ViroVector when the President meets with Madeline and Alice. I'm also going to get a team of IT specialist tech agents to work on taking control of this TITANIA computer."

The Hostage Rescue Team ninjas had impressed Decker when he'd seen them training at Quantico in their jet black portable Racal biological space suits and body armor. He hoped they and their suits wouldn't be needed.

As the meeting drew to a close and Weiss confirmed what everyone had to do, Decker allowed himself to think about tomorrow. On arriving here three hours ago, he had called Barzini. Although forbidden to talk of Crime Zero, he had been able to tell Joey that Kathy and he were OK. Barzini had told him that Matty's funeral had been arranged for tomorrow, and Decker had said he would make it.

He turned to McCloud as he rose from the table. "Bill, keep me in the loop, won't you? I need to go to a funeral tomorrow for a few hours, but I want to be involved in this."

McCloud patted him on the shoulder and gave a dry laugh. "Involved? Shit, Spook, you're stuck right in the middle of this thing."

35

Alice Prince tried to quell the worry gnawing at her stomach. She didn't think it particularly odd that Pamela had asked for their advice on the Iraq epidemic. They were her oldest friends, and ViroVector could offer real practical help. She was only surprised that her advice hadn't been sought before. Finding the pulse box in the Womb was dangerous. But just because Kathy Kerr now knew about Crime Zero didn't mean that Pamela Weiss did.

Alice sat on Madeline's right at the head of the conference table, and from their vantage point they could see the main door of the Smart Suite. Behind them was the screen wall, its array of screens and cameras perusing the room.

Whatever Alice felt, Madeline had become so paranoid and taken such extreme precautions that it made her think the unthinkable. What if the President really did know about their involvement in Crime Zero? The idea filled her with dread.

But if the President did genuinely want help with the Iraq epidemic, then the meeting offered a great opportunity to plant the possibility of what could happen in Weiss's mind, to ready her for the reality of Crime Zero.

Coiling the pendant chain around her little finger, Alice hoped that Madeline's man, Associate Director Jackson, was correct in his hunch about where Luke Decker and Kathy Kerr might be today. They had to be taken out of the equation.

A voice on the intercom told them that the President had arrived and within a matter of moments would be shown into 'he room. Standing but not moving away from the table, Alice watched two staff members open the door and show Pamela Weiss to a seat before leaving again. To Alice's relief Pamela made no move to embrace them both, content with a cool verbal greeting. She looked strained, drawn.

To Alice's surprise Pamela had come alone. No advisers. No backup.

Alice's heart began to beat a little faster.

"How long have we known each other?" asked Pamela with a sad smile. "It must be thirty years."

Alice flashed a nervous glance at Madeline, but the FBI director kept her face expressionless.

"Yes, about that," said Alice.

Pamela nodded. "And we're friends, aren't we?"

"Best of friends," said Madeline.

"And I've never lied to you, you know? I have never purposefully deceived you."

Alice's heart was beating so fast now she was sure Madeline or even Pamela at the other end of the table might hear it.

"And I've never lied to you," replied Madeline.

"What about all the lies on Conscience?"

"They weren't harmful. They were to protect you," said Madeline. Alice couldn't believe Madeline's calm.

Pamela paused then and looked at Alice, those wonderful blue eyes staring right into her soul. "Did you know that the symptoms of the epidemic in Iraq exactly match those exhibited by Axelman and the other death row prisoners at San Quentin?"

Alice didn't know what to say.

"I need your help to solve a problem. I'm going to ask you one question, and if our relationship has meant anything, I need you to tell me the truth—as both your friend and your President." Pamela turned back to Madeline. "Do you know what is behind the Iraq epidemic?"

Alice felt hot and cold rushes down the back of her neck. It was their chance to confess all, to tell Pamela everything and involve her in their plans.

"No," said Madeline with a frown as if the idea were preposterous. "No, of course not. No."

Pamela turned back to her, and Alice thought she saw the glint of tears in her eyes. "What does my other oldest friend say?"

Alice desperately wanted to say yes, but Madeline caught her eye and gave her an icy look.

"No," said Alice, realizing the consequences of her denial even as the syllable left her lips.

Slowly Pamela nodded, still keeping her eyes fixed on Alice. "Would either of you do anything to hurt me?"

"Of course not," said Madeline quickly.

"Or my family?"

"No," said Madeline.

But Alice found it harder to lie so quickly. "No," she whispered eventually.

"So, Alice, help me understand something," said Pamela. Her eyes were definitely moist now. Alice hated confrontation, especially with her friend; she was rigid with tension. "Tell me then, why do you want to murder my husband and sons? Why do you want to kill your own godson?"

Alice gasped, her throat suddenly so tight she could barely breathe.

"Pamela, what are you talking about?" asked Madeline, still calm.

But Alice was far from calm. She began shaking her head. "But I don't want to murder your family."

"Well then, Alice, for the sake of my children and Libby, help me stop Crime Zero."

The silence seemed to last minutes. Alice turned pleadingly to Madeline, but she looked just as shocked.

"You must understand, Pamela," Madeline said, rising to her feet. "We did this for you." She sounded angry more than concerned. "We can explain everything."

At that moment the President rose and walked to the door and opened it. "I want someone else to hear this, another old friend of yours who'll understand the science a lot better than I would."

Alice watched as Kathy Kerr, the second woman she had betrayed, walked into the room.

"Tell us everything," said the President, beckoning for Kathy Kerr to stand beside her. "We're listening."

36

**Hills of Eternity Cemetery, Colma, California.
Sunday, November 9, 11:00 A.M.**

Colma was the world's only incorporated city where the
dead outnumbered the living. Just west of San Francisco
Airport, this necropolis had been home to most of the Bay
Area's cemeteries since 1902, when the city and the county
board of supervisors had outlawed all burials in the city of
San Francisco.

Contemplating this, Luke Decker felt a small shiver as he
helped carry Matty's coffin over the rolling lawns of the
Hills of Eternity Cemetery, one of three specifically Jewish
plots in Colma. When he was a child, a ghoulish teacher had
once told him that if all the human dead from the beginning
of time were added together, the total would still fall short
of the billions alive today. Now he wondered whether, if the
third phase of Crime Zero were allowed to run its deadly
course, that statistic would still be true.

As they neared the grave, Decker and the other pallbear-
ers lowered the coffin. Decker couldn't believe how heavy it
was when Matty had been so small. "You OK?" whispered
Joey Barzini as they laid the coffin on the straps to lower it
into the earth.

Decker nodded and smiled at the big man. He was
touched that in his absence this Catholic had taken it upon
himself to contact all of Matty's friends and help arrange

this funeral in keeping with the Jewish traditions. Decker had never been a religious man, but his mother had brought him up to follow her husband's Catholic faith. Still, he took comfort from the fact that Matty was being buried according to his most cherished values.

As was the custom, the funeral had been arranged as soon as possible—to allow the healing process to begin. Then, following Kavod Ha-met, the Chevra Kaddisha had carefully prepared his body, washing Matty and dressing him in the special hand-sewn soft linen clothes of Tachrichim before placing him in the Oron, the wooden casket.

Despite his sadness and anger at the circumstances, Decker found the funeral and the service that preceded it an oddly joyous occasion. It was a glorious blue-sky day, and more than two hundred people had gathered on the emerald lawns of the Hills of Eternity, including the two FBI agents McCloud had assigned to watch over Decker. At the service a selection of Matty's friends from the San Francisco Symphony had played Matty's favorite passages from Paganini and Debussy. At least Matty's funeral celebrated his zest for life as much as marked his death.

Now as he listened to the Kaddish, Decker felt suddenly alone. To his surprise he thought of how much he would have liked to have had Kathy standing beside him now. It seemed strange that after all they had been through recently, she wasn't here now.

He thought then of what his grandfather had always believed in, Matty's conviction that we were far more than the sum of our genes. He recalled the night Matty had comforted him after learning Axelman was his natural father, touching his face, telling him that he was a good man; that he was more his mother and Matty's son than Karl Axelman's—regardless of blood.

In the madness of Crime Zero Decker realized the wisdom of his grandfather's words. A man could be judged only by his deeds. Nothing else mattered. There were influences brought to bear, from the past and the present, but those deeds were ultimately his choice, his responsibility. For the first time in the longest time Decker felt a kind of peace within his soul.

But as the grave filled with earth, hot tears stung his eyes. Decker was not a vengeful man—he had seen too much and learned too much to think that revenge brought anything more than fleeting satisfaction and then greater pain—but if he ever met Associate Director William Jackson or his co-horts again, he might settle for that.

Blinking back tears of loss, Decker didn't see the Chrysler pull up beneath the copse of trees fifty yards from the edge of the mourners. Three men were in the car. The face of the powerful man in the front passenger seat was par-tially obscured as he held a pair of binoculars to his eyes, studying the crowd. Scanning the heads, he smiled when he alighted upon the flash of blond next to a huge man at the front.

If Luke Decker had turned at that moment, he might have recognized the car and realized that meeting Jackson again wasn't going to be a problem.

Associate Director William Jackson had already found him.

Smart Suite, ViroVector Solutions, Palo Alto.
11:12 A.M.

Standing beside President Weiss in the ViroVector Smart Suite, Kathy Kerr was shocked by how passionately both women believed in what they were doing. And how desper-ate Alice Prince was for President Weiss to understand her reasoning.

Madeline Naylor and Alice Prince had known Kathy for almost ten years, and just over a week ago they had tried to kill her. Yet there was no shame in Naylor's eyes, only ha-tred. Alice Prince wouldn't even look at her. Behind them on the screen wall Kathy noticed the tiny cameras on the cor-ners tracking her and the President, as if TITANIA were studying them.

"You must understand, Pamela," said Prince, standing and

leaning forward as if giving a sermon. Kathy had never seen
her so animated. Behind her lenses her eyes shone with
frightened zeal. "Crime Zero is the cure for all the world's
violence. Within three years we'll virtually eradicate all violent crime, including war. Surely, Pam, you of all people
must realize that with its weapons of mass destruction *Homo
sapiens* is the one species on earth with the power for self-
annihilation. The Iraq crisis, which almost brought you to
the brink of nuclear war, proves that humanity has only one
mortal enemy left to fear: man himself.

"Years ago we needed men. Apart from reproduction they
protected us from predators and supplied food and nourish-
ment. Their aggression and drive helped us develop and
eventually rule the planet. But as a species we have become
too successful too fast. Evolution has lagged behind. Now
that we dominate the earth, men's roles have changed, but
men haven't. Technological advances in a host of areas
mean that we no longer need their protection or even their
hunter-gatherer role. Physical strength, their key asset, is
now redundant. We don't even need them for procreation."

Alice spoke quickly and fluidly, her words bursting forth
in a torrent. Her face glowed as if she had a fever, and she
seemed desperate for Weiss not only to understand her mo-
tives but to approve of them. Even if the President wanted to
interrupt her, Kathy knew it would be in vain. Alice Prince
barely seemed to pause for breath. All the time Pamela
Weiss stood stock-still, her weight seemingly on her toes as
if she were standing in a rushing stream, braced against a re-
lentless current.

"Even men's drive, which years ago was such a positive
asset," continued Alice, "means they aren't content to nurture our position as the lead species and husband the resources of the planet. Now they turn their predatory and
protective impulses on each other. Pamela, they are no
longer an asset to the species but a liability. Over ninety percent of all violent crimes are committed by men. The rest
usually involve them. Virtually every war has been waged
and fought by men for no purpose that benefits us. We are a
species imploding in on itself because men haven't evolved.

"Evolution needs help, and with Crime Zero we can give it. Don't you see? In three years only women and children need exist. All the corrected boys will grow into and sire a new breed of men more genetically relevant to today's needs. Within one single generation the world will be born anew, its future assured. No more violent crime, no more wars, no more mass destruction. Don't you see?"

Before the President or Kathy could reply, Madeline spoke. Her voice was calmer and more pragmatic than Alice's but still weighty with a searing conviction. Madeline's dark eyes shone like polished jet, and her usually pale face was flushed. "Think about it, Pamela, one purge, one cull, and the world will be changed for the better. And it'll happen; we've tested it. After Iraq we know that men will be rendered incapable of acts of violence. Crime Zero Phase Two stopped what could have become World War Three. We also know that no children below puberty will be harmed. Boys will be allowed to grow into men, but better men. There need be no more rapes, no more senseless murders—"

"No more Libbys," interrupted Alice.

"We won't need the FBI," continued Madeline, "or armies, or weapons. Christ, you wouldn't believe the things I've seen in the bureau and in the courts, the abominations men perform for no real motive. Their violence doesn't even bring them any significant benefit. Pamela, Crime Zero is the only way to stop this. We are protecting man from destroying himself. If ever there was a necessary evil, then this is it. Can't you see? This isn't about killing people; it's about *saving* them. It's about saving us all."

"But why didn't you just go with Project Conscience?" asked Kathy, trying to make sense of their insane logic. "I could almost understand your deciding unilaterally to infect everyone with the Conscience vector. But killing almost two and a half billion people in order to eradicate violence—"

"You're missing the point," said Alice desperately, as if Kathy *must* understand her. "Project Conscience was always going to be too little too late. All men alive today are genetically *and* environmentally tainted. Men have become a cancer. They were once healthy cells in the 'body human,' but now they are threatening the very existence of the species. To cure cancer, you must *remove* the malignant cells, and you must remove them *all* because any remaining cells will spread the disease. We must start afresh with a new wave who will benefit the 'body human,' not undermine it. We must do this precisely because we don't want to eradicate men. In order to protect them, we must help them evolve."

"Put it into context," urged Naylor. "What's a few lost decades and deaths in the grand scheme of things? We've been evolving for thousands of years, and if we act now, we'll survive to evolve for thousands more. In thirty or forty years *men* will see the wisdom of what we've done. They'll live in a more equal, matriarchal society, and their aggressive, destructive past will be a bad memory."

Naylor gripped her hands together. "Pamela, you can, you will lead the transition. You are currently the only female leader of a major power. You are perfectly placed to lead this country and the world through the transition."

Weiss's face was gray with shock as if her old friends were strangers she was seeing for the first time. "But what about the good men? Not *all* men are bad! What about my husband? What about my sons, Alice? Sam is your godson, for chrissakes, and he's just reached puberty. How can you justify killing all of *them*? Killing my children won't bring your child back!"

Kathy saw Alice falter and look down, sadness creasing her face.

"Everything has a cost," said Naylor. "Surely you understand that? Nothing comes free."

"Alice, there must be vaccine for Phase Two and Phase Three," demanded Kathy. "You create an antisense vaccine for every vector you develop. You've always told me it was good practice in case they mutated and needed to be neutralized."

"Alice"—the President was almost pleading—"it's not too late. We can still stop the deaths in Iraq. You can still help end this madness."

Alice Prince glanced uncertainly at Naylor. Kathy tried to read her look but couldn't.

"There is no cure for Crime Zero," stated Madeline firmly. "Crime Zero *is* the cure. And, Pamela, you have to accept that."

It was too much for Kathy. Instinctively she moved down the table toward the two women. As she walked toward them, Weiss turned to the door and opened it. Bill McCloud and four armed men in black body armor entered the room. "I can't believe I got you both so wrong," she said to Madeline and Alice. "How could you have ever thought I wanted any part of this abomination?" She turned to Bill. "Arrest them and keep them under armed guard."

"You won't stop Crime Zero, Pamela," said Madeline. "You can't escape your destiny."

Alice looked down at her feet. A study of discomfort.

"Oh, yes, she bloody well can," said Kathy, standing two feet from Naylor.

Then Naylor opened her right hand and revealed a small black tablet that resembled a TV remote. "I think Phase Three should start now," she said.

At that point Kathy lunged for Naylor and the remote.

Or tried to.

Her hand missed, and she almost lost her balance. Steadying herself, she took one step forward and knocked into Naylor. Except Kathy didn't knock into her; she didn't make any contact at all.

In a split second of confusion Kathy looked down and saw the black pad on the floor beneath her and registered that the green light was on.

Suddenly everything was clear. She had used the KREE8 technology herself to present and examine enlarged 3-D images of viral vector DNA molecules. She thought of the guard at the gate and the camera lenses watching from the screen wall, which allowed Prince and Naylor to see them via TITANIA.

She turned to the stunned McCloud and an uncomprehending President Weiss. "They're not here," she said slowly, not wanting to believe what had happened. "Neither Madeline Naylor nor Alice is physically here."

"What do you mean?" demanded McCloud, the blood

draining from his face. His men had seen Alice and Madeline enter the campus and were now in charge of the whole site. "They have to be here."

"This is a holopad area. TITANIA's projected their three-D image from another source."

"So where are they?" Weiss stared at the hologram, at the smiling faces of her old friends. "Ali, Madeline, stop this madness. Where in God's name are you?"

"Finishing what we started," said Naylor, looking at the remote. "As I speak, at least six airports worldwide are equipped to release Crime Zero Phase Three into certain bacteriophage air purifier tunnels. And I can activate each of them from here." Then with a wintry smile she and Alice vanished.

Kathy put her head in her hands. "Christ, we've got to find them," she said. "They could . . ." She trailed off, not knowing what to say.

But from the look of horror on Weiss's and McCloud's faces there was no need to say anything.

Executive Suite, San Francisco Airport.
11:47 A.M.

Anger and relief flooded through Madeline Naylor in equal measure: anger that Pamela Weiss had found out about Crime Zero before they could silence Kerr and Decker, but relief that she had made contingency plans. Perhaps Jackson would finish Decker. That would be a bonus. As she packed up the three KREE8 3-D image catchers, she looked out of the window at the main concourse below.

"Cheer up, Ali, it's not the end of the world." She smiled, fingering the remote, which had activated the phage air purifiers. "It's the beginning."

But Alice didn't smile back. "I just wish we hadn't lied. Perhaps we could have convinced Pamela if she still trusted us. If she understood what we were trying to do."

Naylor shook her head. "No way. Pamela was always going to have to be protected from the truth. She's a Demo-

crat, for chrissakes, a liberal. She'd never have gone along
with this willingly. But whether she's willing or not, she has
no choice now. At least we didn't let her stop us."

It had been Naylor's idea to go into ViroVector before
6:30 A.M. with Alice to set up the Smart Suite and then use
their Gold clearance code to exit via one of the two main inspection tunnels beneath the campus to the waiting rental
car. They had immediately driven to the airport and taken a
private executive suite on the mezzanine level above the
main concourse, using one of six valid credit cards Naylor
held in different names. With a conference room and adjoining bathroom the suite afforded them total privacy.

Then, using the suite's supplied digital phone socket,
Alice had computer linked their laptop and the three KREE8
3-D image catchers to TITANIA so that they could appear to
sit in the Smart Suite for their prearranged conference with
Pamela.

"Come on, Alice, we've got to get ready. There's no time
to worry anymore." Naylor reached into one of the two olive
green shoulder bags, which contained everything she would
need as a fugitive, and pulled out the sachets of black and
auburn hair dyes and new contact lenses. Perhaps in a few
years, when the dust had settled, the world would realize the
wisdom of what they'd done and they would be heroes. But
for now they had to disappear.

Naylor walked to the adjoining bathroom and turned to
Alice, who still sat at the conference table, looking off into
space. "We've things to do, and we need to catch that plane."

"Have we done the right thing?" Alice said suddenly.

Naylor walked over to the laptop and clicked onto the
plane departures program. She checked Heathrow first. The
British Airways Flight BA344 from Gate 28 was already
boarding. It was the same with Sydney, Rio, Singapore,
Nairobi, and Los Angeles. She smiled a smile of satisfaction. "Of course we have. Anyway, it's too late to start worrying now. It's out of our control. The evolution has begun."

37

Hills of Eternity Cemetery, Colma.
Sunday, November 9, 12:01 P.M.

A prickling awareness of being watched made Luke Decker
turn his head. Otherwise he would not have seen the car as
he walked back across the lawns to the black Mercedes Joey
Barzini had lent him.

The funeral was over. Most of the mourners had left for
the shiva at Barzini's house, but Decker had wanted some
time alone to say good-bye to Matty before he joined them.
He had sent his two FBI minders on ahead, promising to join
them in twenty minutes.

After climbing into the Mercedes, he adjusted his
rearview mirror and studied the gray Chrysler parked a hundred yards away behind a copse of trees. There were three
men. A black man sat in the front passenger seat.

Associate Director William Jackson.

Decker gunned the engine into life and slowly pulled
away, all the time keeping his eyes on the Chrysler. He felt
no fear, only a cold sense of purpose. The car behind him
wasn't a threat. It was an opportunity.

In his mind he recalled the winding lanes that led out of
the vast complex of cemeteries and tried to pick the spot
where Jackson would make his move. And then select the
place he would make his.

He checked the gun in his jacket and clicked his seat belt

into place. Behind him he could see the Chrysler pulling closer, but he made no move to increase his speed, keeping at a sedate twenty miles an hour. The road ahead was deserted, and beyond the gates of the Hills of Eternity the main road leading to the other cemeteries looked equally abandoned. He and the three men behind seemed to be the only living souls in this city of the dead.

The Chrysler was only a few yards behind. He could see Jackson's face clearly now. He was smiling.

After pulling out of the gates, Decker turned right down the main tree-lined artery that cut through the patchwork of cemeteries. Still keeping his speed at twenty, Decker waited for the Chrysler to come closer. He could see indecision on the driver's weasely face. Did the man speed up and overtake him, or did he pull up alongside, or wait? Jackson didn't seem to be giving him any guidance.

So Decker made up his mind for him. He suddenly braked to a standstill, put the Mercedes into reverse, and slammed his foot on the gas.

The impact was bone-crunching, but Decker was prepared for it. As the Chrysler stalled and Jackson pulled the driver's head off the dashboard, Decker pushed the Mercedes's automatic gearshift into drive and again slammed his foot on the gas. He had gone three hundred yards down the deserted straight road before the Chrysler started up again. But instead of trying to make good his getaway, Decker again slammed on the brakes, jumped out of the car, and walked into the middle of the road. He retrieved his gun, held it in both hands, and locked its barrel on the approaching Chrysler. The car accelerated. He wouldn't miss. He had hit far more difficult targets in practice.

The first bullet took out the front left tire, pulling the car left immediately. He didn't need a second. The Chrysler almost turned on its side as it spun around and hit a large, gnarled oak. Decker ran to the wreckage and barely noticed the unconscious driver or the third man slumped in the rear seat. Jackson was fumbling with the door, trying to get out. He had a large gash on his forehead, and his left arm appeared broken.

Decker opened the door, pulled him out of the car, and deposited him on the bruised grass verge. He pushed the barrel of the SIG into the back of Jackson's neck and leaned down toward him.

"Why the hell did you have to break his fucking fingers?"

"It wasn't my fault," Jackson whimpered, his nasal whine incensing Decker. "Director Naylor made me do it. I had to find you. If he'd told us where you were, he'd have been OK."

Decker tightened his finger on the trigger. "Well, you've found me now."

"But I wasn't going to kill you. They wanted me to take you to the airport if I found you and Kathy. They called me to—"

A question suddenly cut through the heat of Decker's rage. "When did they call you?"

"I don't know. A few hours ago."

"And you were supposed to take me to the airport?"

"Yeah, to meet them."

Decker suddenly felt calm, numbingly calm. He reached into his left pocket, pulled out his cell phone, and called Bill McCloud's number. Before he could say anything, McCloud told him about Naylor's and Prince's disappearing act.

"They could be anywhere," said McCloud, his drawl uncharacteristically strained. "According to our IT guys, they could have pulled off their hologram stunt from anywhere with a digital phone socket. The IT guys have taken control of most of TITANIA, but apparently a whole lot of its higher functions require some other kind of clearance. They're working on it, but until then we don't know where the hell they are."

"I think I do," said Decker abruptly.

"Yeah?" McCloud sounded stunned.

"I've got William Jackson here, and he says they're at the airport."

"Shit. We'll get it closed down immediately and cordoned off. We'll do it from the outside in, so we don't alert anybody inside." Decker heard McCloud turn from the phone and bark an order.

He came back on the line. "We can have the whole airport sealed within minutes. But we've got to get close to Naylor and Prince before they set anything off—assuming they haven't done so already."

"I've got an idea," said Decker. "But I'll need some help."

"Whatever you need. What do you want to do?"

"The only thing I can: use myself as bait. Prince and Naylor have told Jackson to take me to them." Decker pushed his gun into Jackson's neck. "And I'm going to make sure my friend here does exactly what he's told."

Executive Suite, San Francisco Airport.
12:11 P.M.

It took Madeline Naylor completely by surprise. Not one of her contingency plans could have covered it.

She stood in the private bathroom admiring her short copper-flecked hair and black roots in the mirror above the basin. Her immaculate shoulder-length white hair was gone. Naylor had dyed her hair twice, to look like a natural brunette who had colored her hair. It worked. She was pleased with how different it made her look. Blue contacts helped the transformation, as did the long floral dress. She rarely wore dresses and never floral prints.

"Your turn, Alice," she said, entering the conference room.

But Alice hadn't changed. She hadn't even moved.

"Come on, you've done nothing."

"I know."

"Well, hurry up! We need to get going."

Alice frowned and fiddled with the pendant around her neck. She seemed distracted.

"Alice . . ."

The ring interrupted her. Naylor went over to the green bags and fished out her cell phone.

"Yes." She exhaled the word into the handset.

"I've got Decker," said Jackson. The reception was poor. But despite the static, she could still hear his nasal voice.

"You said you wanted him. I've got him at the airport. The new mall's construction site on the east mezzanine by the Calvin Klein billboard. It's quiet."

Naylor frowned. She didn't need this now.

"Who is it?" asked Alice.

"Jackson, he's got Decker." Naylor spoke back into the phone. "Kill him."

"Wait!" shouted Alice suddenly, snatching the phone from her. "No, leave him. I want to speak to him. Where is he?"

Naylor laughed in disbelief. "You can't speak to him. Are you out of your mind? There's no time." She tried to grab the phone back, but Alice wouldn't release it until she'd made her arrangement with Jackson and hung up. Then Alice turned her back on Naylor and rested on the bags.

Naylor was really angry now. She had never seen Alice so defiant before. "Alice, you aren't seeing Decker. You're getting changed and leaving *now*!"

"No, I'm not," said Alice quietly, her hand in one of the bags.

Naylor moved toward her then, but before she could reach her, Alice turned around, a small pistol in her shaking hands. "Madeline, I don't want to shoot you, but I promise you I will. Just let me go."

Naylor didn't know what to say; she could only stare at her friend. Alice's round face was red, and her eyes were moist with tears. Naylor had no doubt at all that if she rushed her, her gentle, shy friend would shoot her. "I don't understand. What are you trying to do?"

"Step back into the bathroom."

Naylor did as she was told. "We've done everything we planned to do. What the hell's wrong?"

Alice closed the bathroom door and locked the door from the outside. Naylor could hear her take the key out and put it in her pocket. "I'll come back for you afterward," Naylor heard her say through the door.

Naylor couldn't believe this was happening. "Just tell me what the hell you're going to do, for chrissakes."

There was a pause and the faint echo of a sob. Then slowly in a faltering voice, Alice explained.

As soon as she did, Madeline Naylor lunged at the bathroom door with all her force, trying to break it down.

38

San Francisco Airport.
Sunday, November 9, 12:27 P.M.

Alice Prince could think of no other way but this. Madeline would understand when she calmed down. She had to.

Walking across the concourse teeming with busy travelers, Alice looked up at the Calvin Klein billboard and the unpainted concrete pillars of the deserted site for the new shopping mall on the east mezzanine level.

She stepped over a strip of blue tape and a sign saying CONSTRUCTION WORK. PLEASE KEEP OUT, opened a door, and walked up a flight of service stairs, negotiating an obstacle course of paint tins and abandoned ladders left by workers.

Alice Prince regretted using the gun with Madeline. But she had no choice. Madeline was just too dominant. She'd always had a hold over her, twisting everything around. Ever since they were children. Ever since Madeline had explained why it was right to punish Alice's father. Just remembering the day on the ice made Alice's chest tighten. It also convinced her that she was right to do what she was doing now.

The frozen lake close to her house in Baddington is beautiful, and Alice loves skating there. Except when her father joins her. Alice doesn't know if she loves her father because when he gets drunk, he hits her mother and her. But she's used to it now, so she's embarrassed that her friend Madeline knows.

In January a week before her fifteenth birthday Alice goes skating on the lake with Madeline. It's late on a Saturday afternoon, and it's so cold her breath almost freezes solid. The sky is pale blue, and the small lake, lined with neat fir trees, dazzles in the late-afternoon sun. The far end is roped off with a sign saying KEEP OFF: THIN ICE.

Because of the cold, only a few other skaters are on the ice, so the two girls have most of the lake to themselves.

Until her father comes out to join them. She can tell at once that he's drunk because he immediately orders her to skate with him. She tries to leave, but Madeline holds her back. Madeline wears a bright red jacket and hood with her white hair sticking out like icicles. Her dark eyes stare at Alice's father, and she confidently skates over to him with Alice in tow. Like two ducklings, they follow him around on the ice.

Alice's father is a large man with a red nose and face. His rheumy eyes stare out from under a furry Russian hat that makes him look like an angry grizzly. "Follow me," he shouts, "both of you!"

Then he proceeds to skate joylessly around the ice. Her father is a good skater, and as he goes around, he increases his speed. It's a game Alice knows well. Eventually her father will gain such a lead that he will lap her, and when he passes, he will push her over, laughing as he exhorts her to go faster.

But today it's different because Madeline is with her. Unlike Alice, Madeline is an athlete. She skates like the wind, and as she glides on the ice, she tucks Alice in behind her slipstream and carries her along with her.

The faster her father skates, the faster Madeline goes. And Alice is sure that Madeline isn't even trying. She just matches his pace, no quicker, no slower. They keep their distance on the ice. But her father is stubborn. He skates without respite for an hour, trying to close the gap.

As it gets late, the lake is deserted by the few remaining skaters. But behind Madeline, Alice feels exhilarated and safe. It is as if she had wings on her feet that could take her away from harm.

It takes another ten minutes before he tires of the game, realizing he can't win. The last stragglers have gone, and he suddenly stops and points to the unsafe end of the lake.

"Skate by the rope," he orders. His eyes have that cruel, bullying look she hates. "Or are you too scared?"

But she's not frightened with Madeline by her side. Then Madeline pushes the game further. "I'll skate to the *other* side of the rope if you follow me," she says to Alice's father. "Or are *you* too scared?"

His expression changes then, and he frowns. He approaches them, and Alice is scared. Then Madeline turns and, taking her hand, leads her away toward the rope.

"Come back here," he shouts.

But Madeline just pulls her forward, their skates hissing on the ice. For the first time in her life Alice feels a surge of power. It doesn't matter what he does to her after she gets home; at this moment the fire of defiance runs through her veins.

"No," Alice yells back. "Come and get me."

Then, ignoring the sign, Madeline crouches and skates under the waist-high rope, pulling Alice along behind. Cutting her skates into the ice, she stops and turns back to her father.

He glowers at her from the other side of the rope. "Alice, come back here. Do what I say. Now!"

"Don't move," whispers Madeline beside her. "You're safe here." Madeline's eyes are bright, and she has a thin, excited smile on her frozen face. Alice looks down, and the ice is so thin here she can see the dark water beneath her skates.

Madeline suddenly shouts at Alice's father, "If you want to hit Alice, you'll have to come here to do it."

His face reddens with rage.

"Be careful, Madeline," Alice says. She knows how vicious her father can be. "He might hurt you too."

Madeline shakes her head. "He won't hurt me. Watch."

Alice admires her courage but doesn't like the look on her face.

"We're waiting," Madeline taunts. "Or are you too scared?"

He waits for a moment, not believing they can be so defiant. Then he snarls like an animal and steps over the rope. Carefully he rests his first skate on the thin ice, and then his second. When he realizes the ice is taking his weight, he gives them a horrible smile. "Who's scared now?" he says, lunging for Alice.

For a second she is frightened, but then she hears a crack, and Madeline pulls her farther along the rope, and they step over to the safe side.

It happens in seconds.

One moment he is standing there scowling at her, and then he's falling through the ice, clawing on to the side of the hole, trying to pull himself back onto the slippery surface of the lake. She waits for his splashing to stop before skating closer to the breach.

"Pass me the rope," he orders her. His face is furious, but for the first time ever she can also see fear in his eyes.

She stands and looks down on him, but before she can move to him, Madeline holds her back. "Just watch!" she whispers.

"Hurry," her father cries. "I can't hold on much longer." His voice becomes more pleading as he realizes that she isn't rushing to his assistance. He looks up at her, his hands trying to keep their hold on the treacherous ice. His eyes now show naked terror. "Please, Alice, help your papa," he pleads. "Help me. Throw me the rope."

But she can't move. Madeline isn't exactly holding her back, but she legitimizes Alice's inaction. Because looking down on her father, seeing him beg makes Alice feel good. She can't remember how many times he has towered over her, ignoring her pleas.

Still, as she watches his fingers slip on the ice and sees him slide deeper and deeper into the freezing water, she wants to go to him, to help him.

But Madeline is saying in her ear, "Let him go. Let him slide out of your life. You don't need him. You don't love him. He only brings you pain." As he sinks, he starts to cry, but she can't move. Madeline isn't even touching her, but Alice feels as if she's pulling her back.

"Help me," he screams in his panic.

Alice is too paralyzed to help.

He struggles and tries to scream one more time, but he slips farther, and the water drowns his cries. Alice stands on the ice, watching as her father's flailing body floats under the ice beneath her feet. As she stares in horror, Madeline takes her hand and leads her from the lake. "You don't need a father," Madeline reassures her. "I haven't got a father. We just need each other. Your secret's safe. You've done nothing wrong."

But that wasn't true. Deep down Alice had always known that she'd done something wrong. Something so evil that ten years ago her daughter had been taken from her as punishment. All her life she had been in Madeline's thrall, bound to her by guilt. She had always believed that Madeline must be right about everything; to believe otherwise was to face the truth that allowing her father's death was wrong. But now she accepted it *was* wrong—like so much else.

When she reached the service door on the mezzanine level, Alice paused beside the paint tins and boxes in the stairwell. Jackson had said he would leave Decker by the Calvin Klein poster. After slowly opening the door, she stepped out, ignoring a large sign, PLEASE KEEP OUT. WORK IN PROGRESS.

Turning to her left, Alice looked through a break in the advertising boards, over the balcony to the teeming concourse below. At that moment a group of businessmen in dark suits entered through the main doors. They were obviously from some kind of convention and were late for their flights because they stormed impatiently through the crowd, cutting a dark swath through women and children, almost knocking over a baby in a carriage.

As her eyes blurred, the milling throng no longer resembled humans at all, but cells in a petri dish. Some of those cells were good and healthy, but others were malignant—male. She imagined the dark, invasive male cells being eradicated and the remaining cells having more space to move. Then she imagined them all moving at a kinder, more peaceful pace, working together rather than struggling against one another. The vision briefly pleased and reassured Alice, but then she looked again, and the reassuring warmth left her.

Turning, she saw Decker sitting against a pillar next to the Calvin Klein billboard just as Jackson had promised. Dressed in a black suit, he was gagged, and his hands were tied behind his back. When she looked into his green eyes, he seemed surprised more than scared. He kept glancing beyond her as if expecting there to be someone else.

She bent down to his level and reached forward to pull off the tape that covered his mouth. It wasn't strong tape and came away easily. His lips were dry beneath it.

"Where's Naylor?" Decker asked. There was no time for subtlety. The whole plan was to have her here too. If they took Prince, but Naylor was free and she had Phase 3 . . .

Alice smiled. "She's not important. She's safe."

Decker tried to remain calm. After forcing Jackson to call Naylor, Decker had left him to McCloud's men and rushed here. McCloud had already sealed the airport, and although Decker couldn't see any of the ninjas, he knew they were close, waiting to pounce.

"What have you done with Phase Three?" he asked.

When Alice told him, his heart sank.

Then she put her face close to his and explained everything else. As he listened, he leaned forward, unsure he was hearing correctly. Then Alice reached for the teardrop amulet around her neck and made as if to bite it.

At that moment Decker saw two of McCloud's ninjas appear over Alice's shoulder, their guns trained on her, antivirus bleach sprays at the ready.

Suddenly everything slowed down.

Alice followed his eye. Snapped a look over her shoulder. Stood up, pulled the amulet from its chain, and broke it into two parts with her teeth. One part bore a tiny needle.

The ninjas ran at her.

"No," he screamed at them. Could see panic in Alice's eyes.

She moved back, against the waist-high parapet. She slipped backward. Made no attempt to steady herself. Kept both hands locked on the amulet. Suddenly she was falling backward over the parapet.

Decker reached for her, clutching at the ruptured amulet, its contents dripping onto the crowd below.

Senses heightened, he imagined seeing fine droplets float through the air. Beautiful in the refracted light, falling toward people oblivious of them on the concourse below.

"No," he shouted again, throwing himself at Alice Prince. She spread her arms wide. Received him in her embrace as she fell backward over the mezzanine.

"Spook," McCloud shouted behind him. But he too was falling now. Alice beneath him, jabbing the ampule needle into his arm. Below him everyone was screaming.

Alice smiled, clasping his face to hers, wrapping her body around his. "For Libby," she whispered.

Then there was nothing.

Alice Prince's body had jumped with shock when she saw the men in biosuits and guns. But as soon as she realized it was a trap and there was no way out, her terror left her.

She felt no fear of death. She would soon be reunited with Libby. And she had done all she could. It only seemed right that Decker, the son of her daughter's killer, should be the one.

Even as she positioned herself beneath Decker's body and crashed into the cart of luggage beneath her, snapping her neck, dying instantly, Alice was smiling.

Madeline Naylor was too late. She couldn't believe it. She stood stunned in the teeming crowd, watching the two bodies fall through the air toward her. The sound of impact was that of two heavy mattresses falling on dry kindling wood, a sickening cracking thud.

After breaking her way through the flimsy bathroom door, she had rushed here, trying to stop Alice and save her

from herself. But she had failed. Her friend was dead. Alice
was gone.

Dazed, she pushed through the babbling crowd to see the
two bodies lying on a pile of broken luggage. Decker was
sprawled over Alice in a parody of two spent lovers. Squinting, she stared at Alice's neck. She turned away.

On autopilot she registered the ninjas in Racal suits
swarming around the bodies with bleach sprays and covering the main exits. Their unworldly appearance added to her
sense of unreality. But even now she still sensed the danger.
Her disguise wasn't foolproof, and they would be looking
for her. She had to get out fast. Her mind automatically
clicked through all the processes required to close down an
airport. She remembered the exercise she'd run at JFK.

She pulled the green tote bag over her shoulder, pushed
her hand inside, and reached for the Glock. Then, keeping
her hand on its grip, she walked slowly through the large
milling crowds on the main concourse, heading for the service door by the Barnes & Noble bookstore. Most of the ninjas were preoccupied with keeping the crowds from leaving
the main exits. No one seemed to be watching as she stole
away down into the labyrinth of service tunnels below.

Alice had mentioned once how the AirShield maintenance men who serviced the bacteriophage air purifier cartridges had a locker and shower room down below the
concourse. At the bottom of the stairs Naylor found herself
in a large corridor with pipes running along the walls and
strip lights on the ceiling. Just as she was about to turn right,
she saw a sign pointing left toward service lockers. Six company logos were on the sign; the top one was AirShield's.

The door was locked, but it was so flimsy she easily
kicked her way in. In the small dark room she put on an Air-
Shield overall and baseball cap and consulted an airport plan
stuck on the wall behind a grimy plastic shield. Bending
back the shield, she pulled the map out. There was one pas-
sageway that would take her past the baggage handling area
and out under the runways toward the perimeter fence at
maintenance exit 3C. From there she stood the best chance
of escape.

Striding down long corridors beneath flickering spines of fluorescent strip lights, she ignored the few people she passed, and calculated how much time she had before the FBI managed to seal the whole airport. From Jackson's phone call, probably part of a trap, McCloud had had ample time to cover most of the main points of entrance and exit. Exercises she had run in the past had always taken no more than fifteen minutes to close down a large airport. Containing suspected airborne pathogens was more difficult, though. Every man in the front line of containment had to wear full biohazard protection. And men had to be concentrated where the biggest population of passengers was. The outer perimeters were left thin, at least for the first hour or so.

Following the map, she saw a large junction ahead, from which all the main passageways under the runway branched out. If she were organizing the containment, she would have placed a man there to cut off those routes. Knowing McCloud and the standard procedures, she knew that was precisely what he and his agents had done. Naylor could try to go around, or she could use the junction to her advantage.

Slowing to a walk, she wiped the sweat from her brow. The large exposed pipes that ran down the right of the corridor were hot. And McCloud would have closed down the air-conditioning to prevent the distribution of contaminated air. Naylor stopped ten yards from the underground junction and rested her green tote bag on the floor. She stood listening for a moment before she heard the two voices: a man and woman. She listened for another minute to make sure they were alone. Then she began to walk toward the junction. She made no attempt to be particularly quiet. She just walked slowly and calmly, a maintenance employee in overalls going about her daily work.

She saw the eerie figure in the black space suit before he saw her, but she made no attempt to avoid him.

"Halt, FBI," said the man when he spotted her. His voice sounded strange through the suit's speaker as if he were on a long-distance phone line. "Sorry, ma'am, but you can't come this way. You've got to go back to the main building."

"What's going on?" she asked, roughening her voice, hoping the man wouldn't recognize her. "I got to go check a thousand things." She reached into her tote. "Look, I got a pass and everything."

The man leveled his gun at her, and the woman agent came and stood beside him. "This isn't about passes," she said. "You can't go any farther. Just go back now. We don't want any trouble."

"What's wrong?" Naylor asked, feigning fear. "Why you dressed like that?"

The man lowered his gun and smiled at her through his glass visor. It was a kind, reassuring smile. "Don't worry. Go back to the main building, and everything will be explained to you."

She shrugged then. "OK."

"Take care, now," said the man, already turning away with his partner.

Naylor's gun was out of her tote in less than a second, and both FBI agents—*her* agents—were dead in under four.

Within two minutes she was wearing the female agent's black biological space suit and using her headset to track the other agents' movements. In just over sixteen minutes she was outside the cordon sanitaire and in a stolen car making her way to the city.

Crime Zero Phase 3 was out. But she had heard something on the headset. Something about Alice Prince and Decker that meant she couldn't rest yet. As she drove, she tried not to think about Alice. There would be time enough to mourn her. But first she had to protect her legacy.

Part 3

Crime Zero

39

Flight BA186, Calcutta, India.
Monday, November 10, 8:00 A.M.

Flight BA186 from London to Calcutta was the first flight carrying passengers infected by a bacteriophage air purifier tunnel contaminated with Crime Zero Phase 3. For everyone on board the infection would begin unobtrusively enough, a slight cold and a cough.

Every virus has a chosen host cell, whether it is the leaf of a tobacco plant in mosaic disease or the CD4 subset of T lymphocytes in a human sufferer of AIDS. The genetically engineered Crime Zero Phase 3 virus was no different. It was an airborne virus transmitted by respiratory infection, and the first cells it targeted were the lungs. Once it had been ingested there, it sought out the relevant target cells in the brain's hypothalamus, the respiratory tracts, and, in the case of males, the testes. It then began to subvert those cells' DNA with its own. Using the genetic clues it found there, the virus then unbundled its own genetic contents for replication within the human host in three different ways.

In the 118 female passengers on board BA186 the virus would generate no symptoms, except the mild cough that would last for a few days and help transmit the infection.

In the thirty-six prepubescent boy passengers the cough would be the only uncomfortable symptom. Within days the viral vector would unload a battery of control sequences into target cells in the brain's hypothalamus. These control sequences would fine-tune the seventeen interdependent genes mainly responsible for aggression and inhibition within the boys. Their genomes would alter, levels of the inhibiting neurotransmitter serotonin increasing, if deficient, or maintaining, if naturally adequate, the level of the more stimulating transmitters, such as dopamine and noradrenaline modifying, if too high. Potential testosterone levels would also be managed to within predetermined tolerances. Unknowingly the boys would be subtly changed. The default of violent aggression shifted to pacific cooperation. Each would find it easier to "behave well." They would exhibit no other symptoms.

In the 210 males over puberty the cough would mutate into other symptoms, the onset of which would depend upon age. The initial genetic programming would be the same as the boys.' And each male would stabilize in this less aggressive state, in the similar way a person with HIV might stabilize before contracting full-blown AIDS.

Meltdown would be determined by the age-indicative telomeres on the tips of their chromosomes. The youngest would enter meltdown and die within seven or eight days, the oldest in three years.

In the onset of meltdown the virus's dominant genetic code would boost the inhibiting levels of serotonin still higher while instructing full expression of the fuel neurotransmitters and stimulating androgens to kick in, flooding the men's systems.

Immediate physical symptoms of meltdown would include those associated with extreme clinical anxiety, hair loss, acne, and shrinking of the testes. Psychological symptoms would include chronic anxiety, hallucinations, paranoid delusions, and obsessive ruminations. Death by brain hemorrhage would arrive mercifully within a matter of days. A proportion would take their own lives.

All the men on Flight BA186 would die in the next three years, but not before each husband, father, brother, son, lover, and grandfather had passed Crime Zero to whoever came within breathing distance of them.

Within a matter of days the single flight from London to Calcutta would carry Crime Zero to every continent in the world. The number of humans infected would already be in the hundreds of millions. Within a week only the most remote areas of the globe would be uninfected. Then the youngest of the men on the flight would start to die.

ViroVector Solutions, Palo Alto.
The Same Day, 3:00 A.M.

The other scientists were already calling it a loop virus. But to Kathy Kerr it looked more like a hangman's noose, an indiscriminate viral executioner that would lynch all men unless it was stopped. The blowup photograph from an electron microscope was pinned to the door of the Level 1 laboratory conference room in the outer ring of ViroVector's biolab complex. It featured Luke Decker's blood at a magnification of one hundred thousand. The picture was dominated by what looked like a loop with a curled devil's tail. It was the Crime Zero virus, and Luke Decker's blood was teeming with it.

Kathy was still troubled by the clear genetic differences between the virus Alice had infected Luke with and Crime Zero Phase 3. But when she'd suggested studying them more closely, Bibb and the others had argued that although Luke remained in a coma, there were more pressing matters to contend with. Prince had probably developed various versions of Crime Zero, and the one she carried in her pendant was simply an earlier version, sharing greater similarities to the Phase 1 vector than Phase 3. Despite her nagging doubts, Kathy knew she needed to focus on Phase 3.

"A week's impossible. No way!" said Jim Balke, ViroVector's short and scruffy operations director, who ran the large-scale production plant on-site. He nervously rubbed his already red eyes and took another shot of coffee. "We're going to have to aim at a more realistic target. We have to accept that people are going to die. Lots of them. We can't do anything about that."

"But that's the whole point of why we're here." Sharon Bibb groaned. "To see how we can limit the numbers." Her dark hair was pulled off her narrow face, and the stress showed in her eyes. In front of her an open laptop and piles of paper were evidence of the last few hours of work. On her left the brilliant Schlossberg twins, Mel and Al, brought in from her team at the CDC in Atlanta, scribbled away on charts, showing each other what they were working on but saying nothing as they communicated. It was past three in the morning, and all around the room the walls were plastered with sheets of flip-chart paper. Every sheet was covered with brainstormed ideas scrawled by the team.

"But a week's just not going to happen," Balke said again. "You'd be lucky to do it in a year. Even if we had the vaccine now, it would take the whole pharmaceutical industry six months just to produce and distribute enough to treat the U.S. We're not going to have time to test it."

"For God's sake, Jim," growled Major General Tom Allardyce, squaring his jaw and rising from his seat to pace around the room. Two other USAMRIID scientists sat at the far end of the table, peering over a laptop, frantically checking antisense oligonucleotide sequences against Crime Zero's genome, searching for clues that would lead to a vaccine. "Of course a week's too damn short. But we've got no choice! If you want to start accepting deaths now, fine. But quit moaning. When we come up with a cure, other countries will help produce it. Ever since Crime Zero's gone live, the President's informed all heads of state. Each has agreed with the U.S. not to say anything to their people yet but to start making contingency plans. The Russians have already offered their production facilities and weaponization expertise. Jim, your role is crucial in determining *how* we can scale up production from shake flasks."

Kathy Kerr rubbed her temples and looked at the flip chart by the door. Two axes were scribbled on it in blue marker pen. A steep exponential curve in red ink ran from the origin of the graph. The horizontal axis represented time—yesterday's date, November 9, was written in as time zero—and the vertical axis represented the population of men banded by age. Three black lines connected the red line with the horizontal time line; the first at seven days, the second at one year, and the third at three years. By the first line was the scribbled legend "Men start dying—30 million per week"; by the second, "1.2 billion plus men dead." There were only three words by the third line: "All men gone."

She took a deep breath and tried to take some comfort from the caliber of the team assembled around her. As well as Sharon Bibb and Allardyce, each had two of his or her brightest and best there. The last person in the room was the pessimistic Jim Balke. In a perverse way Kathy was glad he was being so downbeat; it seemed to fire up the others.

All the team were dressed in surgical greens, and not one of them had slept since McCloud's agents had confirmed that an air purifier tunnel at Los Angeles's airport had been contaminated with Crime Zero and that at least two planeloads of infected passengers had spread the virus. Other major international airports were being checked, and Crime Zero had been detected at London's Heathrow, but that was academic. One contamination was enough. Crime Zero was out. The world was hot.

"Let's focus on the main things we've got to do," said Kathy. She turned to the two USAMRIID scientists working on the laptop. One was a large, quiet man with a thick red beard named Floyd Harte. The other, Rose Patterson, was a slim black woman with huge eyes and an intellect to match. "For the base vaccine we've got to concentrate on developing antisense oligonucleotides to block Crime Zero's genetic instructions. And yes, that's going to take time. But I still say Alice may have developed one already. She usually did. Once the IT boys have got Gold clearance for TITANIA we can look for the code there. We might find a shortcut."

Kathy looked at Jim Balke. "And when we think of how to distribute this vaccine to the world, we shouldn't assume it has to be via a syringe injected individually into every person. What we need to do is fight fire with fire. We need to develop a viral vector that spreads the vaccine for us."

"Yes, that might work," said Al Schlossberg suddenly, turning to his twin, Mel. Johns Hopkins–educated virologists, both were six feet four inches tall with dark, curly hair, round steel-rimmed glasses, and prominent Adam's apples. Out of their more usual greens they wore matching bow ties. They were rarely seen apart and were brilliant enough to prove the maxim that two heads were better than one.

Mel seemed to muse on what Al was saying. "Yes, it could, but we'd need to . . ."

Al nodded. "Of course, but if we . . ."

"Yes, that might do it," replied Mel. Both spoke in dead-pan voices and assumed that everyone else was privy to their seemingly telepathic mutterings.

"What might work?" Bibb muttered in frustration.

"Well," said Al, as if talking about the weather, "we know that Crime Zero Phase Three uses a toughened influenza orthomyxoviridae virus, genera A, subtype H2N28, carrying the H2 and N28 antigens on its spikes."

"It's a good choice for a vector"—his twin seamlessly continued—"because this genus is most often associated with serious epidemics and killer pandemics. Its drop nuclei are less than four microns in diameter and will remain suspended in the air for hours after being expelled."

Al resumed. "Its viral resistance to drying has been improved, so it will keep moist in aerosolized droplets for longer even than the robust measles virus." He paused. "So what we need to do is find or develop a vector with even better infectious properties, in order to spread our vaccine through the population as fast as possible. Then in the same way as Crime Zero spreads disease, we can get people to spread the vaccine."

"But I still don't see how we're going to be able to make enough of it," moaned Jim Balke. He was clearly worried how his two large but by no means infinite production facilities at the north of the ViroVector campus were going to produce what was needed.

"But, Jim, that's the whole point," said Kathy. "What we must do is create an infectious vector that distributes itself, a contagious cure if you like. Crime Zero is spreading via the population. To have any chance of combating it, we must make the cure do the same. So the absolute amount we produce won't need to be vast so long as the vector is both extremely fast and extremely efficient. If the Crime Zero flu vector is a family car, then our vaccine will need to be a Ferrari."

Kathy paused then and checked the notes on the table in front of her. She had to quell a surge of panic when she saw the number of stages they had to cover in order to reach a solution—if they could even develop an antidote in the first place. But she forced herself to sound positive. "Once we have a vaccine and a vector, we'll have to splice them together to form a viable vaccine. Once we have that and Jim's ensured we can scale up production, we need to get it out there."

Kathy turned to Tom Allardyce. "Obviously your people will be helping with the early stages, but your expertise is vital for the weaponization part of the process."

"Understood," Allardyce said. "We are already selecting a cohort of infected volunteers for testing the mass-produced cure. And in conjunction with the British, Israelis, and Russians we're working on the logistics of spreading the vaccine once we have the go-ahead. It will obviously be dependent on what you guys come up with, but we are already exploring everything from bomblet and warhead design and production to aircraft availability and weather patterns. But rest assured of one thing: If you can come up with the vaccine, we'll get it out there."

Kathy nodded, trying to look as confident as he did. That was the damned problem. They had to come up with the cure. She opened the laptop in front of her and began to type in the main action points. "OK, if the USAMRIID team of Rose and Floyd focus with me on the antisense vaccine, Sharon and Al and Mel can focus on finding a vector. The production issues are with Jim, and Tom has responsibility for the weaponization logistics." She looked around the room, and everyone nodded. "OK, I propose that we remeet every six hours to discuss progress and share problems. Anything else?"

"One thing," said Allardyce, "what are we going to call this?"

Floyd Harte, the quiet USAMRIID scientist, raised a hesitant arm like a child in class. "The way I see it, men all over the world are now effectively on death row. Some have got an earlier execution date than others, but they're all going to be dead in three years. What we're trying to do here is get them a reprieve."

Everyone nodded.

"Well then," said Kathy, typing her notes of the meeting into her laptop, "that's what we'll call it: Project Reprieve."

40

The Fairview Hotel, Fisherman's Wharf, San
Francisco.
Monday, November 10, 9:18 A.M.

Billy Caruso watched the woman open the swinging doors,
enter the gloomy hotel lobby, and walk across the faded,
threadbare carpet toward him. Already he was checking her
out. Billy was one of life's spectators and proud of it. In his
forty-two years, boy and man, Billy had seen all of life pass
through his family's small hotel, the underbelly of life anyway. Nothing shocked him anymore, and he prided himself
on knowing a person's story just by looking at him.

He divided his clientele into two: those who paid for
rooms by the hour—mostly hookers and their johns—and
those who stayed longer, often much longer. One guy—said
his name was Frank Smith, not that Billy cared—stayed almost a month in room 11. Then early last Tuesday morning
Billy had woken to the screeching of tires, followed by three
gunshots. Billy knew when to stay out of sight and hadn't
called the police or anything. The next morning he'd shown
no surprise when he'd found a large wiseguy waiting at the
checkout with a bundle of dollars. "Mr. Smith's checked
out," the guy said, handing over the wad. "His room needs a
cleaning."

The thing is Billy had known from first looking at "Mr.
Smith" that he was on the lam from the mob. Everything

319

about him cried it: the bulging sports bag, the dark glasses, the smell of booze, and the shaking hands. But it was when the glasses came off and Billy saw the man's eyes that he'd known the man was living on borrowed time. They were scared eyes, and they looked half dead already.

Watching the woman approach, Billy took another Chiclet from the package on the scratched check-in desk and began chewing the gum. Billy rarely drank, never took drugs, and only took a hooker when his wife was out of town, which was rarer than hearing the pope fart. Billy got his kicks from watching life, not living it. It was safer.

"So, how can I help you?" he asked with a smile. Like his mama always said, manners don't cost nothing.

"I need a room."

He studied her closely. She'd dyed her hair a kind of copper color, but her dark roots showed through underneath. She was tall and skinny, and that helped disguise her age. Could be anything from forty to sixty. She wore a lightweight cardigan over a long floral dress. She carried a fully packed green tote bag in her right hand. She wore an obligatory pair of dark glasses. Billy reckoned that at least 80 percent of his clientele wore dark glasses. Which was kind of weird, considering how gloomy his lobby was.

"Staying long?" he asked, already guessing the noncommittal answer.

"Just a few days." Her voice sounded shaky.

"Name?"

"Simone Gibson."

Yeah, right, thought Billy, and he was Martin Luther King.

"How you paying?" Again he knew she'd say cash. And as he guessed she would, she reached into her bag and immediately pulled out some bills to give to him. Her hands trembled as she handed over the money. She seemed desperate to get to the room. He guessed that if he rolled up one of those cardigan sleeves, he would find a network of needle holes. A strung-out junkie, probably an old pro on the run from her pimp.

Now that he had guessed her story Billy lost interest, idly

wondering how soon it would take her pimp to find her. Or
whether she was too old for him to bother.

"Room eleven," he said, handing over the key, guessing
that she wouldn't notice the stain on the rug. If she complained, he'd just tell her it was ketchup. Picking another
Chiclet and popping it in his mouth, he hoped the next guest
would provide more of a challenge. Some people were too
damn obvious.

As soon as Madeline Naylor entered room 11, she locked
the door behind her and wedged it shut with one of the
chairs. Not bothering to unpack, she opened the tote bag
and set up her laptop on the rickety desk by the window.
She had stored the car and the black biological space suit
she'd taken off the FBI ninja at the airport in a long-term
garage.

It took her two minutes to plug the matte black laptop into
both the power and phone sockets, switch it on, and dial TI-
TANIA's access number. She didn't bother to use her Gold
clearance code in case it had been closed down or Mc-
Cloud's people were monitoring. Instead she carefully
tapped ten keys in the correct order, opening an electronic
back door Alice often used to get into TITANIA, giving access to all files. It was doubtful the FBI IT people would
ever find this, and even if they did, they couldn't use it to
trace her.

On the laptop screen a list of options suddenly appeared
against a turquoise background. Ghosted into the background like a watermark was the ViroVector logo.

Quickly she clicked the search icon at the top of the
screen. She had to find the file quickly in case Kathy Kerr
and the others had managed to get in. She still couldn't believe Alice had done this and not told her about it.

She typed "Crime Zero Antidote" into the search box.

Within seconds a response came back from TITANIA.
One file found on secure X drive. Entitled "Crime Zero
Phase 3 Modified Antisense Construct."

Naylor smiled. She could see her face reflected in the
turquoise screen. Fingers dancing on the keys and trackball,

she answered the necessary queries and carried out her command. The urgent task had been done.

Next she called up the ViroVector plans. A map of the site appeared on-screen, showing all above and below ground facilities, including access tunnels.

After clicking the personnel icon, she saw a list itemizing everybody on-site. A large proportion had the prefix "visitor," and Naylor guessed that many were agents drafted in to secure the building. Later she could cross-reference some of the names with the FBI personnel database. It would be vital to identify exactly whom she was up against. Using the trackball, she selected two names on the list: Kathy Kerr and Luke Decker. Kerr flashed red, and Decker green. Then she clicked the location icon.

There was a pause as TITANIA checked her door sensor records. Then a red dot flashed on the plan in the outer circle of the underground lab facility. While Naylor watched, the dot moved into the center of the rings as Kerr made her way through the doors toward the Womb. It gave Naylor a sense of power to follow the movements of her prey.

The green dot flashed deep underground below the biolab complex. This dot wasn't moving. Decker was in the Level 4 BioSafety containment hospital. Watching those two flashing dots crystalized Naylor's mission and the reason why she couldn't flee and sit out the coming years of transition. To protect Crime Zero, she had to extinguish both those dots.

But for now she must rest. She stood and moved across to the bed. It was uncomfortable, but she didn't care. Using the TV remote on the bedside table, she clicked on to CNN. On-screen a man stood before a crowd of jubilant women waving placards. Most of the women wore T-shirts with slogans such as "Womankind ManUnkind" and "The Fairer Sex Is the Only Sex" printed on them.

The male reporter was saying: "With concern growing that the so-called Peace Plague has spread beyond Iraq, some factions in the U.S. actually welcome the disease, *hoping* it spreads to our shores. So far all documented deaths have been male, and some women's groups now see this as a final reckoning for all the centuries of what they term 'male tyranny.' "

Naylor shook her head. "Oh, Alice, why did you have to go do it?" she said. A wave of sadness flowed through her.

As she thought of her friend, she watched the women begin to chant on-screen. When they put aside their petty allegiances to a particular lover or family member, every woman secretly agreed that men were expendable. Deep down they all knew that everything evil in the world came from men; they just didn't want to admit it. "Ali, everyone would have understood. You would have been a heroine."

Naylor's eyelids were heavy, but she was at least resolved on a course of action. When she had rested and made the necessary preparations, she would destroy the only remaining threats to Crime Zero. Then the world could start using its energies to build a new future rather than fight to preserve its diseased past.

41

ViroVector Solutions, Palo Alto.
Thursday, November 13, 2:06 P.M.

Kathy Kerr stared at the blank screen, unable to believe her eyes. "What do you mean it's been deleted?"

Louis Stransky, the tech agent working on TITANIA, gave a pained shrug. "Like I said, Kathy. We've got Gold clearance. TITANIA's ours now. But the file's gone. There was one there, though, because Alice Prince made a directory. Still, it's not there now."

Kathy's shoulders slumped as she sat in front of the screen in the Level 1 conference room. She'd hardly slept for days, using the bunk provided in the dome upstairs to snatch only an hour or two. Since Monday she, Harte, and Patterson had been trying to sequence and understand the instructions carried by Crime Zero. Only once this was done could they define and build a safe vaccine. But the more they ran the complex iterations on the Genescope, the more Kathy realized that they would need more time, a lot more time.

Secretly she had been banking on Alice Prince's vaccine. Knowing her methods, Kathy had thought it would only be a question of finding it. When Stransky had called her in the Womb to tell her he'd gained control of TITANIA's Gold clearance, she had been convinced the search was over. But it wasn't. The file had been deleted, and Kathy didn't know where else to look for a shortcut. The only approach left was to continue the painstaking processes required to build a safe antisense construct from scratch, all the time knowing that tens of millions of men would be dying as the time passed.

"Do we know who deleted it? Or when?"

Stransky shook his head. "Nope. It was a complete delete, no trace. But it had to have been recent, or the empty directory would have been automatically deleted too. If you're thinking about Madeline Naylor, I've canceled her Gold clearance, so she shouldn't be able to get in now."

An urgent beeping suddenly sounded, but Kathy was so lost in her thoughts that she barely noticed it.

Stransky said, "Aren't you going to check that?"

"What?"

"It's your pager."

Blankly she reached down to her waistband and the pager attached there. She peered at the liquid crystal display and read the words typed there. For a moment her mood lifted.

Decker was finally awake.

**Biosafety Level 4 Hospital, ViroVector Solutions.
2:21 P.M.**

He had been buried alive. He was about to be reborn.

In the gloom, through the translucent nightmarish walls, he could see white ghosts staring in at him. The rushing in his ears sounded like his own blood flowing in his veins. The smell of chemicals and disinfectant hung in the air.

He was one of his father's embalmed victims, imprisoned in some transparent underground prison. That was why he felt so much pain, why his whole body ached.

He turned to his left but found it difficult to move. He was wired up to a series of beeping chrome instruments and monitors. The rushing sound came from an air pipe to the right of his head. He rolled over and was rewarded with excruciating shooting pains down his left side, which rose above the general ache enveloping his whole body. The pain in his chest took his breath away, leaving him gasping as if he'd been rescued from drowning.

The pain helped clear his head, helped him focus. He was in a bed enclosed in a plastic bubble. To his left inserted in the plastic wall was a pair of reversible gloves, his sole contact with the outside world.

The bed was the only one in a small, featureless room. The white ghost floated to his left, just out of his peripheral vision. Then it stepped closer to him and smiled through a glass faceplate. It told him in a strange distant voice that he was OK and that he should rest.

But it wasn't a ghost at all. It was a woman in a white space suit. Why was she in a suit? Why was he in here?

With a groan he compared this dark, surreal waking with all the times he used to wake in Matty's home. No bright sunlight crept in here. He wondered for a moment if he'd ever see the sun rise again. However hard he listened, he couldn't conjure up the sound of his grandfather's violin; he heard only the rasping rhythm of the bed's air pump and the dull beep of instruments.

Despite this, he felt a strange sense of well-being. Like water settling in a pond, his disturbed mind became clearer. He slowly remembered fragments of what had happened: the airport, Alice Prince, the amulet around her neck, and the fall. But there was something else, something more important, that his fractured memory was edging toward.

42

White Heat Science Park, Palo Alto.
Thursday, November 13, 2:30 P.M.

The emerald green rental Jeep Cherokee pulled up at the top
of the rise overlooking the Science Park and the adjoining
ViroVector campus.

Through the binoculars Madeline Naylor could see that
there were no media vans camped outside; that was good.
Most of the TV stations had assumed that USAMRIID in
Maryland and the CDC in Atlanta were the focal points for
combating the Peace Plague, and the authorities hadn't dis-
abused them of that. It annoyed Naylor that Pamela Weiss
still hadn't announced Crime Zero's release, to start preparing people for the inevitable.

The Science Park next to ViroVector had been cordoned
off. Police sat by the main gates, and no one was allowed in
or out. So she couldn't go in via the inspection tunnels on
the perimeter fences, as she'd originally planned. But that
didn't bother her. After much preparation she knew what she
was going to do.

On the backseat of the Jeep two bags contained all she
would need. And on the passenger seat next to her was a pile
of four printouts. A woman's face smiled out from a block
of text on the top one. Across the head were the words "FBI
Personnel Database. Highly Confidential."

Just then a black van drove down the main road. The windows were tinted, and there was a strange air filter device on the roof. She recognized it as one of the specially equipped biohazard vans used by the FBI to transport agents through contaminated areas. She watched as it turned into the main gate of the ViroVector campus. It stopped by the main dome, and she saw three figures in black Racal biosuits get out. All were female. According to TITANIA's lists of on-site personnel, every FBI ninja on duty around the campus was a female agent. No risks were being taken, and they wore full Racal space suits all the time, not to protect them from contamination but to stop them from contaminating any of the male project team inside. This way the female agents didn't have to be confined to campus. They could work in shifts and go back out into the contaminated world.

The arrangement suited Madeline Naylor perfectly.

Biosafety Level 4 Hospital, ViroVector Solutions, Palo Alto.
2:35 P.M.

Looking at Luke Decker, Kathy Kerr bit back her disappointment and frustration at Alice's deleted file. She was relieved Decker had surfaced from his coma and could only guess how bad he felt.

She wanted to reassure him that it wasn't Alice's amulet that had released the virus. In fact Kathy wasn't even sure how really contagious was the version of Crime Zero with which Alice had infected Decker. He had been put in the slammer only as a precaution, so he could be nursed through his coma and the broken arm and fractured ribs from his fall could be treated.

Entering the isolation room, she saw him lying in the plastic-enclosed bed, his head swathed in bandages. He looked so alone, lying in the bubble, cut off from human touch. She wished she could reach in and save him from his disease as immediately as he had rescued her at the Sanctuary. In that moment seeing him completely vulnerable made her realize that she didn't want to lose him again.

"Hello, Luke," she said. "How are you feeling?"

His smile took her by surprise. She wondered what painkillers he had been given.

"Oh, I've been better," he said. His voice sounded weak. She had to strain past the ear mufflers protecting her from the airflow in her suit to hear him. Suddenly he frowned as if trying to remember something. "Come closer, Kathy. I'm sure there's something I should tell you."

"Don't worry about it," she said. "It'll come to you." She sat down on a chair beside the bed, placed her right glove through one of the reversible gloves in the side of the bubble, and held his hand. She felt him grip her tightly through the layers of latex. "Before you try to tell me anything, there are a few things you should know."

Slowly she explained how Alice Prince and a stack of luggage had broken his fall. Alice Prince was dead, but he had escaped with a fractured arm, a row of cracked ribs, concussion, and some spectacular bruises. Then she told him about Crime Zero. That it was now spreading uncontrollably around the world. That it was just a question of time before the body count started.

As he lay there, she told him Prince had infected him with an earlier version of Crime Zero. And that he had been isolated in case he was contagious and would infect the core team at ViroVector working on a vaccine. She reassured him that at his age the lethal stage shouldn't kick in for a year. By then they might have something.

"What about Madeline Naylor?" he whispered.

She shook her head. "We don't know where she is, but McCloud's convinced she'll be caught."

As she spoke, Decker frowned and then let out a sigh of revelation, as if finally understanding or remembering something important.

"I think you do have the vaccine," he whispered.

"No, Luke, I don't," she said. Perhaps she shouldn't have tried to tell him so much. Decker had only just come out of his coma. "We will get the vaccine, but I haven't got it yet. There was an antidote on TITANIA, but it was deleted."

"No, no, it's not on the computer."

Kathy frowned, not understanding. "Well, where is it then?"

Decker gave her a puzzled smile, disentangled his good hand from hers, and pointed to himself. "I think it's in here," he said.

It was so clear to Decker now as he looked at the shock on Kathy's face. Before she could even ask him to explain, and despite his stricken breathing, he told her about his meeting with Alice Prince at the airport.

"She gave me the vaccine, Kathy. She told me so. It was in the amulet. Somehow she realized who she was hurting. She wanted me to say sorry to Weiss and ensure her godson was OK."

Kathy looked stunned when Decker finished his halting story. He could tell she didn't want to let herself believe it in case it wasn't true. "But how do you know she wasn't lying?"

"I just know, Kathy. Why would she? She was about to die."

"But it looks remarkably like a version of Crime Zero. And your genes have already begun changing; your serotonin levels are up, and your testosterone and catecholamine levels are being modified." Then Kathy seemed to think of something. "But if it was an antidote construct, it could act in an opposite way to Crime Zero. And perhaps your early symptoms are—"

"Kathy," interrupted Decker, "I don't know what the hell you're talking about. You're the expert. Why don't you just infect me with Crime Zero Phase Three and see what happens? If I've already got the virus, who cares, and if I've got the antidote, we might learn something."

Kathy didn't respond at first.

"C'mon, Kathy, I feel useless in here, and this is something I can do to help. So just do me a favor. Give me the goddamn bug, and let me make a contribution to the war effort."

Calcutta, India.
The Same Day, 3:11 P.M.

The two Indian boys swimming at the Tollygunge Club were separated by two years. The elder brother, Babu Anand, was fourteen. He had been the youngest male over puberty on the BA186 flight from Heathrow. He coughed frequently as he swam.

Four days after infection the Crime Zero virus had unloaded its DNA into the cells lining his lungs and respiratory passages. It had moved to the cells in his testes and the hypothalamus in his brain. Each of these target sites was now an amplification zone, reproducing more and more for the virus's DNA.

His younger brother had also been infected, but he had not yet reached puberty. The virus was benevolent. He would be corrected and spared.

But as far as Crime Zero was concerned the older brother was a man, distinguished from other men only by the fatally long telomeres of youth. His life was about to be over before it had begun.

43

**Smart Suite, ViroVector Solutions, Palo Alto.
Saturday, November 15, 2:18 P.M.**

Kathy held up the test tube in her right hand and all twelve pairs of eyes in the Smart Suite, including those of the U.S. President, stared at it. There were still two huge issues to resolve, but Kathy found it amazing that this inch-high sample of cloudy liquid in her hand could contain the salvation of humankind.

"How does it work?" asked the President from the White House. Pamela Weiss's face looked out from one of the four screens on the wall in the Smart Suite. Todd Sullivan, her chief of staff, sat with her. Jack Bloom of the National Security Agency's Doomsday Committee and General Linus Cleaver, the chairman of the Joint Chiefs, looked out from two other screens, and Director McCloud from a fourth. All were in Washington.

In the Smart Suite itself the rest of the core team sat around the conference table. The only absentee was Luke Decker.

"The vaccine works on two levels," said Kathy. "First it cancels out the harmful DNA instructions being sent by Crime Zero, then it inserts new instructions." She turned to the screen wall. "TITANIA, show the hologram." Immediately a multicolored spiral of DNA appeared, rotating above the holopad at the end of the table. The rungs that made up the spiral staircase suddenly split, and each side of the double helix broke away like a zipper opening. These then linked with another shorter piece of DNA with opposing nucleotide bases to form two spirals. "As cells divide, the DNA inside the chromosomes splits and reforms as you see here. Each side of the rungs, or nucleotide pairs, can bond only in a certain way. By using a matching antisense section in the vaccine, it tracks down and binds to the sequence of genetic material Crime Zero has changed, canceling it out." Again the DNA hologram began to split, but this time a new section of DNA floated in and bonded itself to the unzipping sequence, effectively neutralizing it. "Once this has been achieved a second section is introduced to recalibrate the gene expressions back to safe levels."

"Excellent, but how do we know it works?" asked Bloom. His usually pale face was chalk white, and his eyes were sunken in puffy, darkened sockets. Kathy could only guess what he and his team had been doing to plan for Armageddon since their last meeting. "Have you tested the vaccine yet?" he asked.

She paused before explaining how Decker had received it from Alice Prince, emphasizing that saving Pamela Weiss's family, particularly Alice's godson, had been a key motivator. The President nodded at this, but if she was moved by Alice's gesture she didn't show it. "When Luke came around, he told me what had happened. And to test whether he did indeed have the vaccine in his blood, he asked me to infect him with Crime Zero Phase Three; so I did."

"And what happened?" asked the President.

"See for yourself." Kathy walked to the main door of the Smart Suite and opened it, letting Decker enter and take the seat next to her. His left arm was in a cast, and he had a slight limp, but the bandage on his head had been removed. "Luke is unaffected by Crime Zero," said Kathy. "Just as you saw on the hologram, the virus is canceled out because the vaccine in his blood identifies and repairs any cells affected by Crime Zero."

There was a sudden spontaneous round of applause around the room. Even Jack Bloom smiled.

"So what now?" asked Pamela when the commotion died down. She had the look of someone who had just received good news but knew that there was more bad news wrapped up inside it. "I assume that little drop of stuff isn't going to save the world."

Kathy nodded. "You're right. But before we get on to how we get the vaccine into the population, you should be aware of a small twist, which explains why we thought Luke had originally been infected with Crime Zero." She cleared her throat. Decker knew what she was going to say next, and she knew he was pissed off about it. "This vaccine was developed by Alice Prince, and she's given it an interesting side effect. The vaccine does cure men of the lethal effects of Crime Zero, but it also gives them what amounts to a treatment of Project Conscience. Men and boys aren't returned to how they were before being infected. Instead the vaccine modifies their genomes to stay within certain tolerances in a virtually identical way to my FDA-approved Conscience serum—except it affects their germ cells. In essence all males will become recombinant organisms. They will contain foreign DNA."

"Meaning what exactly?" asked Todd Sullivan.

Decker answered him. His voice was calm, but Kathy could hear the strain underlying every word. "Meaning that you can't save men without changing them forever. Men and boys and their children will no longer be as naturally violent or aggressive as they once were. In short, men will never be the same again. *I* will never be the same again."

There was silence for some moments before Pamela Weiss asked, "How do you feel, Luke?"

"I feel OK, I think. Believe you me, I still feel anger and aggression—especially about this. But apparently I'm now instinctively more likely to choose less violent options. Only time will tell what that means."

Pamela Weiss turned back to Kathy. "And what's the alternative?"

Kathy exchanged a quick look with Bibb and Allardyce and the others. "We've discussed this," said Kathy, "and we reckon that with luck we could probably create a new antisense construct within a few months, but there's no guarantee it won't have other, possibly worse side effects."

"By then, of course," said Allardyce, "we'll have already lost hundreds of millions of men. Whatever we do, people are going to start dying in the next couple of days. This compromise is the only way to save the bulk of lives."

"And," said Kathy, holding up the test tube, "the serum we got from Luke is designed to be injected into the patient. Even if we agreed to go with it and accept the side effects, it would take us years to produce and distribute enough to inject into every infected individual in the world." She turned to Jim Balke, who was nodding vehemently.

"So," continued Kathy, "the only way around this problem is not to rely on injections but to insert the antisense DNA vaccine into a genetically engineered viral vector that is spread and caught in the same way as the disease. That's what Sharon's team has been working on."

Kathy turned to Sharon Bibb and retook her seat. The twins, Bibb, and she had been up most of the night discussing the options. They had all ended up at the same place. If they went with the imperfect vaccine, they still needed quickly to find a vector that was not only airborne but robust enough to survive for long periods in air, as well as being highly infectious. The one vector they all came back to seemed perfect in every way, except for two major drawbacks. The first could be overcome with genetic engineering, but the second was more serious. Their only hope was that Pamela Weiss might know a way around it.

Bibb stood and brushed back her black hair. Like all of them, she looked pale and tired, but there was an underlying strength in her voice. "In essence," said Bibb, "we need to use a vector even more infectious, rapid, and robust than the influenza vector used by Crime Zero. This would allow Tom's people in conjunction with other world air forces to distribute relatively small amounts of bomblets over major population centers using known weather systems. We could also use the same airport air purifier tunnels Prince and Naylor used to spread Crime Zero."

"So have you found it yet?" asked General Cleaver. "This wonder vector for Reprieve?"

"We think so, but there are two issues with it. First it's lethal—to both males and females. We need to ensure we remove all the virus's harmful genes before replacing them with the therapeutic DNA vaccine. Otherwise we could end up not only failing to save men but endangering women too."

"OK, let's assume you stop the cure from killing the patient," said Bloom. "What's the other problem?"

Bibb cleared her throat. "The virus we need to spread the cure is smallpox. But according to international law, it was made extinct back in June 1999. We at the CDC and the Russians at Koltsovo had the only remaining stocks, but now all have been destroyed." Bibb paused and looked meaningfully at the President. "Apparently."

"What do you mean, 'apparently'?" asked Weiss. "As far as I'm aware, we destroyed all our stocks."

"We did," confirmed Bloom. He spoke as if expressing a fact, not an opinion. It was clear that he knew things that even the President was protected from. "The question is, did the Russians destroy theirs? Their biological warfare program was always more aggressive than ours, and they were frequently caught breaking the Biological Warfare and Toxin Convention of '72—by both us and the British."

President Weiss paused for a moment and then frowned in concentration. "Let's get this straight. I've got a meeting with the UN Security Council scheduled later, and I want to make sure I know what our options are. Basically, in order to stand any chance at all of saving the male population, we're going to have to use an antidote that will genetically alter them forever. Whether they like it or not?"

Kathy nodded, as did Bibb beside her.

"And even if we do go with this imperfect antidote," continued Weiss, "the only way to ensure it gets through the population fast enough to save anybody is by getting hold of some of the smallpox virus, so you can genetically tame it to become an infectious carrier of the cure?"

"Right," said Bibb.

Weiss let out a deep breath. "OK, I need to speak to the Russian president."

Allardyce nodded. "We'd already taken the liberty of locating President Tabchov. We've explained that you need to speak to him regarding the crisis." Immediately the fifth screen on the wall dividing the Smart Suite from TITANIA's Cold Room fizzed into life, and a heavily jowled face stared out at them.

"President Tabchov, this is President Weiss," said Pamela Weiss. "You know the urgency of the situation, and there is little time for pleasantries. We need your help with a pressing matter." Briefly Weiss outlined what had been discussed. She spoke clearly and with a firm grasp of the issues. The Russian president listened silently, and when Pamela Weiss finished, his broad face broke into a half-smile.

"So you wish to ask whether the Russians destroyed their stocks of smallpox as agreed? Or whether we lied."

"I wouldn't put it so bluntly," said Weiss with a similar smile. "Let's just say that any remaining stocks of the smallpox virus need to be located for the benefit of all mankind. Any help in locating those stocks would be to our mutual advantage."

For a moment the huge face froze on-screen, showing no emotion or expression of any kind. Then it flickered into life again, and Tabchov turned to his left. There followed a heated debate in Russian with an off-screen adviser that lasted almost five minutes before the Russian president turned back to face them. Kathy could feel her heart racing, hoping. It seemed contradictory then that they were relying on a dreaded plague from the Middle Ages to help combat the most technically advanced genetically engineered virus ever created.

"I am sorry," he said with a slow shake of his head. "But despite your obvious prejudices, we did indeed destroy our stocks." Kathy could feel a palpable slump in the room's morale. "However," said Tabchov, raising a large hand, "a number of our best scientists defected from our virological research program in the late nineties. Many were not entirely scrupulous and went for money. We suspect that some took more than their expertise with them." Tabchov turned again to his unseen adviser as if to confirm something. "There is one such person who may have what you seek." He paused then, and the heavy slabs of his face shifted to form a sad smile of acknowledgment. "What we *all* now seek."

Sutter Street, San Francisco.
Sunday, November 16, 3:00 A.M.

Lana Bauer always slept naked. She had done so ever since she was a kid. And now she slept like a baby in her apartment on Sutter Street. For the first time in weeks she had the whole weekend to herself. Tonight she had gone out for a few drinks and actually got drunk.

As she slept, she dreamed of her job. It had been even more tiring than usual recently. It was only her third major assignment, and it was weird. She didn't know exactly what was going on at the place, but it was important. She knew that much.

The window by her bed was open, and the night air blew the curtains into the room. The gentle movement had become background noise. So when the figure on the fire escape outside pulled the window open a few inches more and climbed into the room, Lana Bauer barely stirred.

She didn't even wake when the hand was placed over her mouth. Only the click of the gun pierced her unconscious dreams.

She opened her eyes and was alert in an instant. A gun barrel pointed at her right eye, a hand clamped over her mouth. Above her a tall figure looked down from the darkness.

"I need to ask you some questions," the figure said. "I suggest you answer them."

Two hours later Lana Bauer was dead, a bullet buried in the frontal lobe of her brain.

44

Al Manak Baby Milk Factory, Iraq.
Sunday, November 16, 7:16 A.M.

The world had turned upside down. Civilians were protecting themselves from their own infected soldiers. Enemies were becoming allies, and now plagues of death were offering elixirs of life. But Yevgenia Krotova did not complain as she marched down the long dark corridors of the Al Manak baby milk factory in the north of Baghdad, the largest of Iraq's seven biological warfare laboratories.

The recent death of the Iraqi president from the Peace Plague had removed the immediate threat of execution from Yevgenia and her family for her failure to stop the disease. But she still feared for their safety. Deaths in Iraq were already estimated in the high tens of thousands with many more, particularly infected soldiers, dying in the isolated and hastily constructed concentration camps in the desert. The measures were brutal but necessary, and it now appeared that some kind of containment had been reached.

Yet now the Americans had contacted the new rais, offering money and help to rebuild his shattered country, specifically seeking access to Yevgenia Krotova's treasures to combat an airborne strain of the disease roaming the world beyond Iraq's quarantine borders. They had warned that a death toll of biblical proportions was only days away, but with her help they could vaccinate the world, including Iraq, against this mystery scourge.

As she descended into the hidden labs beneath the factory, the irony that the key to stopping this apocalypse lay with her and the lethal work she had been conducting over the last ten years was not lost on Yevgenia Krotova.

After showering and donning her protective suit, Yevgenia went down into the gloomy maze of concrete storage tunnels where her arsenal of pathogens was kept. Opening a six-inch-thick steel door, disguised to deter UNSCOM inspectors, she walked down another corridor, passing a large room with dented steel walls, the underground testing site for explosive biological warheads. Continuing to the end of the corridor, she came to another steel door. Unlocking this, she found herself in a room surrounded by racks of glass vials. She went immediately to the far wall, reached up to the top shelf, and lifted a rack onto the steel worktable in the center of the room. Here she examined four vials: her four horsemen of the apocalypse.

The first was Ebola. The second was a toughened, more lasting strain to yield a 100 percent death rate. The third was the doomsday virus that had encouraged the last Iraqi president to invade Kuwait and defy the Americans. It was a chimera, a blend of Ebola and other viruses that made it airborne. This chimera had only been possible because of the contents of the fourth vial, a virus so rare it was virtually unique. It was this that had made the Iraqis pay Yevgenia so much blood money to get her here. And now it seemed as if God, not the devil, had been looking over her shoulder when she smuggled it out of Russia. Holding up the vial, she studied the toughened strain of smallpox, marveling at how this medieval scourge of mankind might become its savior.

**Isolation Ward 4, Ballygunge Hospital, Calcutta, India.
The Same Day, 11:28 P.M.**

By day seven Crime Zero had fully established itself within the cells of Babu Anand's hypothalamus and testes.

Because of the fourteen-year-old's youth, he enjoyed virtually no time in the first stage of the virus. The telomeres on his chromosomes and the SRY gene on his Y chromosome immediately triggered the final and fatal stage.

The surge of androgens was so high and so fast that weeping pustules broke out on his face within hours. His hair began falling out in clumps, and his voice deepened.

Rushed to the hospital, he convulsed in his bed, manifesting physical symptoms of acute anxiety as vast levels of adrenaline began to course through his system. The other brain fuels, dopamine and norepinephrine, which stimulated cerebral activity, also kicked in, rocketing to intolerable levels. Simultaneously the influx of the inhibitor serotonin was now so high his blood was saturated with MAO.

His brain was frying in an electrical thunderstorm brought about by massive and conflicting neural traffic, trying to contend with peaking aggressive stimuli while experiencing steel-clawed emotional inhibition. Revving on full power while braking at the same time, his inflamed brain began to rupture as it attempted the impossible task of accommodating these opposing forces.

Hallucinations, terror, and guilt now dominated what was. left of his disintegrating mind.

As his brain imploded, crushing itself, his blood pressure shot up in the shock response known as the Cushing reflex. It heralded his imminent death. His brain had to have blood to survive, and as the swelling from the inflammation closed off vital arteries, the pressure rose further, so his body drove its blood pressure higher to meet the rise in brain pressure, to force blood into the brain. The resulting terminal spike in blood pressure triggered a series of hemorrhages throughout his body and ultimately his brain. A hemorrhagic nosebleed marked his point of death.

His final minutes did not go unnoticed by the authorities. Within an hour of his admission to the hospital the Indian government's senior medical officers had registered his mystery symptoms, along with the results of various tests.

And before Babu Anand's body was cold, an encrypted message was being sent to all the leaders of the world.

Crime Zero Phase 3 had claimed its first victim. And it was only the beginning.

45

The Womb, ViroVector Solutions, Palo Alto.
Sunday, November 16, 9:17 P.M.

"Take a look, Luke. It's beautiful," said Kathy Kerr. In the darkened Womb the electron microscope bathed her helmet and visor in a green aura.

Taking Kathy's place and gazing down into the submicroscopic cellular landscape, Decker couldn't see any beauty in the virus. The Conscience vector Kathy had shown him earlier looked like a shimmering halo, and Crime Zero like a coiled noose, whereas this Project Reprieve vector looked like a deformed half-moon.

According to Kathy, the complex viral vector he was looking at was a hybrid, containing DNA from the antidote in his body and the smallpox vector they had received from Iraq. It had been lovingly crafted and was potentially the DNA antisense vaccine with the power to save mankind. But it still wasn't beautiful.

Within an hour of the conversation between the U.S. and Russian presidents, Iraq had been contacted. The new rais had been more reasonable than the last and, because of the crisis in his country, had been more malleable. But he had still been highly suspicious of the American motives, initially refusing to admit there were any stocks of smallpox in the country. Eventually, after Pamela Weiss had promised to help fund the rebuilding of Iraq's infrastructure and to cure the plague devastating his country, they had come to an agreement.

The real revelation, however, hadn't been the discovery that Iraq did indeed have smallpox stocks, a relief in itself, but the toughened strain Yevgenia Krotova had sent them. It was perfect for their uses, so much so that Kathy warned how if they paused to consider the implications of someone of Krotova's skill helping Iraq's biowarfare program, no one would sleep easily again.

The Schlossberg twins had laid much of the groundwork over the last week, and when the engineered virus arrived, Kathy, Sharon Bibb, and their teams had been able to short-cut the splicing process, merging the antisense sequence with the smallpox envelope genes. They were now satisfied that all the necessary genetic characteristics were in place and that each of the inserted sections should express their instructions when reaching its target cells. Jim Balke had since run off a batch of weapons-grade viral droplets in the pilot biroreactor. This is what Decker was looking at now.

"I think we can do it," said Kathy beside him. Her tired face was aglow with excitement behind her faceplate. "We've got to test that it's safe and it works. But if it does, then we could stop Crime Zero. This is good, Luke. Don't you think?"

"Yeah, of course. It's great." But he still felt uncomfortable. For the last few days he had been trying to come to understand the implications of this "cure." He still felt angry that his genes had been changed. He didn't enjoy possessing Axelman's genes, but they were his, and he was just coming to terms with them. Now genetics had robbed him of his right to grapple with his own past.

"What's wrong, Luke?" Kathy said, watching him carefully.

"I don't know. You're right; this is the best, the *only* option. But I can't help feeling it's wrong somehow."

"How can it be wrong? Assuming this thing works, we'll save all men."

"That's the point. You won't. At least not men as they were. Men as we know them will still die. I can't help thinking that the survivors will be different people—perhaps better, perhaps worse, but *different* in some way. I'll be different. Perhaps I already am." He wanted Kathy to argue with him, so he could get these concerns out of his system. But she said nothing, just stood there and nodded, as if to acknowledge the point he was making.

"Don't you see?" he went on. "Despite what Alice Prince and Madeline Naylor believe, men serve a purpose. Yes, men are more aggressive than women are and commit most of the crimes, and they want to dominate rather than negotiate. Yes, they seek sensation and take risks. But it's precisely this drive and aggression that make them challenge the oceans, the galaxies, and everything from religion to unjust rulers. For good or ill, men, *not women,* have been the agents of change and of civilization, not exclusively but for the most part. Project Conscience on hardened criminals is one thing, but taming the spirit of every present and future male is something else entirely. The implications for the future could be disastrous."

"Surely not as disastrous as what will happen if we do nothing," said Kathy

"Of course," he conceded, "but it still sucks."

Kathy smiled. "Look, I know this is a compromise. But I'll tell you one thing, Luke. I'd rather have you here with a few genes changed than dead. And there's something else to consider. This change, whether it's Conscience or the more drastic Crime Zero, will affect civilization more than any other initiative in our history. But it *wasn't* conceived or implemented by men. Perhaps in a perverse way this proves that women have more drive than men credit them with. Who knows? Far from being doomed, perhaps humanity will benefit from having both genders share the driving seat for a change."

Decker shrugged. "I hope you're right."

Kathy hoped she was right as well. A week had passed since Crime Zero had gone live and people would soon start dying, and continue to die in increasing numbers, unless the vaccine was released—side effects or no side effects.

Suddenly the door to the Womb hissed open, and Kathy saw two blue Chemturion space suits enter. She recognized the wearers as Sharon Bibb and Major General Tom Allardyce.

Allardyce was rubbing his gloved hands together, as excited as Kathy imagined a career military type ever got. "It's all set," he said. "We've got twenty infected male volunteers, all military personnel. All have agreed to be exposed to the Reprieve smallpox vaccine. Each has been fitted with a gene sequence and blood test wristband. The predictive gene scans and blood readings should tell us if they're in the clear by tomorrow morning. We're already recruiting female subjects, and once we know it works on men, we'll test it on them—to ensure it's safe. So by tomorrow night, assuming all the tests are positive, we might, no, *should* have a vaccine to deliver.

"Strategic production sites have been set up here, in the U.K., Russia, China, Iraq, Brazil, and Australia. They are waiting for the go-ahead from the tests, and then each will receive a transfer file giving the full genetic sequence and production spec for the vaccine. They in turn will supply squadrons of military and commercial aircraft from most major nations, which will bomb every significant population center on earth. By analyzing global weather patterns to harness the airflow effects they have on microclimates, we'll be able to target the airborne spread. And this assault will be supplemented by the use of bacteriophage air purifier tunnels at every major hub airport. Over the next week we'll blanket-bomb the world. Crime Zero will have no place to hide."

"So you'll only release the samples and gene sequence of the vaccine once you're sure it's safe and effective?" asked Decker.

"You bet," said Allardyce. "For all we know, the vaccine could be useless or, worse, lethal. So we're keeping it under strict control until we know it's OK." He walked over to a white box in the corner of the Womb by the Genescope. It had no monitor, only a series of lights, a large red button, and a keypad down one side. It looked as if it had been recently installed. "This is an SDU, a Secure Data Unit. It's not linked to TITANIA or any network until a six-letter code is keyed in and that red button is depressed; then and only then will the data stored on its drive be sent down secure lines to the designated production sites. Until that happens, it's effectively a bulletproof, hackerproof strongbox for data.

"As well as the data all the samples, including those produced by Jim Balke in the BioSafety Level Four pilot plant area, are now here in the safe or with the test subjects down in the slammer. Effectively every piece of data and material relating to the vaccine now resides here in the central core of the lab complex."

"In that case," said Decker with a wry grin, "if the vaccine works, let's hope nothing happens to this place."

Allardyce smiled behind his visor. "I wouldn't worry about that. This is one of the most secure places on earth."

Kathy was more concerned about timing. "Can't we test the vaccine faster? You said you had to wait to test it on men before testing it on women. Why?"

Sharon Bibb answered, "Female volunteers are less easy to find, and frankly we don't want to risk women's lives until we know Reprieve works on men. Crime Zero won't harm women, but Reprieve could—especially if we haven't properly attenuated the smallpox vector Krotova gave us."

Kathy frowned at this. "But every minute could be crucial. There are almost three hundred million teenage men in the world. The youngest of these will die a week after infection. That means that anytime now our youngest males are going to start dropping like flies. We've got to test women now. Each hour represents hundreds of thousands of lives."

"Hang on a minute," said Allardyce. "Wait till we get an OK from the men. If Reprieve doesn't work or, worse, it kills them, then there's no point putting women at risk."

Suddenly the computer by Alice Prince's safe began to beep.

"What the hell's that?" growled Allardyce, turning to view the monitor.

"It's a message," said Bibb as Kathy watched the short terse report come up on screen.

"Shit," said Decker softly as he read the text.

On the screen was a picture of a young Indian boy. According to the classified report, he was the first recorded casualty of Crime Zero and had died a little over an hour ago. Time had run out. The death toll had begun.

Then Kathy made a decision.

46

ViroVector Solutions, Palo Alto.
Monday, November 17, 2:12 A.M.

No one challenged the tall FBI ninja in the black biological suit. At the main gate where her suit militated against using the DNA sensor, she knew the correct personal access codes to punch into the ancillary keypad. Once inside the campus she gave her personal call sign and knew all the pass codes when challenged by central security via her headset.

It was after two in the morning, and the campus was dead. The ninja, with the badge "Special Agent Lana Bauer" on her suit, knew from her headset where most of the other agents were and how to avoid them. Hardly anyone passed her as she made her way to the silent dome. Those who did ignored her.

Madeline Naylor felt no fear, only a cold sense of purpose, as she paused outside the dome and adjusted her grip on her bag. Ahead of her a scientist in a white coat left the doors of the dome open for some fresh air. He made no move to approach her or even acknowledge her. It was as if her suit depersonalized her, made her invisible. She had found Lana Bauer's address in her FBI personnel files. She lived alone and in San Francisco. Her apartment had been easy to find. Before she died, Bauer had told her all she needed to know about security on-site, including all the codes and guard movements.

Between one and six in the morning the place was deserted, with people sleeping in the departments in the upper part of the dome. TITANIA was relied on to alert the guards who patrolled the grounds if there was an intruder. But Bauer had said that no intruders were really expected.

Naylor hadn't wanted to kill her, but she had no option. Anything else was too risky. She put two bullets in her head, then wrapped her body in a rug and rolled it under her bed. Bauer would be found soon enough, but after tonight it wouldn't matter.

Madeline Naylor thought again of Luke Decker and Kathy Kerr. Alice Prince had told her she was going to give the vaccine to Decker. And Naylor knew Kerr had the knowledge to exploit it. Between them they were dangerous.

Naylor couldn't see how Kerr could stop Crime Zero at a global level, but she might be able to create a vaccine that would seriously limit its impact. And unless Crime Zero was total, it was pointless. If some malignant cells remained—however few they were—then in time the cancer would return.

Biosafety Level 4 Hospital, ViroVector Solutions

Kathy Kerr checked the clock on the instruments by her bed: 2:25 A.M. She hadn't slept a wink. Her decision may have been a terrible error.

Since no one could do anything until the test results on the twenty men came in, the core team had taken the opportunity to get some sleep in the dome. When they had gone, she'd stolen back to the Womb and taken a sample of the Reprieve vaccine. Leaving a note by the Genescope explaining what she'd done, she'd then come down here to one of the isolation rooms.

She had inhaled the Reprieve Smallpox vaccine four hours ago and had been lying in her bubble ever since. Ever since she learned that the first victim of Crime Zero had died, she knew she had to act, to test the vaccine on herself. If she was OK and it worked on the men, they would save time and hundreds of thousands of extra lives. She hadn't told the others what she'd planned because they would have tried to prevent her. Back then she'd been so sure it was the right thing to do and felt so confident Reprieve would work.

Now she wasn't sure at all.

She checked the chrome bracelet on her left wrist. A small sensor and needle on its inner edge were monitoring her blood and her DNA. The bracelet had a liquid crystal display with two small windows about the size of a digital watch face. One LCD window would show the status of her blood, and the other her genome. Currently both were blank. In two or three more hours the screen would flash with information telling her if she was OK or there were complications. Those complications could be immediately lethal or longer-term genetic mutations that would affect her later in life—however brief that life might be.

She knew that elsewhere in the large ward of the slammer, twenty men were also being tested. But she felt no real kinship with them. They were infected, effectively dying, taking the Reprieve vaccine as a last resort. She, on the other hand, was under no threat. And she knew only too well the terrible complications that could arise if the genetic vaccine went AWOL and played havoc with her DNA. What she was doing was right, she was sure of it, but the thought of contracting a mutant strain of smallpox or some awful hybrid of that disease and Crime Zero chilled her blood. She felt the urge to scratch her face just at the thought of smallpox bubbling under her skin.

Until this moment she'd had little time to think of anything but fighting the disease. Every waking moment had been focused on that aim, and any chance to sleep had been taken without any real thought. But now sleep wouldn't come, and her mind was free to reflect on matters beyond the virus. For the first time since this began she felt overwhelmed by the enormity of what had happened, by what *was* happening.

She found it hard to believe that fewer than three weeks had elapsed since Madeline Naylor tried to lock her away in the Sanctuary. If she died, who would tell her family in Scotland what had happened? Would it matter anyway if Crime Zero ravaged the planet? And what would she do if she survived and the Reprieve vaccine worked? Her dream of Conscience would have been realized in a way far more ambitious and absolute than she'd ever dreamed or wanted. What would she do next?

By asking herself these questions and dwelling on the future, she managed to keep at bay her fear of the present. But only just.

Then she saw the door to her isolation room open and a tall figure in a space suit slip inside. Squinting in the half-light, she peered through her creased plastic bubble at the approaching figure. It seemed to pause for a moment, and Kathy craned to see the person's face, but in the shadowy reflective glow she couldn't see into the visor. She tensed when the figure reached for the plastic wall of her bubble. Then, when the helmet turned, she saw the face.

"I thought you'd be doing something stupid like this," said Decker.

Kathy didn't know what to say.

"Anyway," Decker said, sitting down on the chair beside the bubble, "since you've gone and done it, I thought you could do with some company. I know what it's like being stuck in there. It certainly isn't a barrel of laughs."

47

The Decontamination Room, ViroVector Solutions,
Palo Alto.
Two Hours Later

Sharon Bibb felt exhausted as she pulled on her blue biohazard suit in the decon room between the Biohazard Level
3 laboratories and Level 4. The room consisted of a row of
lockers, showers, and toilets, and a rack of biohazard space
suits. There were two basins at one end with a row of bleach
bottles and various virus-killing chemicals lining the wall. It
was four-thirty in the morning, and everywhere was quiet.
After her earlier meeting with Allardyce, Kathy Kerr, and
Luke Decker, she had gone up into the main dome to grab a
bite to eat and a few hours' sleep in the makeshift sleeping
quarters set up in the dome.

She had agreed with Allardyce that at five o'clock this
morning she would check on the twenty male subjects. If the
results were good, she would alert Allardyce. After present-
ing their results to the core team and gaining permission
from the President, they could then key in the code to the Secure Data Unit and send the protected gene sequence and
production specifications of the Reprieve vector to the various production sites around the world. Only Allardyce,
Kathy Kerr, and she knew the code.

She yawned twice. God, she hadn't been this tired since
handling the Ebola breakout in the Congo back in '99. She

hadn't seen her husband or two kids back in Atlanta for almost two weeks either. Just the thought of losing her husband to Crime Zero brought a rush of panic to her thoughts. The Reprieve vaccine would work. It must work.

Instinctively and carefully checking her suit for any tears, she paused before the door that led to the central Hot Zone of the complex, containing the BioSafety Level 4 labs and the Womb and the elevator going down to the BioSafety Level 4 hospital and morgue.

She became aware of someone else being in the decon room with her only after she'd keyed in the six-character password and presented her eye to be scanned through the faceplate of her helmet. With mufflers on her ears to protect her from the suit's rushing air supply she only just heard the rustle behind her. But before she could turn, the door began to open in front of her, and she felt something hard push into her back.

"Don't turn around," snarled a cold female voice behind her. "I saw you key in the code, so I need only one of your eyes to get the rest of the way. I can either come with you as your guest or you can refuse to cooperate. In which case I'll take out your eye and get into the Womb alone. The choice is yours."

Sharon Bibb was too shocked to say anything, and before she could even frame a response, she had been pushed through the door into the glass corridor beyond. Wildly she looked through the glass partitions into the Level 4 laboratories, but she was alone. Everyone else was up in the dome asleep.

"Go on," said the woman behind her as they passed the elevators to the slammer and the submarine below, pushing her toward the door at the end of the corridor.

A wave of relief flowed through Madeline Naylor. She was so close now. The black biohazard symbol and the large red BioSafety Level 5 emblazoned on the glass door of the Womb seemed to beckon her on.

After getting into ViroVector, Naylor had patiently made her way to the center of the biolab complex, using the radio to avoid any other agents. It seemed as if the agents had been placed at all the key points on the perimeter, but few, if any, were in the lab complex itself at this time of night—probably to avoid getting in the scientists' way. However, the difficult part was still to come: She had to gain access to the central Hot Zone of the complex, where the Womb was. She didn't have access codes for that and would need retina identification.

Using her knowledge of the labs from the numerous times she had accompanied Alice Prince to the Womb, she made her way through the less secure outer rings of the complex. As she stole her way from BioSafety Level 1 to 3, each lab had been a deserted white library of chrome and glass with only the hum of apparatus and air conditioners to disturb the silence. Eventually she had reached the decon room, the gateway to the Hot Zone, and waited patiently behind the row of lockers for someone to arrive and take her in.

Dr. Sharon Bibb—her name written on the front of her suit—had been that person.

"Go on," Naylor said, pushing her toward the door of the Womb. "Open it. I'm right behind you."

Bibb paused for a moment, and Naylor could tell that the shock was wearing off and the scientist was thinking of self-preservation.

"Do it now," she snarled, pushing her gun firmly into Bibb's side, not giving her time to think.

With steady fingers Bibb keyed in the code on the keypad by the door, then stood still while the laser scanned her retina. As the door slid open, Naylor checked her watch. People would start to wake in the next hour or so. She would have to hurry if she wanted to plant the explosive and escape before detonating it. Hefting the tote bag in her left hand, she felt the reassuring weight of the device inside. It was small and simple but would be enough to rupture one of the reinforced glass walls. TITANIA should then go into Close Down mode, sealing the entire Hot Zone with airtight thermo-resistant sutured panels, containing the Level 4 and Level 5 labs, as well as the hospital and mortuary. Then, unless an override code was keyed in from outside, TITANIA would release a shower of virus-killing bleaches and chemicals into the contained area, followed by an ultraviolet light show and finally a firestorm of three thousand degrees to destroy any living organism in the Hot Zone. No human, plague, or vaccine would survive.

When the door to the Womb fully opened, Naylor pushed Bibb through and followed her in. The first thing she noticed was the recently installed Secure Data Unit. She had used one often enough in the bureau. It was only ever used to store data that were too sensitive or valuable to risk being lost or illegally accessed. Copies were rarely made of files in an SDU. It could only mean that whatever progress Kathy Kerr had made on a vaccine was in that box. It was isolated here.

"Now," she said, dropping her bag on the floor and pressing her gun into Bibb's visor, "tell me how much progress you've made. And tell me where I can find Kathy Kerr?"

Then she saw the note by the Genescope. It was from Kathy Kerr. It answered all her questions.

Luke Decker woke with a start. At first he didn't know where he was, the glass was so close to his face. And the rushing noise was so loud in his ears. Then he realized he was in a biohazard suit and had fallen asleep in the chair next to Kathy's bubble.

He turned to the digital clock on the chrome instruments by the bed: 4:47. Quickly he turned to Kathy. She was lying in a ball, her dark hair splayed over the pillow, her mouth half open. He tried to see the bracelet around her wrist, but it was obscured under the covers.

"Kathy," he said, "wake up!"

Her eyes opened, and she looked panicked for a second.

"How are you feeling? How's the bracelet?"

Her eyes widened, suddenly fully awake. She whipped her hand out from under the covers, exposing her bracelet. Both LCD windows, the blood and genome indicators, were green.

"What does it mean?" he asked, suddenly nervous.

Kathy looked at him, a look of disbelief on her face; then

she smiled. "I'm in the clear. I don't know if Reprieve actually works, but it's safe. Green means that the odds of its causing any harm are so low as to be statistically insignificant."

"In that case," he said, picking up her discarded space suit and passing it to her, "let's get the hell out of here."

48

ViroVector Solutions, Palo Alto.
4:58 A.M.

Kathy Kerr could barely contain a sense of impending triumph as she and Luke Decker traveled in the elevator to the lab complex above. Both wore white hospital biohazard suits. Minutes ago they had rushed to the main ward in the slammer and checked the male test subjects. All were asleep, but their gene readings were showing huge improvements.

Kathy was beginning to believe that they were actually going to prevent the biological cataclysm. She looked at Decker, thinking of how he had come to sit with her last night. She felt an overwhelming sense of partnership. Together they had uncovered Crime Zero and fought against all the odds to foil it. And now they were close, so close, to stopping it.

As the elevator doors opened, Decker stepped out and turned left toward the BioSafety Level 5 door of the Womb. Through the angled glass Kathy could make out part of the interior. The sight of the blue Chemturion space suit leaning over one of the work surfaces made her quicken her step. "Look, Sharon's up. Let's give her the good news. Then we'll alert Tom and the others."

She keyed in the code to the Womb and allowed her eye to be scanned. When the door hissed quietly open, she slipped in, Decker following close behind.

Kathy didn't understand the strange way Sharon Bibb was leaning against the Genescope at first. So she moved nearer. She saw the bullet hole through Sharon Bibb's helmet and realized she was dead at virtually the exact same time she saw the black FBI biohazard space suit. The figure was turned away from her, crouching over what looked like a square box of steel, before the glass-fronted refrigerator, which contained many of the world's most virulent and lethal viruses, including Ebola and Marburg.

Stunned, Kathy stood frozen to the ground as the black helmet turned toward her. And although Madeline Naylor's dark eyes looked surprised when she saw her, the onetime FBI director was smiling.

It took Luke Decker a few seconds to take in the situation. Nine yards ahead of him Madeline Naylor crouched over what looked like a small bomb. Four yards behind Naylor, in the no-man's-land between them, was her bag. And on it her gun.

Kathy stood to his right. The Secure Data Unit, which contained all the Reprieve vaccine data that now urgently needed to be dispatched, was on his left. But he didn't know the code. Only Kathy did.

He could tell Naylor had weighed up the situation too. She seemed torn between finishing priming the bomb and reaching for the gun.

Kathy looked straight at the SDU, obviously realizing it was vital to send out the data or all could be lost.

For a long breathless moment no one moved. Each just stared at the other.

Then Decker turned to Kathy, and as he dashed for the gun, he shouted at her, "Send the data. Now!"

Suddenly all three of them were moving as fast across the sheer white tiles as their clumsy suits allowed.

He collided with Naylor as they lunged for the gun, pushing the bag across the tiles and sending them both clattering to the floor.

Decker groaned as his bruised body hit the floor and his broken arm smashed against Naylor's helmet. Directly in front of him he could see Naylor staring at him from behind her faceplate with venomous hatred. To his right he could see the bomb. The black box had a digital display showing the number 9:01 in red digits, presumably a countdown in minutes.

Naylor was now looking beyond him at Kathy, who was standing over the Secure Data Unit, keying the send code into the keypad. Scrabbling to her feet, Naylor kicked his broken arm, and Decker heard a bone crack. For a second he could do nothing but writhe in the white heat of agony. Naylor grabbed at Kathy and pushed her away from the SDU before she could press the large red send button that would deliver the transfer files to the production sites around the world.

Gritting his teeth, Decker grabbed for the bomb with his good hand. But it was a sealed device with a one-way switch. He was no bomb expert, but even his basic explosives training told him that this was designed for ease of use and the utmost simplicity. Once the timer was set, the sealed device would go off at the designated time, and nothing would stop it. The only way to avoid the explosion was to get the hell out of the way.

Then he saw Madeline's Glock under the safe. It must have been propelled along the floor when they collided. He pushed his good arm under the safe and tried to reach for it, but his fingertips touched it only enough to push it farther away. He changed his angle and gained another inch, just enough to pull it out. Then he heard glass smashing behind him. And when he turned and aimed at Naylor, he realized it wasn't going to be that easy.

Madeline Naylor closed her hands around Kathy Kerr's helmet and felt the rage eat into her, twisting her entrails, tightening her chest.

Sharon Bibb wouldn't tell her much before she died, but Kathy Kerr's note had explained enough. Naylor had been delighted that Kathy Kerr was in the hospital suite because the bomb explosion would kill her. All the data in the SDU and the samples of the vaccine would be destroyed too. And when the bomb prompted TITANIA to close everything down and purge the hot core of the complex, all electronic and organic trace of the vaccine should be destroyed, along with Kathy Kerr. It was an ideal solution.

But then Decker and Kerr had entered the Womb.

Decker was injured, so pushing him away hadn't been difficult, but Kathy had almost keyed in the send codes to transmit the vaccine files to whoever was expecting them. It was vital that the files didn't get out, that everything be destroyed. So she had made a decision, leaped at Kathy, pushing her away from the SDU.

Kathy struggled hard, but Naylor smashed the back of Kathy's helmet through the glass door of one of the refrigerators, dazing her and sending rows upon rows of vials crashing to the ground, releasing every major virus from Ebola to Marburg to Hanta. Madeline held Kathy facedown in a headlock, her face as close to the virus-drenched floor as the thickness of the glass of her visor.

But now Decker had her gun.

"Put it down, Decker," she yelled. "Or I'll rip her helmet off. This place is so hot she'll die in minutes."

"We could all die in minutes," said Decker with irritating calm. He stood holding the gun aimed at her. "Six minutes now, according to your bomb. Kathy, are you OK?"

But Kathy, obviously concussed, said nothing. Her body felt heavy when Naylor lifted her as a shield in front of her.

Suddenly through the glass walls she saw three people in blue space suits rushing down the corridor, through the Level 4 laboratory area to the Womb. Naylor thought through the options, then realized she had no choice. She would die. But before she did, she would ensure this place was destroyed and Crime Zero protected. Pulling Kathy closer to her, she stretched for the lock by the door. There was a hissing noise as two dead bolts slid into place. Now the Womb could be opened only from the inside.

"Decker," she said, "if you make any move toward the SDU, I'll kill her."

Kathy's silence wasn't helping Decker at all. For a start he wasn't sure whether she had keyed in all the code into the

SDU. And he didn't even know what the code was. He could only stare at the large red button, knowing that if he pressed it without the full code, nothing would happen. And if he moved toward it, Madeline would undoubtedly kill Kathy. Decker's only hope was that Kathy would come around before the bomb went off in five minutes.

Outside, he could see Allardyce and the Schlossberg twins pawing the glass, helplessly looking in. If only he could hear them, Allardyce could give him the code.

"I thought you were against violent crime, Naylor," he said, "yet you've already killed more people than most of the murderers I've hunted down. And if you get your way with Crime Zero, you'll be responsible for more murders than all men combined, living and dead. My whole gender won't have been as effective at killing as you were. Does that make sense? One woman—the head of the great law-enforcing FBI—murdering every adult member of the opposite sex simply because she's against murder?"

"How would you understand?" Naylor said through clenched teeth. "Your father raped and killed young girls. Of course you don't see the necessity of purging your own kind."

Kathy seemed to stir, and through the glass of her faceplate Decker could see her eyes trying to focus. If he pressed the red button, he *might* save almost two and a half billion men, but he would *definitely* kill Kathy. He had to wait for her to confirm the code. "Of course I see the need to hunt down and destroy the evil among us," he said to Naylor. "I've done it all my working life. But a violent criminal is anyone who has committed a violent crime, not simply a man. A violent criminal is someone like you."

Naylor was visibly rattled, making her loosen her grip on Kathy and focus on him.

He raised his voice now, almost shouting, continually glancing at Kathy as he spoke. "The real irony is that *you* are the violent scum you're so against. You should purge yourself rather than anyone else."

Naylor gave him a venomous smile. "It doesn't matter what you think now. In a few minutes this place and everything in it will be destroyed. Crime Zero will prevail. My only regret is that I will be unable to experience the benefits. But then that's a small price to pay to know that all your meddling has been in vain."

Suddenly Kathy spoke. "The code's in," she said. "Press the button."

For a second Decker looked at her, then at Naylor.

"If you make one move toward it, I'll kill her," Naylor said.

The deal had changed. Pressing the button would save the lives of millions, *billions* of men. It would also kill Kathy. Logically the choice was simple, but this had gone way beyond logic. In that instant he realized how much she meant to him and what he was about to lose. He also knew there was no choice.

Outside the Womb a crowd of scientists had gathered, frozen by the scene in front of them.

"How strong's the glass in here?" he asked.

"Very," said Kathy.

Before Naylor had a chance to react, he moved his good arm, took aim at the red metal button on the SDU and fired. For a moment Naylor's concentration was broken, and Kathy tore herself from the distracted Naylor's grip. She reached for the door. Naylor threw herself at Decker, her eyes narrow with rage, her voice shrill like a wounded beast. "No," she screamed. "No."

He only had time to see the green light go on beneath the keypad, telling him that the data had been sent, before Naylor was on him. She tore at him as though possessed, pushing him to the floor, knocking the gun from his hand. Behind her he could hear Kathy press the release button on the door's dead bolts and call to him, "Luke. Luke."

"Go," he shouted, "leave me."

Pushing Naylor back with his good arm, he raised himself to his knees. To his left he saw the small bomb. A minute remained on the timer's countdown. In anger he reached for it, clutching the black box in his gloved hand, and then, as Madeline Naylor came for him again, he brought it crashing down on her faceplate and smashed it. Rising to his feet, he could hear her screams mingle with the hiss of air escaping from her helmet. Kathy was beside him now, pulling him toward the door.

"Come on," she shouted. "I'm not leaving without you."

Behind him he could see Naylor staggering to her feet, her demented eyes already red from the contaminated air. In her right hand she held a shard of glass from her faceplate, which she wielded like a knife. He had to reach the door, but he knew just one rupture in his suit from her blade would mean death. Kathy had the door to the Womb open, knew that only seconds remained on the bomb. Making one final surge, he pushed forward, sweeping Kathy ahead of him, through the doorway and into the corridor beyond. Allardyce and the others were there pulling them out and away. Turning back for a split second, he saw Naylor make a final grab at him, her eyes ablaze with hatred, missing by inches as the door sprang shut, crushing her outstretched arm.

Madeline could not believe it. Sitting on the floor of the Womb, she wheezed in the foul, contaminated air and stared at her crushed arm. She didn't care that she had only seconds left before the bomb detonated.

This wasn't how it was supposed to be. Her vision of Crime Zero was now ruined. Many men would still die—millions even—*but not all of them.*

To her mind, if just one adult male survived Crime Zero, the purity of her vision was tarnished. Eradicating all men was a great deed that would ensure the survival of the species. But to kill some was little more than a sordid act of murder.

She was suddenly racked with remorse not because she had killed so many men but because she had killed so few.

As she heard the bomb's detonation switch click, she cried out in pain and frustration, realizing that she had changed nothing.

But even as her body was ripped apart by the explosion and TITANIA sealed off the Hot Zone, purging it of all life with chemicals and heat, Madeline Naylor was wrong.

She had changed everything.

*   *   *

As he catapulted himself out of the Womb, Decker was
dragged by Allardyce down the corridor toward the door
leading out of the Hot Zone, to the decon room and safety.
The steel door seemed to take an age to open and even
longer to close again. But standing beside Kathy and the
others in the decon room, he heard and felt the explosion rip
through the center of the complex and saw TITANIA instantly bring heavy black screens down over the door
through which they had just come, sealing in the Hot Zone
before purging it from within.

Decker's last image as Kathy began to spray bleach on his
suit in the decon showers was of Naylor's two eyes staring
at him. He would remember the hatred he saw there for the
rest of his life.

49

Pentagon War Room, Arlington, Virginia.
Sunday, November 23, 11:06 A.M.

The vast chamber of the Pentagon War Room dwarfed the
Smart Suite at ViroVector. The floor was filled with rows of
computers at which sat uniformed men and women processing information. The vast front wall, which seemed to
curve like the horizon, was more than fifty feet high and
twice as wide. It was tiled with screens. The central one, ten
feet wide by eight feet tall, showed a projection of the
world.

The other, smaller screens had legends beneath them indicating the locations. Many showed United States Air
Force fields both in the States and abroad. There were shots
from the news networks around the world, but the rest
showed the air forces of other nations, including Britain,
France, Israel, and even Iraq, all focusing on one shared
mission.

Since the Reprieve vaccine had been dispatched to all the
production sites across the world six days ago, all subsequent test and production trials had been successful. Under
Major General Allardyce's stewardship the necessary
bomblets were produced to the correct specification. And
pending approval, a global armada of aircraft was assembled
to distribute the vaccine.

Three days previously at a UN meeting in New York,

Pamela Weiss had outlined the risks and benefits of the planned vaccine to all the world leaders. She had also announced the latest death toll from the airborne Crime Zero. Globally it was already in the millions, a generation of young men just out of puberty. No country had been spared.

There was some debate about the long-term implications of the side effects, but all agreed that the benefits far outweighed the risks. For the first time in the history of the United Nations every country without exception, regardless of politics, religion, or historical enmity, had signed the resolution. Following the proposal, agreement was reached in a record fourteen minutes.

No precise figure was placed on the global armada, but it was confidently estimated to exceed half a million commercial and military aircraft. It was the largest bombing mission the world had ever seen. Many optimists predicted it would be the last.

As the first bomblets were dropped, the map on the vast central screen erupted with tiny red pinpricks. London glowed red, and Paris, followed by most of mainland Europe. The United States and Canada were soon the same, as were South America and the vast tracts of Africa and Asia. The dots were small on these larger, less populated lands, concentrating on the major cities. But the dots grew and were distorted in line with the prevailing winds, spreading the vaccine far and wide. Soon the dots were merging into one another, creating almost blanket coverage.

As Kathy Kerr stood with Luke Decker at the back of the chamber in the raised viewing area, she shook her head in disbelief.

Nothing would be the same again. Just as the spreading red represented salvation, so it represented a revolution—or perhaps a self-inflicted evolution.

Man had changed irrevocably, had been forced to evolve, in effect creating a new species. *Homo sapiens* was dead. A new man was being born.

"What will the future bring, Kathy?" Decker asked, staring at the screen.

She took his hand and smiled at him. "I don't know, but I hope it's good."

He squeezed her hand in his. "God! So do I. So do I."

Epilogue

San Francisco.
One Hundred Years Later, November 23, 2108

The man was old, but the house was older. He laid down the violin and moved his chair closer to the open windows that overlooked the bay. The celebrations were starting in earnest now. The sky was a riot of fireworks that lit up the night. The children had probably already joined the crowds down by the bridge. He could have gone too, but he preferred to stay here and look up into the skies.

He turned and wheeled the telescope by his side to a better angle. As he looked through the glass, the multicolored explosions were almost blinding in their intensity. It seemed strange to celebrate the Pax Centennia, the hundred years of peace, with explosions. There had even been talk of digging up the ancient armaments and building huge bonfires—beacons of peace.

With stiff legs he stood from his chair and walked to the ancient piano. Of all the photographs, one stood out. It showed a smiling couple holding a baby in their arms. An old church loomed in the background, and a striking, familiar-looking woman stood beside them. The picture made him smile with pride. Not many people could claim to have had a U.S. President at his christening. He studied the picture and wondered what they would have made of the last hundred years—his hundred years.

There had been much talk this year on the centenary of the Change. Not so much of the costs: Eighteen million young men had died, the equivalent of three Holocausts. That was ancient history now. Instead many of the World Council made presentations evaluating its benefits. Most were happy to have enjoyed an unprecedented period of global peace and prosperity. However, some lamented that technological progress wasn't what it used to be without the catalyst of war, that Blake had been right when he'd said there could be no progress without conflict.

His father, Luke, used to tell him stories of a different world, of hunting down men so evil he could only imagine them. But he also used to talk of adventure and courage and the honorable desire to fight for what was right. Even his mother, Kathy, often spoke of the *need* at times to fight for what you believed in.

He moved back to the telescope and pointed it to the heavens, past the puny human pyrotechnics to the majestic planets beyond. He focused on Venus and then the nearest star, Proxima Centauri, a mere twenty-four million million miles away. He imagined what someone there would see if he aimed his telescopes at Earth: A medium-size planet orbiting around an average star in the outer suburbs of an ordinary spiral galaxy, itself one of a million million galaxies.

A shadow passed over Proxima Centauri, and his old shoulders trembled. Suddenly he saw the universe as no more than a vast world: the galaxies, its continents; the planets, its countries.

In his mind's eye he looked at Earth from space again. He saw a lone planet, rich in resources.

A peaceful, decent planet that had risen above the base need for aggression.

He saw a planet that no longer knew how to defend itself.